TRICK

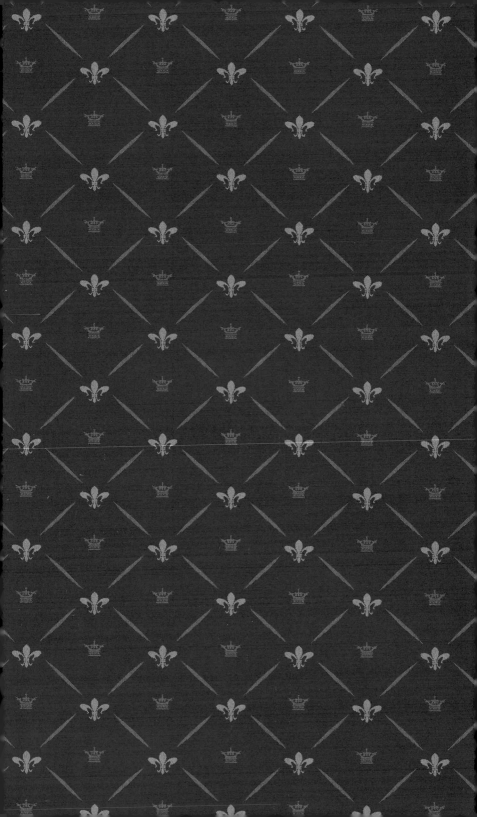

TRICK

FOOLISH KINGDOMS
DARK SEASONS WORLD

1

NATALIA JASTER

Books by Natalia Jaster

FOOLISH KINGDOMS SERIES

Trick (Book 1)

Ruin (Book 2)

Burn (Book 3)

Dare (Book 4)

Lie (Book 5)

Dream (Book 6)

SELFISH MYTHS SERIES

Touch (Book 1)

Torn (Book 2)

Tempt (Book 3)

Transcend (Book 4)

VICIOUS FAERIES SERIES

Kiss the Fae (Book 1)

Hunt the Fae (Book 2)

Curse the Fae (Book 3)

Defy the Fae (Book 4)

Second edition © 2022 Natalia Jaster

First edition © 2015 Natalia Jaster

ISBN: 978-1-957824-01-7

Cover design by AC Graphics

Chapter headings & scene breaks by Noverantale

Poet Character Art by Mageonduty

Typesetting by Roman Jaster

Body text set in Filosofia by Zuzana Licko

Content and trigger warnings can be found at nataliajaster.com/trick

For Roman, my beloved troublemaker

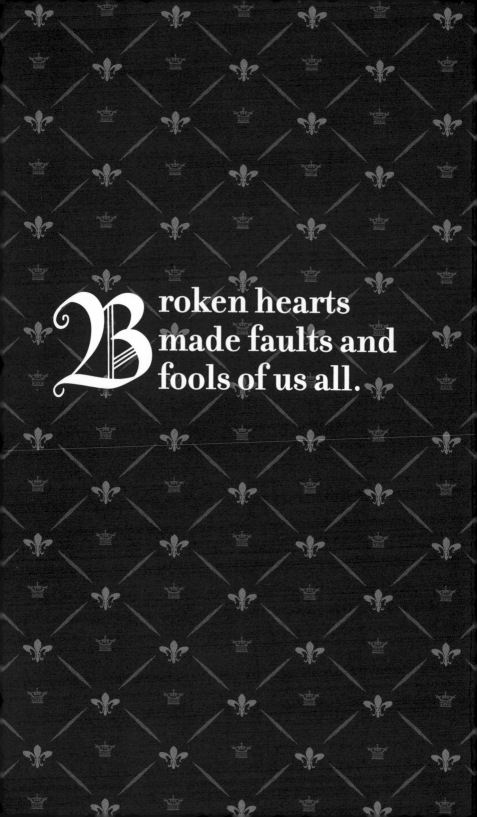

Broken hearts made faults and fools of us all.

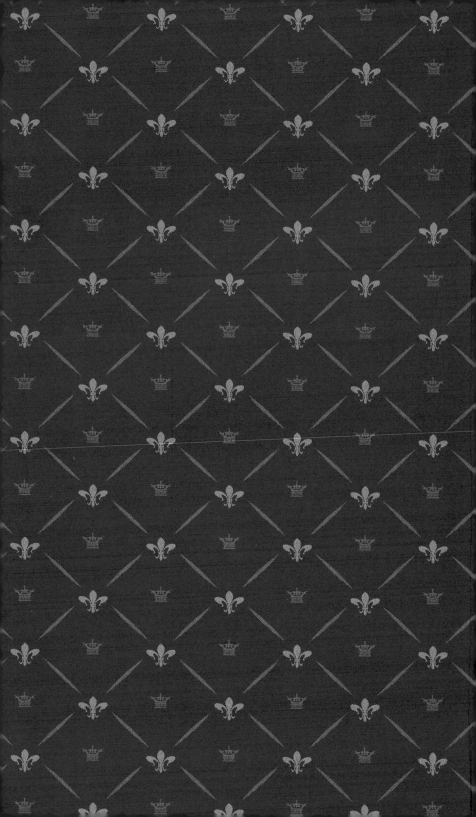

PROLOGUE

Poet

Come here, my sweeting. I have a story to share. I shall amuse you, I promise. 'Tis what I do best. If you consider my costume, with its silken frills and leather thrills, my specialties will be more obvious.

Aye. That's right. Come to me.

And fear not, for I'm renowned. My voice is smooth, my words are spiced, and my smile wickedly pretty. Courtiers say as much whilst lifting goblets to their mouths. Their teeth scrape over the cup rims, their lips tinted from wine as they talk of my skills—the ones I perform in throne rooms, as well as in beds.

I know what people say, for I'm attuned to the whispers in this sensuous court. Rumors drift through the halls, the details carried along on erotic breezes, easy to catch if you're sly.

Have I not mentioned I live in a castle? You'll learn more about that soon.

Indeed, I have your attention. Splendid.

My name is Poet. What is yours?

Hush. Let me guess.

Now allow me to list my attributes. I can flip across a floor like liquid, mock behind your back, and steal your moans with a touch. I speak with the silver tongue of a trickster. If you ask nicely, I'll delight you with a rhyme, a few lines of verse spun for your pleasure.

If you ask even nicer, I might grace you with that rhyme in private—as you like.

I'm a trinket, an accessory of the Crown. I'm a riddle, a brilliant whore, a hidden agenda.

The better to outwit you.

I'm the finest jest you'll ever know. If you irritate me, I'll strike you down with words, for swords are the toys of knights, whilst I use more penetrating weapons.

That doesn't mean I don't know how to handle a blade. For I can. And I have. Many times, I've kept one close whilst slipping undetected from this court, my silhouette passing in and out of shadows, with the guards none the wiser. A weapon has been necessary on those nights, and reaching my priceless destination, my dangerous little secret, has been worth the risk.

Still, my wit is sharper than a blade—and even lovelier than a fuck. And ah, that is the greatest triumph, because it brings even the most artful of this kingdom to their knees.

For only a clever man knows how to play the fool.

Yet none of these skills can deceive a strong will. Recently, I've learned that lesson well.

I had seen her. I'd been watching her.

Soon, I would have her. Yet even sooner, I would lose myself in her.

So let me tell you how I picked a sinful battle against a powerful opponent.

Not a king. Nor a queen.

Nay. I chose their daughter.

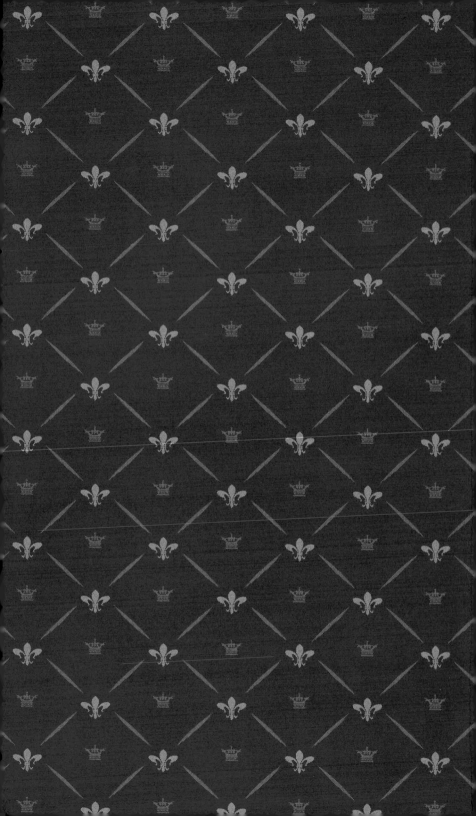

I

Briar

I took a deep, floral breath and held it.

Held it good and tight.

Outside the castle walls, sunset drenched the horizon in shades of deep red and feverish gold. Pitched roofs germinating with moss from the lower town formed a northern crescent around this palace. And surrounding both, rolling hills sprawled across the vista, where blossoms shivered and grasses clapped with noise.

Beyond that stood the wildflower forest.

Gripping the balcony's ledge, I exhaled and squinted at the view. According to the tales, that famed woodland inspired the most reckless of cravings. Within certain glades and hollows, the air emitted fragrances that spurned people to all manner of impulsive acts.

Provocative things happened in that wild. Equally provoking things occurred in this court.

My fingers tightened on the rim. I studied the panorama carpeted in fringes of greenery like something out of faerie lore. Father used to say most fondly how this place brought out the nymph in everyone. In me, especially.

But if Father were alive today, if he knew me now, he would be wrong.

I retreated from the vista and entered the confines of my suite. The interiors were adorned with peony bouquets and linen bedding as light as moth wings. Shades of dark green flourished through the space, the kind of color that seemed to awaken you the moment your eyes landed on it.

Forest green, the lush color of Spring.

I was raised on sensible brown. Autumn, a land of sense and serenity. My nation and my refuge.

One month. One month in this sinful court, and then I would return home.

My traveling trunk had been unpacked. Wrapped in a dressing gown, I stepped toward the wardrobe to choose a dress for the evening.

As my eyes stumbled across the bed, my feet stalled. A scarlet ribbon lay sprawled atop one of the pillows, as if someone had draped it there.

I turned a full circle, scrutinizing the room.

No one. Alone.

The only other person who had recently occupied this suite had been a maid, a chatty bird of a female who'd come bearing towels and gossip. True, the ribbon could have been a random oversight, one of her misplaced mending supplies. Except I could not remember the strip of fabric being there minutes ago, long after the servant had left.

No, somebody else had been in my suite. Someone who'd had the *nerve* to trespass without my permission. And they wanted me to know it.

I was no stranger to this kingdom, with its taste for revelry—not counting excess and debauchery—but this was odd. And brazen. Even a noble wouldn't take such an anonymous liberty. And I should have heard the noise from the balcony.

Pursing my lips, I marched toward the bed, snatched the ribbon from its perch, and dropped it into the nearest drawer. There. Onward. I would address the cheeky item later.

The door swooped open. Mother skipped inside, flew straight to the bed, and threw herself onto it. "Mmm," she cooed, her eyelids fluttering closed as she pawed at the duvet. "Your bed is comfortable."

I set my hands on my hips. "Mother."

"All these feathers."

"Mother."

"Yes, dearest Daughter?"

"You are not sleeping here tonight."

She snuggled into the down like a feline. "So soft. So queenly. I shall have a good rest this evening."

"I know you heard me."

Queen Avalea of Autumn released a dramatic whine. "You don't understand. It's a full moon in Spring and bad luck to sleep alone. We must join forces. A woman never knows when a phantom or an incubus might sneak into her chambers to claim her in the dead of night."

"You're of age now," I deadpanned. "You'll manage on your own."

"So strict to your mama. What have I done to deserve it, Briar?"

As she feigned a pout, a wave of tenderness gusted through my chest. I loved her. She loved me. That wasn't the problem.

Father was the problem. His memory lived between us, slumbering in our rooms and feasting at our table. Daily, he strung us together and tore us apart.

A long time ago, I'd done my worst to him. I could not undo it, and he was gone. But no matter how many years passed, no matter how I tried to atone and fix myself, to be perfect for the leftovers of our family, the guilt was eternal.

I did not deserve Mother's affection. Nor would I permit myself to get attached.

She made a show of stirring, not just with her sparkling eyes but with her whole body, with her limbs stretching to the foot of the bed and the crisp scent of apples infused into her hair—red like mine, but aged to rust.

Aside from our tresses, we were nothing alike. When I was born, the people of Autumn had foreseen another jewel, a female graced with Mother's ripe, curvy attributes.

They got me instead.

To the naive and the uninspired, princesses were supposed to be lovely, from their manicured toes to their polished crowns. A princess possessed the desired traits: long curls, a rosette mouth, actual height. Royals were the pinnacle of beauty.

No one imagined an heiress homely or plain. Or Seasons forbid, sharp. A princess was the bud of the flower, not the thorn.

Well. This unanimous assumption was quite stupid.

In any case, Autumn had not anticipated a female like me. A knobby twenty-year-old bramble with steely irises, pinched features, and the body of a twig. I didn't see a problem with this, except it made me appear too much like my dead father and not enough like my living mother. Our subjects wanted the future queen to be honorable, but also a duplicate of Mother—radiant, voluptuous, and overflowing with what they called sociability.

She was a wise ruler, but she had her amiable ways of getting things done. And I would have my own someday, exercising sound judgment and a steadfast mind. I wouldn't require the people's adoration, only their respect and loyalty.

"Uh-oh," Mother said. "You look cross. What is it this time?" The mattress cushioned her figure as she patted the space beside her. "Come. Join me and speak your mind."

The image of Mother spreading her arms to my troubles choked me with longing. Her hope to share my bed had nothing to do with full moons, apparitions, or legends such as incubi, and everything to do with resurrecting the closeness we used to have, back when I was a child. We'd been a complete family then, before this place held painful memories.

I wanted to curl up with her and explain myself. I wanted to protest that she should have left me behind in Autumn, where I could help run the kingdom in her absence instead of leaving it to our advisors.

However, the very act of confiding anything—to anyone—made me queasy.

The mystery gift bestowed upon me was another vexing matter. But if I showed the ribbon to Mother, she would only tease me for taking the gesture too seriously.

Known as the wiliest and most wanton of courts, Spring flourished a world away from the perpetual Autumn foliage of my own home. Every year, the Royals traveled to this region for the Peace Talks, a truce gathering between The Dark Seasons. It was an important cause, yet an invisible weight pressed my shoulders down. Anticipating the welcome feast tonight gnawed through me. I did not relish drinking or dancing.

Most certainly not dancing.

A princess never puts herself first.

Indeed. I had no right to brood. This trip wasn't about me.

I retreated to the wardrobe. "We need to get ready for the feast."

Except I was the only one not dressed. And it had come out sterner than I'd intended.

A mirror hung above the dressing table. In the pane's reflection, Mother flinched, the sight chafing me with remorse. I opened my mouth to apologize just as she forced a smile onto her face. She swung her legs over the mattress and sashayed toward me, her ample hips jutting from side to side, as though she'd been conceived in this risqué court instead of in Autumn.

How did she move that way so effortlessly? How did she make herself malleable, worthy of our conservative homeland yet skilled at blending in with this indiscreet land like a chameleon?

I twisted to face the wardrobe. The hangers were inundated with the toasty colors of Autumn, plus a few alternatives customized for Spring. From the selection, I grabbed a stately gown of hazel damask with exquisite tailoring and simple, clean lines. The notched collar would offset the short sleeves, and the lavish textile would elevate the straightforward cut from industrious to celebratory.

No trim. No beading. No nonsense.

"Is that what you're wearing?" Mother inquired.

Every single vertebra prickled. "Yes."

17

"Then I'll rephrase: That won't do. Not in this court."

Reaching over my shoulder, Mother thrust her hand into the wardrobe and withdrew one of the alternatives, a new design she'd ordered from the seamstresses. I dutifully allowed her to button me up. The pine green silk gown had elbow-length sleeves, a *low* square neckline, and a tight bodice that inflated my breasts to their full capacity. The hem bustled around my knees while a longer skirt of lighter, complimentary green silk flared out beneath, the folds reminiscent of inverted petals.

Two embellishments followed: a gold belt whittled into leaves and a matching pair of hair clips. Mother argued with me. She insisted the clips sweep only half the layers off my face, enabling the rest to tumble carelessly down my back, in the fashion of Spring.

The prospect curdled my stomach. An Autumn female did no such thing—plaits and headdresses reigned in my land—and allowing my hair to run rampant was a recipe for tangles. In addition, it would draw the sort of male attention I did not care for.

At the dressing table, I tore a brush through my hair, affixed my locks into a braid at the crown of my head, and secured it with the clips. "I'm a future monarch, not a mermaid."

Mother flung up her arms. "Oh, Briar. I give up."

Not a moment later, company arrived in a whirlwind of satin. Seven courtiers, all my age and with sun-kissed complexions ranging from peachy to dark, in stark contrast to my pale skin.

The Queen of Spring's ladies.

The clique strutted into the room, their hips swinging and their gazes confident. Upon seeing the queen, they grinned and dashed across the space. When they finally remembered to stop, the ladies bumped into each other, then burst into impish chortles.

Cadence. Freya. Lisette. Vale. Posy. Questa. Rhiannon.

They dipped into a graceful row of curtsies, each one cooing, "Your Majesty" and "Majesty" and so forth until all seven had performed their greetings.

A pause followed. I waited as the Seven finally remembered themselves. "Your Highness," they said to me in unison, same congenial octave they'd afforded Mother.

They flocked to her, surrounding the queen l chirping over each other in enthusiasm. "Welcome back," and missed you," and "There's going to be such levity at the feast tonight," and "I'm in lust," and "She's always in lust," and "But I'm in *exceptional* lust," and "No, the *real* word for it is obsession."

The Seven listed the revelers attending tonight's event, from noblemen to female soldiers. However, they kept cycling back to the entertainment, hinting at a savory performance while withholding the details. They cast each other knowing glances and raved over the delicious secret of it.

A fine line existed between distinguished fun and Spring fun. Frivolous at best. Indecent at worst. Visions of a sword-swallower wrapped in a loin cloth and greased in oil flitted through my head. That, and an erotic dance that involved even less clothing.

I pinned myself to the dressing table's chair, watching as the effervescent group modeled their gowns and spread their skirts wide. Wrist bangles jingled from their arms. One of the outfits boasted a high slit and a visible garter hugging the female's thighs.

As if to buoy themselves, three of the ladies imitated a classic Spring dance in prelude to the evening. The trio hummed a tune, circling one another in a formation that managed to exude spirit, allure, and sensuality.

In between conversing with the other females, Mother smiled and offered compliments to the dancers.

I kept quiet, squeezing my hands in my lap.

"Join them, Briar," Mother encouraged. "Go on. For me."

I had wounded her once already. I could not refuse.

Even so, this would not end well.

After a moment's hesitation, I stood and approached the trinity of swaying figures while fighting to keep my chin aloft. While the ladies spun, I moved as though made of wood. Each ligament tensed, no better than if I'd been nailed together.

Mother rose from her perch by the hooded fireplace. "If you'll excuse me," she announced, the belt tassels around her waist knocking together. "Do keep Briar company."

She bobbed her finger toward me and mouthed a silent *Stay*, then left.

I suffered inwardly. I was quite sure the others did as well.

The three dancing females refrained from verbally reacting as I treaded on their toes. Instead, they beamed to my face, though the trio swapped very different looks over my shoulder.

Posy had been blessed with plush curves like Mother, a nose as tiny as her namesake, and a string of inked blossoms looping along her collarbone.

Vale's dark skin complimented her burgundy irises, which matched the shade of her hair.

Cadence's evergreen tresses cascaded down her swanlike figure.

Rhiannon and Lisette kept talking. Freya and Questa joined in the dance, which enabled Posy to detach herself and use the opportunity to snoop at my possessions. She appraised everything from my shoes, aligned in a neat row beside the wardrobe, to my signature quill and a stack of my favorite illuminated manuscripts.

Satisfied, Posy trotted to the window and unfastened it. Not an instant into her daydream, the female gasped, "Oh, my Seasons. It's him!"

The dance broke apart. Pandemonium ensued. The ladies stampeded to the sill—what in the *world*?—and squished their heads through the gap.

"Your Highness, you must have a look," Posy whispered.

"A long, stiff, smutty look," Freya purred.

"Your Highness, may we watch him from your balcony?" Questa pleaded.

"Are you mad?" Vale asked, winding her dark arm around Posy's waist. "From there, he'll hear us."

"If Posy's virginal squeal didn't alert him already," Rhiannon said.

"He'll see us, too," Lisette added.

"No, he won't," Questa vouched. "Stop catastrophizing."

Cadence ran her finger across the sill. "Devil, take me hard."

"Or take me prisoner," Vale amended, earning a round of chuckles.

"Your Highness," Posy chirped. "You'll miss him."

No, I would not. I took my time reaching them, hardly in the mood to fuss over some buck. The group parted, allowing me to peek out the window and feign interest for their sake. The view spanned not only the hills of Spring, but also one of the gardens below.

And like a sudden quickening of the pulse, there he was.

2

Briar

Somewhere in Spring's lower town, a storyteller penned a fable, a florist arranged stems, and a nobleman slipped into a courtesan's bed. I hardly required clairvoyance to see this, much less a telescope. Life carried on, drifting aimlessly like the clouds.

Yet it stopped.

Life halted like a breath. Time stood still in the garden, where a figure stalked through the gate, his shape filling the void as if he owned the space. Two sentinels snapped to attention, their poleaxes clicking in place as the male silhouette sauntered past them.

Sunset had given way to twilight. Deep shadows draped over the lawn while several torches threw hot amber light across the grounds. Like those flames, the figure's tall, athletic outline penetrated the darkness. He moved like a phantom—smooth and elusive, impossible to grab a hold of.

Restlessness crackled though me as I watched him bypass the guards. This garden was restricted to Royals, yet he'd waltzed in.

Above black leather pants, a long coat swatted his calves as he moved. The garment molded to his shoulders, and the cuffs were rolled up his forearms, both details alluding to a muscled body beneath. His red standing collar burned through the murk with defiance, like a broken rule.

Despite my vantage point, I knew expensive fabric when I saw it. He dressed too fine to be a servant yet too glibly to be a noble, even at this brazen court.

Someone who existed outside those perimeters, then? One of the prominent court artists?

Shy of a torchlit beam, he stalled. Though shadows concealed his features, he stood there, sensing something. After a second, his head slid toward a hedge, where another form materialized.

The woman idled between the bushes, her dress cinched tightly and her feet bare. She ducked her head—tresses the color of rosewood, from what I could tell—and gave the male a sidelong glance. If I had to guess from the dip of her chin and the thrust of one hip, I would peg her demeanor as coquettish and perhaps a little daring.

But the longer the male figure watched her, the quicker his attention seemed to strip the woman of certainty. Her posture wavered, suddenly intimidated.

My companions and I stared.

After a moment's contemplation, the figure made his decision. He plucked an orchid from one of the garden beds and twirled it absently between his fingers like a toy. Then he prowled toward her.

The woman inched back but held her ground as he halted inches from her. While gliding the orchid petals down her profile, the dark figure watched as the woman buckled from the contact. And as he moved forward like a predator, she moved back like prey, the motions in tandem.

They vanished into the hedges. A moment later, a tremulous, feminine moan splintered through the air.

Heat rushed up my throat. The Seven wrestled each other for a glimpse, but it was no use. We couldn't see them anymore from this prospect.

"Lucky bitch," Cadence muttered, indifferent to my shocked glare.

"I didn't recognize her," Posy said. "It takes cheek to get past sentinels guarding the Royal wing, much less to approach *him*. She must be a courtesan."

"Pfft. As if he needs to pay for a whore," Vale revoked. "I'd say she's a resident dancer. She has the body of one."

"No," Cadence scoffed. "He doesn't fuck court performers."

"How do you know?"

"Everyone knows."

Another moan skittered through the lawn. At the sound, I bristled.

One, how dare these ladies speak so freely in my presence. Two, how dare I take part in voyeurism.

I berated my conscience and was about to wrench the casement closed when the male re-emerged. He strode from the hedges without pause, as though nothing had transpired in there. Resuming his original path, he proceeded down the garden lane. Torchlights sketched the dark layers of hair teasing his nape, plus a stack of ribbon-like bracelets encircling one of his wrists.

The woman didn't return. The orchid he'd stolen was nowhere in sight.

I frowned. This amounted to crumbs. What inspired me to keep observing him, as if more obscene displays might happen any second, I didn't know.

The princess in me huffed aloud.

And that's when he stopped walking.

Clamping their hands over their mouths, the ladies ducked. Because I hadn't thought to do the same thing, I stood there, visible and grasping the sill.

The stranger's head slanted sideways, tilting faintly in the direction of my balcony. I sensed his eyes skewering the ground in concentration, listening rather than looking.

The angle revealed traces of his profile. I prided myself on having keen eyesight and caught the fiendish twitch of his lips.

He heard me. He knows I've been watching.

I thought he might turn and look up. Instead, the specter snapped his fingers lightly, as though in deliberation, then kept going. He crossed the garden, that long coat whipping around his frame, then vanished like fog through a door leading into the north wing.

The Seven popped back up. Cadence made a feral noise reminiscent of a cat in heat. "I know other places he can snap those fingers."

"You are shallow," Vale chuckled.

Candace shrugged. "Not where it matters to Poet."

I would have startled at the crude remark, had I not been distracted. Poet.

Was that his name? What sort of pretentious moniker was that?

Again, the pants and coat didn't pass for a servant's livery or noble's attire, but a person belonging to an entirely different class. A male who sported a lavish standing collar, black leathers, and a set of ribbon bracelets around his wrist.

One of them had been red. Scarlet.

Cadence misread my expression, and her lips slanted in derision. "Sorry, Your Highness. That was shady of me."

She didn't sound or look like she regretted the lewd comment. "I must dress," I heard myself say, too gripped by anxiousness—I wanted a second look at that ribbon in my drawer—to remember that I was already clothed.

My announcement ushered the females out the door. As they trotted down the hall, a muffled *prude* combined with the courtiers' answering sniggers wormed their way into my suite.

Privately, I winced but kept my chin raised.

Unlike every other female Royal, Mother and I didn't keep a retinue of ladies-in-waiting at our disposal. By tradition, practical and simple Autumn required only one for each of us.

However, Mother's lady was very much pregnant, and mine had taken ill and been unable to accompany me. This meant the clan that just exited the room would take up the gauntlet, should they be requested.

Well. Mother could have any one of them, if only for appearance's sake.

For my part, I'd been granted the privilege to rule a kingdom. I could certainly tighten a corset by myself.

As for the ribbon, I strode to the dresser, fished the scarlet fabric from inside, and draped it across my wrist. The shade blazed as hotly as the one that specter had been wearing.

In The Dark Seasons, the gift of a ribbon symbolized a person's esteem for someone they admired. But this didn't feel like a gift. It seemed like a tease.

Or something more dangerous—like a target.

3

Briar

My skirt fanned around my legs and brushed the corridor's tiled floor. In the hallway, ivy entwined the pillars and crept up the edifices the same way it did over the castle's exterior. Alcoves exhibited stained glass windows that depicted the court's numerous gardens.

I checked over my shoulder, making sure none of my assigned guards had caught sight of my departure. Despite the hidden passage leading to and from my suite—a safety measure constructed within a wall panel, as in every Royal apartment—one couldn't be too certain of fleeing undetected.

The absence of moving shadows reassured me. I swerved forward, found the right outlet, and exited the castle. From there, I picked my way across one of the lawns and down a lengthy path toward the ruins of a tower.

It used to be connected to the stronghold centuries ago. Today, weeds shrouded the crumbling walls and fabricated an ancient garden. Fallen chunks of masonry and blooming hyacinths carpeted the expanse, and the once-great towers rose to only half their original heights. The structures loomed like broken teeth in a backdrop of stars. Centuries had reduced some foundations to mere splinters of stone, the facades embroidered in foliage.

Yet I liked it here. I liked the age of this rubbled memorial, the history it carried on its shoulders.

People rarely came here, which made it ideal for secrecy. I loved meeting him in this place—the timelessness of it.

One. Two. Three.

"Psst," came the signal from behind.

My mood lifted. Rather than *psst* back—I was no longer a child—I wheeled toward the sound and tapped my foot rhythmically. I doubted it reached his ears, no matter how finely tuned. But there were too few instances in which I used my feet in a jaunty manner.

"Minion," I whispered.

"Master," he whispered back.

"Minstrel."

"Monarch."

Fingers tickled me in the ribs. I whirled to find Eliot kneeling, a lopsided grin spanning his face before he bowed his head. "Your Supreme Highness," he quipped.

Momentarily, my own grin faltered. We'd been reuniting in this manner since that wonderful and terrible day when we were twelve years old. Yet I worried we couldn't remain like this forever, exploiting our ranks in idle amusement.

"Soooo," Eliot wondered. "May I rise?"

"You may," I recited.

The second he got to his feet, the facade dropped. We chuckled, snatched each other into a tight hug, and I sank into his embrace. That unforgettable market afternoon from our childhood—and the weeks, months, and years of disguised letters that followed—tethered us to one another despite the distance.

Unforgettable Eliot. The sole reason I looked forward to visiting Spring. My one true friend.

And a transgression.

Treat one another with dignity, but do not stray from your class. Marry within your station and Season. Live and die there.

The Seasons maintained that standard. Our allied lands freed us from marriages of convenience. If any of us found ourselves in dire straits and required aid, we negotiated in other ways. An age-old treaty saw to that.

Monarchs could wed as they chose and to whichever lover they wished, so long as those choices reflected their ranks. Casual romps between hierarchies weren't taken seriously, but anything beyond that was forbidden.

Intimate friendships, for instance.

Naturally, people breached this rule behind closed doors. As a princess setting an example for her land, no one suspected me of being such a person. Regardless, I allowed myself this single indulgence. It was worth the risk and always would be.

"Briar," he murmured into my shoulder.

"Eliot," I replied.

Our given names. Much better. Far worse.

I yearned to have a brother. If only he and I shared the same bloodline, lived in the same court, we would not have to hide like this.

Eliot tried to pull back, but I held him fast. "Not yet."

"Aren't I the lucky one." He obliged, clasping me to him. "It's my private duty to keep the Princess of Autumn sane among this depraved lot. How is this for a hug? I've been practicing. That is, I haven't been practicing on other heiresses. Not that there are any others to practice with, and even if there were, they'd smack the shit out of me if I touched them. Not that I would touch them, because well, maidens aren't my fancy—except for you. But what I mean is, it's been a long time, so I want to get the moment right. Is it right?"

Eliot tended to ramble. When we were younger, I'd sought to tame his digressions but eventually learned it would be easier to clear a moat with a ladle.

"Your embrace is unmatched," I answered, then realized with contrition that I hadn't disputed his remark about keeping me composed while in the clutches of Spring. Eliot was more to me than a crutch.

"Not everything about Spring is depraved," I conceded. "Only most of it."

"Still stubborn, aren't you? You act like you've never been here. It's as if you're afraid the walls will devour you, which they won't unless you're having one hell of a nightmare, or unless we're speaking figuratively, or unless you have kinks I don't know about."

Before he went on a tangent, I stepped back. "Let me see you properly."

We surveyed each other. He had grown statuesque, whereas my legs had failed to stretch. Otherwise, Eliot looked the same. Gilded locks. Charming dimples. Wistful eyes. At twenty like me, his physique cut a fine figure in the elegant musician's garb, his black checkered coat etched in bronze.

The makings of a lute tattoo covered the side of his neck, while the rest of the concealed design wrapped around the edge of his shoulder. His ballads proved a bit fanciful in their lyrics, with notions of courtly seduction and such prattle, but the melodies were nice.

"I approve," I said. "You outshine a Royal any day."

He grinned. "How long do we have?"

"About fifteen minutes before I must rush back. My escorts will be knocking soon after."

"I'd say it must be nice having a set of bulky men brandishing weapons and flanking you like a sandwich on a regular basis. But from your sour puss, I doubt you'd agree."

I crossed my arms and teased, "What makes you think they're all men? They could be women."

"True. I was fantasizing. It happens." Eliot eyed the braid crowning my head. "I'll never understand Autumn. What do you mean by this style? You're a guest of Spring, you know. Ladies wear their hair loose here."

"I am not a lady."

He chuckled too loudly. I shushed him while trying not to laugh back, which was difficult. I hadn't heard his infectious humor in a year, and I'd missed it. Eliot was one of those people who made others chortle simply from listening to his mirth. It didn't matter if the joke or comment were truly funny. I would make a wry comment, and he would find it uproarious, and soon I would be joining him.

We once guffawed for a full minute. I'd never forgotten that.

The familiar scents of woodsmoke and sage wafted from his skin, mingling with new aromas. I detected notes of amber and vetiver, which didn't come naturally from him.

No, they came from someone else.

His flushed skin. His swollen lips. His intoxicated eyes.

"You've been wooed," I blurted, the revelation jumping off my tongue.

Eliot's grin deepened. "Wooed? Such a genteel word for sex. Not that sex was involved—yet."

"Involved, how? And with whom?"

Sheepish, he glanced at his boots and went uncharacteristically mute. It was not romantic between us. Eliot preferred males, and I preferred anything but romance.

"Don't insult me by faking coyness," I probed. "Tell me about him this instant."

"Not a damn chance. I can't do him justice. I'll get the details wrong."

"You will not."

"Because you say so?"

"Being a Royal does have its perks."

Eliot slouched against the wall, ardor cutting an uncensored path through his face. "Where do I start? He's gorgeous. He inspires me. When we entertain—"

"He's a musician?"

"I'm the musician. Poet's more than that."

Poet again. That specter who'd been fondling a woman mere hours before—or perhaps, after—feeding on Eliot's mouth. It seemed many were besotted with this bloodhound, which couldn't bode well for my friend.

"More than that," I quoted Eliot. "How much more?"

"Oh hell, don't make me answer," he begged. "I don't want to ruin it. Anyway, you'll have to see for yourself at the feast."

My forehead crinkled like paper. Since when did Eliot refrain from elaborating on his thoughts?

"Will I like him?" I asked, already knowing the answer. "Will I give my blessing?"

"Absolutely not." He smoothed out his ensemble. "So do I look different? They say one does after falling under a person's spell, but I haven't glanced at my reflection to check. Does it make me look more muscular? I've heard desire of this magnitude has that effect, but you can't believe everything the gossips say. They're stupid drunk most of the time. Much of what they tell me is bullshit, which is disappointing."

That was more like him. Nevertheless ...

"Dammit, Briar. Don't scowl at me like that," he groaned. "You're sure to be the only one who despises him. Everyone from aristocrats, to fauna keepers, to artists are at Poet's mercy. If they're not salivating over his face, they're gawking at his coc—never mind," Eliot backpedaled, seeing the reproachful look on my face. "And if they're not fetishizing his body, Poet's words alone will get them to bend over and spread—"

I slapped his arm and spoke over his yelp. "For Season's sake. Spring residents and their filthy vocabularies."

"All right, but there's no reason to get physical," he complained while rubbing his arm. "You've been gone a while, and my tongue keeps getting older."

"Enough about your tongue. You were saying?"

"I was saying not to fret. Your blessing won't be necessary. Poet hardly commits, this court is his playground, and Seasons help anyone who gets his attention."

"His playground."

"To say the least. Poet's not only the court's special weapon, but he's also their greatest temptation—the kingdom's celebrity and the court's libertine. He has no problem with this, and he makes no bones about it, which means I'm the fool's fool."

"Meaning?"

"Meaning, obsession is my destiny. I'm officially whipped. I only wish I had your willpower." Eliot scratched the back of his neck and forced a laugh. "Maybe you could teach me how to resist a man's sexual prowess. Is that teachable?"

I wouldn't know. No man has ever been rude enough to proposition me.

Eliot's despair was palpable, a fine layer of sorrow hiding beneath the humorous tone. This carnivorous Poet person had seduced my friend without returning his affections.

I knew what it did to Eliot's spirit whenever someone deceived him. During last year's Peace Talks, a repugnant knight had taken Eliot's virginity and then cast him aside without a second thought. I'd yearned with the burning intensity of an inferno to mash my fist into that knight's face for disregarding my friend. In any case, the man was long gone now, patrolling an outlying estate for reasons I couldn't care less about.

I had no experience to fall back on, but I knew enough to conclude that consummation should be treated with significance. It should have greater value. Case in point, I would never understand this court's flavor for vagrant promiscuity. It had done nothing to protect Eliot, despite him having grown up here.

What I'd witnessed in the orchid garden weighed on my mind like bricks. Eliot tried to put up a front, but he possessed an open soul and wore his heart on his sleeve, unlike the rest of his kin. One-night stands didn't exist in his head. Spring roots aside, he lacked the armor for rejection.

I took his hand and squeezed it. "You are invaluable. And someday, your perfect match will see that. Until then, if you're as obsessed as you claim, it's because you choose to be. Feelings can be controlled. It's in your power to rise above them."

Eliot peeked between his blond waves. "You think so?"

33

I knew so. Or for his sake, I hoped so, because I feared seeing him hurt again.

How I wished everyone knew what Eliot meant to me. But although I hated keeping our relationship a secret, I did it willingly. He was my one exception to the rules. Other than with him, I would not defy this world.

No one else was worth the risk. No one else would ever tempt me.

In the great hall, candles spilled ambient light across the space, and the guests moved about in boisterous fits and bursts. The vaulted ceiling's glass panels offered a view of the night sky, while the melody of a pan flute skipped its way through the commotion.

Though, not everyone was talking. One man in a fox mask backed another male against a wall and drew his tongue up the recipient's neck. Several attendants donned other animal masks, from the black feathers of a crow to the muzzle of a lion.

In another corner, an older woman dropped a petal atop a younger man's tongue. As he swallowed, his eyes became glassy with euphoria, which signaled it wasn't just any petal.

At the threshold, I swerved away from the scene, only to stumble across several more uninhibited episodes. A couple fed one another wedges of stone fruit and watched each other during every prolonged bite. Another pair fidgeted with one another's clothing, their hands fondling each trim of fabric within reaching distance, to the point where the top of a breast pushed from a neckline, and a pert nipple studded into view. Meanwhile, a man traced his thumb along a knight's lips, thus dabbing a bead of wine from the crook before swiping it across his own tongue.

So much Spring in one place. Nowhere to avoid it.

Anxiety trickled through me. Moisture beaded my palms. Yet blessedly, my heart hid safely within my chest as it knocked, knocked, knocked.

By now, I knew what to expect of this court. This was nothing compared to the audacities that would occur later. Every act was a tease, an appetizer, a promise of things to come once the hours deepened and darkened.

But this time, why did I feel surprised by these displays? Why did my posture buckle?

Since last year, had I merely forgotten—or blocked out—this culture's lack of virtue? Or during my past visits, had I been too young to notice or care about these finer points, much less allow them to scorch the tips of my ears?

I composed my features and stifled the urge to duck my head. No one here would appreciate the discretion. Everyone who witnessed me try would only smirk behind their fans.

Mist coated the air and floated to the rafters. The ripe scent of berries perfumed the hall.

A pair of courtiers kissed open-mouthed across their table, the tips of their tongues sliding against one another. Fleetingly, they broke apart and heaved. Then the female's teeth nipped at the male's lower lip before they dove in again. Mouths angled and clamped together, moving in a sinuous rhythm.

Yes, I must have blotted out these images in the past. Otherwise, I would have remembered mouths kissing that way—that hard and that long.

It wasn't done in Autumn. At least, not in public. Moreover, I had always refused to hear the details of Eliot's experiences.

I stood on the threshold and gaped at the couple.

Just then, the weight of someone's gaze seized me. Like an invisible cord, it slithered around my waist and tugged—not like an enticement but a challenge.

I pried my attention from the lusty sight and scanned the hall with furrowed brows, only to find the guests absorbed in each other. Honestly, the weight could be coming from anywhere. Its presence snuck up my neck like fingers, daring me to shiver.

I ignored the impulse and leveled my chin. Nevertheless, my flesh prickled like a traitor. Annoyed, I twitched rather harshly, fighting the disturbance.

"Her Royal Highness, Princess of Autumn."

A hall's worth of faces swerved in my direction. Thankfully, no one noticed how I'd been staring at the couple. No one except the source of that invisible weight.

A princess does not recoil.

A princess adapts wherever she goes.

I scrunched my lips together and stepped forward, layers of pine silk stroking my calves. Figures bowed and curtsied as I promenaded into the fox den.

Once I managed several steps, the bustle of activity resumed. As it did, that anonymous weight lifted, its retreat pulling a long-constrained breath from my lungs.

The Seven chattered to my left. Vale and Posy wove their fingers together and pecked one another's cheeks, and Cadence ribbed them affectionately. The ladies fed each other strawberries dripping with cream. They wore silk gowns in a prism of colors, with off-the-shoulder necklines exposing the swells of their cleavage, and floral buds ornamented their free-flowing tresses.

I patted the braid in my hair.

What did those females talk about in confidence? Would they tell me if I asked them? Or would they lie because I was a future ruler, and they had no choice but to be cordial?

The Royals of the Seasons presided from the dais.

Silvia and Doria of Winter. The eldest of the monarchs. Spectacles perched on their noses, white hair frothed from their heads, and decades of regal authority creased the women's faces.

Rhys and Giselle of Summer. A union of vitality. A robust husband in his late-thirties and a wife ten years his junior. Rhys had a jungle for a mustache and Giselle a whistle-like voice, so that she constantly sounded surprised.

Basil and Fatima of Spring. At twenty-six years of age, they were a jovial pair of monarchs who enjoyed finishing one another's sentences, laughing from the pits of their stomachs, and nuzzling their noses together.

Avalea of Autumn. The widowed Royal.

The lone sight of my mother clenched my heart. Of course, she wanted me here with her. She had no one else, having been robbed of a husband from the time I was twelve.

My fault. Forever.

Privately, I craved home, where my thoughts had no time to detour and every bit of time for routine.

Publicly, I greeted the Royals and took my seat beside Mother. While settling down, I resigned myself to suffer politely until midnight, like the good heiress I was.

Visitors could be guaranteed three things at this feast. The first, an overdose of Spring fare to rouse the taste buds. Apricots in fluted dishes. Asparagus drenched in sauce. Pies bloated with pork. I chewed, distracted by the view of countless mouths drinking, swallowing, and engaging in far more blatant activities.

The second guarantee, sensuality. That was what Spring liked to call it.

Though I'd witnessed this facet already, the prospect increased with every moment. A trio shared a long pipe as thin as a reed, from which floral-scented smoke plumed; the fondling couple from earlier now bared two breasts from the woman's bodice; and the latter pair hadn't yet peeled themselves from the liplock.

The third guarantee was music. Eliot appeared, lute in hand. This was a minstrel's domain, where words tumbled out of him to his heart's content, and everyone listened. He once confided to me that he should like to die singing.

I'd been jealous about that. I didn't know how I wanted to die, what I wanted to be doing when it happened.

Nor did I wish to ponder death. My father had done enough of that thing called dying.

Eliot began to play, his fingers deftly plucking the strings. He sang like honey, thick and sweet and pouring into the hall. It was all

I could do not to lean forward, prop my elbows on the table, and rest my chin in my hands, proper table manners be damned.

The song described a forbidden tryst between lovers of opposing social ranks. I paid less attention to the lyrics than to my friend's tenor.

When the song ended, I led the applause. This was our tradition, a detail camouflaged within the gaiety, my promise to trumpet him before anyone else did. He and I swapped a brief, conspiratorial look. I clapped and clapped and clapped.

Then I stopped.

Servants doused every mounted torch and candlestick, blanketing us in darkness. Twilight stole through the glass dome, illuminating the spot where Eliot had been, now replaced by a curtain of mist rising from two cauldrons set at opposite ends of the performance floor.

Within the haze stood a masculine outline. The figure was tall, a silhouette glazed in the half-light. From what I could tell, the specter wore dark hose stitched in metallic thread and no shirt, his naked torso sculpted with muscles.

He bowed with his arms spread, glossy black paint flashing from his fingernails. Something about the pose seemed both illicit and mocking.

My eyes slid across that carved male body, which shifted like a smoke—fluid, untouchable, and capable of blindsiding a person. Serpentine motions. Toned physique. With those attributes, he could likely spin into a full axis while balancing a stack of bricks.

Also, those movements matched the same provocative ones from the garden.

My breath hitched. Instantly, I knew.

I *knew* who he was.

From an unseen corner, the chords from Eliot's lute twined through the room again. The figure in the mist started to dance, slowly but without a sequence. With his head thrown back, he became a vapor, writhing and disorderly.

As the stranger twisted, skin and sinew flashed. The brackets of his shoulder blades cut through the miasma, and the ridges of his forearms flexed, candlelight burnishing every contracting part of him. Smooth grids of flesh tightened and released, pulling taut and then yielding with each turn.

The guests fell silent. I fell into a different sort of trap, one that overwhelmed me with restlessness. I had never moved that way or witnessed anyone do so.

What did it require, what sacrifice did the body make, to become such a limitless thing? Was it possible for a body to bend so far off its hinges that it snapped free and flew away?

It must take stamina to carry on like that, with little pause to draw breath, to suck in a lungful of it. Yet he made it look effortless, as if oxygen were an afterthought.

I wondered what it would take to deplete him of air. To push his limits until he wiped himself out and collapsed, panting and spent.

The line of his jaw flickered in and out of sight. I swallowed, my tongue suddenly parched, thirst overwhelming my palate.

To my shame, I wasn't in the minority. The revelers stared hard at him, their expressions reminiscent of corn kernels ready to pop.

Every mortal with a beating heart, a pair of eyes, and a set of genitals savored the whipcord view. Males leaned forward, one of them knocking over his tankard in the process. Females watched in a daze, as though they'd been glamoured by dark magic. Someone sighed, and another person draped a finger across their neckline, as if the room's temperature had spiked.

The dancer's abdominals stretched and constricted, ropes of cobbled flesh glossed in perspiration. For an instant, those muscles finally siphoned air. They expanded and deflated, heavily and hotly, as a fine sheen of moisture coated his sternum.

Beneath my skirts, my knees pressed together. They clasped until it hurt, trapping an inexplicable rush of humidity.

Other physical things occurred under my dress. Confusing things that stunned and horrified me. The cleft between my legs warmed, blood gushing to the apex of my thighs, and a curious but gentle ache filled the intimate seam.

In protest, I bit my lower lip. In desperation, I shifted in my seat.

Thankfully, the mortifying tension in my core receded, even if the heat sweltering my inner folds didn't. I snatched my chalice and guzzled water, my throat pumping and the liquid cooling my insides. Carefully, I set down the vessel.

For Season's sake, what had come over me? Once upon a time, I used to be an excitable girl, back when I was too young to know the difference between passion and prudence. That is, until I paid the price for it.

So never again.

The dark figure stopped, as did the music.

This gave me the chance to remember I detested him out of loyalty to Eliot. My friend, who could not see past enchantment to choose his paramours wisely.

That rake. The wrong choice.

In the dome's rays, the male pressed a finger to his lips. *Hush*, he might have said.

One of the servants must have been cued, because they threw him a small globe. When the figure caught the ball, another round of music started, with Eliot's lute and the pan flutist joining forces, along with someone pounding a drum. To their rhythm, the stranger sent the globe careening down his arm.

Then both arms swayed, cording together and sliding apart in rapid waves, casting an intricate path for the ball to trace. From palm to palm, elbow to elbow, shoulder to shoulder.

He tossed the sphere sideways behind him. When the opposite hand captured it, one ball became two. As he juggled them, the pair multiplied into three balls. Then four, then five, then six. The male pitched them in wayward directions, around his waist, in loops above his head. All this while dancing and rolling across the ground.

He caught the spheres with the tops of his bare toes, in the nape of his neck, in the dip of his lower back. He used his whole body.

It ended too soon. One by one, as they landed in his hands, he tossed out his props for the guests to catch.

And when the room settled down, the specter flicked his wrist, producing a thin candle. He blew on it, igniting the wick, the flame popping out of nowhere. The fog and his dexterous fingers must have kept us from noticing some pair of flint and steel, because there was no way he could have—

The revelers gasped. The male vaulted into a series of single-handed flips across the hall while carrying the burning taper with him. His biceps and abdomen flexed as he broke through the mist, his body lashing like a rope.

Coming straight toward me.

My heart galloped. I veered, my back ramming into the chair.

Tankards toppled from the table and clattered to the floor. Dishes slid to the banquet's edge, in danger of crashing.

Shocked, I glanced down and registered the tablecloth suffocating in my death-grip. I had unconsciously yanked on it, sending everything into disarray.

The elastic male landed on one hand and both knees. He wasn't kneeling in front of me as I had anticipated. Instead, he fronted my mother, to whom he proffered the flickering candle with a bowed head.

King Basil of Spring gained his feet. "My fellow monarchs of the Seasons," he boasted. "I give you Poet, the Court Jester of Spring."

Nobles erupted into applauses and hoots, male and female knights hammered their knuckles on the tables, and the Seven squeaked like aroused mice. The clamor made the ground rumble.

The figure lifted his head, revealing himself in the toasted glow of the room.

And I released the tablecloth. I might have dropped my chalice of nectar, had I been holding it.

I'd expected a pleasant face.

That was not what greeted me.

4

Briar

I saw vicious, green irises. I saw wicked lips and a great deal of trouble.

A long, black diamond pierced through one amused eye. A simpler thread of kohl lined the other orb.

He was older than me, perhaps exceeding my age by one or two years.

Poet. A jester. A beautiful one.

How did I not realize what he was the moment his limbs had pivoted?

It must have been the absence of a costume. His appearance defied tradition, lacking the typical motley ensemble of flaps, bell cap, and jester's staff.

Instead, he'd outfitted himself in dark hose trimmed with whorls of fine thread—authentic, expensive, gold thread—and nothing else. The chiseled plains of his torso rose and fell, his attributes exposed and taking up far too much space in the room.

He ignored me. Instead, the jester focused on my mother, his arm extended to offer her the candle in a droll imitation of chivalry. With a genial laugh, she accepted the light and wedged it into the nearest pillar.

As the guests raved, Poet rose to his feet, spread his arms wide, and gave a series of flamboyant bows to each table. His grin revealed a slightly crooked upper tooth, the naughty canine peeking out from the rest of his teeth.

Honestly, I had no exclusive cause to dislike him. Not when I scarcely knew him.

It was because of Eliot, I told myself. Absolutely because of Eliot, who stood in the corner with the other minstrels, his gaze melting like butter all over Poet. All because this rake of a jester was using my friend.

One of the servants tossed Poet a pouch. From it, he withdrew six more candles and distributed them to the monarchs, as tokens of welcome. Using my mother's taper, they created their own flames, partially brightening the hall once more.

With a final bow, the jester turned, excluding me from the gesture. I pretended not to care. I even went so far as to audibly harrumph.

I should have kept my mouth shut.

Poet paused mid-saunter, catching the sound.

The moment suspended itself like a held breath. Then he twirled— literally twirled around—and the ribbons encircling his wrist flapped. With that, he scanned the room as though remembering something important.

Hmm, that devious expression said. *I've neglected someone. Who could it be?*

His eyes scrolled across the hall, those notorious irises searching the crowd. The Seven snickered while I resisted the urge to throw a scowl in their direction.

The jester's gaze floated across the congregation, then latched onto me. Those coltish orbs glittered with a threatening sort of mischief—and familiarity, as if they had already memorized my features, as if he'd caught sight of me long before I caught sight of him. The density of his stare pushed into me, the pressure similar to the invisible weight from earlier.

An alarm bell rung in my head as endless pairs of eyes fixated on us. Refusing to cower, I raised my chin. Our audience watched as the jester strolled toward me while slipping a hand into the pouch. Petulant though it was, I would accept the stupid candle and then purposefully leave it unlit. It would send a message that I found his stunts lacking and unworthy of compliments.

My palm turned over for the taper. Poet dug through the pouch, then pantomimed checking a bunch of pockets he didn't have, then glanced under his feet. He came up empty-handed. In a show of mockery, he shrugged at poor little me and twisted from my pathetic, outstretched palm. It hovered, open but rejected.

A public judgment. A direct cut.

The room burst into guffaws. Eliot, the traitor, pressed a fist to his mouth to conceal his chuckles. My mother offered me an entertained but conciliatory smile.

I contemplated the ribbon in my drawer. It could be used for many things besides expressing admiration for someone. To choke them, for example. To bind their wrists and cut off their circulation.

A pair of barefooted acrobats balancing atop large hoops rolled into the hall. The male and female wore only tight pants that clung to their limbs, the woman's breasts and pink nipples just as exposed as her partner's chest.

At Poet's signal, they slid to the ground and proceeded to spin the hoops over their heads. As the background act and music continued, the guests strayed, abandoning their meals in the pursuit of frivolity.

The candles dimmed, their mellow light gilding the vast space and creating shadowed corners. As darkened niches multiplied, the feast shapeshifted into a bacchanal. Several revelers played a dice game in which the loser pouted her lips and unlaced her bodice. A languid pair tangled like snakes, their hips locked and gyrating slowly as they danced. Two knights seemed to have misplaced their weapons as they crushed themselves together, fused their mouths into one, and rutted against a pillar while a small crowd watched.

Without a backward glance, Poet quit the hall. The moment he was gone, gravity settled, and it became easier to suck in air. And as time dragged on, my breathing relaxed. Doubtless, that was the last I'd see of him.

That I continued to crane my neck and check the main doors made no sense, nor did my anticipation, which deflated with every second he remained absent. Although my exhalations grew steadier, my shoulders lowered a notch. For some reason, the environment lost what little appeal it had, as if he had stolen it, pirated it before I'd known it was there.

Never mind. I should be so grateful.

However, the devil returned less than an hour later.

My shoulders tensed the second he entered. He was freshly dressed, having changed into raven leather pants, a fitted jacket embellished with red studs, and black boots.

Poet's magnetic presence drew the revelers like an intoxicant, as potent and unhealthy as a guilty pleasure. But rather than unforgivable admiration, I felt a motivated thrill, a competitive spark fizzing through me. The more opportunities to observe him, the more chances to stake out his weak spots.

That trickster would pay for humiliating me. Perhaps not tonight, but soon.

The heads of every guest turned, following the man's progress as he ambled through the crowd. Some mooned over him and sought to gain his favor through sultry looks or witty conversations. Others shrank back, as if they feared catching his undivided attention.

In The Dark Seasons, the term "born fool" was universal across the courts. Although I detested giving anyone such labels, these individuals were divided into two classes: the "mad" and the "simpleton," and both belonged to the Crown.

The people whom this world called mad were deemed dangers to society. They were locked away in dungeons and oubliettes, the cells located either within each castle or across the lands.

The people whom this world called simpletons were forced into service in various ways, depending on the kingdom. Spring used those born souls for amusement. Basil and Fatima distributed them across the nation to traveling troupes or nobles who favored that sort of entertainment at their secluded estates. For that reason, there were no such individuals living in Spring's palace.

But in this Season, a third type of so-called "fool" existed. A professional one.

The jester.

A licensed figure and the product of training. Unlike born souls, jesters weren't owned by their sovereigns. They were high-ranking players specializing in the arts of candor, performance, and the turning of a phrase. As a trade, they journeyed with the sunset carnivals and midnight festivals that reigned across Spring.

All except the Court Jester. Being the most prized of his craft, he resided at court, where he was appointed to entertain the Crown, with the added liberty to counsel and influence the monarchy.

That was what Eliot had meant while referring to the jester as the Crown's special weapon. Being the most popular person in the room gave Poet power. It made him a prominent fixture when it came to political and social chess.

I snatched a fork, my grip tightening around the stem. A man should be either a Royal's trusted advisor or an artisan, not one and the same.

Eliot had once mentioned to me in a letter that the previous jester died of a fever, shortly after the last Peace Talks. Apparently, Poet had replaced him.

My friend's playing faltered as his attention strayed to Poet, who propped himself casually on the edge of the Seven's table. Posy appeared to be pleading with him, simpering while he shook his head, stole a strawberry off Vale's plate, and popped it into his mouth. Still chewing, he left the ravenous females staring after him, their gazes dripping with lust.

Not just a political and social influencer, but a widely desired one.

My knife skewered a slab of glazed ham. By some miracle, I'd witnessed the scene and still managed to keep my food down.

"Are you well?" Mother asked, studying me.

"Yes," I gritted out.

"I'm told he plans to charm us with prose tomorrow. He seems to have quite an effect on his audience."

"Pass the salt, please."

"I see how your eyes dissect him."

"Him, who?"

"And your chin crinkles like parchment when you're riled, dearest. Don't allow a few harmless candles to do that. Laugh at it." She wiggled in her seat, shifting toward me. "Here, I'll show you how to laugh."

I set down my napkin before she could do anything of the sort. "If you'll excuse me, I'm finished."

Mother's face fell. She stiffened in her chair. "Fine. Go."

Her curt tone made me flinch with regret. I opened my mouth to apologize, but she swerved away and inserted herself into a conversion with Summer's queen.

At the same time, a window of opportunity presented itself. The mingling, dancing, and inebriated guests created a dense throng—easy to slip away from. I flattened my lips but seized the chance, shoving back my chair, inclining my head toward the dais of occupied Royals, and descending the platform. After glancing around, I blended in and skirted along the perimeter to the exit.

I'd arrived at the feast with several escorts. Outside of sneaking through the secret passage from my room to meet Eliot, I lived and breathed among guards and coteries and entourages. Oftentimes, it was a wonder they didn't stalk me into the bathroom.

But for once, I didn't care about propriety. I made haste without bidding Eliot a covert farewell. On the way, my shoulder grazed someone else's. A noble wearing a horse mask turned my way and winked behind the visor.

"Princess," he crooned, ducking his head in a less than discreet manner.

I set my jaw and inched past him, then squeezed behind another groping couple and slipped through a crack in the main doors.

Beyond the threshold, I suppressed a sigh of relief. For as many residents dwelled in a castle, it grew quiet at night. One needed to strain to hear the clanking of armor, murmured conversation, and stuttered moans, all distant as though tucked behind cupboards.

Nevertheless, I hardly wished to be overheard and get caught. I wanted to preserve this moment, this rare freedom from prying eyes.

I grasped several layers of skirts and fled. My breath beat out a staccato rhythm, and the fabric of my dress brushed the floor. Torches slanted from the walls, flames hopping into the air and embossing the passages. I wandered, embarrassed by my attitude toward a stranger, worried about my friend's heart, and guilty over my rudeness to Mother.

My heels tapped the floor. At least fifteen minutes must have passed before I realized I'd detoured into an unfamiliar section of the palace, a passage of glinting mirrors and iron-banded chandeliers. If one stood at the right angle, one could see infinite reflections of oneself.

I scrutinized my likeness. Mother was right. My chin did crinkle when someone got on my nerves.

Remembering the jester's dancing style, I attempted a shimmy, then gave up. Bracing my hands on my hips, I shook my head and chided myself, "You jest, Briar."

"On the contrary, Princess. That's my job."

My eyes flew to the edge of the mirror. I froze as a silken male voice spoke.

"She leaves her throne.
She leaves her home.
At night, she roams.
The dark, her own.
Alas, Princess.
You're not alone."

5

Briar

Proof that I should not dance, not even by myself. I stood rooted in place, my cheeks burning with mortification. In the mirror, I watched him materialize behind me.

It was not that he appeared from the shadows so much as he stepped into the light, as if the room had been waiting for him.

First, the balcony. Then the great hall. And now here.

Poet leaned casually against the nearest wall and crooked one leg, angling it behind the other, the booted toe pointing against the floor.

A pose both lazy and intentional, sinister and sinful. A devil who carried himself like a dancer.

At any second, he could shift positions or close the distance between us. In doing so, the jester could turn this moment into something immoral.

Verdant eyes roamed the length, width, and depth of me. Whatever conclusions he drew from there, the painted diamond eclipsing half his countenance seemed to obscure his thoughts. He tipped his chin, a small divot forming beside his mouth.

His rudeness knew no bounds if he thought it was acceptable to ridicule a Royal in front of her peers, then trail her into the recesses of this complex. I linked my hands in front of me and leveled him with a glower. This rake needed to be reminded of his place and with whom he was dealing.

In a syrupy tone, the jester said, "Highness."

"Sirrah," I clipped, deliberately choosing to address him by an inferior status.

An answering grin wormed its way across his face, his crooked canine poking out like a trick. At the sight of it, a thousand queer things happened in my chest. My pulse stalled, then jolted back to life, to name only one hazard.

He stalked forward. I recovered in time, jerking from the mirror to face him. The proximity magnified his height, which introduced me to his amber-and-vetiver scent.

I sidestepped him, trying to put distance between us. Yet Poet continued to advance, matching each of my movements until we began circling each other.

"Would you like me to show you how it's done?" he offered.

"How *what* is done?" I asked.

"How to twirl, twist, turn. You were off to an interesting start."

"No, thank you."

The jester tsked in a low voice. "Such a polite, purebred young lady. Thank me when I'm finished with you, sweeting. It would be my pleasure—the jester and the princess locked in motion, our bodies going round and round."

"I do not care for dancing."

"Oh, trust me. Based on what I saw, no one would dare to assume you frequently gyrate your hips."

"And I do not appreciate being spied on," I snapped.

"I assure you, jesters don't spy. They don't need to, for they have nothing to hide and nothing to seek. People give themselves away freely, for they are not as discreet as they think. Meanwhile, we jesters hear and see all, for that is our craft."

"I know what you're doing. Spare me the comely words."

"But I saved them just for you."

"You've wasted the effort. However, if you're suffocating for attention, I can name seven ladies who would lap up your prose."

"Is that so? I do appreciate a woman's company. Only seven, though? That's offensive. Speaking of snooping," he baited, "I take it you mean the damsels who fawned from your window as you were watching me."

My right foot tripped. I pictured myself landing flat on the ground, suctioned there like a starfish. The nimble jester reached out to break my fall, but I regained my balance before his fingers made contact with my elbow.

We continued to prowl around one another. Our features multiplied in the mirrors.

"A princess does not spy," I stated. "She observes."

"Oh? Enlighten me, then," he prompted. "What did you *observe* from the window?"

"I cannot recall. The landscape had distracted me."

"Which landscape? Mine or the countryside's?" With his eyes glinting, the knave cupped a hand to his mouth and whispered, "Be careful how you answer, sweeting. I'm memorizing what you say, in case you're wondering."

"I am not."

As though choreographed, he stopped. I floundered in my tracks, nettled that I'd allowed him to take the lead in the first place.

"By the way, *that*—" he circled his index finger between us, "—was a dance."

"It does not count. I was not concentrating."

"Precisely. That's the reason it worked." He tilted his head, layers of dark, disheveled hair slanting with the action. "My name's Poet."

"Why?" I asked, my tone accusatory.

He grinned. There was a pause in which he stared, and I waited. Then I lost my patience. "The question was meant to be answered."

"I'm sure it was."

"I know who you are."

51

"Everyone knows who I am," he proclaimed with a dismissive wave. "The atrocity is that King Basil and Queen Fatima rarely announce me the right way at these revels. No chariots. No blaring trumpets. No pomp and circumstance."

"No fireworks," I mocked, pretending to lament with him. "No naked escorts."

His mouth twitched. "You're getting warmer."

I burst into a half-laugh, half-sneer. "You're a subject of the Crown. You're lucky you warrant an introduction at all."

I would try to forgive myself for that unkindness later. My breeding and conscience should have known better than to belittle his position.

His gaze narrowed, bathed in hot auburn from the flames. His reply trampled over the spot where my apology should be. "With pleasure and with skill—" he stole my hand and bent his head, his breath coasting across my knuckles, "—I am decidedly more than that."

The touch provoked the strangest response, swooping me on an ocean wave. My head spun, so that my insides tumbled over themselves.

Poet must have registered the change. When his gaze slanted from my hand to my face, a deceptive shadow etched his features—the very picture of a dark and sly jester. His fingers flexed against mine like an offer or a bargain. If I allowed it, those digits might squeeze and pull me closer, and this dance would transform, and that ocean wave would consume me.

I stood still, caught between recoiling and sinking my hand further into his—not to let this stranger draw me into him, but to tug *him* into *me*.

The notion caused me to stiffen. Just like that, the wave broke.

The jester's grip eased, and he straightened. "Ah. What is this? Have words forsaken you, sweeting?"

I yanked my fingers away. "You cannot address me in that manner."

"Perish the thought. But something more compatible, I agree. Sweet Thorn, perhaps? 'Tis the best I can do on short notice."

"Keep away from Eliot."

Poet's lashes flapped in surprise. I'd spoken too freely. To call one of the court artists by his given name risked exposing my closeness to Eliot.

So be it, if it meant protecting him.

My foe recovered quickly. "Ah, Eliot. Maker of melodies, player of lutes, singer of destinies." Poet quirked a brow. "Keep away from him in what manner?"

"He's ... my friend."

"Found one worthy of the term, did you?"

In the decades to come, I would congratulate myself for standing tall against such audacity. He'd been told about my aloofness and had decided to be impertinent about it.

Well. So what?

On the other hand, how dare he! Based on how the jester peered at me, the hurt I felt must have revealed itself to him, creeping out somewhere between my clenched fists and compressed mouth. What he saw wiped the mirth from his face.

"Your request was serious," he said, bemused.

"Of course, it was serious," I hissed. "It doesn't matter how popular you are, or how many props you can juggle, or how many flips you can dizzy us with, or how mesmerized Eliot is by you, or that he's aware of your licentious whims. You are a callous, arrogant scoundrel who thinks he can do whatever he wants, with whomever he wants, and believes he's impenetrable because his words are covered in a gaudy layer of gilt.

"Eliot's heart is priceless. He will not be privy to a meaningless seduction, or I will tell your sovereigns how you accosted me in this hallway. I will boot you to the dungeon myself, and for good measure, I will find my own candle and shove it down your throat. Mark my words."

Poet stared at me, calm and contemplative. "Hmm. Now we're getting somewhere."

"Pardon?" I demanded.

"What an outburst from such a pinnacle of refinement. I scarcely expected a promise to hack off my balls, but still. Have you heard of laughter? 'Twas merely a lark, me excluding you from that trifling favor at the feast. If it insulted you—"

"I don't care about that. I only care that you leave my friend alone."

"Impossible, since we work together."

"And that will be the extent of it. You shall work with him, not fondle him. Are we understood?"

"As you like," he acknowledged. "Except for one thing. Tempting as it would be, I've not seduced the lovely Eliot."

I balked. "I don't believe you."

"'Tis all the same to me, Sweet Thorn."

"Stop calling me that. I forbid it."

"We were scheduled to entertain eight monarchs, and our sorry minstrel was as nervous as a ripe cherry virgin on his wedding night. My banter wasn't helping, so I kissed him to steady his nerves. I won't lie; his tongue tasted delectable, but it was hardly sexual."

Primly, I shook off the terms *ripe*, *virgin*, and *sexual*. I considered doing the same with *cherry*.

"Nerves," I repeated. "You must be jesting."

Poet set his palm on his chest. "Who, me?"

"Eliot has been strumming for the Royals since his youth. He does not get nervous."

"He does when he's performing alongside Spring's court jester in front of every Royal in The Dark Seasons. You're all esteemed, and I've made quite the name for myself this past year. So many high expectations." He mock-sighed. "Life is hard. But during the kiss, my cock was not."

"Hold your tongue," I said, my cheeks blazing. "Evidently, jesters don't see everything, if you failed to notice Eliot's response to you."

"Evidently, you don't know your friend. Not if you took whatever he's told you to heart and then promptly assumed he's been bending over for me. I could have told you he exaggerates, ever the walking love ballad."

"Then you should have known that he would romanticize a kiss,"

I parried, exasperated.

"A trivial kiss," Poet corrected, then shrugged. "My mistake."

That shrug. That flippant twitch of his body, like it was of no great consequence.

When I met Eliot in the hall before the feast, I thought Poet had done fatally intimate things to my friend, had used him for pleasure. Doubt wriggled its way into my head. Of course, Eliot had misinterpreted the kiss and let his feelings get the better of him. But the notion of him fretting about performing for the Royals alongside the famed Poet wasn't far-fetched.

I knew my friend. His emotions overtook him in from one instant to the next. The episode with that knight and Eliot's loss of virginity proved it.

But I did not know Poet. I did not know who he was, only *what* he was—a jester—and what that made him capable of.

He could be lying. He could be doing an excellent job of it.

And perhaps he had the power to read minds. The instant my thoughts surfaced, he moved, strolling toward me until my back hit the wall.

Unanimously, my senses sharpened and dissolved. The corridor beyond dimmed to pitch black, yet I managed to hear our exhalations flee down its path. My skirts rustled against his legs, yet I couldn't recall exactly which gown I wore.

Poet lowered his head and smirked, as if the astute little princess should know better. "A jester doesn't corner a woman. He snares her in the middle of the room, where she belongs."

Linking my fingers with his, he returned us to our original position in the hallway's center. Only this time, he tethered us, clasping his strong hands to mine, stretching our arms out to the sides, and continuing the circle.

I mimicked his steps, too dumbfounded to resist. As we moved, that deceitful smirk twisted into something more wicked.

"My tastes for both sexes are hardly secrets," he informed me. "But I'm not a greedy prick. I have my morals—most of the time. One might say I share myself selectively."

He turned us in the opposite direction. His shoulders adjusted, revolving seamlessly. "In other words, I don't fuck anyone who wears their ardor like the sun, open and shining all over the place. Taking advantage of innocents is what I call scheming, sordid lust." His gaze ensnared mine like a web. "Nay, I'd rather fuck the ones who can handle me."

I ripped my hands from his. "You shouldn't use vulgar language in my presence."

"You're in Spring," he said, as if that should have made it clear.

"And I'm from Autumn," I retorted because *that* should have made it clear as well. "We conduct ourselves differently, in case you haven't been educated on that fact."

"What precisely do you have against *fuck*? 'Tis a lovely word. I do have a fetish for lovely words."

"I don't trust you."

"I don't recall giving a shit," he remarked. "But out of curiosity, what cause do you have to doubt me? Jesters don't lie. Indeed, why should we try? If I wish to fuck with someone, I'll do so candidly. I have nothing to hide and no one who'll stop me."

"You disguise yourself in verse. You barely know me, yet that didn't prevent you from scorning my character in public. *That* is untrustworthy."

Another grin, more of that snaggletooth. "The candles again. You don't want to be here, in this kingdom, with these people. Still, my jest made you feel left out. Oh, but I do believe you earned that. I've been told about you—the proper princess whom her Autumn subjects respect but don't adore. As for the rest, I saw it with my own eyes. I see it as we speak, a righteous riot of freckles multiplied over and over within panes of glass."

"Mirrors are mere surfaces. You do not know me."

As if given a challenge, he sauntered forward. My restless pulse leaped. I stepped back—once.

It wasn't enough. He merely ate up the distance as if it didn't exist, as if no such thing could ever exist between him and what he went after. Our clothes brushed, the noise a hiss in my ears.

"Permit the fool to elaborate," Poet murmured. *"There once lived a princess made of impenetrable knots and impervious thorns. She was thin as a quill, if you will, with eyes like rain, for fear of pain—*nay, I shall cease the rhymes, for they don't become you.

"How about a sugary dose of this. *The princess lived among leaves of copper and crimson. They flourished outside her tidy bedchamber, where she stored her heart—steady, solitary, and safe.*

"Ah, but then, at a plentiful feast in the Spring Kingdom, she watched a duo of lovers kissing. Their tongues flailed and flaunted. And the princess scowled, despite such sad yearning blistering beneath her gown. For under the surface, she wondered what it was like to dare, to dance, and to do."

His timbre skated up my spine. Threads of his breath stirred against my throat, causing a ripple effect along my skin. My breasts swelled, the silk of my bodice sliding over the hard studs of his jacket. The abrasion of our clothes grated on my nerves, rough yet oddly stimulating, a sensation I could either pull away from or lean into.

Poet's gaze had been the weight I'd felt in the great hall, as I watched the couple molding their mouths together. He'd seen me.

As I swallowed, those fiendish eyes slid down my neck, trailing the contortion before lifting to my face. "There, there. I've made you flustered." The jester dipped his head nearer to me, so that our breaths mingled. "So do I know you? Am I close?"

A hot stone sizzled low in my belly. "Just because you make a speech sound pretty, that does not make it true."

"And just because you've replied, that doesn't make it an answer." I was about give him another tongue lashing for this insolence when the jester inquired, "Have you ever lost control with someone?" He burrowed closer, his tone dropping another octave. "Have you ever wanted to?"

His inflection seeped into my pores. And I could not speak.

"Have you ever fantasized about flinging yourself into the fire?" the jester murmured, pupils glittering with intrigue behind the diamond cutting through his left eye. "Have you ever imagined being naked and breathless, clasping someone who's as rampant as you are? Ever opened yourself for a man or woman, spread yourself so wide they could reach every deep, tight, and moaning part of you?"

His voice tapered to a purr. "Would you care to know such an upheaval of the body?" And when I could only stare, that devious intonation thinned to nothing but a hushed breath. "Would you allow yourself that pleasure?"

The questions stroked my insides. A strange pressure throbbed in my navel.

Unbidden, my fingers stole out to touch the bands at his wrist. I wanted to unravel them, to feel the frayed edges under the pads of my thumbs, to untighten the knots and see how long they dangled before falling to the floor.

Poet's pupils flared. The black wells dilated and swallowed his irises, a second before those orbs dimmed like snuffed candlelight. At which point, a protective shadow darkened his mien.

Abruptly, he snagged his wrist away, evading my touch at the last instant. His veneer dropped like a curtain, replaced by a venomous twist of his features. The expression promised retribution if I crossed that line.

"'Tis not polite, touching what isn't yours," he cautioned. "Was the ribbon I gave you not enough? Do you want more of me?" His whisper deepened, rustling over my lips like black silk. "Careful what you ask for, Princess."

Once again tonight, my hand hung suspended and empty, denied something this stranger refused to give. Mortified heat seared my flesh. This jester possessed the perilous skill of knocking me from one emotion to the next. The realization extinguished any residual impulse toward the ribbon.

Livid, I strangled my skirt and shoved past him. The dress's green hem snapped around my legs and seethed against the floor as I strode away. With each retreating step, the weight of his gaze lingered on my back.

Of course, the only thing Poet wanted to give me were taunts and deceptions. I'd known for a while now the scarlet ribbon had come from him. And I was smart enough to figure out its purpose.

Whoever caught the Court Jester's attention became his target. If a princess thought she was exempt, she'd better think again. The band of fabric marked me. It was the jester's way of singling out the renowned, stuffy princess.

Well, I would not give him the satisfaction of thinking I cared about his high jinks, nor that I could be marked. Especially not by a jester.

"Good night," a fiendish voice murmured. "Sweet Thorn."

I smashed to a halt. Digging my heels into the floor, I glanced over my shoulder to where the jester lounged with a single, careless shoulder propped against the wall. The chandeliers painted his silhouette in gold and black. Panels of darkness covered half his face, as though he wore a mask, yet those mischievous eyes glowed through the murk.

The corner of his mouth tipped. And there, amid a hundred mirrors, the jester blew me a thousand fiendish kisses.

Poet

Allow me this: I regret nothing.

She deserved what she got. She deserved what I gave.

Jesters don't explain themselves, don't show mercy, don't apologize.

At the feast, the minx could have laughed, and I would have been satisfied. I wouldn't have interrupted her precious little moment in that hallway.

Though I'm pleased she had tempted me. For it turned out to be a rather appealing introduction.

Alas, I hadn't begun to lament my every move, nor drown in every forsaken thing about her. She hadn't devoured me yet.

Oh, not yet. We had only just begun this dangerous dance …

The hellish blast of someone's fist rapping on the door invaded my beauty sleep.

I rolled my naked splendor deeper into the bed, my fingers flicking toward the offensive racket. "Be gone."

The abominable knocking grew louder. The voice attached to that knock forced his words out. "If you please, Poet. The Crown has requested your audience for the Peace Talks."

Fuck. A groan rumbled from my chest. Facing down, I squashed a pillow over the back of my head.

One, the order meant I'd miss early training with the castle's resident troupe, which I oversaw.

Two, the Talks required concentration. That was a problem, considering the precious real estate in my head—now that I'd been woken up—became immediately consumed by this rubbish involving Eliot and the steaming plate of horseshit I'd served myself yesterday.

I favored women, with all that succulent wetness pooling from beneath their skirts. Other times, I sampled with fervor a masculine mouth, a muscled weight pinned beneath me as I thrusted my hips into a welcoming male body.

Granted, I was picky about sex. I fancied myself cautious. I rarely traversed from one bed to the next without foresight and a keen understanding of my playmates.

I'd learned my lesson there once already. It wouldn't happen again.

And I liked Eliot. However, I never mixed professionalism with pleasure, and I knew enough about the minstrel's tendencies to overreact. Even more reason why I should have noticed the change after taking his lips for a jaunt.

Instead, I had walked away from him too fast last afternoon. I'd behaved as if he were one of my conquests, letting him take a flying leap to conclusions.

Cursed kiss. The meddling princess had been right.

I tossed the pillow from my head, whipped back around to face the ceiling, and feathered my knuckles over my abdomen.

Princess Briar. Now there was a more intricate puzzle.

Briar—a brisk, no-nonsense name. Despite its lack of flair, it was confident without trying hard. 'Twas the sort of lasting name that held its head high and withstood the elements. Indeed, it suited her.

If a man groaned that name, the sound would be guttural—a husky eruption of noise.

"Poet?" the guard repeated. "Be aware, I've been instructed to 'throw your naked ass' over my shoulder if you delay."

The coverlet puddled around my waist as I sat up. "Is that right?"

The poor, intimidated sod continued, "Or if you, 'so much as pause to tidy your hair.'"

Come now. That was uncalled for, to threaten my grooming habits.

I sighed loudly, dramatically, and inconveniently. Sliding out of bed, I rotated my shoulders, then stretched my arms overhead to loosen the kinks. In general, I loathed tension in the body.

The fur rug inside my wardrobe brushed my feet as I stepped inside and debated what to wear. For another twenty minutes, the throne room could piss off. No way did I plan on showing myself without looking halfway primped.

Being graced with standards, I shunned the traditional jester's costume. Unfortunately, the other trained fools in this land preferred that absurdity of an outfit, claiming it distinguished their office. Well, whatever they fancied. And I did enjoy looking the best of them all, as the Court Jester should.

I dressed attentively, scrutinizing whether my jacket hung off my frame to its greatest effect. Whilst inspecting the sleeves, my gaze strayed to the ribbons hugging my wrist.

My lips crooked, even whilst a knife speared my chest. Daily, I lived and breathed for this pain, which covered me like a second skin. I needed the hurt, needed to keep it close like a weapon.

A vision from last night assaulted my mind, a flash of the princess reaching out to grab the bracelets, her fingers straining toward me. Her attempt had thrown me off balance, the air had grown static, and I'd felt her impending touch like a vice—a threat that could easily become a bad habit.

Pathetically, my reflexes had faltered. I should have retreated faster. That part of my life would be touched by no one, especially not by a Royal.

Oh, I knew when I was being watched. The feast hadn't been the first time she had laid eyes on me. Even before then, she'd been shielded by her window and surrounded by the queen's ladies, spying on me in the orchid garden.

I'd repaid the chit for her nosiness later, observing her from the shadows as she stalled at great hall's threshold. For an heiress, she was a prickly thing with barbed diction, not a smooth edge to her tongue, and a perennial frown. She seemed to have that expression prepared in advance, as if everything and everyone would inevitably make her scowl—or make her uncomfortable.

What a shame to squander rapturous red hair on a shrewish personality. Whatever the hell they put in the Royal bathwater in Autumn, it had rinsed the levity from her pores.

I'd heard enough about Briar from the gossiping tongues in this castle. In fact, her reputation as a bramble had been cooed into my ears up until the day before she arrived.

That was why I'd targeted her.

Accepting secondhand information was a disservice to one's own point of view. I believed in heeding rumors and then figuring shit out for myself. But thus far, everything that had happened proved I'd been right in my choice.

I remembered her primly made bed, with its dainty linens and neat corners, all prepared for its upright, upstanding guest. The scarlet ribbon I'd left on the princess's pillow had unfurled like a tendril of blood—a blemish in the pristine sheets.

The band hadn't come from my wrist, for those were too important to use. On the contrary, I stocked a cache for my recipients, for whom the strips of fabric became markers. I picked those who could be made an example of.

Sometimes it was a dark and direct cut intended for social ridicule or political criticism.

Other times, it was a mirthful tease meant to sway a person's perspective or mood.

And other confidential times, it was a seduction, an enticement—

providing I saw interest, an unspoken invitation in their eyes.

Always, the former targets either lost their clout or their nerve to retaliate. Either that, or they laughed at themselves and reconsidered their viewpoints, because my jests were that good, that perceptive, that well placed.

As for the latter targets who dropped their chamber keys in my pocket, they kept quiet about what I did to them, loving the exclusivity of it.

The princess had been none of those things. Nay, she had been a test. Hellbent on either verifying or revoking her flinty reputation, I made her the first night's quest.

Ultimately, she could have been a good sport and laughed at herself dismissively, thus extinguishing the rumors about her. That would have given her power, a sight I would have enjoyed, an outcome that would have won her widespread approval.

Yet she hadn't laughed, and more's the pity. Thus, her reputation remained intact.

One might say our paths crossed accidentally in the hall of mirrors. Technically, I'd been done with her by then. Targeting the same person more than once got old quickly.

Or one might say I had watched Briar leaving the great hall, as I'd been watching her throughout the feast. Whilst mingling with the court—and trying to recall who the hell I was talking to—that combustible red hair and ramrod posture seized my attention. The instant she had released her chokehold on that poor, innocent dinner fork and shuffled from the room, I'd had an itch.

The devil knows why. Only that she had taken my gesture so vehemently, as if I'd poured acid into her chalice. And how intriguing. No dignified Autumn woman was that corrosive, much less its future ruler.

So one might say I followed the princess. And one might say I hadn't been able to help myself.

What a ripe scene as her silhouette attempted to imitate my dance. She'd done such a miserable job that I fluctuated between amused, flattered, and irritated.

Aye. Indeed, my grand entrance had been worth it.

The Royal's eyebrows had vaulted into her hairline. An astonished bolt of pink had lanced up her cheeks—not out of shyness but an attractive sort of combativeness. Despite how I'd angered Briar, the challenge had also fueled her. Such a radical and primitive reaction for that waspish heiress of Autumn, that prude from the land of Could Not, Should Not, Would Not.

At first glance, her tight face, tight lips, and even tighter temper lured the troublemaker in me. Then her accusations offended the fuck out of me, roused the adversary in me. To say nothing of her interest in my bracelets.

Provoking a skilled fool was a mistake. No one broke the Court Jester's rules and got away with it. Thusly, I'd homed in, wielded my tongue like a blade, and gave the woman a dose of her own candor.

My words hit their mark, ignited a spark.

And wicked hell. I'd enjoyed that part.

Bloody knock number three. "Sir?"

For fuck's sake, I rolled my eyes. *Sir* bored me. I was not *Sir*, but *Poet*.

Sauntering to the vanity table, I dabbed a brush into a vial of kohl and swiped the tip along my lower eyelids. The line of color extended to the edge, below my lashes. A mere thread of black did wonders for enhancing—and disguising.

After quitting the room, I approached the guard who paced outside and muttered complaints to himself. I made a joke, something too amateurish to congratulate myself for. Not my best effort, but I had an excuse since the princess still took up valuable space in my head.

Anyway, the guard's frown dissolved into a snicker. For the price of a sloppy quip, I was forgiven for delaying.

Most times, it was far too easy.

But sometimes, it was more difficult.

Sometimes, a rare challenge came along. And sometimes, that challenge wore a crown.

In the circular throne room, stained glass trees cut through mullioned windows. At the center, the Royals sat around an opulent table.
Papers, illustrated tomes, carafes of nectar, and untouched flagons
of wine graced the wooden surface.

The shrunken Queens of Winter studied me. The ruler of Autumn
glanced down in discreet amusement. Laughter rolled from the
mouths of my Spring sovereigns. The Queen of Summer fanned herself whilst her husband beheaded me with his eyes.

They'd been discussing Lark's Night, the annual sunset carnival
that Spring hosted to celebrate the close of the Peace Talks. The revels would take place in a month, but preparations were well under
way. As a grand gesture of unity, the Royals had discussed allowing
Spring's servants and local commoners to attend the event. A nov-
elty, as it was usually exclusive to the court and contributing artists.

The cantankerous Summer King had objected. Then the asshole
compromised by suggesting "inferiors" could attend the fest's final
hour.

To which, I'd drawled, "Some might say that's like being invited to
the end of an orgy, when the fun's over and everyone has to clean up."

The analogy hadn't impressed him.

I hadn't come up for air since my arrival. I'd blown open the room's
double doors, late to the party, and sang my apologies, then proceeded to agree with certain wisdoms and slay others. I mock-shivered
at hyperbolic concerns about certain bloodlines producing criminal rebellion, waving the Royals' double standards about the natural
world in their faces.

Four hours hence, I'd just planted my ass on Queen Fatima's
throne, hooked both legs over one arm, and linked my hands behind
my head. I'd done this before, to tease Her Majesty and alleviate one
of her occasional bad moods.

Fatima chortled but then cleared her throat. That meant I had one minute to get the fuck out of her chair. I used those sixty seconds to muse, listening to seven quills scratching across parchment and cutlery clattering as servants arranged a roasted pig on the sideboard.

"What is this? A fucking soiree?" the Summer King bitched, thrusting down his quill. "I've had enough. I will not share this room with vermin."

"It's a swine," I corrected, gesturing to the pig with a pear stuffed in its mouth. "If you're still not sure, remove the gag and ask it."

"You tiresome shit. I wasn't talking about the pig."

Ah. How remarkable that he considered my presence a threat. Naturally this monarch preferred the company of charred fauna over me, considering he was also known to keep and pamper an aquarium of sharks in his own throne room, plus a rather bratty chinchilla.

King Rhys reclaimed his quill and beat it against the table like a scepter. "I propose an amended draft stating who may attend these discussions and who may not."

My head flopped toward him. "You don't want me here because you can't handle being made fun of, Your Majesty? Strange, as I've heard kings can handle many things. War and famine, for example."

"We forbid our heirs from these proceedings, yet this glorified knickknack of a jester is here." The man whipped his hand toward me. "Why is that?"

Oh, I could tell them why. "'Tis because I'm prettier than your offspring."

I'd sprinkled enough casual exaggeration into the comment to earn a round of chuckles. True enough, the Royals' successors weren't permitted to these roundtables. Fair enough, Spring's daughter was barely in the nursery. But this rule also explained the absences of the remaining Seasonal heirs and heiresses—apart from the Autumn Princess whose scowl lingered in my head and refused to vacate the premises.

Those steely eyes. That smart, tenacious mouth. That willful tongue.

Wake the fuck up.

Far-too-fetching visions dangled in my head like bait. I shifted in the seat, attempting to purge myself of them.

Spring was the Season of renewal—a distinguished substitute for the word *sexual*, from eroticism to conception. We were the Peace Talks' eternal host kingdom, which meant the Crown could invite whichever advisors they wished to this gathering. King Basil and Queen Fatima valued my judgement on issues from law to trade, disputes to grievances.

Since my appointment, I'd become their darling, the only soul at court able to talk my sovereigns off ledges, to reason with Basil and Fatima, and to approach the monarchs whenever petulance got the better of them.

They trusted me, relied on me. I needed that.

And come now. I hadn't spent this entire morning vomiting humor. I'd supported fine arguments when they arose, and arose they had.

Just not consistently.

Summer could yowl all he wanted about my presence. The Spring Crown would be sure to let him know when they gave a shit.

"This is no place for jests or *fools*." King Rhys's monsoon of a voice rose another octave. "It's a place of progress, lineage, and *standards*. We must pride ourselves on *refinement*. A policy revision of this summit's tenets will seal the matter, ordain us with the inalienable right to *govern* without interference, so we might *focus*, or at the very least be spared a pounding head. To *anyone* who contests—" he pelted me with his gaze, "—the document will be indisputable."

"Indisputable, in case you forget who's in charge," I clarified. "Otherwise, I might become so incensed by the exclusion that I'll protest, rallying artists and courtesans to my side. We'll steal mallets from the armory and loot the vaults. But so long as there's an indisputable piece of parchment, not to worry. My absence in these talks shall protect you from both stress and subsequent meltdowns. I tend to have that effect."

King Rhys squirmed. If he wanted a verbal cock joust, he'd picked the wrong opponent.

I pointed to his chalice of nectar. "I would put some alcohol in that."

"Make him stop," the King of Summer grunted to Spring.

Basil waved me off. "Poet, would you mind lifting your ass from my wife's chair? And give your thoughts a rest. Have an apple," he suggested. "They're a gift from Autumn."

"You're too kind, Majesty." Hopping off the throne, I sidled toward the sideboard flanked by rosy-cheeked pages and supplied with a frenzy of fruits, cheeses, and smoked fish, in addition to the pig.

Certain fare of the Seasons mixed only at a momentous time like this, allowing pears to copulate with blackberries. We limited trade to essential resources. Spring herbs, Summer ropes, Autumn grain, and medicine from Winter, to name a few.

Apart from emergency aid, anything unimportant was excluded. The kingdoms also forbade their people from crossing borders or changing citizenship. As best we could, we lived equally but separately, determined to maintain the natural order of things. Because perish the thought of anything being "unnatural," whatever the fuck that meant.

Selecting a trio of apples, I juggled them for a lazy minute, then kept one and sent the others flying back into the pile. After lowering myself to the dais, I pocketed the pome and lounged against the pedestal table situated between the thrones.

From her seat across the room, the Autumn Queen considered me with a honed gaze. According to gossip, the widow cherished her daughter. After the feast, could Autumn have drawn the conclusion that I'd singled out her offspring for more than a jest?

There once lived a jester, too tempting to resist. Protective of her daughter's chastity, the queen banned him upon pain of public castration from the princess's virginal maidenhead.

As though I would prey on such a prissy conquest. Fucking a princess was dangerous business in too many ways to count. I would never be that stupid.

No touching Royals or resident artists. Everyone else was fair game.

Then again, I was hardly known for being chivalrous. I didn't advertise the ribbons' purpose, but word got around privately, taking the form of confidential rumors. And because my intentions were often unknown, some feared my ribbons whilst others coveted them, enjoying the adrenaline rush.

I inclined my head at Autumn's queen, offering my silent gratitude for the apple. With a neutral expression, she nodded back.

Well, well, well. Dare I say, my assumption about this woman had been wrong. She didn't have a thorn up her ass, not like her daughter, who would have responded differently. The pulse in the princess's neck would have throbbed with disdain.

Thereupon, I imagined pressing my finger into the slant of that female's throat. I imagined counting that sharp pulse, wondering how many beats it would take until her lips parted for air. I imagined getting a sneak peek at that whiplash of a tongue.

How would her shocked gasp sound? How would it look if that tongue swiped across those lips, her mouth glistening?

"Be reasonable, Summer," Queen Fatima chided, snapping me out of it. "Poet isn't just any fool."

Rhys the Rotten huffed. "A trained fool is still a fool. He has no business in the Peace Talks. On that score, forget that Spring has an abundance of artists. Why Your Majesties have need of jesters is beyond me, when you already own simpletons like the rest of us. Now those are real idiots. Better idiots. Surely, they must provide enough amusement."

Fucking condemnation. By better idiots, he meant chattel. Our continent, The Dark Seasons, represented nature without fully accepting the natural world, a notion that poured a rancid flavor down my palate. The courts deemed so-called "simpletons" and the inherently "mad" as legal property of the Crown, viewing such minds as freak accidents of birth, thereby a disgrace. Apparently, the existence of "born fools" brought shame upon the people, who demanded to be distinguished from them.

The Royals claimed and abused such born souls, stripping them of rights. They shackled the mad and made the rest cater to the Seasons' needs, so long as it wasn't counter-productive, so long as they were capable and manageable.

Summer forced their captives to gut fish, weave nets until their fingers bled, and toil as deckhands. Winter used them as hunting bait and science experiments—whilst they were still alive and awake. Autumn assigned them to fields and orchards.

Spring used born souls as diversions. Basil and Fatima handed them over to traveling exhibits and nobles whose tastes for entertainment leaned that way. Comprised of trained acrobats, athletes, and aerialists like myself, the castle's resident ensemble was the only one in Spring that didn't include born souls.

But I had witnessed and loathed their treatment. Dark carnivals and eventide festivals drugged them, then made them brawl each other for sport. They were restrained, heckled in the stocks, bullied until they either collapsed or broke bones, and charged to do pet tricks for spectators.

My jaw locked. Someday, that could happen to ...

Basil raised his finger. "We enjoy variety. Jesters represent every advantage rolled into one person—levity, wisdom, and eroticism. They can imitate a simpleton one hour, be a perceptive advisor the next, and seduce a crowded room by sunset. A counselor at dawn, a bard at noon, a dancer at dusk—"

"And a whore by night," King Rhys finished.

My lips slanted. "Who says I limit my sex binges to the evenings? A lot can be accomplished in a day."

"And you say this as if it's a bad thing," Spring criticized Summer. "It's invaluable."

"It's excessive," Rhys protested.

"It's flattering," I clarified. "It's been my lifelong ambition to be excessive. Ah, the honor, to have a king appraise me that way. Speaking of excess, how are your pet sharks faring?"

Red suffused the man's throat. He mashed his mouth together.

Then it happened. His whiskers twitched with reluctant mirth, which motivated him to raise his chalice in a mock-toast. "Sly bastard. You've made your point."

Certainly. For better or worse, I could have gibed the king some more. Lucky for him, I felt merciful—until he opened his mouth yet again, and his words poisoned the air.

"I might see a jester's appeal to Spring. I grant, there's a versatile elegance to their otherwise annoying breed, whereas simpletons are another matter. As profitable as they are for extra labor, they aren't as malleable or physically appealing to behold. If we had more room in the dungeon, I would lock them with the mad when they're not needed, underground where they can't be seen or heard. Why, they can't even cry respectably."

Slowly, my features tightened like fist. Even slower, my eyes skewered toward him.

Malice crawled across my knuckles. Fortunately for the king, I hadn't brought my blade with me today, otherwise I might have let it slip.

Artifice be damned. I felt my irises darkening to a murderous shade. The king's comparison had sounded as if enslaving human beings versus employing a trained fool dressed in lace and leather was a matter of inconvenience rather than barbarism.

What was the word he prided his kingdom on? Refinement?

Because the rest of this company supported owning born souls, they murmured their empathy with Summer. The only one not engaging was Queen Avalea, who jotted notes and kept her thoughts to herself.

This turned into a slippery moment when reacting viscerally would do spectacular harm. I should have licked my lips and sunk my teeth into the king, right before suggesting the man go fuck himself hard.

The problem was I couldn't trust myself to speak without giving myself away. Not when the ribbons around my wrist clung to me for protection.

I'd earned a vital measure power in this court. My sovereigns wouldn't admit it, but I had more social influence with their subjects than they did.

Yet they didn't take it seriously. Why? Because jesters sided with their rulers, not with themselves. Traditionally and historically, our kind didn't have ambitions beyond revelry, ridicule, and sex.

In their minds, I embodied that rule. Therefore, they presumed I wasn't a threat.

I intended to keep it that way for now. For what I had in mind, I couldn't afford to take risks yet. I needed more time.

To hide the mayhem festering inside me, I swung my head toward the windows. Dust motes swam in the mullioned light. Watching them, I latched onto a memory of tiny hands grasping at similar flecks, small fingers trying to catch them.

Soon enough, my tongue would be primed to go another round and make actual headway. For when had I ever failed to sway a Royal?

Last night, perhaps.

Mentally, I flung that thought out the window before it pissed me off. Yet the image of her flinty eyes and smart, righteous mouth resurfaced, branding itself on me like a lesson that refused to be learned.

7

Poet

$\mathfrak{A}$nger has a profound effect on a person's ingenuity. Looking back, the violence I'd felt in the throne room helped me reclaim my voice later that night, during an intimate affair for the Royals and their peers. They had beseeched me to engage the court, and my words had oozed into the sky, where a canvas of stars flashed above the orchid garden.

As the centerpiece, I outdid myself.

But then l saw her …

"In Summer," I narrated, "the sun rages with heat. Whilst amid the bones of Winter, every crystalline sound is solitary." I cocked a brow at the court's children. "And ready to cast a magic spell."

Gap-toothed mouths wreathed into smiles. I knew someone else who would have loved to hear this recital, set among the gardens' lush shrubs and alcoves. That someone would have also loved the bubbles floating from a collection of wands, which several of the guests wielded. That someone would have loved to be here with me.

I suppressed the ache. *"In Autumn—"*

I had meant to indicate Queen Avalea.

But there stood her daughter.

Briar's wonderful glower cut me off. She wore ivory and amber brocade, the gown divided down the center, from its bodice to the hem. Within the gap, the same material shone through, except the colors were reversed within the pattern, and amber trim encircled her scalloped elbow sleeves.

Impressive. Not the style a Spring lady would flaunt, but in fine taste all the same. If this thorn weren't careful in the future, she would eventually out-dress me.

Covertly, she fussed over the gown. Her fingers plucked at the fitted shoulders, then her palms fluttered over the low neckline, as if desperate to shield her exposed flesh. Just like a proper heiress, except with a frown instead of a blush.

My lips tilted. The neckline befitted Spring, yet the coverage of skin everywhere else smacked of Autumn. Nevertheless, the garment evidently wasn't her personal preference.

Pity that she also insisted on binding her hair. The braided bun, speckled with pearls, scarcely did her justice. Every stitch of that magnificent red hair was shackled in place, to the point where it looked like a migraine waiting to happen.

What attractions existed beneath the tight stitching of that outfit? How easy would it be to dismantle the braid, to unravel it like a brushfire and tangle my fingers in that blaze? What would she do, and how would she sound, if I pulled those flames from their roots?

With purpose, I let my gaze slide over Briar like the tip of a dagger, smoothly and with a hint of peril. My eyes carved through and ran deep. Between us—just between us—I made it obvious, letting my deviant thoughts be known.

Her eyes latched onto mine, translating the anarchy occurring in my head. A flustered tint of pink raced across the neckline she disliked so much. The slender plank of her mouth parted like a latch breaking open, beyond which deep, dark, damp places lurked.

The phenomenon lasted one exquisite second before giving way to visible annoyance. She clamped her thin lips together, as if her mouth was adhered with cement.

Fascinating. I'd never made someone hate me with this much devotion. The ivory, amber, and red shades of her—innocence and fire—drew me in like a moth.

She was a bramble that had never been clipped of its thorns. A stiff taper that had never been lit and melted.

I had believed myself done with her, but I was a fickle being. How could I resist seeing where this challenge led? Besides, I'd grown bored with everyone else.

Nay. I blamed her. Somehow, this female made everyone else boring.

I'd targeted her once already. I could do it again.

Indeed, I could push it further.

Make her squirm.

My voice pinned the princess to the grass. *"In Autumn,"* I repeated, *"color infuses the trees like spices, and ladies interpret dreams by candle-light, the wicks illuminated for the long night."* I piled the next words on my tongue and hurled them at her. *"Burning hot before melting into a lovely disaster."*

Briar's slender throat bobbed, the muscles working in tandem. Were it not for the subtle pump of her neck, I'd have pegged the princess for a statue. But nay, I wasn't naïve. I saw her discomfort and could have dined on it like an appetizer—a gluttonous impulse.

A lovely disaster.

Spreading my arms, I fixed my attention on Basil and Fatima. *"And here in Spring, life blossoms. We pile our plates high, dwell among the flora and fauna, and thrive on sensuous pleasures. So go forth and frolic, sweetings. And praise our sovereigns for this revel. For the love of Spring, I bid you a scandalous welcome."* I bowed. *"And a scandalous adieu."*

The guests toasted and explored the grounds. The children attacked, crashing into my legs and begging me to tell them another story. "Please please please please please please please please pleasepleasepleeeeeease!"

"Alas," I lamented. "I've run out of tales for the night."

"Noooooooooo." they whined.

"But I have an alternative."

With a flourish, I snatched one of the soap wands from a passing servant who carried them in a pail. Because the orbs would last a while before popping, I blew air through the oval tip. A stream of translucent orbs sailed across the garden and coasted into the winding paths. The tykes gave chase, scattering across the gardens whilst their parents made haste to follow.

Spring greeted their guests. Summer joined a game of bowls.

Elderly Winter looked in desperate need of airing out. Silvia and Doria trundled down a walkway as if it would take a pilgrimage to reach the end.

Autumn conversed with a group of attendants who showed her how the bubble wands worked. And where there was Autumn, there should be her daughter.

Should be. Yet wasn't.

The misanthrope hadn't wasted time in disappearing. My eyes scanned the foliage, hunting for those flammable tresses.

The queen's seven ladies danced like flirtatious nymphs. Two of them—Posy and Vale—swatted their hips together.

Cadence joined the pair, gyrating with them. As the only clique member I knew intimately, the female caught my eye beneath her lashes, the cliffs of her cheekbones cut like a gem. She had beckoned me like this on a prior occasion. The outcome had been pleasant, my fingers thrusting slowly between her legs until she came around my knuckles.

Presently, Cadence swayed her tits in an unspoken invitation.

Juggle these, if you please.

My frustration could use a release. Swapping orgasms with her would massage away the tension of today's meeting and whatever else churned inside me of late, including the instincts that had caused me to harass the princess not once, but twice.

I debated where to take Cadence for a repeat offense of our last bout, when two things happened. First, thoughts of the princess swept my attention from the other female, the fantasy Briar's glare eclipsing the reality of Cadence's grin. Second, a dulcet voice wrapped itself around my waist, the sound enamored and hopeful.

"Your speech was magnificent," he said.

Eliot. Fuck.

His presence drizzled into my skin, seeped into my conscience. Because I couldn't give him what he wanted, I had to fix this problem.

That didn't make it any easier to turn and face him. He glowed at me, the eagerness to please splashed across his face. If I opened my arms, he would step into them.

Seasons. All this from one chaste kiss.

Curse me for not recognizing that hectic look of desire earlier. I'd beheld it from Lord Peyton's bride before my head vanished under her skirt and my tongue sank into her cunt. Then a week hence, Lord Peyton himself as I wrapped my lips around his cock and sucked the marital stress out of him.

In any event, I couldn't do this here. I couldn't reject Eliot whilst bubbles swarmed all over the fucking place.

I offered him my hand. "Walk with me."

Eliot accepted it. I led him to a private section of the garden, a crescent of orchid shrubs where the full moon glazed us in silver.

An admirer had intercepted me here yesterday, whilst Briar had been watching from her window. Remembering that, I released Eliot. He probably thought I intended to finish what we started with the kiss. He couldn't know that I did mean to finish it, but not in a frisky way.

I held his gaze. "Eliot—"

"Poet, do you think music would complement your prose? I was fixing to compose something, turning ideas in my head, but would that make it a full composition and not prose anymore? And shit, this isn't coming out right." He scraped his fingers through his hair. "I'm not saying I'll jot anything down, but if I did, if you wanted ... I mean, if you agreed … would that disrupt the narrative?

"I don't want my lute to kill it, only make the prose nicer. Or perhaps, you'd rather I compose something for your verse. Can both work in tandem, like a collaborative effort?" He cleared his throat. "Can they blend together?"

I treaded carefully. "That depends."

"I'd surely like to do that for you," he rushed ahead. "I mean, for the poem."

Lovely Eliot. He had earned an onslaught of fans, those whose tastes leaned toward role play. However, the sirens and serpents of this court had failed to devour him, having underestimated his resolve. I'd heard about the knight who took Eliot's virginity.

The minstrel became cautious after that, refusing to let anyone abuse his affections further. These days, he didn't fall under a person's spell often.

But when he did …

If Eliot weren't as pure, and if I were a lecherous prick, I might explore. I might stalk him into a corner, silence that tireless mouth, and sample the heat brimming there. With lips like those, he had the makings of a sumptuous kisser and an enthusiastic bed partner.

The court would approve of us. Lovers of equal skill. Showpieces for this world to fawn over. He would be right for me, and I him—if my pulse were able to beat that way, to that rhythm.

A jester didn't commit himself, nor lie about his feelings. As much as the prude princess liked to think she knew me, my sex sprees had limits. Ruining Eliot wasn't on my agenda.

Besides, my heart was spoken for. I had room there for only one person.

I'd been gazing at Eliot for too long and with too much misdirected affection. I was sure of it, because he stood there, all brightness and lightness, encouraged by what he saw.

"Eliot, sweeting," I began.

"Poet. If a man calls another man 'sweeting,' is it the same as when he says it to a woman?"

"I call everyone 'my sweeting.' I call everyone 'my lovely.' I call everyone anything I please, for they are all the same to me."

"Oh." He frowned rather cutely. "Right. What I meant—"

"Eliot." I brushed his hair aside, stupidly thinking to comfort him. Even in the dimness, I saw the blood charging up his skin. It deterred me long enough for him to graze his pinky over mine, and his eyes dropped to my lips.

Wicked hell. I never said he wasn't altogether enticing, or that I wore my professionalism like armor. He knew about me, yet he offered himself, riding that impulsive current without concern. Fiendish, selfish me wondered if I'd misjudged his resilience like the rest of them. Perhaps I didn't have to wound him after all and could make him feel good, indulge him without hurting him, for a brief turn until his crush wore off.

I tried again. "There's something I—"

"Yes?" Eliot urged.

"What happened last night—"

Royal footsteps crashed to a halt on the path. A disapproving heat scorched me from the sideline. I caught the red shock of her hair in my peripheral vision, the flaming tresses burning from a shrub to my left.

My mouth tingled. When I had spied on her, it honed her thorns. Yet she could do whatever she wanted, could she?

I pulled back from Eliot and pressed a finger to my mouth. *Hush.*

Striding to the bush, I thrust out my arms and whipped the vegetation apart. My favorite distraction jumped back and glared at me from within the gap.

"Good evening, Princess," I said, then mouthed, *I've missed you.*

That got her going. Hiking up her chin, Briar stepped through the greenery and onto the gravel lane.

Eliot's eyes widened. He bowed, and his voice stiffened with fake formality. "Your Highness."

With a defeated look, she waved him off. "He knows about us, Eliot."

The minstrel's face bunched in confusion as he glanced between me and her.

I couldn't fathom why it took me this long to question it, but how had this Royal come to befriend Eliot? However much I fancied the notion, she didn't strike me as a person who rebelled against the elitist rules of social class.

Eliot stared at the princess, beseeching her with a silent question that made her fidget, which I found oddly endearing. She cared about him, about what he thought and how he felt.

Her eyes tripped over to me, silently imploring. I could guess why. She was deciding how much to confess about our encounter last night. Unsurprisingly, she intended to leave out the good parts.

"Poet was taking a stroll," she said. "He saw us talking at the ruins before the feast."

Eliot blanched. If his eyes had been bulging earlier, they now launched from their sockets. "Did you, um, hear what we said?" he asked me.

"No," she interjected. "He was too far away for that."

Eliot didn't listen to her. As if on the brink of a panic attack, he gaped my way.

I pretended to mull this over. Whilst doing so, I relished seeing the princess cringe. Though, I couldn't say the same about the hyperventilating minstrel beside me.

So they'd met at the ancient garden ruins. From the covert sound of it, this happened on a consistent basis. And whatever they said during their most recent rendezvous must have been about me.

Again, I could guess.

I'd mentioned this to her before: Jesters didn't lie.

I should have amended that rule: Most of the time.

"I didn't hear a thing," I assured Eliot. "But a princess and a minstrel alone together? How could such an intriguing sight not ensnare me?"

"After we said goodbye, I caught him idling and was compelled to explain," the princess bullshitted. "I should have made something up, but I was taken off guard."

Relief swept across Eliot's face. His posture relaxed as he cupped her shoulder. "It's all right. We can trust Poet."

Briar placed her hand over his, unable to meet his gaze.

Huh. Why did she feel the need to keep our real meeting from him? Nothing naked had occurred in the hallway last night. It's not as though I'd backed the princess into a darkened corner, wrenched up her skirt, hefted her against a wall, and strapped her legs around my waist.

Then again, our definitions of scandalous were leagues apart.

I flattened my palm against my chest. "I won't tell a soul."

The minstrel dissolved into a smile, whereas the dubious princess scoffed. "I'd like a word."

Of course, she did. More than one word, probably.

At Eliot's hesitation, she spoke in a gentle tone. "We won't be long. I merely wish to know what happened at the Peace Talks."

'Twas a robust excuse, considering information about the Talks was confidential between the Royals and anyone else who took part. Notwithstanding, it was still a fabrication. Logically, I couldn't tell Briar anything her mother wouldn't be able to, but Eliot's faith in the princess presumably extended beyond such logic. Also, her request justified why she'd want to be alone with me, out of earshot.

Reassured, Eliot smothered me and my conscience with an infatuated look before retreating. The space he left behind filled with a piper's melody, which drifted from the main lawn. At which point, the Royal and I regarded one another.

Briar studied me openly. Black swirls accented the outer corners of my eyes. Obsidian and dark green fleur-de-lis embellished the collar and cuffs of my black ankle-length coat. That I wondered what she thought of my choices created a sour taste in my mouth.

Her ivory-and-amber dress shimmered, but her face didn't. She looked violated, as though I'd deflowered her tidy world views and now sought to corrupt the rest of her.

I debated how hard I'd have to smash into that barricade, to break through it completely. Indeed, I had a craving to find out. Whereas everyone else diluted my impulses once I'd finished targeting them, she kept stirring those impulses back to life.

"Poet," she said.

I spread my arms. "At your service."

"You are despicable."

"Nonsense. You didn't give me time to be despicable."

"I warned you to leave him be."

"You shouldn't tell a jester what to do."

"I am a princess," she declared. "I can make you do whatever I command."

"From any other mouth, that would sound like a dominant-submissive kink."

"From any other mouth, it probably would be."

"If you thought I was going to shatter Eliot in front of you, then you're not as perceptive as you look. This drama is between him and me. And here's another controversial thought. He's not an infant in need of a nipple, and you're not his nursemaid. What the devil gives you the right?"

The princess flushed and swerved her gaze toward the orchids. "It was an accident," she defended. "I didn't trail you here. I wanted some time to myself, and I didn't know what you were about, what you would do to him, or whether I would have to tackle you. I just needed to be sure." She faced me again, her features pinching. "You stalked that woman here, did whatever it was you did to her, and then dismissed her like a trollop."

"I dismiss bigots," I said. "I don't dismiss lovers."

The woman had been a tenant of the lower town who'd confessed to a bet with her friends—to corner the Court Jester and reap a moment of pleasure. Typically, I was the one who did the tempting, not the other way around. But I did enjoy bets and had quite the respect for games. And why deprive the woman of coin?

My tongue had made an exception. I'd backed the female into the hedges and whispered decadence into her ear, the graphic friction of my words alone making her come.

Anyway, the woman would have been fined for trespassing, if not apprehended. Whilst my tongue was equipped to handle the monarchy and influence the masses, I wasn't about to take a chance. Propositioning the Court Jester was common, but violating the Crown's law to succeed was borderline mutinous. The incident would have shamed her.

"I gave her what she wanted," I told the princess. "Then she left through an inconspicuous path so the sentinels wouldn't notice her. You might guess why."

The answer stumped Briar. "Oh. I see."

"Clearly, you don't see."

"Whatever. For all I know, this is where you lure your consorts. This is your official lair of debauchery."

My mouth coiled. "Take care, or you'll start giving me ideas. You don't want to give a jester ideas."

"You were pawing at Eliot."

"Out of compassion."

"Even if I'm wrong about you, which I'm betting against, I will not apologize for assuming. Eliot is too important, and everyone says you either ruin people or steal their virtue. If you're not busy being a trickster, you're busy being a trinket."

To that, I could have made a dozen naughty responses. "Do they, now?" I quirked an eyebrow. "As long as I shine, that is fine."

She grunted. To her credit, I hadn't foreseen the princess defending herself with such raw vulnerability. She and Eliot must know one another well, which made him a chink in her armor.

I had one of those, too. To that end, I wouldn't react any differently than she, if I suspected a stranger of taking advantage. I'd rip them to pieces without a second thought.

"What do you even feel toward the people you target?" she asked.

"A multitude of things," I replied. "I don't target randomly."

"I'm after specifics."

"I'm aware of that."

"You seemed invested last night—with me."

Truer words couldn't be spoken. Yet I wagered that feeling had been mutual. "You're easy to invest in, Princess. Though in the great hall, the guests weren't laughing *at* you. If you had taken my performance lightly, you might have bested me and earned a few admirers in the process."

"I have no time for admirers."

"Coming from a future monarch, that doesn't sound like a wise strategy. Seems you failed to inherit your mother's charms there, not to mention her ambitions."

"I don't care what these people think!" she snapped, her voice shaking like a leaf. "And I don't care what *you* think. I have nothing to be ashamed of. I am who I am. If that's not enough, too bad."

"For someone who doesn't care what Spring thinks of her, that's a rather thunderous response. So eager to rage." I cocked my head and studied her. "Your eyes, how they shout at me."

"The opinions of a jester are irrelevant, since I carry few expectations of their kind as it is."

I paused for effect. "My, my. You superior brat."

Her brows knitted. "Tell me. Do you have family?"

That was unanticipated. And unwelcome.

"I have no relations in this court," I drew out cautiously.

"Well, since I've been judicious in asking first, I shall proceed to deduce the situation. You know what your problem is?"

My lips slanted. This should be interesting.

"You have no one," she said.

My smirk dropped like a drawbridge.

"The courtiers go on and on about you," she said. "For all your notoriety, they tell me you're alone in this court. You have fans galore but no relatives. No one who matters. No one who needs you. What's more, you have no principles. That's a sorry combination."

"Careful, sweet thorn," I murmured, my words as polished as a set of blades. "Now you're being cruel. I have a low tolerance threshold for that."

The princess had the decency to look ashamed. Nonetheless, her repentance came far too late to pacify my tongue. If she wanted a moral rival, so be it.

I stalked forward. My mouth crooked at how long Briar resisted backing away, standing her ground until that became impossible. At last, she broke from her stance. Her heels and my boots scraped the ground until her ass bumped into an ivy-encrusted stone wall.

To be blunt, I closed the last inch of space between us, uninterested in acting cocky on this tourney field. I'd much rather look as pissed off as I felt.

As my frame spanned hers, heat radiated off Briar's form. Even in this dim corner, her hair seared through the darkness. Though, none of this toned down the hitch in her breath.

I made venomous eye contact and reminded her of a crucial fact. "The Spring Crown would disagree with you, seeing as my political prowess and social clout matter quite a lot to them."

She chopped that fact apart like an axe. "You advise them in order to puff yourself up, to regale yourself without having to feel the burden of accountability. You may be clever and forthright, but you don't really care about the people of this land, not any more than they care about you beyond a cheap joke and a meaningless ..." The axe slipped as crimson pooled in her cheeks. "A meaningless ..."

"Allow me," I volunteered. "The phrase you're looking for is a *meaningless fuck*."

She stiffened, her pupils dilating with offense. "A meaningless bout of carnal relations."

"That's one annotated mouthful to describe sex. Likewise, I would argue that orgasms are never meaningless. For a start, they put you in a good mood."

"You are unscrupulous."

"And you seem to have a limited appreciation for the erotic things in life. Never mind *meaningless* when there are many phrases at our disposal." I leaned forward and lowered my voice to a fever pitch, the words leaking out like steam. "Do you know the difference between a hard kiss and sweet fuck? One is deep, the other is long. A noble-man will give you a choice between the two, but a jester will give you both." My voice burrowed into the gritty crawlspace left between us. "And he'll do it at the same time."

Her pulse tripled, that button pounding in her delicate neck.

If I moved closer, what other tiny, tight parts of her would pulsate?

Briar evaded her gaze, glancing toward a distant iron rotunda crammed with roses behind its locked gate. Press a finger into one of the thorns, and they had the power to intoxicate a person to the point of sexual gluttony. With so many striplings running around, that accounted for the structure's bolted door tonight.

This princess must have known not to take Spring's flora at face value, though she wouldn't be fluent in the intricate effects of each species. To say the least, such varieties outnumbered all the toys in the court's pleasure vault.

If we had been standing in that rotunda, I'd have been forced to yank Briar as far from the vines as possible. As it is, the urge prickled up my fingers to pull her attention from the roses altogether.

Quickly, she regrouped and cleared her throat. "You might give your fans pleasure, but would you give your life for any of these peo-ple? Because I would. For my Autumn subjects, I would as well. Can you say that about anyone?"

The ribbons tapped against my wrist, as if to remind me.

As if I needed reminding.

Correcting her would make no difference. This Royal may be friends with a minstrel. She may be loyal to her people, but doubtless she had constraints about who mattered in her narrow world. At the day's end, she was like the rest of them—ignorant.

My story, the *anyone* in it, wouldn't count to her.

Briar took my silence as confirmation. "You can't say it because you're too busy mocking and ridiculing for sport. I have principles. I have a relevant purpose because I take life seriously."

I sneered, "Not to mention you inherited that purpose. How's that serious life working for you? Is it a happy one?"

"It's a responsible one. It's honorable."

"I do enjoy my share of depravity, but what exactly is atrocious about laughing, dancing, feasting, flirting, or fucking? Or at least unwinding that rigid braid of yours? Are you cursed? Are you going to grow fangs if you throw caution to the wind? Are you going to hurt someone?"

"You made a fool of me."

"You make fools of so-called fools," I snarled, my control slipping. "You Royals shackle, labor, and spurn born souls. You assume the right to abuse them. 'Tis fine to leash and drag around the ones you call 'lesser, unnatural' beings, but when someone plays the slightest trick on you, then you have a tantrum. If you can't handle even that, then relinquish your entitlement to the throne so another poor sod can take up the gauntlet."

She blanched. Contrition drained the anger from her complexion.

By nature—pun intended—Autumn was a benevolent nation. But although it may be less vicious, that didn't pardon her kingdom. And she knew it.

Nevertheless, I couldn't decide what I fancied more—the sight of her riled up, flushed by temptation and indignation, or the image of her ashen from humility. At least both proved she had a spleen, as well as a blood temperature above freezing.

The princess licked her lips. The gesture produced a moist sheen that snatched my attention, its heated effect traveling up the length of my cock.

Our torchlit silhouettes collided across the mesh of foliage, making it impossible to tell where her shadow began and mine ended. The common waft of Spring flowers clashed with the heady, intrusive rush of her own scent—fresh parchment and tart apples.

She squared her shoulders. "If I couldn't handle the likes of you, I wouldn't be standing here."

Curse this woman. I'd promised myself I would never lay my hands on a Royal, but raging this near to one, I changed my fucking mind.

"Oh, Sweet Thorn," I husked, stroking my thumb down her arm, searing a path from her shoulder to her wrist. "That's because you're not standing close enough."

Briar sucked in a breath and then leaned in. As her sleeve abraded mine, every whiff of Autumn chipped at my confidence.

Her voice snapped back, as quickly as a deck of cards. "How's this?" she challenged in a whisper.

Applause. Because sometime between last night's hall and this night's garden, she found her nerve. And I lost mine.

Briar

The dressing table mirror threw my reflection back at me. My nightgown hung off my body in layers of pearlescent linen, and the neckline slumped down the knob of one shoulder. The bun in my hair slouched against my neck, the tendrils uprooted and hanging in red vines. I looked as rumpled as the unmade bed across the room.

Yet the crackling fireplace illuminated other raw details, namely the peachy tints mottling my face. Had my complexion ever looked this animated? Stress had to be the culprit. Either that, or I was merely overheated from the blaze.

Behind me, flames spit embers and doused the room in orange. I traced my index finger along the flushed slope of my jaw, then jolted to a halt. What was I doing? It was just a feverish tinge, nothing more and nothing to waste time on.

Beside a pot of lip balm and a set of combs laid out like silverware, a sheaf of parchment rested on the tabletop. I grabbed my quill and tapped the plume against my temple, then dropped my arm. The nib leaked onto the page, leaving a black stain. I had planned to reflect on Autumn's current finances, including list of questions and concerns for Mother and me to examine later.

But my thoughts strayed, as they'd been doing since the garden revel three nights ago. Memories of a confrontation surfaced, crowding my head with unwanted visions. The clovers of his eyes glittering with resentment, combativeness, and something else—something foreign and even more disruptive. The paint twining around those orbs, the design like an iron gate closed off to strangers. That wayward grin playing at the corners of his lips.

Me, wanting to reach over and dab that grin back into a frown.

Him, stepping closer, daring me to try.

And then us, breaking apart and returning to the main lawn separately so the courtiers wouldn't get the wrong impression. My attempt to converse with the Queens of Winter. My mother's gaze, which had caught me glancing at Poet's profile while he roamed from guest to guest.

Eliot, surrounded by the Seven. My friend, reciting the words to an old ballad—as he tended to do whenever in the grips of uncertainty—and then peeking at Poet.

Poet, watching me from across the lawn. Me, fighting to remain placid.

I'd touched him. On purpose.

Never had I pressed myself against someone in such a manner. I hadn't liked it. In fact, *like* seemed a flimsy description, too dull and inadequate for the disorder I'd felt.

The crushing press of my lungs. The itch across my flesh.

In this world, women could inherit thrones without having to marry, or we could choose to bond eternally with someone. We could be knights or seamstresses. We could be warriors, mothers, or both. It was our choice, yet at the same time, it wasn't.

Class still reigned. People were expected to know their place among the ranks.

Nonetheless, the company of a jester had thrown me into a tailspin. I'd felt dizzy and overwhelmed, confident and fierce. Rank and hierarchy had ceased to exist.

Peel away the princess, and there lived a woman. Peel away the woman, and one discovered a heart that either raced or stopped, depending on what a man said or did. Regardless of my authority, the jester could disarm me. He could make me do things I wouldn't normally do, absurd things like touch him back.

I had used impudent tactics to silence Poet. I'd confronted him with a breathy hiss and far too much proximity.

The sensations of being near him reemerged, bringing with them the reluctant stirrings of curiosity. A straining sort of ache nestled low in my body, in a place I only allowed myself to consider in rare moments of helplessness and frustration.

As if tethered to my thoughts, that same intimate place clenched. Suddenly, the upholstered chair felt too smooth, not rough enough to alleviate the twinge. I shifted until my core brushed against a hard spot, a corner that seemed to grip back. The friction ignited a spark, which blasted up my thighs.

I went still, which only worsened the need. And when I nudged my hips once more against the furnishing, the sensation returned, brighter and warmer this time. A shaky puff of air trembled from my mouth, so that I almost seized the table. It felt terrible and wonderful, bad and good, greedy and essential.

The slit between my thighs yearned for another pass. I sank my teeth into my lower lip, because I shouldn't, because it made no sense, because no normal person would do this on a piece of furniture.

Would they? Anyone in Spring would know the answer.

He would know the answer.

The fireplace writhed and tossed scorching colors across the rug. I jutted atop the seat again, a small noise curled from my lips—and I dropped the quill. It thumped against the paper and rolled off the edge.

On a gasp, I froze. Then I launched from my chair. Mortified, I paced a favorable distance from the flames. No respectable Autumn native would debase herself like this.

What had gotten into me? Why had I done *that*?

And why did I want to do it again?

It had to be Spring's doing. The Season was testing me. Being here was compromising my composure and sense.

After several leagues, my skin cooled, the crease in my body calmed down, and blessed sanity returned. With it, another memory came to mind, one I could deal with.

You make fools of so-called fools.

I dumped myself into the chair. Poet's words had been even more potent than his physical presence. And he was right. The smudge of embarrassment I'd felt during the feast did not compare to how we let others be treated.

Others. That was also the problem, that we allowed ourselves to think of anyone as an *other*.

I could easily fill pages contesting our manifestos about equality and humanity. I could write without stopping. I could do that.

Father would advise me to think without dwelling, then write without scrutinizing. His guidance perplexed me, though I missed it so much. In my mind, I saw his face, the crinkling of skin around his platinum eyes, the lopsided tilt of his beard whenever he smiled, and the Y-shaped battle scar across his cheek.

A lump expanded in my throat. Unlike the details of his face, time had eclipsed his voice. The years had dissolved the memory of his baritone, the way water swallowed droplets of blood.

Anguish swam at the corners of my eyes. *I wish you were here.*

The antechamber door creaked open. Quickly, I sucked up the tears and rolled my shoulders into place.

Mother swept into the bedroom. Swaths of eggplant satin hugged her curves, and her feet were unshod. Sometimes the courtiers did that in Spring—ran through the castle barefooted. Complying with their customs would be expected of a visiting queen.

Mother paused behind me. "Is everything all right?" she asked my reflection. "I can't tell if you're glowing or have a temperature."

I mustered a rueful but detached smile. "It's been a long day."

"Then you must rest. I've come to bid you goodnight."

Was it that late already? I glanced at the candle twitching atop the table. Twelve lines marked into the wax indicated the passage of each hour. Indeed, the flame had burned down to the next groove.

"How is my dearest?" Mother inquired.

"Dear," I responded to her likeness.

"You've been behaving in my absence? Staying away from suitors? Avoiding scandals?"

"Yes. Yes. Yes."

"Then I should have raised you better," she quipped, though a hint of truth dangled from her words. She rested her hands on my shoulders and stared at me in the mirror. Sometimes I feared she saw Father's face there, the life I had taken from her.

Being in Spring smothered our relationship further. After that first evening, she had stopped advising me on what to wear and how to behave. Moreover, she ceased making hints about us sharing a suite, sharing private time together, sharing secrets.

I touched the Court Jester. I don't trust him.

I miss Father. I miss home.

I miss you.

"Dearest." Mother released my shoulders, grasped the back of my chair, and bent forward, her profile hovering beside mine. "I only want you to take joy in these days. You could make friends here. Or perhaps there's something in particular you'd like to talk about?"

"I cannot figure out where to begin this analysis," I said, gesturing to the blank parchment.

It wasn't entirely true. I knew where to begin. I just hadn't been able to scribble a single, actual thought.

Her features lifted. She moved to grab a stool from beside the fire. "Would you like my help?"

"I'm tired," I said, halting her motions. "Maybe tomorrow?"

That hopeful expression faltered. "I see. Very well, then. Tomorrow," she conceded. "Don't forget—"

"To blow out the candles," I finished.

We traded awkward smiles. She reached out, her fingers smoothing my hair and adjusting my bun. I swore, the contact felt like waking up and falling asleep, like protection and loneliness.

A castle was such a formal, ceremonial place. But with her, it softened into a home, with comforting bits and pieces strewn about.

Pillows and quilts. Steam from a pot of tea. A hairbrush.

I wondered what she would do if I grabbed a handkerchief from the table and used it to mirthfully smack her wrist, or if I stuck out my tongue and then teased her, or if I uncapped my pot of lip balm and smeared it across her chin, or if I grabbed my quill and wrote my secrets on the parchment for her to see—actions I would have played at years ago.

Instead, Mother left. And I let her go.

A Spring breeze whisked through the window cracks, the fragrances of nightfall and nature flooding my nostrils. Rising, I shuffled toward the glass and opened the casement, inhaling a vista's worth of flora.

Each kingdom had its Crown, its court, its warriors, its servants, its peasants, and its harvesters. But the kingdoms also had different landscapes, mindsets, and specialties.

Humble, charitable Autumn. The land of practicality and tranquility. Our castle, presiding over fields of corn and wheat, and orchards dripping with pears.

The aromas of soil and damp wool. The crunch of leaves. Builders, farmers, and millers.

Introspective, stoic Winter. The glacial land of wisdom. A white world with a blade-like stronghold surrounded by a frozen lake, the placid surface flipping the world upside down.

The sunken dens, the libraries and universities, and the medical halls. Scholars, scribes, and hunters.

Tireless and temperamental Summer. The wrathful land of flames, relentless oceans, and briny air. A fortress chiseled into a cliff beside the waves. The cavernous call of peacocks, aquarium-lined corridors, and indoor waterfalls.

Fishermen and women. Makers of nets, ropes, and sails. And sand drifters, explorers who traveled the kingdom's uncharted seas.

Then there was artful, sinful Spring, with its palace of ivy-covered walls and stained glass murals. Domed ceilings, circular turrets, and round chambers. The numerous gardens, including the one where I clashed with Poet, the blooming ruins where I met Eliot, a coiling labyrinth, an expanse of wisteria arbors, lotus ponds, and too many others to list.

Keepers of flora and fauna. All manner of artists and courtesans.

Each nation possessed its own natural cycle. Seasons within the Seasons.

Winter went through different stages in a year. Months of frost, then snow, then ice.

Summer intensified from sunshine to a heat that glared down on people.

In Autumn, the trees burst with color for part of the year. During later months, the leaves dried up. After that, they fell, cracked and brittle.

Then it started over. The land shed its coat and eventually grew it back.

Spring had its rain and clouds, then blue skies, then growth as the environment blossomed, and then another chill and an onslaught of weeds.

Presently, it was blooming season in Spring.

The sensuous gaiety of life. The wild, unpredictable full moon. The spiraling free fall.

A time to lose control. A time to be bold.

I thought of the ribbon the jester had left me, targeting me as his latest victim. Shutting the window, I stalked over to the wardrobe and grabbed a mahogany wool frock, along with a matching cloak. The hood would shield my face from recognition during the night patrol.

From my dresser drawer, I retrieved his little token of affection. I should have dealt with this sooner.

The jester must have a room somewhere close to Eliot. I used the hidden passage leading from my suite to a mezzanine adorned in potted lilies, then peeked out the doorway to make sure the neighboring walkways were clear. A guard's silhouette vanished around a corner, and I counted several minutes before continuing.

In the glare of a torch sconce, I slipped around the pulsating light, then scurried past a flickering chandelier. From the east wing, I griped my skirt and darted between nooks, behind pillars, and hastened along passages while glancing repeatedly over my shoulder.

Once I reached the right stairwell and hiked three flights of steps, I landed in the artist wing. From there, it proved easy to locate the door belonging to Poet. As the most ostentatious entrance of them all, it flourished in a separate hollow.

It also boasted a plaque that read, *Court Jester*.

Beneath that, *Give me a rhyme, and I shall give you time*.

I rolled my eyes. Show-off.

Keeping the ribbon would send the wrong message and give the man license to meddle with me. The moment he answered the door, I would drop it in his palm and leave—with squared shoulders and definitely before he had the chance to open his mouth.

Leaning back, I swung my head left and right to check the corridor. Rumors were the enemy. The aloof, virginal Princess of Autumn loitering outside the Court Jester's den of vice would not look good.

Since the knocker would echo, my knuckles tapped lightly on the wooden surface instead. I waited, then tried once more.

Nothing. No answer.

Darkness leaked from under the door. Poet didn't seem like the type to be sleeping yet. He might be out doing lord-knew-what, carousing somewhere in these halls or in the town's tavern, having charmed the sentinels into raising the portcullis and letting him through the gate.

He could have taken a trip to one of the local brothels. Perhaps he'd brought Eliot with him, intent on doing more damage to my friend.

Every day at dusk, I'd wrangled a free moment out of my social obligations to meet Eliot at the ruins. Of the many subjects we could have jumped into, he focused on only one. Rather than telling me how his family fared or about his latest musical endeavors, he'd ruminate over Poet and ask my advice.

Thus far, I had kept my answers neutral. I wanted to be wrong about Poet. He could have been telling the truth, that he'd planned on remedying the situation with Eliot before I had interrupted them the other night.

But that had been three days ago. What had Poet been doing since then? If he didn't say something to Eliot soon, I would.

I bumped my knuckles against the facade. The entrance nudged open, the latch's click stunning my ears. The calculative jester wouldn't have forgotten to lock the door, but why else would he leave the room unbolted?

Hesitation and guilt brought me up short. I had done many things in my life, but violating someone's privacy was not one of them. However, if the jester could steal into my quarters with the ribbon, I would do the same.

Warning myself to be quick, I pushed past the door and stepped into his chambers, closing the partition behind me. Moonlight spilled through the bay windows, casting a blue film across the floor.

It was a spacious interior, neatly kept, and adorned in rich shades and textures—an antechamber leading into the bedroom; dark wood paneling; stained glass panes depicting taper candles that matched the ones propped in the wall sconces; and upholstered tapestry chairs and ottomans, which fronted a fireplace wide and tall enough for its resident to stand in.

I tarried, astonished. This lavish set of chambers wasn't the residence of someone with a low rank.

A sideboard held a stemmed bowl of grapes. A corner bookshelf reached the ceiling, the stacks crammed with volumes of history, verse, and pornographic novels. A vanity table overflowed with thin brushes, vials of pigment, and lidded pots.

One passage led to a bathroom with a brass tub and a glass wall overlooking a garden, while the other passage led to a walk-in wardrobe packed with textiles, the shades ranging from black to garnet.

The spiced scent of him infused my lungs.

A heavy trunk stood open, supplied with props of his craft. Amid the clubs, globes, and spiked rings, a baldric held a row of daggers. My fingers grazed the hilt of one knife, then jerked away.

Cabinets embedded into the wardrobe. The upper storage held an organized array of knits and boots and ... I had no idea what to call them.

Frowning, I stepped closer to inspect one of the mantels, where several velvet-lined containers rested side by side. The compartments held a rod with a fringed tassel affixed to the end, an ornate riding crop, a thick silk cord, an elegant red mask trimmed in gold, and a black blindfold. Everything sat there, arranged elegantly like jewels.

Flummoxed, I squinted. Three seconds later, my face slackened in comprehension.

This was Spring. He was the infamous jester.

I knew what these intimate items were.

Promptly, I swerved from the wardrobe and retreated toward the bedroom. Heat sluiced across my face. I could not say whether it stemmed from modesty or repentance.

Likely both. I had no right to impose myself on his personal space like this.

While returning to the bedroom, my eyes stumbled across the tasseled window draperies—and landed on his bed. The elaborate furnishing stood on a central dais, the mattress outfitted in a deep green coverlet and a coordinating mountain of pillows, every element accented in black and gold.

The sight drew me near, my pulse leaping with each invasive step. I had anticipated ruby brocade, fringed curtains, four phallic-looking columns, and a nude self-portrait above the headboard. To the contrary, the only detail that fulfilled my expectations was the dark silk robe. It lay slung across the mattress, the cuffs embroidered with feathers.

I caught my lips quirking and promptly flattened them out.

Although the bed had been made, the sheets were slightly mussed, as if he'd had company last night.

Which men and women have had that privilege? And how often?

I imagined the jester there, naked and hunched over his latest conquest, his body driving into theirs. For some unfathomable reason, the image set my teeth on edge.

Then I thought of Poet sleeping alone, his bare chest exposed, a stack of muscles contorting as he breathed, and his arm flopped above his head. If he rested on his back, the sheets might hang low to reveal the slopes of his hips and the base of his ...

Seasons forgive me. I sucked in a gust of air, shoved my fingers into my pouch, and snatched the ribbon. If the jester meant to target me, I would target him back. I leaned forward, intending to place the scarlet band strategically on the pillows.

The door latch clicked. I lurched upright, then froze as the partition shuddered. Terror and a strange thrill surged through my veins. I bounded off the dais, dashed behind a changing screen, and crouched low.

Footsteps glided into the bedchamber. The jester may live loudly, but he moved quietly.

Gulping, I peeked through a slit in the screen. Poet's profile appeared, his body clad in a long, hooded cloak, along with a plain shirt and hose. No artwork or makeup enhanced his features. At least, none that I could tell, other than kohl lining his eyes and those fingernails enameled to match.

He took three steps, his boots thumping the floor. Then he stopped as if registering something.

Shadows etched his face. Those green eyes ticked in awareness, then slid across the room.

I shrank back and held my breath. Several palpitations later, Poet's shoulders unlocked, and he strode toward the wardrobe.

Moments later, he returned while slipping his hands into a pair of suede gloves and driving a flashing object into the scabbard of his belt. I struggled to identify the item, then regretted as much when I succeeded, alarm and confusion tightening in my gut.

The jester thrust the cloak's hood over his head and stalked from the room.

I lurched to my feet. The ribbon could wait.

I tracked the dark figure as he rounded corners and descended stairways, the hem of his mantle whipping around his legs. Once, twice, the jester angled his head to check the perimeter.

Each time, I leaped out of sight. He strode ahead, opting for vacant passages that cut into the castle like back alleys, unfrequented and unmanned.

Eventually, Poet nudged a stone beneath a windowsill, which prompted the neighboring wall to split. My face cinched. In addition to the secret arteries attached to the Royals' rooms, this fortress had a chain of disguised corridors that would direct people out of the citadel during an invasion. The same held true in every Season, however detailed knowledge of these outlets was restricted to soldiers and the courts' highest-ranking members.

Poet slipped through the crack and dissolved into a tunnel. I darted after him. The shaft was a pupil devoid of light, forcing me to run my hand along the damp walls while tracking his gait.

At the end, slivers of moonlight crept into the conduit and illuminated Poet's outline. He paused outside a barred gate and slid a key into the bolt. The iron groaned open and swung into an herb garden choked with rosemary.

Poet prowled ahead. I counted to ten before exiting and bolting after him across the shrubs.

Through another gate, I emerged into the lower town and ducked behind the gaping door of a public stable. Horses snorted, and the scents of barley and dung slithered up my nostrils. Poet guided one of the stallions to the exit and spoke calmly to it.

Balancing his weight on the stirrup, the jester swung his leg over the horse's obsidian back, then urged it into a moderate gait.

The Crown trusted him. The Season courts lived in peace, but that did not guarantee an eternity of it. We each had our anarchists and murderers. Humans could be bitter or greedy, overcome by grievances or power lust.

Poet toted a weapon and had been skulking through the complex. Surely, the Crown had gifted him with his own stallion, if his chambers and wardrobe were any indication. Yet he insisted on taking an animal from a public stall under the cover of night.

He could be a spy for an unknown group of insurgents. He could be dangerous.

First, I stole a hoof pick—the only portable and sharp item available—from the tack room. My own horse had accompanied me from Autumn, but it was ensconced in the court stables. Instead, I claimed one of the horses, a mare fit to catch up with the jester and the least antsy of my options.

Hastening to saddle her, I ran my palm over the female's back and whispered like my father taught me to. "Shh. It's all right. We're friends, you and me. I give you my word."

The mare relaxed. I might be a stuffy Royal, but I identified with these creatures, and they tended to respond.

I mounted and steered her forward. We passed from the stable and navigated a narrow lane wedged behind the building, which guided us through town. Bawdy laughter and fiddle music filtered from the tavern, while shaky moans and crossing blades echoed from other establishments.

I tightened my grip on the hoof pick and urged the mare faster.

From a rift in the town's main gate, Poet's steed ascended the rolling hills. At the crest, he bled into the wildflower forest—the hub of recklessness, where hidden copses inspired one's impulsive nature.

I should know.

So thinking, I stalled the horse. Our company had traveled through that woodland from Autumn, though we'd journeyed across the safest public avenues. While in Spring, I did my best to otherwise avoid that place.

Somewhere in there, my father had died.

Thankfully, I could not remember where it had happened.

Bracing myself, I dug my heels into the mare, and we plowed after the jester. The wind chased through my hair and licked my cheeks. At the tree line, I wavered once more and then decided. Resigning myself, I secured Poet's ribbon to a bush, lest a search party should need to find me later. They wouldn't associate the item with me, but they *would* link it to the jester.

The route twisted, veering in and out of the moon's ashen glare. At length, Poet abandoned the main thoroughfare and crossed into a thicket. I kept far enough behind, but close enough to pursue the horse's glossy coat. The woods grew dense, twigs tangling into nests and bracken clogging the ground.

Anxiety soaked my palms. I had no plan. I had no idea where, or to whom, he was headed. Had I used my brain, I would have torn strips off my gown to mark a trail.

We kept on like this, heading toward the outlying villages. However, this remote area isolated us from the hamlets. I glanced behind me, then twisted back around, only to jerk on the reins.

Poet was gone.

I guided the mare farther into the snarl of vegetation before halting us again. The animal must have noted the tension in my joints, because she pressed her tail down and snorted. She shifted uneasily, so I slid to the ground and glided my palm over her coat.

Nearby, a brook tumbled and nibbled at its bank. From somewhere above, an owl hooted.

I might as well admit it. I'd lost my quarry. It had to be midnight at this point, which meant I'd have to wait until morning before backtracking home.

My pulse raced. "Don't panic," I told myself and the horse. "We'll be fine."

"Hooo. Hooo," the raptor called from an unseen perch.

"Quiet," I hissed.

"Hoo-hoo-hoooooo."

I paused. That was *so* not an owl.

An obsidian steed trotted out of the shadows, sans its rider, and proceeded to chew on foliage. I reached for the animal's bridle.

"I wouldn't do that if I were you," a masculine timbre warned. "He's a skittish thing."

Whipping around, my gaze connected with a pair of cutthroat eyes.

9

Poet

As I recall, that historic moment hadn't been my finest entrance. Thusly, I'd been hanging upside down, with my legs hooked over a tree branch like an infernal novice because I had lacked quicker options. The princess and I tarried in starlight. Each of us concealed weapons, but mine was fastened in its scabbard, and I hadn't discovered hers yet. That would come shortly.

Wielding deadly tools had always come with the territory for me. Throwing daggers to entertain the masses, for instance. And I'd never left the castle without a blade. Isolated routes. Deceptive nights. Mercenary assholes, political assholes, and drunken assholes. You understand.

But come. I'm vicious toward mortal enemies and naïve targets, not headstrong heiresses. No matter that she'd raised my hackles more times than I could count back then.

Yet how my jaw had ticked. She'd followed me, had gotten too close before I detected her presence, and I was feeling brutal as hell about it.

I wanted to do many things to her that night. Some reasonable, some not.

Does it sound like I'd had malicious intent in mind? Pay attention and find out …

Briar's eyes widened the instant she rounded on me. The woven bun in her hair had gone savage and begun to unravel, red wisps trembling around her shoulders. The vision tugged at a dormant spot in my chest. 'Twas best to ignore that and focus on being pissed off.

I'd had my share of uninvited visitors, usually to my chambers in the dead of night. My status had won me not only adoration but resentment. Thus, people had darkened the Court Jester's door in many ways. Either they offered pleasure—from the perverse to the sensual—which I didn't mind, or threats to slice me open, or petulant bribes, both of which I minded very fucking much.

But never had I been pursued whilst en route to secrecy.

A persistent light simmered in her pupils. A brave and headstrong female, indeed.

A rash one, too. Coming here had been daring of her, and whilst this enabler of a forest was the perfect place for that sort of behavior, it was also negligent. She could have gotten hurt, ambushed, or worse.

Or another mile, and the Royal saboteur could have seen what she shouldn't.

Grabbing the branch, I flipped right side up and landed on my feet. I'd noticed the princess as we entered the woods, and far too late at that. For I should have heeded my interloper long before.

I consumed the inches of space between us and towered over Briar. "You're good," I admitted, then pointed to myself. "But you're not *this* good."

She bristled. "You snuck out."

"Is that how you'd phrase it? I seem to recall being a grown man."

"You snuck out, girded and armed."

Vexing woman. She'd been sniffing my tracks for a while.

"You should have followed the latter of my example. 'Tis one thing, stalking me through the stronghold, but the lower town's alleys?" I tsked. "No one promenades through there at night unless they want to get robbed, stabbed, or fucked."

"Or unless they want to avoid being seen."

I clapped. "Well done. Keeping tabs on me past your bedtime, or perhaps it's a coincidence that you saw me. Either way, I'm here for no special reason. 'Tis a silvery night. A cause for delight—"

The tip of something sharp jabbed between my legs. Glancing down, I was treated to the sight of a hoof pick strategically aimed at my cock. Based on the angle, the head would go first.

I respected a female who could make an otherwise innocent object look deadly.

"Where are you going?" she demanded. "Who are you? And none of this *'tis a secret, 'tis a riddle* rubbish."

"Whatever you assume, give it up. I'm no traitor. I've no time in my busy schedule for treason."

"You are a wordsmith, therefore a liar. I know what your tongue is capable of."

And I knew an opportunity when I heard it. I prowled forward, lowered my voice, and let the words drizzle down her skin. "Now, now," I husked. "You haven't begun to learn what my tongue can do."

A thin strip of color slithered across her cheeks, a scarlet ribbon so faint it unspooled like a dirty little secret. Her posture buckled, a minor shift the lesser acute wouldn't recognize. Myself, I detected it as if the motions were my own. It meant she felt my words between her hips, every slick syllable rooting itself deeply through the slender walls of her cunt.

I savored this precious reaction, so fetching to behold. Unfortunately, the sudden image of Briar's parted thighs flanking my head and the taste of her climax on my tongue inserted itself into my brain.

My cock jumped, thankfully without her noticing. I ground my teeth, because since when have I ever teased a woman or man whilst losing control of myself in the process?

Briar wrestled to keep her gaze aloft, her pulse tapping against her throat. I could punish her for this, for converting every taunt into an unexpected temptation, for preying on truths that didn't belong to her, and for constantly turning my plans against me.

Yet dread and regret weren't the responses I wanted to extract from this Royal. Nay, I wanted that heartbeat, that erratic button pounding in her neck, aching to burst through.

I *wanted* it.

If she were of any other rank, I would make good on this moment. I'd press her against the tree, slip my hand under that skirt, and curl my fingers into the molten slot of her pussy until she came hard and sweetly into my shoulder. I fetishized about how deeply I'd have to reach to penetrate her senses, to draw out her cries, to pry the moans from her.

The fine hairs across my arms raised in protest. Briar wasn't of any other rank. She was an infringement, a breach in my sanity, and a rather inconvenient problem. She'd come this far, which made her a threat. The last thing I could afford was a Royal's suspicion.

Taking advantage of the princess's momentary shock, I swiped the hoof pick from her fingers and proceeded to spin a tale. "Occasionally, I have trouble sleeping, so I fling myself into artistic sojourns. You might have heard about this forest and its power to help with impulsions. The more distance I cover here, the more inspired I become, the better I rest."

I handed the unique murder weapon back to her. "You see? My intentions are as pristine as my wardrobe."

"How strange that you needed a horse from the lower town, when I'm sure the Crown has gladly supplied you with one of your own steeds," she interrogated. "How bizarre that you would take a secret passageway instead of traversing the drawbridge. I'm sure you could have flirted with the guards and convinced them to let you out."

I rolled my eyes. "I'm not about to embarrass myself and give the court fodder for gossip by flaunting my insomnia. Appearances matter, sweeting. In any case, I'm trustworthy."

She lifted her free palm. "Then hand me your blade."

"What for?" I asked. "Mayhap 'tis the jester who can't trust the princess." When she made no reply, I snatched her chin between my thumb and forefinger. "I'm waiting."

"Likewise. If you wish me for to trust you: Hand. Me. The. Blade."

"Sooooo extreme." I squinted at her. "Just how long have you been stalking me?"

Briar flinched. "Since you vacated your bedchamber."

Ah. I should have known the ominous presence in my room had been her, instead of chalking it up to paranoia. I wondered how many corners she'd inspected before regretting her actions—and before the contents of my room flustered her.

"Is that so?" I dipped my head. "And did you see anything you liked?"

Her throat bobbed, her ears suffusing with color. Indeed, the meddlesome little Royal had not only entered my wardrobe but noticed my assortment of pleasure trinkets. This wasn't uncommon in any Spring chamber, though I doubted she knew that.

Then again, I liked to display my treasure trove openly. Her eyes would have unwillingly stumbled across the blindfolds, masks, cords, plumed wands, and other assortments by accident.

As for my stash of ribbons, the princess couldn't have located those unless she'd found the compartment hidden inside my bed's headboard. No worries there.

When she made no reply, I shook my head. "Well, well. I step out for three minutes, and you manage to squeeze your way into exclusive territory."

Guilt flickered across her face. "I-I apologize. I shouldn't have imposed on your absence."

"Hmm. Repenting for the intrusion *whilst* suspecting me of being a criminal *and* holding a weapon to my cock? Such irony. You truly are from Autumn."

"I merely intended to return your ribbon."

"But the color goes so well with your hair."

Her eyes tapered. "You should have been prudent. Isn't that what locks are for?"

"Details. Let's say I was being a heedless rebel, if only for the several minutes it took to loan a pot of eye pigment to one of my fellow dancers. So—" I poured the question all over her, slowly and thickly, "—what did you think of my bed?"

She blinked, flushed, did all the things I wanted her to do.

This proved the princess had inspected where I slept. The prospect of her standing beside the mattress, close to my sheets where I spent my nights naked, appealed to me more than it should. Just like everything else about her.

She recovered and nudged the hoof pick against my leather pants, threatening to dismember one of my best attributes.

I grunted, slanting my groin from the prongs. "Carrying a blade doesn't make me treasonous, Highness. The weapon's merely for dicing through enemies who get in my way, not for skinning nosy princesses. Though, I'm impressed you noticed the knife at all. My room was dark."

Above her, an unidentified critter scurried along a branch, inciting an avalanche of stones. My hand shot out to capture one and then toss it to the Royal, which she caught in her outstretched grasp.

The moment provided important details that she hadn't noticed, but I had. One, the fact that she'd let go of her mare's bridle, allowing the horse to roam freely alongside mine. And two, a hunting trap— an aged model, from what I could tell of its shape—five feet from us.

A shitty premonition crept up on me.

"I pay attention to things," she claimed. At which point, the princess whipped out her arm, pitched the rock off to the side, and sealed our fucking fate.

The stone thwacked into the hunting trap. Its rusty hinges squealed, the teeth snapping shut with a ghastly echo.

The horses reared into action. Their spooked cries pierced through the forest as they bolted into the night.

"Let's play a game," I instigated.

"Don't start," the princess said, panting as we hiked beside the brook.

"You realize we've circled this area twice already."

"I'm aware of that."

"I'm bored," I mock-whined, just to fuck with her.

This tenacious woman deserved to be punished. She had waylaid my evening, kept me from the one beloved thing I anticipated all week—every week—and gotten us stranded. Moreover, having my ears assaulted by righteous dialogue added insult to injury. And mud caked my favorite boots to the fucking ankles.

Two hours later, and we were still searching for the horses. I never used my own stallion from the court stables for these evening trips. Those stalls were under constant surveillance, guarded by cranky bastards who noticed every ant that traveled in and out, and I couldn't risk being seen.

But whilst I had been spared the loss of my personal mount, we'd lost a pair that had been for sale, which meant the stable would lose money.

Notwithstanding, our chances of recovering the fauna were slim. I'd given up an hour ago, for it was too dark to follow their hoof prints. And as terrified as the horses had been, they could push themselves three miles out of range before the gallop sapped their energy.

The princess and I had a rigorous trek back to the court to look forward to. I'd need those hours to contemplate how to sweet-talk us out of this. Justifying why we abducted common steeds, and why we'd been out here together, would be problematic. Dammit, I could strangle this female and flog my own ass.

We trailed the brook, figuring the horses would seek water.

"Indulge me, Sweet Thorn," I said. "I won't take nay for an answer, not until we make our return journey or make camp. Mind you, I vote for the latter."

Briar rounded on me, the hem of her mahogany gown slapping the dirt. "I will not give up yet."

Up close, her forehead shimmered with sweat. Her disheveled appearance was unaccountably different from the figure that usually locked horns with me. The sight made her look approachable ... alluring.

Do not go there again.

I appreciated the woman's determination. However, I also craved a fresh diversion, mostly to keep my admiration from segueing for the hundredth time to her physical attributes.

"We'll call a ceasefire," I said. "I shall ask you a series of questions, and you shall stimulate me with your own inquisition. The first person to lie loses. We're well-versed enough with each other for that."

Dubious, she crossed her arms. "It's a distraction."

"You're a Royal. I'm a juggler. That makes us accustomed to multitasking."

With a sigh, the princess trudged through the undergrowth. Her hips swayed and did attractive things to her skirt, which in turn did cruel things to my bloodstream, which annoyed the shit out of me. The Royal had been routinely getting under my skin since the feast, and I couldn't afford to start obsessing.

I marshalled my concentration. Her silence gave me permission to start interrogating.

Why do you hate Spring? Why do you distrust this Season? Why won't you let anyone in? What are you afraid of?

Who did this to you?

"Why are you friends with Eliot?" I asked.

'Twas the least invasive question on my list.

Still, Briar faltered. "That is none of your concern."

"And that's a paltry response."

"You haven't spoken to him yet," she accused over her shoulder.

"Regrettably so. I haven't been procrastinating, but I haven't been in a hurry to crush Eliot, either. Plus, my sovereigns have kept me busy. There hasn't been a free moment since the orchid garden, and that isn't an answer to my question. You're pitiful at this game."

"Eliot expects nothing of me. When we're alone, I can be anyone with him. I can confess anything, and he'll understand me."

"That sounds more hypothetical than factual. Do you confess everything?"

She shrugged. Waiting for her to continue took a monumental amount of effort, but I didn't want to push it. More than I cared to admit, I wanted her to speak willingly.

"I just know he wouldn't judge me," she said. "We met when we were twelve, at a market in the lower town. My parents—" The princess hedged, her eyebrows slashing downward with suspicion

As I stared back, something in her eyes loosened. Shadows from the branches laced her pale features, the markings reminiscent of scars. According to common knowledge, the Princess of Autumn was twenty, and her father had died eight years ago. She lost him here in Spring, whilst at court.

That didn't mean the public knew the whole story. A few middling details rarely amounted to that.

"They were here for the Peace Talks," she said. "Anyway, at the market, I came upon this group of children making fun of Eliot because he was trying to strum a lute for passersby, but the instrument was too large for his body. So I defended him. I clapped, the first applause he ever got."

A grin slanted through the princess's face, causing her freckles to shift. "I praised him and admonished the children for not appreciating fine music. I requested more songs from Eliot until he drew a crowd, which got the king and queen to notice him. The lute was too big, but he played with charm, which earned him a Royal apprenticeship. His family was so proud."

Eliot's family lived in an outlying village. He wrote to them every week.

"We had a memorable time together, exploring the artists' wares. It was astounding, keeping company with someone who didn't see me as an heiress but just a girl. Because I was there, a merchant let us try on her best costumes, which excited Eliot to no end.

"At another stall, we admired the bird cages. I bought him a berry pie, and he taught me how to master a chord. We stole a quart of mead from one of the booths, but it tasted vile."

When she laughed, the sound crept into me like a vine—a cord that could easily take root and germinate all over the forsaken place.

Without my realizing it, we'd drifted from the brook and veered east, a direction I'd been intending to avoid with her.

She halted when I did. "When my father died that night—"

I made damn sure to keep my expression blank. He died the same night?

"—Eliot found me in the ruins hours later. His apprenticeship would begin the next day, and the Crown had already supplied him with a room in the artist wing. I sent him a message, and when he came to me, I told him I was going to be a new person from then on, not the same one he met. And Eliot said that was okay, then he played me a song until I fell asleep in his lap. I'd saved him, and he saved me.

"For the next eight years, we wrote to each other—long letters every month. I would wear a disguise, sneak into Autumn's lower town, and have them dispatched from there."

The scent of apples and parchment wafted from her hair, soaking into my lungs. I moved nearer but paused when Briar tensed in response. I wasn't used to feeling inadequate or unwanted. Worse, the vision of her curled up in the ruins—a child without a father—caught me by the throat.

"What do you mean, 'a new person'?" I asked, because it didn't sound okay to me. Matter of fact, it sounded all sorts of wrong.

"I am a princess," she clipped. "I cannot afford to be myself."

"In that case, you could have at least gotten creative and shape-shifted into a unicorn. Everyone likes a unicorn."

"My turn," she announced, wheeling to face me. "How old are you?"

"A profligate twenty-one tonight and a provocative twenty-two eventually. Which is more appealing? Take your pick."

"Who apprenticed you?"

"Consider me a prodigy."

"What about your speech? Who educated you?"

I sidestepped that as well. "I taught myself how to speak like a patrician. That's more questions than I got, Highness."

"Where do you come from?"

I slouched against a tree. "You'll forgive me if I remain mysterious, Sweet Thorn. Not that I'm the brooding type—men of the like are dull. Mystery tends to compensate for that. Also, it's sexier. In other words, my history is otherwise unimpressive, and I do prefer to impress."

She grimaced. "At someone else's expense."

Splendid. We were back to criticizing my methods.

I huffed at the fringed branches. "True, I target the bigots, ridicule the hypocrites, and verbally slay the intolerant assholes of this court. As for the rest, the courtiers enjoy themselves. I make fair points and ease the blow with humor, and that brings a measure of understanding—a willing inclination to re-evaluate certain prospects.

"Is that not a noble accomplishment? Are those not the principles you so dearly value? 'Tis my craft to know what people need to hear, what they can handle." I glanced at her. "Like I've said before, I'm a jester. I see everything."

Unfortunately, the princess had quit listening. Her face blanched, and her eyes widened as they fixated on a spot behind me.

She pointed. "Do you see *that*?"

Peeved, I swung around. As I did, a feral growl sheared through the wild. My joints locked at the sight of claws, bared fangs, and a pair of carnivorous, yellow irises.

Oh. Fuck.

Poet

L et me explain what we dealt with. 'Twas a leenix. The predatory forest cat was native to Spring, possessed the lethal grace of a panther, and wielded canines born from hell. It had a bottomless appetite and an incomparable agility the likes of which my reflexes had no prayer against.

In short, I'd met my match. I would have seized this opportunity—sightings of them were rare—to observe our predator's movements if it weren't planning to maul us.

And so, a violent game began ...

The feline flashed its tusks and hissed, the noise scratching through the night. Gray fur bristled down the creature's spine as it brooded on its haunches, itching to spring free off the invisible coils beneath its paws.

With measured steps, I moved in front of the princess. My body shielded her from the leenix whilst I set my hand on the hilt of my blade. I locked gazes with the animal and lowered my voice to a murmur. "Your Highness. If you turn back, you'll be facing west."

A second after processing that instruction, Briar's breath hitched. "No," she rasped. "You cannot be serious."

"The second I snap my fingers, I'll be busy entertaining our distinguished guest. Whilst that's happening, you're going to flee. And I do mean, *flee*. Follow the beaten path that we came from, and when you locate the hunting trap, veer northwest until you hit a narrow lane parallel to the main thoroughfare. It shall conceal you from nightwalkers and other assorted shitheads whilst also guiding you home."

"Poet, no."

Although the next few minutes were bound to hurt, I enjoyed the tremble of my name on her lips. "Do not bring back help. If you do, I shall despise you for it. Indeed, my contempt will be legendary."

She wouldn't understand that, and she wasn't going to obey, but I had to try. Hopefully, despite whatever damage this kitty did to me, I'd still be able to crawl another mile or so from here. I didn't want to be anywhere near this spot when the cavalry arrived. It was too close to what mattered most.

I pictured a little pair of eyes, greener than mine. Soon enough, those eyes would peek outside a window and alight. They would wait for me to arrive, unaware I wasn't coming.

My fists curled. My shoulders tightened.

The leenix had spotted us long before we'd spotted it. Yet I held the creature's gaze.

Trick me, and I shall trick you back.

None of this meant I wasn't scared. Down to the marrow of my bones, I was petrified, but I was also cranky. I had too much to live for, to tolerate this horseshit.

I inclined my head to the fine specimen of a cat and then snapped my fingers to keep its attention. The moment shattered like glass shards—sudden and explosive.

The cat launched toward me with a savage growl, its claws lashing the air. I dove out of the leenix's path, rolled across the ground, and shot to my feet whilst whipping out the blade.

The animal flew at me again, a liquid beam of gray.

It struck. I ducked.

It pounced. I spun.

It gave chase. I ran toward a tree, planted a foot on the trunk, and flung myself into a backflip over the creature's head. The cat was still scraping the bark when I landed behind it and took advantage, striking with the blade and slitting a hind leg.

Crimson spritzed from the gash and sprayed my clothes. The animal yowled and pivoted, the flat of its paw smacking my wrist. Its claws missed my flesh, but the force nearly wrenched my arm out of its socket, and the impact knocked the weapon from my grasp. The blade flashed and catapulted into the darkness.

A whistle cut through the woods, the shrill noise distracting the cat. At the same time, I pivoted and parried around the creature, disorientating the animal and dodging a series of enraged swipes.

Another whistle. Pebbles thwacked against the leenix's skull, punctuated by a feminine "Hey!"

The seething animal vaulted around and bared its canines. Instinctively, it swatted at a mahogany wool skirt, but not before the princess used her hoof pick to stab its shoulder.

More blood spurted from the second wound, pouring in rivulets down the leenix's fur. The injured cat howled, hobbled backward, and dashed into the thicket. The animal would live, but it would hurt for a while.

On a groan, I staggered in place. Then my body tipped forward. I hunched over, clasping my thighs and wheezing.

Wicked fucking hell. I'd told that princess to leave. She could have gotten torn to shreds.

Raising my head, I opened my mouth to flay the woman for her stupidity, but her piercing cries stopped me cold. The princess lay sprawled on the grass. Her body spasmed, puddles of red seeping through her gown and pooling into the earth.

My heart stuttered. I charged ahead, my knees slamming into the dirt beside her. Snatching the hem of her skirt, I wrenched up the fabric and went still.

Her bare thighs quivered. A slash carved through her flesh, the trench leaking blood.

"Fuck," I spat in horror. "Briar."

In a thrice, the choice was stolen from me. The gash on her thigh was neither small, nor shallow. We needed help, and the only place to find it was the last place I wanted to take her.

The place I'd originally been heading to before this chaos began.

II

Briar

ranches swam above me, thick limbs of bark twisting and gnarling together. Dark clusters of trees passed in and out of my vision like moving shadows, the canopies dense with shingled foliage. Several leaves detached from the boughs and fell, raining on me like flakes of ash.

My eyes hooded with a terrible weight. A chilled draft swept through my dress and rustled my hair. I seemed to be floating mid-air, drifting through a strange forest, the sky beyond an oily black. Exposed tree roots plaited, stocky and stitched in filaments of moss.

They seemed familiar.

I tried to suck in air, but my lungs chafed, roasting me from the inside. A desperate noise sawed through the eventide air. I scraped at my throat to ward off the burn, then realized the frantic mewls were coming from me.

My thigh throbbed like a drum. The agony worsened each time I shifted, each time the fabric of my skirt abraded my flesh.

As another whimper curled from my throat, a strong hand cupped my face. A velveteen timbre whispered for me to *breathe*, it's *all right*.

I clung to that voice, my lungs relaxing and filling with fresh oxygen. My nostrils drew in the earthy scents of perspiration and soil, along with notes of amber and vetiver.

Something sticky and moist coated my leg. I must be in trouble. Either that, or I was dreaming.

Where was Father's ghost? Was he here, forever roaming this place?

Where was Mother? I wanted her. I wanted to go home.

Solid arms encased me in their grip. Male heat radiated from the source and seeped into my pores.

My eyelids fluttered. Alarmed orbs shone down on me, the irises a startling color amid the bleakness. Their hue cut through the woodland murk like gems.

"Poet," I mumbled.

"Shh," he intoned.

Yes, it was Poet. That rakish jester and my prevailing enemy.

And there had been a predator—a leenix. It had attacked the jester, and the jester had executed some type of flip to get out of harm's way, but the maneuver hadn't helped. So I wounded the animal, but not before it had swiped at me.

Dizzy. Tired. Shaky.

The grass swam several feet beneath me. I was hovering, my body suspended above the ground. Poet was carrying me.

The jester kept one arm linked under my knees, the other harnessed across my back. His heartbeat hammered into my cheek, the wild tempo reminding me of when he danced in the great hall. I mused whether his pulse had sounded this erratic back then, and I wondered what it sounded like whenever he looked at me.

Words bubbled from my lips. I mumbled something about him being a talented prat, and how much I hated him, and that I was sorry.

I should have apologized to the leenix, too. The poor creature was only hungry.

Had I harmed it fatally? Would the animal live?

My savior rested a finger on my mouth to shush me. He murmured how the wildcat would survive and that I should conserve my energy. His pace accelerated, his weight thudding against the ground as he stalked through the forest.

Suddenly, I cried out. The pain in my thigh stunned me into full consciousness, scorching my flesh where claws had torn through me. My tears soaked Poet's shirt as he panted a rhyme into my temple, his voice a languid caress.

I listened while weeping. And after he finished the recitation, the jester promised we were *almost there, almost there.*

Almost where?

An oval of dim light appeared from nowhere, its golden sheen drizzling through the netting of foliage. As we approached, more details came into view.

A window. A thatched roof.

A cottage.

Poet rapped on the wooden door. It flew open, revealing a face with skin made of burlap and a nest of silver hair. The old woman wore an apron and a turbulent expression that slackened with relief when she saw Poet.

"You bastard," she lectured. "Where have you been? I'm bloody well not getting any younger to be worrying."

"Come now," Poet remarked dryly. "You know how I enjoy being fashionably late."

"Oh, just get the hell in here."

In a series of hectic gestures, she waved him inside. The jester hastened into the womb of the house.

I craned my head and blinked through the haze. The aromas of herbs and crisp woodsmoke infused my senses. Colorful bands of material were tied into knots, forming cords that hung from the ceiling.

To my bemusement, Poet tried and failed to interrupt the old woman's ranting. I caught fragments of her tirade while she fussed with the door's bolt.

"Nicu was in hysterics ..."

"Even Tumble couldn't calm him down ..."

"It was a horror putting the boy to bed ..."

"Fought me tooth and nail ..."

"Don't you go making us fret like that ..."

Suddenly, she swerved from the door—and her gaze landed on me. The wrinkles across her face multiplied, creasing with concern. "Who's this?"

Poet strode to a kitchen nook outfitted with a table and chairs. "Funny you should notice."

She smacked his shoulder while trotting after him. "Don't be smart. I'm not as spry as I used to be. What do you mean, bringing one of your consorts here? And what's wrong with her?" The woman squinted, then her eyes shifted to my leg. "Seasons almighty. Poet—"

I moaned as he eased me into a seat. In a rush, he rattled off blurry, indecipherable things that caused the woman to gasp.

She disappeared and returned with a basket. Kneeling at my feet, she rifled through the contents, her movements urgent.

After that, the woman rolled up her sleeves and lifted the skirt to my hips, exposing my bare limbs and the lace trim of my undergarments. Then she unwrapped the material that had been torn from my gown to make a bandage—when had the jester done that?—and blood dribbled from the cleft.

Orders were tossed at Poet.

"Get me a cloth."

"Get another chair."

"Get out of my way."

Amid delirium, the words *blood loss* and *infection* and *stitches* tolled in my head. I felt the complexion drain from my face and sweat bridge across my palms.

A tiny voice drifted into the fray. "Papa?"

To my left, a fae appeared. A runty figure with an upturned nose and puffy eyes. The little male poked his head out from the hallway, his neck entwined with a log-shaped parcel of fur. A ferret nestled like a shawl along the fae's shoulders, the animal's beady orbs fixating on the scene.

Meanwhile, the fae boy's full lips mashed into a sleepy pucker. At which point, the small pairing blinked at the spectacle occurring in the living room.

The instant the fae spotted me, his eyes sparkled. He stumbled forward, his arms extending in my direction. "Ooooooh," he exclaimed, gleeful.

Poet intercepted. He rushed over and scooped up the fae. Or rather, the child bore an alarming resemblance to a fae, especially with the ferret still attached to his scanty shoulders.

Not that such beings lived on this continent, as far as anyone knew. While I couldn't speak for the world outside The Dark Seasons, magic existed here primarily through nature and the elements. In Autumn, there was a legend about mythical acorns, for instance. And in Summer, lore had spread about an uncharted island and its deadly rainforest.

Upon seeing Poet, the child forgot about me and smothered the jester instead. He and the ferret made an elated fuss, chattering and squeaking with enthusiasm until Poet kissed the child's cheek and whispered, causing the boy to sag as if he'd wiped himself out. The ferret slinked to Poet's shoulder while the boy wound his limbs around the jester's torso, his fingers digging into Poet's back.

I squinted, recognizing the tattered ribbon tied around the boy's wrist.

The child had said *Papa*.

The old woman mentioned a sleeping draught in the cupboard and how the boy wouldn't hear a thing. On that note, she regarded me. "It could help you, too. Do you have allergies?"

"Willow Dime," I slurred, listing the Spring herb that had almost killed me when I was three.

My healer traded a clammy look with Poet and shrugged. "Well, there goes that."

Poet carried the child and fauna sidekick into the corridor, back the way they'd come. The woman spoke to me in gentle tones, but I suffered for an eternity until the jester returned. He produced a jug from an open shelf and coaxed wine down my throat, which I shoved away after two foul gulps.

My breathing grew shallow when I saw the thread, the needle, and the tip.

The healer paused, instrument in hand. "This is going to hurt, miss."

My head bobbed to indicate I understood her. If I spoke, it would come out as a groan. It was a moot point once she bound my arms and ankles to the chair, then gave me a wooden spoon to bite on.

Poet sank into the seat behind mine, rested his chin on my shoulder, and encircled my waist. Whether to restrain or comfort me, I wasn't sure.

"Two frisky little ferrets walk into a whorehouse," he began into my ear.

The older woman doused a cloth with liquid, then pressed the material into the slash. I wailed between my teeth. And I wailed louder as the needle dug into my flesh, and I marveled how that child dreamed through the shrill noises.

A spike punctured my flesh, followed by a tugging sensation. Another searing pain probed my leg. Then another.

The woman's bent head fogged at the edges. The blood on her hands blurred.

My body shivered, freezing and baking all at once. My limb throbbed like a hammer.

I needed to move. I needed to get out of this chair. I hated this chair.

My fingernails dug into the armrests. My teeth gnashed on the spoon, the pressure threatening to crack my molars.

I squirmed and arched backward into Poet, my temple grazing his jaw. He restrained my hips and whispered another naughty joke, and something akin to a laugh and a sob escaped me.

A blade stabbed into my leg. A guttural noise flooded the room.

Right before I fainted.

12

Poet

I remember her whimpers against my throat. Oh, how I remember. She'd taken the pain like a warrior, laughed at my racy joke like a nymph, and then swooned like a princess. Such a relief, for each time she unleashed into the spoon's handle, I had gripped her tighter and cursed fate.

Destiny was appealing in verse. But in reality, it was nothing but a clever deception, a delusion at best, derailing plans swifter than a punch in the face.

The Royal's eyes had vanished into the back of her head. That was it.

Old Jinny had threaded the final stitch. At last, I'd carried the unconscious female to my bed, tucking her in and nestling the duvet beneath that determined chin. Often, she'd proven herself to be divinely unpredictable. So because we were alone, I did something phenomenal. I knelt beside the sleeping woman and stared at her.

Truly stared at her.

And this was how I began to feel ...

Like a fool. For all that I toyed with people, I'd overlooked her exquisite profile and, most importantly, failed to appreciate her integrity. I hadn't foreseen the lengths to which she'd go to help someone she despised. This stifling princess took a leenix blow to protect the very jester she scorned, the person she trusted the least.

No longer busy censuring my very existence, a tempestuous side had emerged. Prickly as a bramble, yet she had blood and courage pumping through her veins.

Also, she dreamed with color tinting her skin. A ripe pink crept across her parted lips, as though she were on the verge of an unconscious moan.

How much darker could that stubborn mouth become? How much wetter?

I snapped the bloody fuck out of it. As much as I had loathed Briar's pain, I hadn't gotten to finish my last joke whilst Old Jinny mended her. A tragedy, since I'd fancied speaking into the Royal's ear, provoking chuckles between the tears.

I had hated seeing her in pain. But I'd enjoyed making her laugh.

It hadn't been a chore to comfort her. Indeed, the latter had been a privilege. For a moment, knowing Briar needed me felt as extraordinary and agonizing as being needed by Jinny and Nicu.

Nicu.

My ribs cinched tightly. Standing, I dragged my gaze from the princess to the small body cocooned in the neighboring bed. His toes stuck out from under the covers because his feet always got too hot. That knoll of messy hair forever smelled of powder and sunlight.

I loved it all. I loved all of my son.

His chest rose and fell, the movements barely detectable. When he was an infant, that chest had consumed me with paranoia. I would stay up all night to make sure he was breathing. I'd place a finger under his nostrils, reassured by those priceless wisps of air that hit my knuckles.

Presently, Tumble snoozed in the crook of Nicu's nape. The ferret's body twisted into a corkscrew, and his whiskers fluttered.

Putting Nicu to sleep whilst Jinny mended the princess had been necessary, but now that our guest hogged the spare bed—the one I used during my visits—'twas best not to leave her with my son. I couldn't take the risk that he'd rouse and attack Briar with hugs, or scurry under the covers with her, hoping to make a friend of the princess and rip her stitches in his enthusiasm.

A pity, indeed. For the trio of humans and fauna made a fetching sight, filling this room with their steady breathing.

I hooked my arms beneath his legs and shoulders, then lifted him off the mattress. Tumble jolted awake and nipped at my cloak in tired protest.

"Hey," I scolded. "We've talked about this. Not the clothes."

The command was more of a reflex than anything, considering blood clotted the mantle. There was no saving this garment, much less the rest of my attire, all of which was sprayed in crimson.

Annoyed, the ferret hopped off the mattress. He scurried beside me as I balanced Nicu with one arm and closed the door behind us with the other. Crossing the hallway, I stepped into the living room.

Jinny sat at the kitchen table and darned one of my shirts, her quick pace verifying that I'd charred her nerves to cinders tonight. She concentrated on the linen and sealed a tear. And how many times had I told her she didn't have to do that for me? I kept a private tailor at court, yet the woman insisted.

The fire snapped and spewed embers onto the grate. The blaze's orange cast stretched across the walls, illuminating the space.

Jinny waited as I swaddled my son by the hearth. Whilst Tumble jumped into the nearby mending basket and wrapped himself around a sock, Nicu flopped over and mumbled in his sleep.

Despite the fur rug and pile of blankets, this wouldn't do. I kept opulent chambers in the castle, with paneling mounted on the walls, feather pillows and silk casings, and a wardrobe that would make an emperor jealous. Yet my family needed a sofa, and my son needed his own bedroom, not a cubicle he shared with me during my visits.

Granted, I had the means. But large or extravagant deliveries to this cottage—to say nothing of commissions or renovations—would be noticed. Drawing public attention to this place was the one thing none of us could afford. So no matter what minor luxuries I brought with me on a weekly basis, it would never be enough.

They deserved better. They deserved a palace.

I wiped Nicu's moist brow with my thumb and then, lacking my usual finesse, dropped into the seat across from the woman who'd been a mother to me since I could crawl.

Jinny jerked her head toward Nicu. "He's yours, all right. Trying to charm the maidens the minute he sees them," she wisecracked, referring to the way he had waddled toward the bleeding Royal in excitement before I'd intervened.

On the table, a mug of tea waited for me, the contents reeking with the scent of ginger. It rekindled a memory of my eight-year-old self, spice flaring on my tongue when Jinny forced me to drink a shitload of it. That had been my punishment for using her cups to practice juggling after she'd told me not to.

I raised the cup in a mock toast. "I suppose I deserve this."

Nonchalantly, she pulled a thread through the shirt and spoke to the material bunched in her hands. "You deserve fire pepper."

I set down the mug and pinched the bridge of my nose. "What the devil is happening?"

"You tell me."

"'Tis a long, inconvenient story."

"You're a master at those. Let's hear it."

"Sadly, I reached my crisis threshold hours ago. I'm tired and haven't the energy to embellish."

"Well, try," Jinny scolded, dropping her arms in her lap. "And leave your fancy talk at the castle gate, my boy."

"I propose we delay the unpleasantries until tomorrow, when we've rested and stuffed ourselves with so much food that we lack the strength to actually talk."

"Poet—"

I threw up my arms. "Why does that suggestion get a *Poet*?"

"You're right. I'm too ancient to be using that dandified court name of yours anyway, Fen—"

My finger shot to my lips. My eyes clicked toward the hallway, which led to the room where Briar slept. I refused to have my real name trumpeted within spitting distance of her. The name was private and only for Jinny to utter.

"The female waylaid me," I defended, lowering my voice.

"But she isn't just any female, is she? I know a lady when I see one."

"She's a princess."

Old Jinny swiveled her head toward me. "Well, your taste has gotten even more expensive," she replied, amazement and apprehension clashing in her voice. "Do you mean she's Briar of Autumn?"

Jinny may be tucked away in this forest, but she'd known about the Peace Talks. Weeks ago, I'd listed the princess as the only Royal successor attending the spree.

Tracing my fingers around the rim of my cup, I toiled through a bland version of the events, starting with her pursuit of me and ending with the leenix. Although I'd told the princess to run, she hadn't listened. Quite the contrary, she got in the way.

She did that in abundance. Everything about her tended to get in the way.

On the other hand, if the princess wanted to turn alpha, that was her choice. I had no quandary there. Certain insipid and unimpressive men in this court would glance down to make sure their balls hadn't fallen off by now, but neither my masculinity, nor my confidence suffered. The jester jewels weren't going anywhere. It was the other vital organs, located in the upper regions of my body, that I'd begun to second-guess.

"Saved your hide, did she?" Jinny translated. "Granted, I'll thank her heroism once I know the rest of her is harmless."

"It is," I said, reclining in the chair and contemplating the fire as it chewed on the logs. "There's no prejudice in that Royal's blood. My fatherly intuition is intact, and it detects compassion."

"Hmm. I wonder if it's truly your fatherly intuition that vouches for her. From where I'm sitting, you're right splotchy."

For fuck's sake. That knowing twinkle of hers was the purest form of teasing.

A protest teetered on my lips. I should have let it out or mocked the situation, but that would have been the intelligent thing to do, and where that princess was concerned, I'd been on a destructive path since the welcome feast.

Trusting the Royal wasn't exactly smart. No matter that Briar rescued me, for a droplet of doubt still trickled through my mind, which I'd deal with once she woke up.

Jinny cut off whatever I could have said. "She can take a wildcat wound, that's for sure."

"My sentiments exactly."

"She lasted a while before keeling over. Much better than you. The day you survive a splinter is the day I become a sorceress."

My eyes slitted. "Let's not exaggerate."

"Reminded me of when you were six."

I groaned. She loved to tell this damned story.

"We'd just returned from a fest," Jinny reminisced. "You and your obsession with sunset carnivals, always watching the jesters, your little face glowing with awe."

"Not always," I reminded her.

The sunset carnivals could be lush, enigmatic, mysterious. They could be gritty and beautiful—darkly enchanting. But they also had their vicious sides, the gruesome parts covered in thick layers of pomp and glitz. It didn't take much to notice once a person opened their fucking eyes and looked closer. Alas, most people didn't.

"No, of course," Jinny agreed. "But that day when we got home, you imitated those jesters for hours, twirling from rock to rock in the grass. And when you fell—"

"I *stumbled*."

"—and scraped yourself raw, I never saw the like when I dabbed a wet cloth on your knees. You howled bloody murder."

My elbow hit the table as I pointed at her. "That part never happened."

"Go ahead. Deny it."

"I'm changing the subject. Apologies for my tardiness."

"You know better'n to think I *don't* know *better*. You gave us a fright, but don't apologize. The only reason you'd ever stay away is if you were hurt or suspected trouble was following you."

I glanced at my son. Guilt cleaved through my ribs, a permanent emotion if there ever was one. "I'll ask Nicu's forgiveness in the morning."

Setting my shirt and her thread on the table, Jinny grabbed my hand. "You mind this. What happened was out of your control. You'd as soon battle an army of leenixes to be here."

This was the story no one at court knew. I had a son, a radiant son for whom I'd willingly rest my neck on the executioner's block. His mother, a raven-haired spitfire, had been crossing through the wildflower forest with her nomadic family when we met.

Wandering from their camp on that fateful dawn, she had found me practicing handstands on a fallen tree trunk. I'd been bare-chested and cut a decent seventeen-year-old figure. Which was why the spitfire—eighteen, she boasted—stayed to watch.

Then she stayed for more after we fumbled past the introductions.

We had challenged one another to a balancing competition on that trunk. By the end of it, I'd lost. She had cheated by hitching up her skirt and feasting her gaze on me so greedily, so smugly, that I'd known where things were headed.

Naturally, my erection agreed with her. In that spirit, I'd found myself grasping that log for dear life whilst the female straddled my cock and rode me until my eyes slid to the back of my brainless head.

Afterward, she walked home with me, sucked my mouth into another kiss, and never returned. However, she was polite enough to leave me a token of her gratitude on Jinny's doorstep nine months later. Oh, the irony of history repeating itself.

Those green irises proved the infant was mine. He didn't know me yet, but he'd gurgled a laugh and extended a pair of chubby arms, demanding to be held. Henceforth, the little one owned me.

He had made another noise, something that sounded like *nicu-uuuu* to my ears, so that's what I called him. I liked the idea of my son naming himself.

In the beginning, it had been easy to miss the signs, for infants did incomprehensible things and wept daily. They could be as temperamental and fussy as Nicu had been. However, his appearance—disproportionate features that belonged in a folktale—had immediately given me pause. He could be a fae with that expansive grin, and the way his wide eyes jumped from his face and his nose condensed into it. I ignored the signs, too anxious to do otherwise.

But it wasn't until Nicu approached his second year that I noticed something singular about his behavior. My son had a giant heart. Yet I hadn't realized how giant until we passed a peddler on the road, whom Nicu sprang to. He'd tackled the shocked man's leg and asked if the stranger wanted to come home with us for dinner and be eternal friends.

That was how Tumble joined our family. I'd purchased the critter to distract Nicu, to pry him from the man's limb.

I had clung to a theory. Living far outside the villages made my son thirsty for attention, as I'd been growing up. As such, Tumble and my son became inseparable. With Nicu isolated and cloistered from other children, Tumble gave him the friendship he'd been deprived of.

In any case, Nicu was about as shy as his father. At a midnight festival, he once trotted out of my sight to greet a stranger and sit on their lap without permission. In such mystical places where dramatics abounded, he managed to blend in and evade suspicion, and his social aggression was excused because of his age—to a point. For his face had given shrewd people cause to look twice.

I might have predicted he'd outgrow his excitability, except I knew my son inside and out. My gut began to feel the permanence of it.

Jinny and I watched him carefully. As he became more extreme—random monologues and inventive, fictional rants that surpassed his years, and utter devotion to anyone crossing paths with us between hamlets and towns—our uncertainties took root.

Who was to say Nicu wouldn't one day stumble into the wrong pair of arms?

We ceased taking him on outings. It ensured that locals forgot about him entirely, as people did when engulfed in their own demons and raptures.

Enter the second act. For not only did Nicu lob his friendliness at whomever he met, but he got lost easily and couldn't tell his bedroom from the kitchen. All manner of spaces, distances, and directions puzzled him.

Enter the third and final act, shy of his third year. I asked him to fetch a bucket for Jinny, and he disappeared outside the cottage, then returned with one of our chickens instead.

"Here," he'd said, handing the animal to a bewildered Jinny.

The scene iced me with terror. It would take a dozen more occurrences like this to be certain, but already I knew. In the intolerant eyes of The Dark Seasons, my son possessed a slanted mind.

At the time, we couldn't afford a physician, much less trust one to examine Nicu in secret. Turning in such undisclosed prey to the Crown amounted to rewards.

Desperate for answers, I traveled to neighboring villages to strike up hypothetical, random conversations with anyone skilled in the healing arts. Feigning nonchalance, I picked their brains but came up empty-handed. I couldn't identify what caused my son's condition, what it was called, or what to do about it.

There was that saying. Keep your enemies close.

A month after the chicken incident, destiny threw me into the monarchy's path, when I entered myself into an acrobatic match at a midnight festival. A knight of Spring had viewed the spectacle and reported me to Basil and Fatima, who in turn summoned me to perform for them.

Within days, I became the new Court Jester.

I straddled two worlds: public and secret.

If my sovereigns knew about Nicu, he'd become their lawful property. So I spent my days making sure that never happened, dazzling the court, worming my way into their good graces and their beds, and earning a small fortune. My precarious job fed and clothed my family. I visited them every week and kept Jinny in supplies.

As long as Nicu remained here, he was protected. As long as I nudged the Crown's funny bone, remained privy to the intricacies of their reign, and maintained influence over them, I had control.

At court, I lived a lavish and influential life. In secret, I worried.

Nay, terror seized me with every cursed breath I drew.

I glanced at Old Jinny. "'Tisn't enough."

With her free hand, she anchored my cheek. "No parent ever thinks what they do is enough. I'm a mother, too, aren't I?"

I relaxed into her palm. "I don't know what I'd do without you."

Her eyes misted. "Oh yes, you do."

She insisted the unendurable but inevitable. The princess and I were to stay put until the threat of an infection passed and she could make the trek back. Not to mention, a rare misfortune brewed—a Spring storm in the middle of blooming season. Brilliant.

After Jinny retired, I snuggled with my son, his fingers bunching my shirt. Rest came and went, slipping through my fingers before I could catch it. The rainy dawn followed, droplets splattering the roof, and soot caked the hearth.

A little someone snickered. A little someone scrambled onto my torso and tugged on my earlobe.

I pretended to be asleep and was rewarded with more ear tugs. Without opening my eyes, I seized Nicu by the ribcage. "Got you!"

My son chirped with glee. He lay flat atop my chest, spanning my width with his twig arms and legs. "No, I've got you! You're my prisoner, Papa!"

"And I surrender willingly. You have no idea, my love."

"I have lots of ideas. Wanna hear one? The rain likes me!"

"Shh." My arms encircled his skimpy waist. "I beseech you. Say you forgive me for being late last night. I didn't mean it."

He tilted his head. "Late from what? Where did you go?"

Never mind. He didn't remember, wasn't pondering why we'd been degraded to the living room.

Speaking of which, Tumble was nowhere in sight. Likely, the ferret had woken buzzing with energy and scaled his way out one of the windows, in search of local critter activity. He would last four hours before exhausting himself and coming back inside. Such was the ferret's enterprising nature, for if not engaged regularly, he grew cantankerous.

Like another tiny person I knew.

"Can we play now?" Nicu asked. "Can I ride on your shoulders today?"

"Your wish is my command."

"Yay! I saw a maiden somewhere in the cottage, but she's gone. She's hanging upside down from a cloud that Jinny knitted in the sky. The maiden's hair is the sun when it's mad. Huzzah."

I couldn't deny my pride at his storytelling abilities. However nonsensical, they surpassed mine.

"Nay, she's here," I whispered. "She's dreaming of flowers as tall as the trees."

"Because that's where she's from," he added. "The maiden has dots all over her cheeks."

"And thorns for ears."

"Really? Is she a bramble?"

"Close. Her name is Briar."

"Like a briar patch?" Nicu's head snapped left and right. "I wanna see her!"

"Later. She's hurt."

"Mmm. She looked scared last night. She was breathing heavy, like, *hehhh, hehhh, hehhh.*" His voice proved uncanny in its flawless imitation of Briar's terror and shallow panting.

"A leenix came upon her," I explained. "Remember what I once told you about them? They're dangerous. They don't want to be petted, so never try."

"Leenix!" he piped.

"Nicu. What did I just say?"

"I don't know. Oh, I do." He altered his voice to sound like me, the timbre accurate to the point of eerie. *"A leenix came upon her. Remember what I once told you about them? They're dangerous. They don't want to be petted, so never try.* I wanna hunt for Jinny's biscuits."

That meant he was hungry. "A leenix means bad tidings," I stressed. "You shouldn't touch one. 'Tis the same with people. Aye?"

"Stay away from people?" he asked in a small voice that cracked my heart. "I, um ..."

"Repeat our last talk," I prompted.

"If you see someone who isn't Papa or Jinny, you must hide," he recited.

"Now remind me. What does *hide* mean?"

He tapped his fingers on my shoulder, tossing those marbles around in his head, because this was the hardest part for him. To Nicu, bounding into someone's path might as well be *hide*. Running toward them might as well be *run away*.

Some days, it wasn't easy with him. Raising him, hoping he would grasp what I tried to teach him, having to repeat myself constantly whilst using the same words. Remembering to keep every object in the same spot, so that he wouldn't confuse items like a knife and a spoon, simply because one was left where the other should have been. Enduring his fits and flare-ups, his bouts of confusion and frustration whenever he didn't comprehend something. Bearing his weight as he climbed all over me, no matter what mood he caught me in, when I sometimes lacked the energy to keep up. Not being here for him every day, coping with remorse and too much love for one person to take.

I confess to days when it tired me.

But always, Nicu's precious traits, all the good of him, outweighed the rest. He was my everything, my musical fae—feisty and funny, bright and imaginative. A treasure, not a trial.

"Hide means no hugging, no talking, and—" Nicu's face withered in

disappointment. "But the briar patch maiden is a person, too. I want her to be my friend."

"Not until I say it's safe," I said. "For I'm the one who decides."

"I know what's safe." Nicu burst into a list of Spring's fauna. "The bronze bear, spotted hare, shadow mare—"

"And the Nicu fae," I said, tickling his sides. "I see you've been practicing your rhymes."

When he came up for air, Nicu rested his chin on my chest. "I miss you when you're late."

The words punctured deeply. I rubbed my nose against his, unable to muster a response that would do him justice.

13

Briar

I lurched upright, gusts of air blasting from my lungs. Grumbling clouds scrolled audibly through my ears, cutting short the night-mare I'd been having about ribbons and thread snarling into a knot, both soaked in crimson like a bloody fist. I blinked, my vision hazy as I tried to identify the bed I lay in and the walls surrounding me.

Not my suite in Autumn. Nor the one in Spring's palace.

This space was the size of a peasant's quarter. A smaller bed nestled in the corner, with a gnome hand-puppet resting on the pillow. Curtains framed the box-shaped window, raindrops splattered the glass, and rivulets distorted the view. Blurry trees wobbled in and out of sight, the muscled trunks topped with awnings of jade leaves.

The wildflower forest, where I had followed Poet last night. I remembered the horses abandoning us, tree roots and crochets of moss, the leenix clawing into my leg, and the jester bringing me somewhere.

Here, to this cottage.

And that silver-haired woman. And the needle.

A coarse blanket cocooned my body and gently scratched my chin. Muted voices sailed in from an unknown part of the house, interrupted by the peal of childish laughter.

The stranger and Poet.

And that fae boy. The one whom I hadn't imagined, after all.

My pulse settled. I should be anxious about what had happened, about our whereabouts, and how long I'd been unconscious. I hadn't trusted Poet when he left the castle, but he'd done nothing to harm me. No, he stepped in front of that leenix and told me to run while he dealt with the creature, knowing it could mean his death.

The jester had also warned me not to bring a rescue party back for him. The request had stumped me. However, thinking of that child, a hunch squatted in my gut.

The boy.

This cottage.

Sheltered in the middle of nowhere.

An elder and a stripling were hardly mercenary companions. Paranoid thoughts of becoming a prisoner receded, along with the possibility of them using me as bargaining chip for some nefarious cause. If any of them wanted to hurt me, they would have done so already.

My cloak hung from a wall peg, and the muffled conversations drifted. The whiff of vegetables coasted into my nostrils, wetting my palate and gnawing on my stomach.

I scooted across the mattress and winced from the tenderness in my thigh. Lifting the blanket, I discovered the blood-speckled cloth around my leg. The older woman had been kind, taking care of the wound.

The bedroom door squeaked. My shoulders tensed as the facade crept open.

A pert nose stuck through the gap, followed by a pair of short fingers grasping the wood, then the fae boy's head popped inside. He had oval ears, a broad mouth, a scab on his wrist—a wrist strung with a scarlet ribbon—and the same clover irises as Poet.

We stared at each other. His gaze hopped all over me, his eyes eclipsing much of his face. The instant he noticed I was awake, he dashed to my side, and his voice rung like a bell.

"You're Summer in my pocket,
and Winter likes to snore,
Spring waits in a locket,
but Autumn is a bore ..."

The words amounted to gibberish. Be that as it may, his melodic tenor rivaled Eliot's. Except where the minstrel hummed like a violin, this child sounded like a flute when he sang.

He finished with a bow, the final confirmation of his lineage and who sired him.

The motion knocked me from my stupor. I smiled and clapped.

Elated, the boy grinned, wide and lovely.

"Where's my hug?" he asked. "Do I get a hug?"

Without waiting for my response, he flung himself at me. I gasped, my tentative arms winding around him. "There, there. Easy now," I said, patting him awkwardly.

Nonplussed, I pulled back and tilted my head. So did he. What a bold request he'd made, sweet but spoken with a ravenous edge to it. Even from one so young, such a frenzied sort of friendliness struck a chord.

The past remarks Poet had made in defense of born souls came rushing back. Apprehension dawned, solidifying inside me. I couldn't be overreacting. In addition to his fantastical features, if the child behaved like this in public, he would draw people's attention like a red flag. In doing so, they might take a closer look.

Something I'd done or said seemed to tame the boy. He relaxed his grip on my clothes but didn't move away. Instead, he blinked at me expectantly.

"You may have earned a hug, but I haven't," I said. "What shall we do about that?"

The boy contemplated. I nodded at him in encouragement.

A hand with dark-lacquered fingernails pushed open the door. Poet stepped inside, his eyes sweeping over us and settling on the child.

Instantly, the jester transformed. The look on his face bespoke of such tenderness that I'd never seen from him.

Instead of introducing us, he tugged on the boy's ear. "Jinny's waiting for you. She wanted you to fetch her shawl from her room, remember?" He cupped a palm beside his mouth and said conspiratorially, "Follow the yellow ribbons. Quick now, and then she'll let you sit by the window. The rain is waiting for your audience."

Giggles bubbled from the child. He skipped off, chortling as Poet smacked his little backside on the way out.

The storm beat its fists against the cottage, the torrent battering the windowpanes as though desperate to get inside. I arranged the blanket around my legs, feeling absurdly Royal in the process.

Poet slouched a shoulder against the jamb. His lucid eyes sketched me, traveling from the layers sticking out like straw from my unkempt braid to the rumpled mahogany gown hanging off my body like a sack. I weathered his attention, resisting the urge to tidy what was left of my plaited locks, as if a groomed appearance would vouch for my trustworthiness. Nonetheless, I felt his scrutiny, the texture of it like a serrated knife angled against my throat.

In his mind, only one person in this room posed a threat. And it wasn't him.

Whatever conclusion he drew, the jester kept it to himself. Without glancing away, he straightened—and closed the door.

The hinges clicked. The sound pinched the space between my shoulder blades.

Poet stalked inside, dragged a chair over to the bed, and sat. He wore loose hose and a fresh shirt with the drawstrings undone. The plunging V revealed his collarbone and the sleek muscles that tracked down his torso, his abdomen stacked like bricks.

Heat slithered up my thighs, unbidden and unwelcome. I shifted on the mattress, awash in shock, mortification, and shame. Because I had already seen his bare chest at the feast, my body's reaction was an enigma I didn't know what to do with.

Threads of black lined the bottoms of Poet's eyes. Apart from that and his coated fingernails, the simplicity of his appearance unsettled me.

His unadorned face. The modest clothing, which lacked ornamentation or finery. That glimpse of skin and sinew.

Seeing the jester this way felt intimate, especially in a compact chamber with no one else here. Lounging in humble attire, he still managed to look imposing, yet in an unfamiliar way.

I had the strangest urge to make him appear even less recognizable, to smudge the black beneath his eyes, to turn it into a flaw. It wasn't about making him less impeccable. No, it was more about disheveling him further and finding out what that looked like.

My eyes flitted away. It was the attack last night. That had to be causing this wholly inappropriate upheaval inside me.

As I twisted back, my spine stiffened.

There. Dignity preserved.

Poet lifted something I hadn't realized he'd been holding—a bread bowl of pureed soup, the aroma of carrots rising from the creamy liquid.

I wondered where the flour had come from. If had been sourced from the castle, then it wouldn't be Spring grain. It would be from Autumn, since Basil and Fatima expected the best, and the best came from Autumn's mills. I'd be able to tell from the taste.

Poet blew on the soup and held out a spoonful. "Open wide, Your Highness. I promise, it's not poisoned." But when I made no reply, he added, "Come now, no need to frown. 'Tis not as though you narrowly escaped an attempted leenix maiming."

I took the bowl and spoon. "I can feed myself."

"Please do. I'm too pretty to be doing a thankless job."

"I did not mean ..." Salvaging what was left of my manners, I set the bowl on my lap. "Chasing you into the forest was a foolish impulse. I was asking for trouble, so thank you for taking care of me. The soup smells wonderful."

"I made it."

I balked. "You?"

"I diced the carrots. I'll have you know, 'tis a crucial task," he defended. "In fairness, I'm the one who should be grateful. You would have been safe if you'd listened to me and ran, and though I wish you had, it's nice to be alive. Because of you, I'm in one piece, and my s …" He trailed off. "You must know, I wasn't thrilled about having my comely face torn off. By the way, it won't do the soup any good to stay in the bowl."

Poet possessed several types of wit. I was beginning to recognize the differences between them. Depending on the tilt of his mouth and the depth of his voice, he exercised that tongue for amusement, seduction, coercion, or annihilation.

Or for disguising the truth.

I dabbed the spoon into the bowl and summoned the courage to ask, "How old is he?"

A crippling silence ensued. As a Royal, answers were handed to me on a platter at my command. I'd never had to humble myself and earn them—a refreshing change that I welcomed.

I met Poet's leery countenance. "I will not utter a word to anyone. I swear it."

Because I never gave my word of honor rashly, I might as well have carved it into stone.

His eyes riveted on me, many things cluttering within that look. Witnessing him like this—defensive, protective, vulnerable—distorted every previous conclusion I'd made about him. Here was the jester, absently touching a particular ribbon at his wrist, which matched the one worn by that child.

This whole time, I'd been wrong to assume. I did not know him at all.

For no explicable reason, I wanted his trust.

Perhaps it was the Royal in me. Maybe I understood what it was like to conceal myself from others. Or perhaps I could not explain it.

Poet waited for several heartbeats before saying, "He's four."

"And may I ask his name?" I broached.

Again, it took him a moment to answer. "Nicu."

"He has your eyes."

"Nature knows what's best."

Still vain as a peacock. We chuckled, but the laughter vanished quickly, as if sliced in half.

I lifted the spoon to my lips, the velvety blend of carrots and cream melting on my tongue. A small noise of appreciation curled from my throat. But the instant that sound twined into the room, Poet's concentration faltered. His eyes sank to my lips, the weight of his attention palpable, like a warm caress, which rose several degrees and simmered across my flesh.

My mouth tingled. And when my neck bobbed, he watched that, too.

A muscle thumped in his jaw. The jester lurched his gaze toward the window.

I did the same while quickly finishing my food.

"Delicate things and fierce things," he mumbled, raindrop shadows dappling his face, candlelight illuminating the rest of him.

"Nicu is ..." I dared not finish, because this story belonged to the jester. I was a breath away from finding out the truth, but if I made the slightest mistake, I wouldn't.

Poet slid his gaze back to me. "Here's a tale of a kindly child who loves making up songs, whispering to the rain, licking sugar off his pinky, and playing word games. He sees and speaks of this world in iridescence. His sidekick is a rather demanding ferret, his favorite color is 'happy orange,' he thinks dust motes are sprites, he'll eat anything so long as it doesn't have a filling, he adores fauna and people, and he wouldn't harm a soul. What else about him matters?"

"I'm not the bigot you imagine me to be."

He canted his head, expecting me to repeat myself.

"Mother treats everyone with benevolence," I explained. "She and my father taught me to do the same."

This couldn't be news to Poet. Although the same social laws prevailed in Autumn, we acted less harshly toward born souls than the other kingdoms. It hardly excused us, but everyone knew Autumn was not violent, except in matters of defense.

What Poet didn't know was that my parents also raised me without prejudice. Like them, I abhorred the injustices leveled at those whom Autumn claimed as property. However, we'd voiced this only behind closed doors while remaining stern in public, my parents having believed few options existed to contest the matter.

I seldom groused about the decisions Mother and Father had made. This was one of the exceptions.

"Princess," Poet deadpanned. "This is not a poem or a song. This is not negotiable. If there's any chance you'll betray my trust, indulge me now. I won't take this step lightly."

I nodded. "I never take any steps lightly."

"Of course not. You would fall."

"Very funny."

"If what I tell you leaves this house, and it harms a hair on my son, I will retaliate. Wherever you stand, I will not hesitate."

"Was that rhyme intentional? I cannot tell."

He'd been staring at me, his features anchored. But then, his mouth twitched. "To say the least, I'm not in a rhyming mood."

"I don't believe that for a second," I stated. "But I do believe your threats are born of love. Likewise, you'll have to believe I'm not a wretch. I agree to your terms, jester. Let us consider this a verbal pledge."

My reply unlocked his jaw. So it began.

Poet leaned forward, arms bracketed on his thighs. He told me how his parents had abandoned him at a midnight festival and about Old Jinny, the woman who stitched my leg. How she'd found Poet in a bassinet behind a pavilion tent, raised him in this cottage, and then helped to bring up Nicu after the child's mother had left him on their doorstep.

Poet clarified Nicu's condition. Not in detail but enough to grasp the situation.

A memory cramped Poet's face. "When Nicu was two, I took him to a midnight festival for the first time. I'll never forget his look of wonder, so beautiful on him." The jester's eyes glazed over, remote and haunted. "But I glanced away for a mere second. When I turned back, he'd disappeared."

Poet withdrew further, deeper into that scene, as if he wasn't in the room any longer. "I can still see it, the empty spot where my son should have been standing—this patch of grass shadowed by someone tipping back a tankard. And I loathe how long it took my goddamn legs to move, and then I was racing, running, raging. The festival stole him from me and wouldn't give him back, and everywhere I looked, he wasn't there. I killed my voice shouting his name, and I hated the sound of it, but I hated more the sound of him not answering."

His mouth curled as though he'd swallowed something putrid. "Fests are magnificent and deplorable. It's where I discovered my passion and my wrath, this place where artists thrived and others suffered. I made sure not to show Nicu the horrible parts, but as I searched for him, I saw what I'd seen many times. The people this world calls 'born fools' were being treated like abominations. They were forced to fight, with spectators betting on them and cheering as the opponents bashed in one another's skulls, because the prisoners' only choices were to either use their fists or lose them on the chopping block.

"An elderly man, who ranted to himself whilst onlookers baited him into further confusion, until he got so agitated and nervous that he pissed himself. And a woman in the stocks being hit with rotten food by children who wanted to win a prize."

My chest hurt. I saw these horrific visions in my mind, each one playing out.

Poet swallowed. "I didn't fully comprehend my son's condition at the time, but I had an inkling. I imagined that fate befalling Nicu. And minutes later, I found him climbing onto an unsuspecting fortune-teller's lap. Furious doesn't begin to express my reaction." He ground his teeth. "I yelled at my son, scared him. He recoiled because he didn't understand, because I was a prick of a father, and I didn't have a clue what the fuck I was doing."

He shook his head. "Nicu wouldn't speak for the rest of the day, afraid to make me angry again. I confess, I've been pushed near to my limits, but I've not raised my voice to him since."

The jester craned his head at me. "He's my heartbeat. He's my greatest achievement." He narrowed his eyes, slitting them like blades, and his voice sliced through the room. "He's *mine*."

His words grew fangs, the implication hard to miss.

Nicu was his. Not the Crown's.

The jester spoke with low, deadly calm. "I couldn't mean this more, Your Highness. I won't let anyone take my son from me. Let no one say he's damaged, inferior, or unworthy because his mind bends in a different way. He doesn't deserve to be owned or ridiculed.

"The cardinal question is this: What are fools? Are they madmen who mutilate their own flesh? Those who see what isn't there? Those whose minds drift in a fog? Some of the mad are indeed violent and must be separated so they can't hurt others or themselves. But dungeons are hardly a humane solution. Likewise, those whom our world calls 'half-wits' and 'simpletons' don't deserve what they get—no born soul does. Unfortunately, we lump everyone together as property because anything unnatural is unnatural, as the Seasons say.

"My opinion? A fool is a man who believes glory can be found at the tip of a sword instead of on the tip of his tongue. 'Tis a person who judges with their eyes closed. 'Tis people who invent aberrations from speculation and rumors. 'Tis bred from ignorance. That is life's cruel trick.

"Being close to my sovereigns is a blessing and curse, you see. For I have influence there. If the Crown adores me, I'll convince them to change their law. I have no qualms with the Royals except for this one thing, and therefore, I have a thousand qualms with them. They want my stories, but not my son's."

His features hardened into cement. "But someday I will force-feed it to them. Someday that's how this shall end, for I'm the puppet who holds the strings."

I stared at him. His performance at the feast had captivated me, but it did not compare to this reality.

Questions abounded. The *hows*, *whys*, and *whats* of his upbringing.

"The puppet who holds the strings," I repeated. "You have power but no freedom."

"You live a half-lie, speak half-truths," he agreed.

"And though they want you to be honest, you cannot speak your mind. They don't want the real you. They want a leader who thinks as they do."

"You play a role."

"Because if not, they'll punish you."

Our gazes stayed pinned, nailed to one another. Rain smacked the window, and thunder cracked through the sky. A significant amount of time passed, tempting me to say more, because it had felt liberating not to hold back.

I returned to the topic at hand. "Does Nicu know about his condition?"

"Ah." Poet reclined in the seat. "We've tried explaining certain things like distance and direction to him, to no avail. Though he remembers every word of what we say, it eventually loses its meaning to him. From that alone, we suspect he wouldn't understand the rest. Mayhap when he's older, but for now Jinny and I focus on giving Nicu a happy life and teaching him how to be safe, how to protect himself in this world. Apart from that, he's buoyantly unaware."

I thought about that and many other things. If I saw no means to challenge the law, I could not imagine a jester would succeed.

Still, Poet was intelligent, persuasive, and passionate.

A spark ignited in me that perhaps ...

Perhaps together we could ...

We could nothing. Not when I'd be leaving court at the month's end.

If he were a citizen of Autumn, we might work together.

But this wasn't Autumn.

When my gaze slid to his ribbons, Poet's mouth quirked. "Nicu made them for me—well, I helped without him knowing it. Tying knots

149

on his own would be a difficulty. You might say I use them as tokens to mark my targets, as symbols of us against them."

Us against them. I cringed, unsure of my place within that statement.

"You'll notice them hanging from the cottage ceiling," he continued. "We use them to help give Nicu direction. It's been working so far."

Just then, an alarming detail invaded my memory. I clasped Poet's arm. "The ribbon you left on my pillow. Poet, I tied it to a bush at the forest border when I followed you. And our footprints," I fretted. "They could lead a search party here."

He tensed until I released him. "If they find the ribbon, it'll draw them toward one of the thoroughfares, but they'll head full west after that, since more crimes are reported from there. That's how Spring patrols. By the time they quit that area, we'll have returned to the court, and a messenger will be dispatched to the outlying unit.

"As for our treasonous tracks, the storm took care of them. We're southeast of the castle, so this area would be the troop's last stop, out of routine as much as superstition. Despite this forest's reputation for inciting naughty behavior, which doesn't usually deter people, I also convinced the court these parts were haunted."

I peered at him, suspicious. "How did you achieve that?"

"I'm Poet," he said, as if that explained everything.

"And monarchy aside, how do you know about official procedures?"

"I'm a glorious kisser—and even better in bed."

Scandalized laughter popped from my lips. "You are impossible."

"Am I?" His stare verged on explicit. Invasive, as though he was scouring my mind, picking through all the disquieting thoughts I'd had about him.

Eager for a distraction, I thrust the spoon into my mouth, only to remember it was empty and that I'd finished the soup.

The jester smirked, then chuckled as I whacked his arm with the spoon.

14

Briar

The rains continued throughout the day. I slept on and off, comforted by a steaming cup of herbal tea that Jinny brought me. In and out, I floated between blackness and clarity.

A masculine shape stared at me from an open doorway. A hand swept its fingers over my brow, murmuring a rhyme to quell my shuddering.

A passing vision of Mother and I, nestling in bed and whispering under a quilt.

A flash of Father snapping at me, then my small body running off into the wildflower forest, then my eyes peeking from a hiding spot as he searched frantically for me.

Sometime during the night, I awakened to find the neighboring mattress vacant. Sweeping my blanket aside, I stood and hobbled to the doorway. Needing reassurance, I checked around the corner and saw them.

Poet and Nicu.

They slept on the living room floor, wrapped up in each other by the dying firelight. The child's head rested on his father's shoulder while Poet breathed evenly into his son's hair. Both wore identical scrunched expressions, so that I practically tasted the charm of it.

I'd been recovering in Nicu's room, the one he shared with his father, which meant I was imposing on Poet's bed. I would have woken them and insisted they return to their rightful place, that I would be fine on the floor, but they looked so peaceful. I did not have the heart to disturb them, and something told me that Poet would have refused anyway.

After stumbling back to his bed, I melted into the mattress. I might have been too delirious on my first night to notice, but now the whiffs of amber and vetiver rose from the pillow.

I flopped over, but whether to avoid the scents or dissolve into them, I couldn't say. As I turned, the coverlet banded around my waist like a pair of arms, solid and strong.

And as the world blurred, a dream accompanied the fall. I felt his warmth filling this bed, his body flexing with every movement, his breath panting against mine, and our limbs entangled. I saw my thighs spreading, his waist snapping into the vent between them, our skin beading with perspiration, my back arching, and my mouth hanging open on a silent cry, and his name dangling off the edge of my quavering lips.

The montage unraveled, replete with visions of us naked. Him and me in this tight, dark room, away from anyone who could hear me clutch his rippling back and shatter beneath him, my voice going hoarse from the accelerated pace of his hips.

Then came images of his eyes, with black lining the rims and an inked diamond cutting through a single orb. The forbidden jester hovering over me, breaking through me, taking me. His hips whipping into mine, his erect length—he would say his cock—pitching into my wet folds, flaring them wide, opening them. His green irises flashing with satisfaction, his pupils on fire, and my reflection coming undone within them.

Him, pinning me to the mattress. Me, riding every thrust of that cock.

Us alone, charging at each other, wanting each other, tearing each other to shreds.

I arched from the fantasy and gasped into consciousness. My eyes whipped open and stumbled across the ceiling while heavy puffs rushed from my lips. My calves were tangled around the blanket, my breasts ached from an inexplicable loss, and the nexus of my thighs pooled with heat. The intimate walls of my core were so wet, they'd saturated my undergarments.

I lay there, an exhausted, overwhelmed, shameful mess. The fabric of my dress chafed my nipples, which had become overly sensitive, and the stifling garment clung to me far too tightly.

Fragments of my dream returned, decadent visions that included moist skin, teeth sinking into someone's lower lip, and skilled fingers tracing my knees—then splitting them apart.

I launched upright, my hand shooting to my chest, desperate to calm my pulse. My stomach coiled with something akin to longing. But unconscious or not, how dare I fabricate such visions of my nemesis while being a guest in this family's hideout—*and* while sleeping so near to Poet and his son.

I shook my head, scattering the illicit imagery like marbles. It was only an illusion, nothing more.

Sunlight oozed into the room and glazed my toes. The clouds had broken into a new day.

I swung my legs off the mattress and stood, then plucked the ends of my dress and grimaced at the soiled material. Dirt smudged the fabric, and several tears marred the skirt. I'd sweated and slept in it for two nights.

Two nights, thus far. Eliot would be pacing. Mother would be panicking, wondering if she'd lost another loved one to Spring's forest.

My eyes screwed shut. We'd leave here soon enough, now that my leg was on the mend.

Resigned, I surveyed the room. Someone had left me a gift folded atop Nicu's bed. The flax-colored dress had front clasps and elbow-length sleeves. A pair of knit socks rested beside the outfit, and both items smelled of lavender.

A cloth, a bar of soap, and a bowl and ewer of water waited on the dresser. Sighing with gratitude, I peeled off my gown, then bathed and threw myself into the fresh garments before lacing my boots.

I should rearrange my braided bun into a new updo. It was only appropriate, in the company of strangers. At least, it would be in Autumn.

Regardless, this was Spring. Plus, after having my locks constrained for this long, the thought of entwining them into another restrictive style threatened to give me a headache.

While unwinding and shaking out my hair, I thought of the Seven. I imagined myself greeting them like this, in all my threadbare, leenix-scarred glory, with my tresses hanging freely down my back.

My lips tilted in amusement. I tiptoed out of the room and got my first conspicuous glimpse of the cottage.

The place was quaint, filled with warm, pigmented colors. Beneath a patterned rug, plush chairs fronted the crackling fireplace. A hooked cauldron dangled inside, and a vase of dried flowers stood on the mantle.

A round table and chairs nestled inside the corner kitchen. A built-in cupboard held a mortar and pestle, along with jars of ground herbs and shavings of bark. Iron pots and bundles of more dried blossoms hung in front of the window, and shelves displayed costly treats like honey and sugar, potentially supplied by Poet's wages.

Four cords of ribbons looped from the ceiling, each meant to guide Nicu to a different area of the cottage. I trailed them to see where they led.

Orange for Nicu's room. Yellow for Jinny's room. Green for the living room. Blue for the bathroom at the back of the house.

Afterward, I stepped outside. Trees speared into the sky, the trunks topped in canopies more verdant than in any other Season. Poppies and daises puckered from the grass, each species of wildflower bunched in tufts rather than scattered everywhere.

The circular cottage was secluded, tucked into a small clearing where a bubbling stream cut through the grass. The flux emitted a gurgling sound while caws resounded from the treetops. And although the ground was still wet from the storm, sunlight unfurled across my face.

"You like berries?"

Stunned, I wheeled toward the older woman who stood beside a pen several paces away. The stall was home to hens pecking at the ground, a speckled horse staring into space, a plot of vegetable beds, and a wagon stationed in the background.

The woman's arm slung over an empty basket that rested on her hip. "Sorry if I startled you."

She had a voice that rose from the earth, the way I'd imagine a root would sound if it could talk. Where most people let their words float away, her speech had a sturdy quality to it.

"Not at all," I lied. "You were saying something about berries?"

"Bundleberries." The woman pumped her thumb toward a bush loaded with rosy morsels. "Spring's best, they are. Mixed with the right ingredients, they're good for baking, blood circulation, battling sleep deprivation, and preventing unwanted pregnancy. What?" she sniggered when crimson leaked into my cheeks. "This is the land of sexual plenty, dearie. It's as easy to procreate as it is to nullify fertility. The flora and their fruits have a role there. Why, I wager these berries can do everything but reverse your age. What other fruit can you say that about?

"Also, they're delicious. My Poet and Nicu love them. I'm not sure about you, so I'm asking before I set a berry biscuit on your plate. I've got a batch steaming and ready, if you like."

I'd polished off the bread bowl yesterday and confirmed it was Autumn grain, which Poet must have brought from Basil and Fatima's stores. We exported it from Autumn, and a few barrels had accompanied Mother and me on our journey here. The biscuits Jinny offered were likely of the same quality.

When my stomach grumbled, the woman beamed. "Sounds like a yes to me. Good morning, Your Highness."

It took a moment for my tongue to continue functioning. "Oh, there's no need to call me that. And um, good morning. My name is Briar."

"You sure?"

"Unless my parents have been lying to me."

"I meant, are you sure about giving me leave with your name? Even in frisky Spring, it isn't proper, Highness."

"I'm too tired for proper."

"From the loose style of your hair, I'd say so. Would be a shame anyway, restraining such a fiery color inside a braid." She shifted her basket to the opposite hip. "Look at me, forgetting introductions. My boys call my Old Jinny. I take it curtsying isn't necessary? My bones can't take it."

I smiled. "I'm grateful to you for taking care of my leg. And the food and clothes. Oh, and the washing supplies."

"Don't be silly. It wasn't any trouble. We've got a bathroom where you can have a proper wash later, but I figured the ewer was better for a start, especially with you just waking up. Mind you don't get those stitches wet, though."

"I'll be careful."

"Good. And I've had that frock since I was your age. Also, the bit about your leg wasn't a chore. When Poet first came along, I had no money for a doctor. Now we have the coin but no healer we can trust with Nicu. I had to learn how to minister to my boys, and I had to learn fast. Being surrounded by medicines of the soil helped, so I've managed." She wagged a finger at me. "You're lucky you haven't gotten infected. A hale one, you are. You'll be walking finer than Poet by tomorrow."

I resisted the temptation to let my eyes wander. "Where is he?"

"Just missed him. He took Nicu and Tumble to pick me a batch of yarrow."

Poet had told me about the ferret who kept Nicu company here. As for Jinny, I could imagine how much upkeep this cottage and its crops required. Growing up among fields and orchards, I was famil-

156

iar with such tasks.

I gestured to the berry bush. "May I help you?"

Jinny frowned, the trenches in her face deepening. "This work isn't suited for a princess."

"I prefer to labor with my hands. In Autumn, I take part in the harvest."

"You work the fields?" she asked, taken aback.

"To rule the fields is to know them. Besides, I'd love something to do instead of sitting around. I've never gathered bundleberries before."

"Then I'll be the one to teach you after breakfast. Only, take care with your leg. Sit in the grass and gather from the bottom. I'll mind the top of the bushes."

After I ate and washed the biscuit down with black tea, Jinny demonstrated how to pluck the berries from above the base of their stems. She went as far as to cover my hands with her wilted ones. "Let me show you."

My fingers went rigid. "Actually, I-I'm fine."

But she ignored me. "You have to be gentle to keep them from popping and draining of juice, see?" She molded our hands together, her skin warmer than mine. "My mother taught me it's all in the sleight of hand. If done right, we'll have the gift of sweetness."

Her tone softened, reverential and conspiratorial, as though imparting a secret.

I had a grandaunt back home, a matriarch I liked very much but who seldom visited. Apart from that, Mother and I only had each other.

How long had it been since we shared a moment like this? How long since I allowed it?

A lump bloated in my throat. I relaxed, yielding to Jinny's instruction.

Once she released me, I found my rhythm. We worked in silence, moving from shrub to shrub while occasionally sampling the fruit. Although I remained seated, my joints groaned, and sweat beaded in patches across the dress.

Jinny told me about the flora of Spring. This land wasn't nearly as advanced in medicine as Winter—no other Season could make that claim—but every kingdom grew its own magic.

In Spring, nature yielded basic restoratives, from cures to antidotes. Those, in addition to robust hallucinogenics, aphrodisiacs, contraceptives, and preventatives against diseases that developed from copulation. Though this being the Season of rebirth, the latter ailment was rare.

The woman didn't pry or ask me questions about myself. It felt surreal being someplace where no one could find me, instead of cloistered in a fortress, fraught with schedules and obligations and etiquette.

Not that I minded those things. Routines were reliable, customs steadfast.

Yet it felt nice to be free of prying eyes and gazes consuming me wherever I went. The weight of everyone's attention leaked from my shoulders.

Truth be told, I wished I had more time for harvesting back home. I liked to feel my hands burrowing into the earth, contributing to its lifecycle. The dirtier my fingers got, the more a defiant sort of curiosity sprouted inside me, the sensation tickling my stomach.

Jinny made a noise of bemusement. "Never thought I'd see a day when a princess got her fingernails caked. Never thought I'd see a day when Poet ripened for a Royal, neither."

I jerked upright, knocking over the basket. "It's not that way between us."

She must know such a thing was forbidden anyway. However powerful, renowned, and desired Poet was, tradition outweighed that. Our differences in rank placed us worlds apart, and anything serious would be impossible, even if we wanted it.

Which neither of us did.

Jinny's face pinched. Evidently, she heard my unspoken thoughts. But before I could beg her pardon, she said, "He was offered a lordship."

I stopped myself from crushing a handful of berries and squirting juice everywhere. "Basil and Fatima offered to give Poet a title?"

"Property, too. Upon retirement, that is. It happens when a jester becomes as worshipped as him. My boy walks into a room, and every head turns. It doesn't matter who holds the highest office. Either they're lusting after him, or they're waiting with baited breaths, eager to find out what he'll do or say."

"So you've been to court."

"Nah. I may not attend, but I don't need to. My son's fame has traveled, and he's confirmed or denied every bit of gossip to me. Also, it's hard not to imagine." She shook her head wryly and turned the basket right side up. "As for King Basil and Queen Fatima, he's their most valued asset. When people have that much prestige, they get right spoiled. It wouldn't be the first time in history."

Fair enough. I'd always known this, yet still. "Poet never said anything."

"When was he supposed to do that?" she countered, then shrugged. "Besides, what does it matter? Poet respectfully—and carefully—rejected the offer. So that he wouldn't insult the Crown, the trickster had made it sound like he couldn't bear to be away from them, even in the future."

I balked. "But why?"

The woman raised her eyebrows and gave me a look that said, *Why do you think?*

Oh. A knob inside my chest twisted. Having a title would yield more influence, but it would also garner more watchful eyes than his popularity had already won him, which could endanger the secrets he tried to keep. It would mean increased public responsibilities and less time with his family.

Property for Nicu and Jinny upon retirement wouldn't safeguard them. Not with a bevy of indiscreet—and likely intolerant—servants bustling through the halls. Moreover, it would mean a separation from the Crown, which was where Poet needed to be if he wanted to best protect Nicu.

Near his monarchs, Poet could monitor them for decades, steer them in whatever direction he wanted. But away from his king and queen, he would lose that leverage.

I understood this. It was a delicate balance, a power play that required tact and proximity.

The jester might call it a juggling act.

I caught Jinny watching me and flushed. "I never meant to imply my class was too good for his," I hastened to say. "It's just not—"

"Allowed," she deduced. "But what's allowed and what happens aren't always the same."

"We're merely tolerating each other."

"Let me guess how this started. You didn't happen to find a ribbon waiting when you arrived at the castle, did you?" And because my visible astonishment spoke for itself, she grunted. "We don't keep secrets from each other. I'm mighty aware of what he does with those ribbons. Can't say I agree with it, but he's a grown man, and I know why he does it."

The woman dumped another handful of berries into her basket. "I've known that scoundrel since he was a wee thing. Poet's an arrogant one, vain as can be, and he's got more lovers than a mother wants to count, but he's also got a strong heart. He worships his son, would sever his limbs to keep that child safe, and would crush anyone who got in his way. He's careful there, always has been.

"If he hated you, he would have gotten you stitched up quickly. Then he would have carried you like a sack of barley over his shoulder, back to court no matter the hour or how long it took, just so you wouldn't be around long enough to notice Nicu." She paused for effect. "But he kept you here. He told you about his sapling, and you've seen the runt for yourself."

Poet formally introduced me to Nicu yesterday, after our talk. Nicu had taken to calling me Briar Patch.

"That tyke will hug the lungs out of strangers," Jinny confessed. "He can list every herb in these parts, but ask him where to find them, and he won't know what you're talking about. Ask him where north is, and he'll point to your feet. Ask him where I sleep, and he won't be able to tell you without checking the ceiling cords. Poet trusts you knowing this. Respects you, even."

She leaned back, musing. "Look at you, picking berries in the mud with me, saying I can call you by your name." Her gaze probed mine. "You're a Royal who thinks differently about people. Am I right?"

Comprehending what she really asked, I nodded.

She nodded back. "And don't think I believe that drivel about you and Poet. You're tolerating each other, you say? There's the kind of static that tears people apart, and there's the kind that draws people together like moths to flames, no matter how they try to prevent it. He's got the sexual whims of a satyr, born with a tongue to spice tarts and spread legs, but those things never kept his attention for this long. Dismissing that won't do either of you any good, so have a care."

I swerved toward the bushes and fixated on my task. It would be rude to correct her, so I did not bother.

We worked until twilight embossed the trees with a gray-blue light. Poet and Nicu must have returned sometime before then without us noticing, because their voices drifted from the kitchen as we entered. The child sat perched on the counter and clapped with glee while his father juggled nectarines around his head.

Jinny beamed, affection loosening the wrinkles across her face. She wiped her hands loudly. "Well. Now I know why my nectarines always have bruises."

Then Nicu saw me and squealed, "Briar Patch!"

To which Poet swung around, a criticism no doubt poised on his lips. But then he halted, and his eyes skated over my figure. Mortification scalded my flesh. Bits of soil caked my fingernails, grit and berry stains mottled the dress I'd borrowed, and sweat coated my skin beneath the slumped neckline, the top clasps having come undone.

Also, my hair hung freely. It must resemble a hedge by now. The locks tumbled over my shoulders in messy red thickets, the tresses snarled and clumped.

If anyone at court saw me this way, I would never hear the end of it. Disgrace would brand me for the rest of my days in Spring.

Poet donned leather pants and a vest that clung to his frame, the sleeveless garment flaunting a pair of biceps that could have been hewn from rock. Compared with that, I looked a shambles.

Yet instead of smirking in triumph, issuing a snarky comment about my appearance, and then bribing me over this candid moment, the jester merely stared. The pome rested in his hand, forgotten. Those green irises tracked across my face, skimming my hair as if he'd never seen the color before.

My stomach lurched. A fluttery sensation rushed up my body.

As we inspected one another from across the cottage, the temperature seemed to rise either from the fireplace or the boiling cauldron hooked inside.

An aged throat cleared. The noise sawed through our trance. Even so, Jinny's visage crinkled in amusement.

We sat around the table, the aromas of beef, carrots, and bay leaves permeating the kitchen. Poet and Jinny were vigilant to keep every object—from forks to napkins—in the same spots, no matter how often they were used, to prevent inconsistencies from misdirecting Nicu.

I paid attention and did the same, which earned me several incomprehensible looks from his father.

During the meal, each family member attempted to dominate the conversation, inundating the kitchen with anecdotes, wisecracks, and stories. At one point, Jinny told me, "My Poet wasn't always a sly one. The first time he practiced flipping—"

Poet palmed his face in abject misery. "Didn't we just talk about this? I told you to stop with that bloody story."

This only fueled my curiosity. "What happened?"

But halfway through the tale, Poet leaned across the table. "That does it."

He tossed down his napkin with a flourish and tried to clamp his hand over Jinny's mouth. This resulted in a wrestling match, a bunch of cackles on her part and laughter on Nicu's part.

I smiled and watched them banter. Contentment wrapped around me like a shawl, coupled with an envious ache I couldn't reconcile.

Baked cherries accompanied the stew. I raised a steaming orb to my mouth, draped it on my tongue, and bit. Sweetness and tartness mingled on my palate.

As I chewed, I felt his attention like a tangible, secretive thing. It fixated on the motions of my jaw, the muscles of my throat as I swallowed, and the press of the napkin to my lips.

I carried the memory of that look to bed, which took up residence in my mind long into the night. Some hours later, I woke to an uncomfortable dryness in my mouth. Drowsy but parched, I padded from the room and into the kitchen, shuffling as quietly as possible.

It was too dark to see the living room, where Poet and his son were sleeping. Nonetheless, a solitary beam of moonlight lanced through the small kitchen window. It was enough to guide me. I'd seen a pitcher of water on the counter earlier, but rifling through the preserve jars and flour canisters yielded no success.

"Looking for something, Princess?" a suave voice inquired.

15

Briar

I whirled, a gasp catching in my throat.

Poet resided on the opposite side of the kitchen, his frame clad in loose pants and nothing else. Idling within that slash of indigo light, the jester leaned against the counter, hands grasping the rims on either end.

My eyes dropped to the taut nipples pitting from his chest, then staggered to the wisps of hair trailing down his navel before I had the presence of mind to glance away.

"I'm sorry," I mumbled, my voice as unsteady as a teacup wobbling atop a saucer. "I didn't realize anyone was awake."

He didn't speak, just kept watching me. In my periphery, his torso contracted with every inhalation, siphoning in and out.

I swept my gaze over the shelves, the cupboard, the crockery—any place my attention could safely land on. Stress climbed up my fingers. Restless, I wheeled away from him and snatched the nearest object I could reach, a dishrag that I proceeded to fold.

"I couldn't sleep," I said, fighting to keep the words level, to keep them upright before they slipped and overturned.

Still, no response. The air thickened, so dense it could crush a boulder.

Unfortunately, folding the rag didn't take long enough. So I smoothed out the wrinkles next, as if I could bring some order to this moment.

"I'm unaccustomed to people not knowing where I am at all times." My outtakes grew heavy, weighed down by the silence. "But I like it."

Repeatedly, I raced my palms over the cloth. "That's not why I came in here, though." A breeze sailed through the window, rustling the ends of my hair. "Anyway, I hope I didn't disturb you."

The quiet persisted. *He* persisted.

I had never been this conscious of my proximity to someone before. Not so much the distance separating us, but rather the number of steps it would take to close it.

I'd never been this alone with a man before.

I flattened my palms atop the cloth. Slowly, I pushed it across the counter, away from the edge. "Did I disturb you?"

"That, you did," the jester murmured from behind. "You've been doing a routine job of keeping me up, sweeting."

My stomach dropped to my knees. His reply brushed my spine like a plume. It didn't just close the distance but extinguished it altogether.

Keeping my back averted would mark me as a coward. I turned on my heel, my eyes clicking back to him.

He hadn't moved. He hadn't needed to.

Merely by opening his mouth, the jester penetrated me everywhere.

His pants hung indecently low, baring the shadows of his hipbones, which sloped into the waistband. His pectorals rose and fell, the flesh as smooth as marble. And with that heavy-lidded expression and mussed hair, he looked as rumpled as a blanket—ravished, as though he'd recently exited a lover's chamber.

I had been keeping him awake, he'd said. The notion shouldn't invigorate me, but it did.

I might be inexperienced, but I wasn't naive after spending time in Spring. I knew what he meant.

But I also knew my place. And while I couldn't control the drumming of my pulse, I could control everything else. So I refused to entertain the comment by asking him to clarify, to imply it mattered. Instead, I lifted my chin like any Royal would. "I was thirsty."

I expected mischief or mockery, some form of additional teasing. However, Poet continued to stare at me deadpan, looking anything but amused.

Then I remembered the nightgown. Despite the darkness, the funnel of light piercing through the window illuminated everything important, most notably the garment's sheerness. The fabric was little more than yards of film, its diaphanous folds accentuating the swells of my breasts and the straight lines of my hips.

One sleeve hung off my shoulder, baring the skin there. Worse, the neckline plunged further than any male, other than a physician, had ever seen.

My unbound hair cascaded around me. To be sure, the red must be breaching the murk, as my freckles certainly were, because they always did. I didn't need a mirror to guess this.

My nipples poked through the nightgown, the pointed tips evident. Heat scorched my cheeks, and I crossed my arms, but it was too late.

Midnight glossed the kitchen and etched the lines of Poet's face. He'd certainly seen men and women wearing less, yet his gaze roved from the nightgown to my hair. In fact, he watched me like he'd done before dinner, except his eyes were a dozen shades deeper.

His fingers remained fastened to the counter, as though someone had bolted them down. Because of this, the ribbons encircling his wrist strained, in danger of snapping.

If I had kept my own ribbon, perhaps I'd still be one of his targets. An unbidden part of me wanted to unravel one of those bracelets, to claim it as my own, to throw him off guard.

No one marks me unless I want them to.

Something must have unspooled across my face, because Poet broke from his position. With deliberate slowness, the jester released the counter and sauntered my way like a panther.

Foreboding and anticipation seized me. My buttocks pressed harder into the ledge as he approached.

Stalling inches from me, Poet tipped his head down. His intakes and my outtakes amplified in this room. If I requested it, he would stand aside and let me pass. Yet the words drained from my consciousness, and every righteous inclination I'd been bred with fled my mind.

With his eyes nailed to me, Poet extended his arm past my shoulder. The telltale scrape of earthenware breached the silence, and only briefly did he look away to concentrate on something, the action bringing his profile into sharp relief.

Splashes resounded. Then his gaze found me again, and he raised a cup between us, offering it. Absently, I took the vessel, gripping it as Poet tapped his own cup to mine in a mock toast.

"Need something to wet your tongue, do you?" he inquired, then lowered his voice to the faintest whisper. "So do I."

My throat bobbed. A week ago, I would have ordered him to watch his mouth in my presence. But now, the jester's comment oozed beneath the nightgown and stoked the blood churning through my system.

It was true that males didn't notice me—not like this. As a princess, courtiers and noblemen surveyed me with interest of the ambitious and practical sort. Technically, I was the most eligible and regal match any gentleman could make. That was how the court looked at me.

As something to be attained. As a path to sovereignty.

But men hadn't looked at me as Poet was doing. Like I wasn't something but someone. Someone with curves and lips, with words and wants.

Never had a man made me feel so keenly aware of the shape of my mouth or the weight of my breasts, which hung heavily and erect under the nightgown. Never had a man visibly devoured me like this, like I was somebody to crave, to consume. Never had a man made me feel desired, beyond all measure of civility.

From the moment I walked in and saw him, I should have covered myself, should have preserved what remained of my modesty. However, a rebellious need eddied through me. It twined up my thighs, the molten sensation flooding the private slit between my legs.

Many of his admirers dreamed of finding themselves sequestered with him in the dark. Many would have coveted the chance to catch his eye, to have his undivided attention.

Poet's gaze fused with mine. Together, we lifted the cups to our mouths and drank. Water sloshed down my throat, and Poet's neck pumped, the combined sounds gushing through my ears.

Those pupils glinted at me over the rim, then sunk to my mouth as we lowered our cups. Wetness coated my lips. Of its own volition, my tongue swabbed at the corners, a gesture his eyes traced.

Poet's chest inflated, his abdomen hitching. "Have you had your fill?" he whispered. "Or would you like more?"

So much happened under the gown. Fluid dripped into the recess between my thighs, my pulse hammered like an unbridled thing, and my gaze strayed across his slightly parted mouth. Those soft arches glistened, so very near, so very fiendish.

So very wrong.

With a refined dignity I could only attribute to years of training, I set the cup on the counter, the contents half full. Then I composed my features and nodded to him. "A princess knows her limits."

Poet absorbed the words, turned them over, then inclined his head. We moved in sync, me scooting past him, and him stepping out of the way. But as I vacated the kitchen, his lingering silence coasted up my spine like fingers.

Poet

I shall only say this.

Had we been alone in the cottage, that night would have turned out differently.

Had the princess given me a trace of permission, the counter would have been swiped of its dishes.

Had she given the slightest indication, she would have been hauled off the ground—and that fucking water glass would have shattered to the floor.

Briar

The next day, I continued to harvest crops with Jinny. All the while, I watched him.

The jester propped his son on his lap, asked the child questions, and listened to the boy chatter.

The jester lifted and twirled the fae in the air, with Tumble scurrying around their feet.

The jester hefted Nicu from my hip each time the child interrupted my work and made a fuss over me. He flopped the boy over his shoulder, his arm contracting as he carried Nicu, ignoring the child's tantrum and my assurances that it was fine, that I liked Nicu's company.

The jester kept a constant eye on his son, snatching Nicu into his arms when the jovial child chased a wasp and got too close.

The jester filled a wooden basin with water, gave Nicu an outdoor bath at the boy's request, and recited a poem while drying the child's shaggy hair.

There was Poet, utterly enamored with his son.

There was me, utterly stricken by it.

By early evening, I couldn't take it anymore and retreated to the stream. Water flopped down the bank, the flux licking the stones. The setting sun oozed through the trees and cloaked the grass with burnished light. I had detested these woods for eight years and never trusted myself to go near them again.

Unexpectedly, something had changed. I had witnessed happiness here—the brave kind, the sort I didn't have any longer but missed.

My soul pitied Poet and Nicu for the intolerance they had to endure. My heart envied how they smiled and laughed despite the constant separation. My bunched fists wanted to protect them. Most of all, my clenched stomach worried about them.

What could I do to help their plight? Did Poet even need my help? What would happen if they got caught?

I removed my boots and dipped my feet into the chilly current. Goosebumps raced across my legs, and the water glinted around my toes. I snatched a pebble from the ground, then rolled it between my thumb and forefinger while contemplating.

No, Poet did not need my help, since we were hardly friends. He hadn't confided in me out of closeness. I'd forced this situation on him. If it had been up to the jester, I would have never set eyes on this cottage, nor the people who lived inside it.

The knowledge was a blister, raw and stinging my flesh.

The stream rushed across my toes and lapped at the bank. The breeze carried his scent, which permeated my senses.

Finally, I was learning how to detect his presence. Soon, I would know how best to avoid him. Or how to catch him before he caught me.

While turning to face the jester, the skirt of my dress brushed my thighs.

Poet lounged against the column of a tree, his shoulder slumping into the bark. Grass rustled around his scuffed boots. The wrinkled dip of his neckline flapped like a set of wings.

With that lazy pose, those eyes smudged in black, and the tousled clothing, this male looked untidy yet impeccable, casual and sensual all at once. He stood there like a misstep waiting to happen, like a compulsion I could get used to.

My breath hitched, suspended on a precipice. That's how it felt to be near him—unsteady and unpredictable. If I lost my balance, the fall would be steep, and the landing would hurt.

As I'd learned the previous evening, Quiet Poet made an Inconceivable Poet. His slanted head and silent expression asked, *What are you thinking about?*

I hoped mine said, *Anything but you.*

I hadn't lied to Jinny. A social and political chasm existed between him and me.

But I did lie to her. Stripped of finery, we could have been commoners, a man and woman free of hierarchy and laws. I wanted to draft a contract with myself, to stop my impressions of him from getting worse. Because after last night, they could only get worse.

The memory of us in the kitchen.

Scarcely dressed and staring.

His body, hard and hot.

My body, wet for him.

In the dark, so close.

Nothing had happened. But because of that, it felt as if everything had happened.

Shivers vibrated up my spine. Remorse trailed in its wake, pinching my vertebrae back into place.

If Poet was thinking about that moment in the kitchen, he didn't show it. Rather, he cocked his head. "Am I interrupting?"

I flipped my skirt over my bare calves. "Is that ever a concern for you?"

His mouth tilted, giving me the answer.

To combat the awkwardness, I stood and tossed the pebble I'd been holding into the stream. It skipped across the surface and plunged, drops of water spraying the air. I snatched more pebbles and whisked them against the ripples, then watched as they bounced and splashed like shards of glass.

It had been forever since I'd idled in a forest. Especially in this one.

On a whim, I tilted my head and held out a palm full of pebbles.

"Afraid to test your skills against a Royal?"

Poet tamped down his surprise. "You make me sound like a pomp-ous prick."

"Rest assured, you've earned that reputation on your own."

"If we indulge any further, I might corrupt you."

My words flitted out, as light as air. "You sought me, not the other way around. And I'm the one issuing a challenge."

"Hmm. If I didn't know better, I'd say you were toying with me," Poet observed. "Who are you, and what you have done with the Autumn Princess?"

"She's here, about to beat you with relish."

Those mischievous lips tipped to the side. He studied me for far too long, so long that I felt his attention like a private caress.

At last, Poet straightened from the tree and moved toward me. He took a pebble from my hand, our fingers sweeping against one another and causing that forsaken place inside me to liquify further.

I squared my shoulders.

After a pause and another penetrating glance, Poet flicked the stone above his head, and caught it behind his back with the opposite hand. "Beat me, you say? Perish the thought," he said, then casually flicked the rock.

We watched as it vaulted forward and plunked into the steam with a dismal thud.

"Wow," I joked.

"Hush," he ordered.

Poet closed his eyes and whipped out his arm. The pebble launched into the air, then pivoted and grazed the surface like a tease. After the fourth bump, it spun and dove into the water.

He whirled and stuck his tongue out at me, the action triggering my sportive side.

We competed, tossing rubble into the bank without speaking. After the impropriety of hours ago, this was a welcome shift—simple, easy, and uncomplicated. The time slipped by in companionable silence. The rolling pebbles, babbling stream, and wordless challenges to see

173

who could master a better throw distracted us.

"I insist you tell me where learned your tricks," I said. "You don't grow up in isolation and miraculously learn how to read, pen verse, speak like a noble, juggle daggers, and dance. And do not get me started on learning politics to the point of advising the monarchy after only one year of residency."

The jester shrugged. "Fests and revels are in my blood. I have a love-hate relationship with them. My birth parents thought it a fine idea to dump me in a rather animated place, and I became obsessed whilst growing up, having been lost and found in one.

"Mayhap I dragged Jinny to carnivals because I was searching for my parents, but I went home amazed by the sights and sounds—and haunted by them. I was torn, so I avoided the areas where they baited born souls. Instead, I studied the performers and understood how they moved. I can't explain it. I gave myself a slew of cuts, bruises, and fractures, but I replicated the artists' movements until I could do them blindfolded.

"When I was old enough to venture out on my own, I made it a routine. Every week, I'd find the next attraction by walking there or sneaking rides on wagons. I paid attention to every jester, acrobat, aerialist, and dancer, and I charmed them into teaching me.

"Then at home, I practiced and experimented. When I grew proficient enough, I became a performer. That's how I earned money to help Jinny.

"I listened to storytellers and musicians. I eavesdropped on the titled and soaked up their speech. Whatever I heard stuck in my mind. I don't know why or how, but lucky me."

Careful not to aggravate my stitched leg, I gingerly plucked another stone from the grass. "You learned purely from listening to them?"

"Isn't that how we learn language to begin with? Stranger things have happened, Princess. Fair words and verse attracted me, so I devoted myself to them."

I furrowed my brow. "People cannot advance themselves without tutors or books. They need experience and official training."

"Don't be a snob, Highness. You've been doing so well, wearing your hair down and everything."

"I'm being pragmatic. I was bred in a castle. You're negating my studies."

"Nay, I'm saying there are other ways to be taught." He sounded insulted. "One can achieve whatever they want if passionate about it and as fortunate, or sneaky, as I was. I learned to read by stealing anything with writing on it—scrolls, announcements, discarded letters—and teaching myself.

"And I grew up among the common folk, who had plenty of opinions about the court, the monarchy, and their governing rules. Thereupon, I digested what people had to say and then formed my own ideas, and I discovered a knack for expressing those ideas by twisting my words.

"After the Crown summoned me, I submerged myself deeper into the craft. Even before that, from the moment I saw what born souls were forced into, I thought about how I could stop it from continuing. Do I get to learn your secrets next?"

No, he didn't. Not in these woods.

Nonetheless, I hesitated. "What would you care to know?"

However partial, my willingness caught Poet off guard. He opened his mouth but then closed it, apparently changing his mind about whatever he'd been ready to ask.

"Your favorite Season," he said at last.

A chuckle burst from my lips. "Well, now you're getting too personal."

The jester's mouth quirked, a wily divot burrowing into his cheek.

We continued our game of throwing pebbles while listing our favorite things, the rule being they had to be simple pleasures, and they couldn't involve family or friends, because that was too easy.

Me: the tartness of green apples, the creak of carriage wheels, the scent of campfires, the gleam of an illuminated manuscript, and droplets of ink.

Him: the taste of wine, the touch of velvet against his skin, the tip of a brush sliding across his face, a man or woman's moan before they came, and the soaked heat of a kiss.

Those last two points led to images of Poet tasting someone, splaying them wide, and pulling noises from their mouth with every lurch of his hips. My blood spiked, the sensation grating and enthralling. I didn't like picturing him with some imaginary bed partner, yet curiosity wedged its way in.

The conversation shifted to individual talents. Poet's eyes gleamed as he juggled a stone, then tossed it. "I know how to curl my tongue."

I hurled my own stone, then rounded on him and scowled. "You're trying to get a reaction from me."

Those pupils deepened. "Is it working?"

Damn him. He knew where he was steering my thoughts. I remembered what he'd said in the forest, after he caught me following him.

You haven't begun to learn what my tongue can do.

Also, what he'd said last night.

Need something to wet your tongue, do you?

So do I.

My bloodstream accelerated. It sweltered in my navel, then lower, and lower still. This fiend didn't need to reach out and touch me. His words did plenty, sunk deeply enough.

"I can wiggle my ears," I blurted out.

His features transformed, shifting from molten to jovial. "I insist you show me."

"Certainly not," I clipped.

"Why? Can't stand to indulge the notorious whims of this jester?"

"Absolutely not."

"Worried I'll never let you live it down?"

"*Definitely* not."

"Thank Seasons," he sighed. "I've developed a fetish for your strength of will. It does things to me."

"I don't want to do things to you."

The protest jumped out of me and filled the atmosphere to capacity. Water trickled down the brook, and an owl flitted through the trees, the raptor's trajectory rustling the leaves. Yet my words lingered much louder than any background noise.

"Oh?" Poet queried. "I'm glad you cleared that up."

His puckish expression didn't alter, yet the pulse at his neck sped up.

Either that, or it was a trick of remaining light from the twilit sky. Nearly an hour had swept by, the sunset long over and mellow blue shadows draping over the woods. Soon, darkness would fall. After that, we wouldn't be able to see the water anymore.

I shook my head and grunted, "This is foolish."

"I'll be the judge of what's foolish," he remarked. "That's what I'm known for. Then again, I'm off duty." His lips slanted. "Be foolish with me, Briar."

I wavered. While avoiding his amused gaze, I flapped my ears once and swiftly. Unable to believe what I'd just done, I dropped my face into my hands. Mortified laughter tripped from my mouth, the chuckles muffled against my palms.

Silence.

Thick, heady silence.

I lifted my head and met a pair of turbulent eyes, which reflected the proof that I'd gotten carried away. He gazed back, rapt as though he'd never heard that noise before, the sound of laughter—and pleasure.

"You should do that more often," he said. "Make those noises."

A deprived sensation clenched in my chest. I cleared my throat. "I won."

Poet blinked, then flung his head back and chuckled. The echo of his mirth slid between my ribs.

I folded in my lips, containing a dry laugh. Inwardly, I agreed with the sentiment. I liked hearing him make those noises, too.

Strolling back to the cottage, I reaped the rewards of my victory. I recapped my best throwing moves and his worst, as though we'd been in a jousting match.

Poet tried to revoke my point system. I accused him of being a sore loser.

The rest of the way, we lapsed into another bout of quiet, this one comfortable. I savored the unspoken truce we'd reached. Traipsing through the forest, I hadn't felt this carefree in ages, not even with Eliot.

I liked this version of Poet. I think he liked this version of me.

Minutes later, he halted and stared at the cottage. Smoke puffed from the chimney, wisps dissolving into the quarter-moon and carrying the savory aromas of dinner.

"He deserves more than me," Poet said.

I swung my gaze to his pensive profile. "That's not true."

"There's nothing bad about Nicu. He's spectacular, yet his condition endangers him, and that's my fault. For I'm the one who made him."

The instant I touched his sleeve, his eyes snapped toward me. "You've told me what you believe a fool is," I said. "But there's more. A fool is a man who sees his worth in a mirror, and in the faces of a crowd, but is oblivious to it elsewhere—where it counts above all, in the eyes of those who matter the most to him. Don't insult yourself that way."

There was another reason I vowed to keep his secret safe. I knew what it was like to be responsible for the fate of someone I loved. Just as well, I knew the bite of letting others down and owing them far more than I was able to give.

The difference was, Poet didn't deserve that anguish.

Seasons, I admired his resilience. He had the stomach to make the world laugh, when that same world would laugh at his son. To say anything he wanted, while saying nothing about his life. To be the desired "fool," while his son remained the condemned one. To let everyone think he had no depth of character, that he embodied only humor, seduction, and sin.

More than being captured in his stare, I sought to catch him in mine. When Jinny had stitched me, I'd bled and wept in front of Poet. I sprayed his face with spittle. He witnessed me delirious and suffering, then entrusted his secrets to me.

Poet had seen me loud. And now I'd seen him quiet.

Being this honest with someone felt like a luxury. I must have been starved for it, because right then, years of decorum vanished.

"I've addressed the whole of my kingdom," I told him. "I've reassured peasants and rallied armies with my mother. But with no one around, I've managed to stay your tongue, and it feels just as remarkable." I glanced away. "And it's awful."

"Appalling," Poet amended. "Appalling is a better word."

"Does that mean you're confirming or denying my effect on you?"

"Frankly, denying your effect on me is getting old quickly."

My head veered back to him, only to find Poet's gaze fastened on me. Instantly, I felt its scorching effect, a tingling sort of burn, tangible in its intensity.

Of its own accord, my gaze dropped to his mouth, transfixed by their fullness.

Nicu dashed outside. His father and I splintered apart, the moment shattering.

"Papa," the child squeaked. "I ate my dinner without you. Wanna see me dance? Look! You too, Briar Patch!"

Poet swerved toward him and cautioned, "Nicu, not so fast—"

The child had barely come to a full stop. He flung himself into a spin, tilted like a cart off its traces, and crashed to the ground. Immediately, his face lifted to check our reactions.

Poet crossed his arms, a lighthearted gibe ready to spring from his lips. But when the boy's eyes shifted to me, I couldn't help it. I knew the turmoil shone across my face like a bad omen.

Nicu burst into tears.

Grasping my skirt, I bolted toward him. I reached him before Poet had the chance, and the weeping child spilled into my arms. I drew my thumbs across his sodden cheeks and lowered my gaze, persuading him to look at me.

"Come now," I shared. "My falls are much worse than yours. In fact, they're sorry to behold."

Nicu's wide eyes flashed with doubt as he whimpered, "Are you lying to me?"

"Not in the least."

He sniffled, then fiddled with my hair and listened as I described a time when I'd been practicing dance steps for a grand ball, only to topple into an Autumn tumbleweed. I made it sound funnier than it had been.

"I'm afraid to dance now," I confessed.

"Why?" Nicu asked.

"I don't want to fall again and be embarrassed. But you?" I poked his belly. "You're brave. You'll get right back up and try again. It would be a shame not to, because even the birds must risk crashing before they can fly. Your father has fallen, too. He just won't admit it."

"Old Jinny will tell us about that, if we ask her," Nicu whispered, cupping his hands around his mouth.

"Then we shall," I whispered back.

The boy's teary, lopsided grin undid me. I had thought rendering Poet speechless had been a triumph, but I hadn't known the half of it until I'd made Nicu smile.

"No conspiring, you two." Poet approached us, playing along. "Just because I can't fall as brilliantly, 'tis unfair to rib me about it."

The boy giggled. "The Briar Patch told on you, Papa. You can't walk straaaaaaight."

"Ouch. Take pity on my shortcomings, I beg of you."

"Nope."

"Well said, my love." Poet held out his hand to Nicu. "'Tis the hour for your pillow."

Enticed by the added promise of a bedtime story, Nicu peeled himself from me. I started to follow them as they headed inside but halted when Poet's gaze cut my way—and he tossed me a violent look over his shoulder.

Stay here, he mouthed.

The words stung like incisions across my skin, so that I wavered in place.

The coddling must have vexed Poet. The fall hadn't been that bad, so Nicu might not have cried if I hadn't encouraged him to.

Or this had to do with his condition. Perhaps I'd said something wrong.

Eons later, Poet returned. He shut the front door and strode from the house, his eyes leveled on me like a target.

I steeled myself for a lecture as he stalked toward me. Then I yelped as the jester seized my wrist. "What—"

Without a word, he charged across the grass while lugging me with him. Not forcefully. Not gently. He dragged us past the cottage, through the crochet of trees, and into a dense passage out of range.

"Now see here," I blustered, jerking my hand back to no avail. "I am not a beast of burden. Let go!"

Without glancing back, Poet blithely flicked my arm out to the side. I tugged on my sleeve to straighten the material, then rolled my shoulders and marched after him.

We cleared the woods again and emerged into a compact meadow that dipped into a slight incline and cupped us in its palm. Bordering tree branches quavered and stretched overhead, the boughs shingled in jade foliage. Budding darkness leaked into the atmosphere, dousing the wild in a cobalt sheen. Another ten minutes or so, and we wouldn't be able to see.

Trepidation slowed my steps. Since the leenix attack, I had overlooked this forest's capabilities, what the lore said about hidden hollows eliciting reckless impulses. This could be one of those places.

Poet prowled ahead, as though he might trample anything that got in his way, innocent or not. He put several leagues between us, then halted.

Because I'd forgotten my boots at the stream, mud streaked my unshod feet and stained the hem of Jinny's dress. I paused, uncertain. "Where are we?"

Poet expelled a dry puff of air. "I'm a wicked one, but I'm not a lecher, Princess. You think I'd take you someplace that compromised your senses?"

Days ago when I found that ribbon on my pillow, my answer would have been different.

Now? Of course not. I shouldn't have presumed.

"Does the woodland really do that?" But when he made no reply, I sighed and spoke to the jester's back. "I'm sorry about Nicu. I meant no offense. I only thought—"

"Briar," Poet warned, his shoulder blades stiffening the instant my voice reached him. "I wouldn't continue if I were you."

I bristled and stormed up to him, stopping inches from his tall form. "And I wouldn't tell me what to do."

"And for once in our lives, I'm serious: Stop."

"Stop what? Look, I know I should have asked you first. It wasn't my place without your permission, but—"

"Oh, fuck my permission," Poet hissed, then rounded on me and whisked a finger against my lips. "We're finished talking, sweeting. So very fucking finished."

Then he grabbed my face—and his mouth slammed against mine.

18

Briar

His mouth seized me, the heat of his lips snatching my breath. An objection swelled and died in my throat, silenced by the deep angle of Poet's head, the tilt of his jaw, and the taste of wine.

His fingers speared into my hair, blazing a trail through the roots. I grabbed his waist, intending to haul myself away from him. But those strong fingers clamped to the back of my head, the effect spine-tingling.

I shuddered, letting this happen, allowing *him* to happen.

Unleashing a strangled whimper, my restraint broke and flung it-self over the edge. I hurled myself into the kiss, slung my arms around the brackets of his shoulders, and hooked my hands behind his neck.

My body crushed against his. My breasts scraped the bared cliff of his torso, nipples rushing against his skin.

A hum vibrated from Poet's chest and into my mouth. With a groan, he pried the seam of my lips apart. His mouth clutched mine, damp heat emanating between us.

We sealed together, our lips clinging, our tongues on the verge of threading. With abandon, my fingers raced up his scalp, urging him for it, for more, for right now.

He split me wider, about take me fully into the heat of him, to flex that tongue deeply, to draw me into madness.

My head swam. I anticipated it, felt the onslaught so near, the contact so close. Tremors racked my body, tearing me from my foundation—and flinging me to the ground.

I ripped my mouth from his. My palm sliced the air, aiming for his cheek and the promise of a resounding crack that would strike the treetops. In a flash, I imagined Poet's head whipping sideways, a furious mark branding his skin.

But the jester's serpentine reflexes saw it coming. He moved with inhuman speed and caught my wrist. And curse this rake, he did so without taking his eyes off me.

My palm ceased inches from his face. With my wrist shackled in his grip, Poet jerked me into him. "I didn't know you cared," he murmured.

His breath grazed my lips, hot and heavy. I gasped as that silken rasp cut a path through my clothes and stroked the crease between my legs. Warmth poured into that forbidden notch, a wet rush that coated my inner walls.

I shoved him back, wheeled away, and retreated.

If I kept going, and if I left the jester behind, my body would recover.

If I went even farther, and if I didn't stop, he and I would be separated by the expanse of woodland, then eventually by the halls of Spring's palace.

I made it as far as the meadow's threshold. There, I gazed down at myself as if expecting to find a disaster. Heat dashed up my neck, but whether from desire or fury, I had no idea. I couldn't pick through the sensations to tell which were right and wrong, which were me and which were him.

In the grass, Poet's shadow pooled with my own, submerging him into me. He loomed, his soft shirt buffeting my rigid spine. The temperature brimming from his chest simmered from behind.

Agitation gripped my throat. My breasts pressed into the bodice, which suddenly felt tighter, rougher, so that my nipples pitted against the constrictive fabric.

Seasons forgive me. If I turned, the jester would see what he'd done.

Yet it would be effortless for my head to loll back and find relief on his shoulder. To grant him permission like every other admirer, consort, and virgin he's had.

Poet's shallow outtakes rustled through my hair, tickling my skull and plying my arms with goosebumps. A hint of his mouth traced my temple, the scant touch a temptation and a threat. With every inflamed second that passed, my resolve slipped another notch.

Tension coiled in the narrow space between us. It radiated from there, a taut pressure on the verge of snapping.

Slowly, he reached around me. Black enameled his fingernails, and one of the bracelets clinging to his wrist bled scarlet into the half-light. The pad of his thumb played across my lips, sketching their shape until my mouth quavered, loosening like a chink.

As my lips parted of their own volition, Poet hummed in approval. "That's more like it."

Then he used his fingers to tilt my chin, giving him access to my ear. His mouth idled over the shell, a maneuver that coaxed the fight out of me.

My lungs compressed. I hissed, but the sound came out fractured. "What are you doing?"

"Everything," the jester husked. "And if you wish, everything I wanted to do to you last night."

That indecent voice probed the nexus of my thighs, coaxing a mortifying response from my core. A terrible ache bloomed there, my walls clenching. Wetness dripped from me, slick and seeping through my undergarments.

Poet paused and waited for me to decide. When I didn't pull away, couldn't pull away, wouldn't pull away, he did his worst. He palmed my hips, and his tongue flicked the dainty lobe of my ear, dislodging a gasp from my throat.

My lips unhinged, and my head slumped against his shoulder.

The jester toyed with my flesh, tracing the edges and curves with his mouth. Like a brushfire, the upheaval of his lips tingled down my skin, from the roots of my hair to the tips of my fingers and toes.

The ground dissipated. My eyelids fluttered, and my vision rolled backward, and my hysterical heart pounded so hard I thought it might crack through my breast.

Then he sunk his teeth into me. And I sunk my nails into my palms.

Then he bit my lobe. And I bit my lip.

Yet I failed to stifle the barest moan. The noise slipped from my throat and tripped into the air. "This can't be right," I heaved. "This can't be happening."

Poet dipped his head, his mouth sketching the length of my neck as he intoned, "The mystical corners of this woodland aren't as vile as you assume. They merely enhance what's already inside you. Nevertheless, I told you. This meadow is pure."

So this was real? Was I relieved or disturbed?

It was all I could do not to reach back and cling to him, to ground my backside into his pelvis until he grew hard for me. It required all semblance of willpower not to twist and subdue the jester with my mouth, to vanquish him with the same grievous touches.

He prolonged this torture, his lips thrusting humidity against the crook of my neck. My knees dissolved, so that my limbs threatened to give out.

"We can't," I said, the protest barely audible.

"Sweet Thorn," he whispered. "We both know better. Give this another few seconds, and neither of us will give a fuck."

"I disagree."

"The princess disagrees. The woman trapped within doesn't."

The cord severed. I broke from the spell, whirled on my heels, and pushed him. "How dare you presume to tell a Royal who she is. I don't need you to dissect or fix me!"

Poet hadn't so much as budged from the impact of my hands. "Where to start," he mused, stepping nearer, our chests bumping. "I'm not talking to a Royal, I'm talking to a woman, for that has a more charming ring to it. I'm not presuming, I'm provoking. And I didn't say you needed fixing. I'm denying you're broken to begin with."

"Fix. Change. It doesn't matter what you meant!" I leaned into him, pinching my thumb and forefinger together. "What you know is *this much* about carrying a kingdom, countless lives, and centuries of ancestry on your shoulders."

"Just to clarify, we were referring to a kiss. You haven't received word that Autumn is being invaded, correct?"

"Aren't you the clever one."

"But enough about me," he exaggerated. "What I see is a woman with bandages on her leg, not a crown on her head. She defended the jester whom she despises and befriended the child whom society expects her to shackle. She dances in front of mirrors. She cherishes a minstrel. That makes an authentic heart, and that's what makes a leader.

"She began as the jester's target but ended up tricking him instead. That's what makes her stunning, and that's why I can't stop myself from obsessing over her. Too bad for the world, she'd rather let people believe her as cold as a block of marble."

"You lead two lives, yet you have the gall to accuse me of pretending. You have no right!"

"My excuse is three feet tall and has my eyes. What's yours?"

My excuse had my eyes, too. But he was dead.

"I'm not trying to change you," Poet bit out. "I'm trying to unearth what's already there. You're the tragedy who doesn't realize it."

"Do not patronize me."

"Please," he flouted. "'Tis my craft to patronize everybody."

It had been a long three days. My father drew his final breath in this forest. My mother had no idea where I was or if I was safe. My best friend believed himself hopelessly in love with the ... the *asshole* I had betrayed our friendship with. I'd been led astray, sliced open by a cat, stitched by a stranger, serenaded by a child whose freedom depended on my silence, and been kissed—dear Autumn, my first kiss—and criticized by a juggler.

With a battle cry, I launched at him.

We careened into the mud. Poet grunted in surprise as we smacked the ground, the carpet of grass and pockets of dirt sparing us from cracking our heads open. His height and dexterity would have overpowered my lack of both, were it not for my temper.

I growled and clamped my legs around him. Muck splattered our clothing as we rolled once, twice.

I landed on top of him, my thighs splitting around his waist and my fists ramming into his chest. "How's that for reflexes! Not so nimble and quick anymore, are you?"

Poet seethed and wrested my hands from him, then locked my elbows behind my back. I writhed and squirmed, trying to break his hold.

"Fucking hell," he spat. "Briar, your stitches."

Clarity returned. I went still, my body snapping to attention. Though I didn't feel pain or see blood, I'd neglected my injury.

Defeated, I collapsed and sagged on top of him. His chest inflated, hard and heaving beneath me. We lay there wheezing and smudged in dirt, with his heartbeat drumming into my cheek.

All at once, darkness fell. Deep blues and purples swarmed the thicket, and the quarter-moon iced the treetops.

My fingers came to rest on his neck, a pulse point that quickened the moment I touched him there. A defiant, ambitious, and frenzied sort of desire welled inside me. Without his concession, I thumbed the spot.

Poet stalled. His throat pumped, and he gripped my hips, causing them to buck.

Another lapse reared its fiendish head, worse this time. Him, worn out under me, with nowhere to go. My limbs splayed over his thighs and my soft body pinning his solid frame to the earth.

I knew nothing of giving physical pleasure, except for what I'd overheard spoken between courtiers and ladies-in-waiting. In certain, uncensored moments, I had wondered about all the things I was missing.

I craned my head and met Poet's hooded gaze. Slowly, I crawled higher up his frame.

His mussed clothes burned against mine. His neckline slung off one shoulder, two round nipples tightened under the fabric, and palpitations rammed into his upper frame.

Our breathing grew shallow, rapid, and hectic. Yet I didn't stop until I'd aligned myself with him, my legs broadening around his waist. My skirt fanned over us, so that my bare thighs spread across his pants, the abrasion against my flesh tantalizing.

Within seconds, a firm ridge distended between us, so near to my core. An electric current shot through me as my folds grazed the hard length of his erect phallus. Though, a less pious term immediately filtered through my frazzled mind.

I feel him.

I feel his cock.

Poet gnashed his teeth, trapping a hiss between them. "Briar."

His eyes glinted—dark, turmoiled, and pent-up. And then clarity dawned. I wasn't a mere flirtation, a target of mockery, or a meaningless conquest.

Not anymore.

He wouldn't be riveted on me this way if I were. He wouldn't be monitoring my every move, as though I could destroy him, as though he desired and dreaded that.

What would it be like to turn the tables? How would it feel to rub against him until he melted? What would it feel like to have that ample erection surging right through the slit of my drawers and striking repeatedly into me?

The images cemented my nipples and wetted me anew. In response, Poet's cock rose, thick and hot—and unmistakably my doing.

He wants more.

He wants me.

Triumph spurred me on. I curled myself into him, branding him with my own heat.

Then my mouth found his.

With the lightest brush, the jester's lips quivered, tasting of spice, wine, and rain. Oxygen pumped out of him, erratic and heavy.

Then he moved in kind, meeting me halfway. We etched one other's lips with more urgency.

My need jumped in response, and my core throbbed. I sprawled over the jester, winding myself around him.

And in my weakness, I found a new type of power—the means to shut him up.

Poet

I have no words for it. Remembering those days, I can't think straight.

The princess, waking in my bed and pulling secrets from my lips.

The princess, working alongside Jinny in the dirt, unfazed by the prospect of filthy hands.

The princess with her hair flowing freely, the inflamed locks mussed as if she'd just been given a deep, dark orgasm.

The princess in that damn sheer nightgown, the crescents of her breasts pushing against the fabric as she stood in the kitchen, on the opposite side of a line that begged to be crossed.

The princess, interrogating me whilst refusing to expose herself, to let me in.

The princess, comforting my son and, hence, beating the shit out of my heart.

The princess's thighs straddling me, rousing my blood and my body.

In my haven, the princess was no longer a princess. In my arms, she became the most painful of thorns. Against my mouth, she became Briar.

Briar, fucking kissing me …

She melted, pouring herself all over me and laying siege to my cursed mouth. Her lips parted. The delicate seam opened like a tease and made contact with my flesh, the slight press of skin a shock to the system. Like that, her mouth trembled against mine, brushing the contours with a tentative and unhurried pace.

I lay still, my pulse a battering ram. Our breaths wavered, suspended. My eyes threatened to seal shut, and a warning hiss got stuck in my throat. Every working part of me stalled, save for the instantaneous rise and thickening of my cock.

Briar's ministrations grew in confidence. She skimmed her lower lip over the bow of my upper one, then slanted her damn mouth toward the crook. The path this woman took left a burning trail in her wake, sparks crackling under my skin. This barest of touches did more to ruin me than any plunge into a wet and waiting body ever had.

True, I had instigated this chaos. Even truer, she'd taken it farther.

At some point, the corrupter had become the corrupted. The seducer had become the seduced.

She dominated this now. I wouldn't have wanted it any other way.

Need climbed up my fingers. Temptation curled my knuckles until my hands fisted her skirt. Hellfire, my teeth ached, eager to bite, to sink my teeth into this Royal.

The promise of anarchy seized me by the lungs. Then her tits dragged across my chest, those pert nipples toughened into pellets through the bodice, and I nearly blacked out. Desire vaulted from my sac to the roof of my erection, the taunts hardening me to the point of anguish.

I seethed into her mouth. "You're playing a treacherous game, Princess."

The response trembled out of Briar like a small flame, one that could detonate into an inferno at any moment. "Then play it with me," she dared.

Wicked. Hell.

We paused. Then we launched at one another.

The tension shattered like glass. I released the skirt, palmed her ass, and hoisted Briar against me. On a shocked gasp, she flung herself at my chest and drove her fingers into my hair.

We yanked each other close. And our mouths collided.

My lips snatched hers, catching and consuming her breath. With a deft tilt of my head, I sealed our mouths and rolled us into a decadent pace. I grasped at Briar's lips, undulating with them, swiping against them.

My tongue slid across her ridge, begging for entrance. A whimper snuck from her throat, more potent than a drug. If I'd ever doubted such a scant noise could render me useless, she converted me into a believer and swiftly turned me into a glutton.

I fastened my mouth with hers, then promptly splayed her apart and flexed my tongue between the seam of her lips. The moment I did, another stunned noise rippled from Briar.

That's it, Princess.

Give me that sound. Give me your taste.

I stroked into her, lapping into the hot depths of her mouth. Briar keened, moaning into the kiss, the noise fracturing across my tongue. She sank into me and took it, took me into her. Devil almighty, her wet tongue tasted of ripe apples, equally candied and tart—so erotically sweet.

My muscles shuddered. My cock rose higher, grew broader.

I burrowed my lips into Briar's, driving our mouths together. My tongue swabbed into the depths of her. Then she hooked her own tongue onto mine, tentatively, experimentally.

The kiss erupted.

I groaned, hefted her ass with my palms, and crushed my lips against hers. Curtains of red hair flanked me as our mouths rushed at one another, the tempo of our tongues hectic.

Briar followed my lead. She rocked her lips with mine, yielding under their weight, clutching them until I couldn't tell where either of us ended or began.

Nor did I want to know. Nay, I wanted us like this. I wanted our bodies entangled, our mouths enfolded, our minds emptied.

Briar's skirt flared around my waist, exposing the scorching heat between her thighs. The linen material under her dress scraped against my pants. Her pert little cunt rubbed over my cock, the damp warmth doing epic damage to my sanity.

Seasons, she was so wet. Her arousal seeped through the fabric.

Briar whined, the sound torn at the edges. Based on the frayed noise, the humid temperature of her slit, and the way she dissolved above me, she had grown beautifully, indecently slick. My head fogged with visions of her soaked beneath the dress, the tight bud of her clit swelling, and the lovely cleft of her body flushing, opening.

My cock thrummed. I hoped to hell this cruel woman felt it.

But just in case, I whisked my hips into hers. The sinuous movement splayed her wider, so that I lurched the hard column of my cock into the vent of her legs and ground against that cinched place inside her.

A stunned noise cracked from Briar's throat. Shivers tracked down her body, but she didn't retreat, didn't shy away.

Nay, not this female. Rather, she leaned into it whilst her tongue rode mine.

Her hands knifed through my hair as my own fingers destroyed her locks. A vine of lust wound up my spine, a dozen thorns pricking me. And that was before she responded in kind by jutting her hips against me, reflexively swiping her covered pussy over my erection.

Fuck me. I was done for.

With a grunt, I vaulted upright off the grass and brought her with me, her body astride mine. I went after her taste like a demon. My lips pried hers apart as I slanted my head, pushing this further, my tongue striking into her. With every flex, I prodded at Briar's gasps, pumped my tongue against them.

The noises toppled out, a rhapsodic strum of music as I licked through her. Lapping at those sounds, the kiss escalated. Each piston mimicked the thrust of hips, the pulse of sex.

I worked my jaw into her, my tongue slipping in and out of her mouth, making sure she felt that same decadent sensation. I didn't care if I wasn't inside her, because she wasn't leaving here without knowing a hint of what I could do to her, how far I could reach. Thus, I speared in so deeply, so thoroughly, making sure this prudent princess felt every pitch of my tongue not just between her lips, but between her thighs.

Briar moaned into my mouth. Strapped around me, her thighs shook. She grabbed my face and bore down, her lips clinging to mine.

Her waist moved on instinct. She resumed those torturous thrusts, innocently yet viciously done, swiftly accomplished. The princess whimpered from the friction, and I seethed into her mouth. My waist connected with hers in a teasing, suggestive cadence, not quite fucking through our clothes but rather a close mimicry of it, the prelude enough to make a severe impact.

Mud streaked our limbs, our arms, our hands. Dirt stained her cheeks and chin, my neck and jaw.

Our nostrils flared, and our tongues went wild. In the dark, fed up and pent up, I couldn't tell anymore if we were kissing or fighting. Though, I hardly gave a shit. All I cared about was making her feel it—every ounce of painful pleasure.

Tremors ratcheted over Briar's spine. All the whilst, she welcomed my greedy pulls at her mouth, swept her tongue with my own.

But when that wasn't enough, I wrapped my mouth around that tongue and sucked. I drew on the tip, tugging as if it were that delicate bud between her legs.

Her moan splintered against me, as though chipped apart.

Yes.

I wouldn't release her until I had drained that precious sound for all it was worth, until I'd tasted every bit of it, until she was mine.

Mine.

Retreating, I nipped on her lower lip, seeking to punish her for this turn of events. Yet another moan sent me reeling. Those forbidden hips kept grinding into me, her undergarments dry-rutting against my pants, her cunt skidding over my cock.

Again.

On a groan, I grabbed Briar's right knee, hitched it over my waist, and hauled her forward. And my kiss slammed back into her. Our mouths crashed, mine clenching hers, our tongues snaring together.

The frail material under her skirt did little to obscure the shape of her folds as she bounded on my lap. My erection lifted, so hard it might as well be forged of stone. Even less substantial, my pants could have been made of paper, for all they concealed. My cock shoved into them, its length and girth rendering the closed garment practically obsolete.

I hardly cared. Nor did Briar, who swatted her hips. The outline of her pussy flung at my cock, the wet line of her body skating against the rigid stem of mine. Repeatedly, I reeled her into me at a measured pace, and our mouths layered as we rammed our waists against each other, hot jolts sprinting to the pome of my erection with each pass. The column traced her clit through her drawers, enough for me to feel the stud.

I groaned, licked into her, sloped my hips into that spot. With a tilt of my waist, the outline of my tip probed the compact bit of flesh.

Briar gave a cry, the sound fraying across my tongue. A curse strayed across my tongue but never made it out, for my mouth clung to hers. Instead, I chased that sound with more punctures of my hips, hitting her from below and tasting her moans from above.

Embers tracked the width of my shoulder blades. My sac throbbed against the warmth of her cunt.

The kiss deepened in cadence to our waists, which ran rampant, unable to stop, unwilling to let go. I whisked Briar against me, and she threw herself into it. Her fingers charged through my hair, and her mouth dropped heady noises into mine.

Aye, Your Highness. Take what your jester gives you.

All that separated her pussy and my cock were two panels of thin fabric. Yet how clearly I felt the contours of Briar, her walls dampening the textile, and how deftly she felt me thickening for that wetness. How trivial our clothes were compared to this.

I could kiss her until we both passed out. I could make her come whilst doing so.

With a growl, I shackled my hold on her ass and plowed her into me. Briar chanted, kissing me back, riding me back. Her fingers left my hair and splayed over my jaw, her frame abrading my torso.

I hummed. My tongue speared through her lips as I ground my hips between her thighs.

Thus, all wicked fucking hell broke loose.

Our mouths, tongues, and hips bucked. We threw our waists and lips into it, into the mayhem, and—

And like a bolt of lightning, Briar ripped her mouth from mine.

20

Poet

I'm supposed to admit guilt and ask forgiveness. I'm supposed to call it a mistake.

Based on how often I had been hurling myself into stupidity's waiting arms, you would think I'd made a deal with the devil.

Except the devil was me.

Again, jesters don't apologize. Rather, I will say this. It would be impossible to repent a muddy, maddening kiss that depletes one of air and intellect, a kiss that makes a mockery of reason.

Neither would it beget much of a tale if I'd regretted having a taste of her, since remorse would have made life simple. For then I could have walked away with bruised lips, but with the divine trinity intact—my conscience, my cunning, and my cock.

Instead, I self-destructed. Mind, body, and black soul …

Briar tore off my lap. She toppled onto the grass, then staggered to her feet. To complete the drama, her hand shot to her mouth.

198

What Have I Done? scrawled in pink across her face.

Seasons almighty. I flattened my palms into the mud, attempted to stifle their damnable shaking, and waited until my blood cooled and my erection deflated. It took a while. I wasn't used to feeling unsated by the aftermath, never needed to recover before.

My joints quaked from the impact of Briar—from the loss of her. Moreover, my head levitated, then crashed to earth as though I had been tossed from a vortex. It felt like I'd been slapped out of a euphoric hallucination that only certain petals could otherwise achieve.

Eventide descended fully, stalking its way into the meadow. That was how long we'd been making a hot mess of each other. Once I managed to calm myself, I picked through my reserves. My thoughts scavenged for witticisms or wisecracks, none of them adequate, all of them rubbish.

I opted for role-play instead and fake-gasped, "You beast."

The princess's hand fell. Her eyes narrowed to slits.

I held out my fingers like a damsel, and she played the hero, helping me to stand. Nonetheless, disquiet wedged itself between us. We attempted to rid ourselves of the dirt, smacking at our clothes and combing through our hair, not that it did much good.

Of all the sullied places that caught my notice, mud smudged her wrist. As I wiped it with my sleeve, the princess went rigid. Her self-loathing was impossible to miss, because at least one of us had to set the moral example.

Yet for some reason, her reaction drove a stake through my chest. To cover it up, I gave her a once-over. "You're filthier than me."

Briar drew back. "I do not care."

There went the mortal remains of my ego. Because I was an eternal prick, I couldn't tell if I'd been trying to lighten the mood or sabotage it further, to get her to laugh or scowl. Both options had merit, though only one of them felt like a dangerous reflex.

"Did you lie?" she asked.

The question brought me up short. I met her flinty eyes and noticed her arms had crossed. She closed herself off like a drawbridge, like I might contaminate her—me or the woodland.

A monstrous thought occurred to me, one that I'd forgotten. Sometimes after a storm, the elements of this forest traveled and permeated different areas. That included more than windblown seeds or pollen. It meant the essence of recklessness could have migrated— threads of them, at least. That would have been enough to provoke anyone to abandon sense.

"Did you lie to me?" Briar repeated, her pupils tremulous, vulnerable in a way they'd never been.

I wanted to fix that look, to smooth the crinkle between her brows with my thumb. "No," I said, then admitted, "But I might have underestimated one bitty fact."

I told Briar of my suspicions, which only made those platinum eyes quaver more. It lasted seconds before she fortified herself, fastening her arms tighter. "Then it wasn't real."

"Wasn't it?" I contested.

"I guess we'll never know."

"That depends on what happens between us when we leave here."

The princess marched past me, her shoulder knocking against mine on the way. "Nothing will happen," she mumbled before retreating into the thicket.

I braced my hands on my hips, and a corner of my jaw ticked. She might have been right, except for one crucial fact that I'd already told her. The wild didn't corrupt.

Nay, it intensified what was already there.

We withdrew to the cottage, where Nicu and Tumble were already asleep. Old Jinny kept quiet about our grimy state because she didn't need to comment. She knew me. Therefore, she *knew*.

Dignity in question—I read the princess's mind—but chin held high, Briar weathered the unspoken judgment as though receiving it from a pack of monarchs. She knew that Jinny knew, and Jinny knew that Briar knew, and I knew that they both knew. And so fucking forth.

Jinny might have teased me last night, but she had dedicated years to the role of my harshest critic. From behind the princess's back, my cherished keeper raised a solitary eyebrow at me.

I translated that look. It was the approximation of, *I didn't raise you to be a shithead.*

Indeed, Jinny hadn't. Doubtless, she would have verbally skinned my hide if she weren't busy serving royalty a meal.

To the world, the princess masked herself well, but she could be impetuous when nature ran its course. And I happened to be irresistible. Jinny had a right to worry, so I put her at ease with a covert shake of my head.

Unlike at court, bathrooms in the countryside didn't have water and heat pumping through the walls unless the residents were nobles, wealthy merchants, or magicians. Jinny and I had installed a system underground. It ran from the stream and connected to a lever in the cottage's smallest chamber, which we'd turned into a bathroom.

Having access to perks in the castle, I'd been able to store a few amenities here. With several droplets of a brew derived from Winter, the water frothed from the tub and threw steam into the air.

As I finished adding the mixture, my shoulders pinched, detecting her presence behind me. Turning, I found Briar shuffling her feet on the threshold. Her hair looked like it had been through a typhoon, courtesy of my hands. Dirt caked the dress, stained her bare toes, and swept across her cheeks.

Mother of all Seasons.

My eyes clamped onto hers and stayed there. If I so much as glimpsed her mouth, which was still inflated from the kiss, I wouldn't have a chance in hell of leaving this room in one piece. Neither would she.

As it was, I wanted to strip her, drag a sponge over her skin, and squeeze the material until it gushed soapy liquid down her naked body. I longed to watch the rivulets race across her figure, a tiny bead dangling off the pink tip of her breast. I yearned to wash her clean, my tongue following the sponge's path until I made another wreck of her. The craving lurched from my tongue to my sac.

Briar's eyes tripped over to the bronze tub pressed against the opposite wall beneath the lever, then crept back to me. "I did not mean to interrupt. Jinny said a bath had been prepared, and I thought—"

"She was right." Somehow, I got my wooden legs to move. Unhooking a towel from the wall, I stopped inches from her and offered the cloth. "'Tis all yours."

Absently, Briar accepted the towel. She wasn't the type to fuss, so she merely clenched the textile whilst struggling to cool the flush creeping across her throat. Likely, she'd assumed Jinny had run the bath for her.

Moisture filled the room. I imagined steam rising from the water behind me.

Briar cleared that filthy throat. "Thank you."

I inclined my head. "Be careful with your stitches. If you need help—"

"I'll call Jinny."

Aye. That should have been what I was going to suggest.

I nodded, sauntered past her, and got the fuck out of there. Whilst stalking through the house, I sliced my fingers through my hair. A frantic, foreign type of desire shredded through me. Not only did I wish to help bathe her, to coast my fingers over her bare, wet flesh. Nay, I wanted to wash the muck from her hair, to rinse her skin until she tingled with satisfaction.

I wanted to take care of her.

For the next twenty forsaken minutes, I didn't think about the princess peeling those clothes from her body. I didn't think about the soiled garments landing on the floor beside her feet. I didn't think about the slosh of water as she dipped herself into the tub. I didn't think about her watching out for that injured leg, making sure she propped it on the tub's rim, and how the position would part her thighs. I didn't think about the tub drenching her, foam rushing over her navel and between her legs. And I didn't fucking think about her sigh of pleasure.

Instead of waiting for the mist to clear after her bath, then refilling the tub for my own needs, I charged outside to the stream. There,

I ripped off my clothes and dunked myself into the icy flux.

That night, I slipped under the blanket with my son, resigning myself to sleep deprivation. It wasn't that bad. It gave me six lucid hours to listen to the melody of his sleep-talk. The distraction kept me from reliving the memory of Briar's moans as her tongue yielded beneath mine and the intoxicating heat of her cunt. If I were sleeping alone, those visions would ruin me and ensure hours of pumping my length to the brink, until my wrist broke.

As the sun hooked onto the sky, its rays yawned through the forest. Bleary-eyed, I hiked to a neighboring village. Jinny had a horse, but she needed it, so I purchased one to cart the royal bane of my existence home. The breed was worth more than the pair Briar and I had taken, which meant we could donate it to the stables afterward.

As usual, my looming departure caused an upheaval. I spent an hour trying to calm Nicu. He wept, his heart flooding the cottage and my own heart dangling from the end of a noose.

Nicu thought I spent my days earning coin at sunset carnivals and midnight festivals. Someday, I would tell him the truth, but I found no need for it now. He wouldn't understand. Indeed, I couldn't say whether he would later.

I said goodbye to my son, and he wailed. This was our fate every week, because our world saw him as a crime of nature, and I served the court heartily and hatefully. That was our story.

My jokes had no effect on Nicu this time. Why? Because the princess was leaving as well. My son cried that she couldn't go, because she was his friend, and he didn't want to lose her.

Briar did the wrong thing. Her gaze flickered to me in indecision, requesting guidance.

Nicu would not see her after today. Not if I had anything to do with it.

So what did this female do to further confound me? She knelt before my child and achieved the impossible, quieting him with a balmy smile and a speech bred from empathy.

"I miss my father, too. But I must be brave about it," she said. "And

I think you can be brave. Let's try together. Before you know it, your papa will return. He's always done so, isn't that right?"

"Yes," Nicu hiccupped whilst fisting her sleeves and resting his profile in the crook of her neck.

"Then you are lucky," the princess admitted, her misty expression betraying her.

On the dusty floor, she let his tears drizzle down her bodice. No one, not even my masterful self, had relaxed my son so swiftly and with so little effort. The princess had magic. Her performance demanded my respect, reaped my envy, and infused my blood.

I wanted to kiss her again. I wanted to do more than kiss her. I wanted to target her for reasons other than ridicule. I wanted to drag her to a shadowed corner, wrench up her skirt, and take her until she combusted. I wanted to make her beg, to make her plead for more. I wanted to ply her slowly, deeply. I wanted to shred her moans to pieces. I wanted to make her come long and loud with my name on her lips.

I wanted to show her just how much I was capable of. For she had no idea, apart from that fleeting taste in the meadow.

More than that, I wanted to dismiss this feeling. I wanted to mock it, reduce it to a joke. I wanted to resent her for interfering, to punish her for being here, for doing whatever the devil it was she was doing to me.

Then I wanted to have her all over again. I wanted to make her pleasure my sole ambition, to fit myself inside her until she branded my skin.

My jaw clenched. I caught Jinny staring and snapped out of the haze.

"Tell the briar patch maiden a story," I suggested, kneeling beside the pair. "Something she can take with her."

Nicu perked up and dazzled us with nonsensical beauty. The princess embraced and thanked him, then pried herself from my son.

Letting him go took visible effort on her part. I knew the feeling.

I kissed my son's face until Jinny hinted I should leave before he started crying again. I tightened the ribbon on Nicu's wrist. Just one more kiss, one more clasp.

I left. For the thousandth time, I left him.

The forest consumed Nicu's face huddled with Tumble in the window, the overgrowth screening the cottage from view. I guided the horse through the hedges. At the sound of Briar's huff, I smirked to myself and mentally counted to three.

"I can walk," she protested. "A horse was an unnecessary expense."

"I do appreciate a frugal princess," I remarked. "However, aren't you forgetting something?"

I glanced over my shoulder, to where the Briar sat astride the animal. A strip of cloth shielded her eyes, and another cloth secured her wrists to the saddle's pommel, lest she should get ideas about removing the blindfold. But although my gut knew Briar wouldn't divulge the cottage's location, I took no chances when it came to my son.

Nonetheless, my decision was backfiring. Normally, I reserved such instruments for erotic pastimes, among the other trinkets in my collection. Consequently, seeing the fabric stretched across Briar's steely orbs evoked visions of her tied up, ribbons tethering her as she arched off my bed, with a mask concealing her eyes and her mouth open on a silent, shocked moan.

"I meant, I can walk if you take off this thing," she clarified. "I won't tell anyone about the cottage."

The hitch in her voice sounded wounded. I choked the rein and twisted ahead. "I'm sure you wouldn't. Hence, call me a paranoid father."

The princess absorbed that. "Fair enough," she conceded, her words reinforced by logic. "But a horse was still too extravagant for this trip."

I scoffed. "As opposed to all the princesses and court jesters who arrive at court saddled on a mule?"

"You know what I meant. A stout pony would have sufficed."

"Go ahead. Deny me the chance to be a hero."

Another pause followed, then she mumbled, "You don't need me for that."

Briar didn't elaborate, and I didn't push her for an explanation. Putting it mildly, I lacked the verbal stamina, for I'd had my fill of her. And I was still thinking about her blindfolded, stripped bare, and spread out like a feast on my sheets.

We kept going. Between resting and our ride's slow gait, the journey took three times as long as it should have.

'Twas the kind of overripe Spring day that felt like a sham, the air pregnant with the aromatic nausea of sweet peas. I concentrated on the crunch of dead branches underfoot, a beetle snacking on the corpse of its mate, and the earthy waft of the horse's coat penetrating my nostrils. The sun lurked through the trees like a warning, threatening to lash us with glaring light at any moment.

Which it did when we reached the castle—my stage and my cage. It rose above the hills, crenelations lining the parapet walks like teeth, residents entering and exiting the open-mouthed drawbridge, glass spires stabbing the sky, and ivy clinging to the round towers. From the turrets, dozens of flags whipped at the clouds.

I tallied certain perks, such as my spacious chambers, my wardrobe, and my retainer of admirers. Nothing compared to my son, but these comforts somewhat blunted the pain. The attention frequently lavished on me, the way I tucked everyone in the palm of my hand, was exquisite. To that end, I needed another bath, a soul-deep stretch, and a long draught of fine wine.

I untied Briar. Spring's fortress loomed as we passed under the barbican and into the clamor. Horns shrieked, guards stampeded across the walkway to attend us, and a retinue of servants cluttered the scene, the crowd swarming us like sheep.

Whilst being ushered to the throne room, Briar and I swapped glances. In the wild, we'd cobbled together our story during the only moment in which we talked. Now our gazes locked. The wildflower forest, the cottage, the stream, the meadow, there and gone.

Again, jesters didn't lie.

And again, not routinely, nor outright.

Instead, we deceived with omission or evasion. Unless, of course, fabrication was the only option.

I nodded to Briar. *Let me do the lying.*

She nodded back. Good princess.

Bad jester. I still wanted to take her, ruin her, make her burn.

Basil and Fatima launched from their thrones. They trundled toward Briar first, expressing their relief. Then they took my hands, beaming and bursting with questions.

I bowed and hatched a tale. The princess had journeyed from the complex to pay homage to her father in the forest, where he was known to have died. When I saw her departure from a window, I got nosy.

The princess had wished for privacy, an impossible thing in general, and even more so had she ridden her own horse from the court stables. Thus, she'd borrowed a steed from the public stalls in the lower town, intending to compensate the owner later.

Like a troublemaker, I followed suit. Thereupon, we lost our mounts and had our showdown with the leenix.

A woodland recluse found us, gave us shelter, and stitched the princess's leg. And nay, the solitary woman didn't want to be thanked or receive a reward.

Her Highness impaled me with a look, smarting because I'd included her deceased father in the falsehood, not to mention dishonestly citing her for instigating the events to begin with. Well, apologies. She knew she'd have a better excuse to be in the wilderness than I would. Notwithstanding, we'd been over this earlier, and she'd known what to expect.

It wasn't my best effort. But since Briar sported a bandage, no one questioned us about the particulars.

My ally lost her composure only when Avalea of Autumn flew into the room. Briar's posture faltered as her mother gathered her into a petrified embrace. The queen clasped her daughter tightly and echoed, "My girl. My girl."

Even as Briar held her mother, the princess also held herself back from grasping too tightly. Indeed, she'd had more difficulty saying goodbye to my son than greeting her own flesh and blood.

Avalea inundated me with words of gratitude. The Spring Crown insisted on a celebratory feast, at nightfall tomorrow, and allowed us to rest in the meantime. They led the princess and me in opposite directions, and thank merciful fuck, and damnation. I thrust myself into a tub, into bed, and the next day, into better fashion choices.

We didn't see each other until the evening, when a note slipped beneath my door and her handwriting bled across the parchment.

The east tower catches the afterlight.

Whilst reading the message, I smirked. If she intended to communicate this way, she'd need to whet her skills.

That particular tower smelled of cold wax and gave a wider berth than the others. I mounted the spiral staircase and found her dressed in a waterfall of cinnamon silk—a richly spiced dye—with her neck roped in jewels and her hair confined in a circlet of braids. Eventide fell through the arrow slits, the stars illuminating her fidgety fingers.

I'd chosen a billowing shirt under a gray leather vest with an upright fluted collar trimmed in a thicket of lace. The garment split open at the waist and cascaded into two panels that framed charcoal pants and high boots.

Armored in fine tailoring and with black streaking my eyes, I felt ready for her. I curved my hand beside my mouth, lowered my voice to a broody, baritone whisper, and played off her covert message. *"But the afterlight—"*

Briar spun around with a yelp.

"—won't catch us," I finished. "Say that three times quickly, and I'll grant you a wish."

She sagged into the wall. "Reverting to your splendor, I see."

"Aren't we all."

"No. I don't think I can see you the same way anymore."

"I might have a similar problem regarding a certain Royal." I linked my fingers behind me and paused on the stair below her. "I enjoy looking up to you like this. Do you enjoy looking down on me?"

"Is that a trick question?"

"Every question is a trick question."

She stared at me through eyes that I longed to steal, to see what she saw. My deviant reflexes wanted to crush her against the stones and map the crease of her lips with my tongue. This woman was becoming a vice, a fixation, a stimulant—something indulgently bad for me. And I did enjoy things that were bad for me.

But more than that, I enjoyed being something bad for her.

"We are hardly alike," she said, her words tiptoeing into the darkness.

"That's true here and false elsewhere," I observed.

"I had a speech prepared."

I scoffed. "Speeches are an insult to intuition."

"Among other things, they also show we care enough to make an effort," she rebuked. "Anything that matters takes time."

I did a double take. She was right.

Briar checked the stairway. "Once more, I wanted to assure you that I'm trustworthy. I'll keep all I've learned to myself."

"Aye," I stated. "You will."

Because whatever barriers we confronted, they didn't compare to Nicu's plight. As he grew older, his problems would escalate, and the cocksuckers of this country would make him pay more dearly for being allegedly different than she and I ever would for sharing a kiss.

This near to her, I inhaled tart apples and fresh soil—remnants of the meadow, of her scent. The fragrance clouded my head like an opiate—tempting, unhealthy, and addictive if I got used to it.

The effect would pass. It had to.

For my son's sake, I couldn't afford to get on the Crown's bad side. Being intimately acquainted with the Autumn Princess's moans amounted to me pissing on their laws, fundamentals I planned to attack someday.

"Have you seen Eliot?" she blurted out.

I quirked a brow. I hadn't yet seen the minstrel because I'd been out cold ever since our return. "I'll get to that. I'll talk to him."

"You must have been missed," Briar commented. "By many."

Ah. Her expression declared, *I won't be one of a dozen.*

This princess may think she wasn't special, merely because of the ribbons and my tendency to go down on patrons. Yet what she failed to grasp was that none of my lovers had ever witnessed me uncensored the way she had.

No one else had met my son.

On the other hand, this woman had me pegged. Surely, many had missed me. The walls and halls of Spring would be a dismal place otherwise.

Regardless, it couldn't happen for her and me. That was the point.

When I didn't deny her comment, the princess's expression hardened. "So you'll leave Eliot out of your flings. And you won't flaunt your conquests in front of him. Otherwise, it could cause harm."

"Funny," I sneered. "Here, I thought we were talking about the minstrel."

Briar's glower faltered. "What happened with you was a moment of weakness."

"Was it, now? For whom?"

"For both of us. The forest—"

"You forgot the part where I said the woodland enhances what's already inside you."

"Which was still afflicted," she reasoned. "We'd been recovering from dire circumstances. We were overwhelmed and sought a release from the trauma, so no matter what, our actions were compromised. Even if they weren't, that would be criminal."

"I suppose that's an unfortunate truth."

"But we're back now. We're above this." Her throat bobbed. "It didn't mean anything."

I took one step closer, testing the boundary. As predicted, she remained still. Yet her breathing hitched.

It didn't mean anything.

Only two words fit in my mouth. "Of course."

"Right," she clipped.

It didn't mean anything. It would be criminal.

At least, I understood one half of what she meant. If our brief dalliance went further and got exposed, the court would doubt its foundation and how it began. That would lead to questions, which would lead to inquisitions.

None would think twice about the infamous Court Jester making a sexual target of someone they deemed a stuffy innocent. But if that innocent were a Royal? And if that stuffy target were Briar of Autumn? Oh that, they wouldn't comprehend.

I singled out courtiers, not future sovereigns. And she was the last female in The Dark Seasons anyone would expect to melt into my arms.

Aligning myself with this heiress could place my carefully orchestrated plans in jeopardy. In turn, that would destroy any chance of swaying the monarchy, of paving the way for Nicu to have a better, safer future.

So no, this wasn't merely about Eliot or a potential scandal. If we lost our respective powers, how could I get what I wanted? And how could she ever help me? That was what Briar was saying.

Not only would the outcome hurt my son. It would hurt this princess, ruin her beyond measure. If that happened, she would suffer.

Protectiveness curled my knuckles. If anyone wounded her, I'd be forced to do bodily damage to them. Inflict the slightest harm to Briar, and I would tear them to shreds.

That warning extended to yours truly. Being with me threatened to weaken her influence.

For once, I wanted something in this court that I couldn't have. For all my power, this was one exception where my cunning words wouldn't get it for me.

Even if that weren't so, the more important dealbreaker was this: She didn't want me.

Briar had enjoyed my touch and my taste. But given the choice, this princess would rather it never happened again. And I was many things, but a predator wasn't one of them. I didn't lure unwilling partners to my bed.

The aftereffects of this moment lingered. Later, it killed my appetite during the feast, as the princess and I sat among nobility, her mother at her side and the seven ladies at my own. I ignored her presence, as Her Highness ignored mine.

Eliot watched us from the corner, where he strummed his lute. His devoted brown eyes hopped from her to me, drinking us in with relief.

Longing for a story, the Crown requested the tale of our disappearance. I obliged, becoming the jester they worshipped. Rising with a flourish to their applause, I sauntered to the head of the assembly, in my element, where I belonged.

Rage and yearning fueled my actions. Daring a glimpse of that scorching red hair and those stoical features, I took a breath and a bow.

21

Briar

Father used to say that change took time, but he was wrong. It did not take any time at all to change me.

The glimpse of a family. One parent's death and another's embrace.

A child's tears. A confession. A wound.

An honest opinion. An unintended betrayal.

A touch—an instant that burned until you remembered to jolt away.

Those quick moments changed people. And what took time was accepting that change.

Standing on my balcony, I thought about revelry, sensuality, and recklessness, about being human and being a leader. I thought about the scarlet ribbon, which I no longer had, because I'd left it in the woods, tied to a bush.

I dragged my fingers across my lips. I still felt the heat of his mouth and the solid plains of his body. The shape of his cock growing for me, its outline rubbing skillfully against my folds through our clothing, the hardness probing my clitoris. The hysterical pleasure, the crash just before it went too far, before the sensations had a chance to erupt.

The lasting aftershocks of unfulfilled hunger.

I may have stopped it. Yet I still felt the jester everywhere.

Mother refused to leave my side. She kept encircling my waist or smoothing down my hair. Each contact threatened me with tears to match the ones prickling her eyes.

She doted. She shooed the maid away and readied my bath herself.

Was I hungry? Would I like my favorite steamed plums?

How was my leg? Would another pillow help?

Whenever I thought to brush Mother off, her eager face changed my mind. I was famished. My leg would survive. Yes, another pillow, please.

When I retired, she pulled a chair beside my bed.

"I am fine, Mother," I insisted.

"I know," she said, draping a fur blanket over her seat. "I'll stay for only a few minutes."

"Mother—"

"It's no trouble."

At dawn, I awakened to find her still there, slumped over with her mouth open and her eyes closed. I allowed myself a private smile, chasing it away with a frown of disapproval once she stirred.

Eliot met me at the ruins. He rushed into the space, and we charged toward each other, crashing into a hug. As we became a sloppy heap of arms, he ranted into my shoulder. Imagining Poet and I were lost to him had been sickening. The monarchy had been in an uproar, questioning everyone about our disappearance.

Eliot asked how I fared and whether he was crushing me with his embrace.

My heart thought, *I've had what you desire. I've tasted his tongue and wrapped myself around his body. I've felt the rhythmic pulse of his erection against me, and I've wanted more ever since, wanted it so badly I shook from the need of it. And I still want it, still envision it, still crave it. And none of this was supposed to happen, and I can't talk to you about it, and I'm sorry for stealing him from you, if only briefly.*

Please. Forgive me.

We burrowed into a corner on the grass, with our fingers entwined and our bodies huddled together. My cheek took refuge against his sleeve, which had achieved a dreamy softness from years of repeated washing.

Eliot lifted the hem of my skirt, exposed my thigh, and whistled at my stitches. With anyone else outside my intimate sphere, showing this much skin would have been indecent.

"How many times have I told you, you're not an immortal?" he teased.

"It's merely a scratch," I told him. "I'm more durable than the other princesses you know."

"And you weren't scared."

"Not with the jester as my shield."

At the mention of Poet, Eliot peered at me. "So he's ensnared you, too."

I composed my features. "I'm not sure what you mean."

"You don't want to tell me what happened, so it must be the sort of trauma worthy of songs. In which case, he must've had time to influence you, if you're using jokes to hide the truth, but I can take it, believe me. You don't have to protect me from the gory details. Not that it won't bruise my soul to know the turmoil you went through, but you're my friend, and I want to know so I can comfort you. I mean, if anything else happened worth mentioning, I'll stomach it. I'm a big guy—well, not a giant, but you get my meaning."

Remorse gnawed on my ribs. In eight years, I had shared with him every possible truth.

I leaned back and gazed at him. "There's nothing more to tell."

The castle had two training grounds. One for knights. One for performers.

I passed the latter with Mother during a morning walk, a rare moment of freedom for her as the sun crawled into the sky and spilled gold across the verdant turf.

She vented about something the Queen of Summer had said. "And I asked her to clarify what she'd meant ... and she had the audacity to suggest ... and I couldn't believe ..."

My head slanted toward the adjacent lawn, where railings enclosed the practice field. Spring's resident troupe practiced on the green. Twelve limber bodies rotated staffs and danced, their scantily clad forms spinning like disks. They balanced on low beams and flipped with their graceful limbs extended.

Six women. Five men.

One jester.

He dangled from a tree, using his arms to pull his body upward until his chin passed a branch, then lowered himself again. He did this repeatedly. Up and down. Down and up. His arms and torso flexed, ropes of muscles shaking with exertion and covered in a layer of sweat.

A bead of perspiration drizzled passed to his navel and into the low waistband of his pants. His biceps inflated, contracting with every repetition. Shadows accented the grooves of his spine, which swelled into a taut backside.

I had straddled that lap and strung myself around those arms. I'd felt the urgency and strength of those hands when they tore through my hair. I clutched those panting lips with my own. I had felt his length strain, hard and firm against me.

On an exhale, the jester dropped to the ground and swiped a skin pouch from the grass. Uncorking it, he tipped his head back and drank. As his throat pumped, my mouth watered. A deep-rooted ache burdened me, the pulse in my core making it difficult to walk with grace.

The jester's abdomen constricted as he twisted and flung his arm in a wide arc, tossing the skin sideways over his head to another acrobat. He did this without warning, but the female caught it without breaking her twirl.

They laughed. Poet strode over to her, aimed his pointer finger to ground, and circled it in a silent request. She winked at him and obediently executed another spin while he tilted his head and assessed the motions. Despite her saucy gesture, there was nothing flirtatious about the scene. They took their craft seriously, their expressions as concentrated as the rest of the troupe.

Poet spoke to her, offering some form of guidance while using his hands to describe a complex movement. And after she mimicked his instructions, the woman bumped her elbow against Poet's and said something that made him smirk.

"Briar?" Mother inquired, the weight of her stare heavy. "Briar, are you listening?"

I blinked and was about to swerve her way. I needed to apologize and recuperate what remained of my concentration.

Except we had crossed into Poet's line of vision.

His body tensed, arms and back locking like mechanisms. Anticipation flared within me, a disastrous and self-indulgent impulse if there ever was one. His head tilted a fraction over his shoulder, so that his rigid jaw became visible, as though he might glance my way.

My breath stalled. But after a moment, his frame unwound, as if ridding himself of an unwelcome crick. Poet continued advising the female without affording me a glance.

As I promenaded, the distance between us grew again. But then I craned my head when I thought he wasn't looking. And at that exact moment, he did the same.

Our eyes stumbled across one another like thrusts of lightning, sudden and perilous. In those fleeting seconds, our gazes held fast. They collided, like fists and lips.

In the mornings, I interrogated Mother for recaps of the Peace Talks. In the evenings, the maid laced me into elegant gowns.

In between, I kept busy. I ensured that my schedule was full, including throne room appearances to witness the Crown hold court; a royal tour of the armory and a personal one of the kitchens, where I thanked the staff for their hospitality and acquainted myself with their names and smiles; festive meals attended by Poet; private meetings with Eliot; the Seven nudging me for details about spending three nights with Poet in the woods; and a jousting tournament that Poet opened with a booming speech.

But many nights, I stared into space. Like now.

This privileged life had taught me all the regal words I needed to rule. Except these days, I wondered about the honest words I'd never considered, the ones collecting in my throat.

I don't know. I'm scared.

Don't leave. Come back. Let me go.

I crossed into the dimly lit passage, en route to the archive library and intending to address a stack of letters from advisers in Autumn. Most of the correspondence regarded social disputes, and Mother let me take charge of such missives while she was occupied. Beyond that, I planned to research historical doctrines concerning the treatment of born souls, in the hopes of finding loopholes or any bits of information Poet could use in his favor.

Around a corner, my footsteps slowed, then stopped altogether. The letters I'd been holding crumpled in my grip.

In an alcove outfitted with lounge chairs and settees, Poet reclined against an ivy-entwined pillar. Clad in a black velvet coat with rouge-colored lapels, he seemed distracted. His profile angled away from me, the cut of his jaw sloped toward the mullioned window.

He wasn't alone.

A nobleman approached the jester, his chin anchored as if gathering his courage. In a low pitch, the man mumbled something before setting his hand on the post and leaning in. Lust cluttered his face as he tilted toward Poet, then lifted a finger toward a stray lock of Poet's hair.

That nudged the jester's attention from whatever he'd been thinking about. Those expeditious reflexes kicked in. His arm flapped up, the back of his hand blocking the man's fingers before he could make contact.

A thrilled expression alighted the nobleman's countenance, as if he was playing with a set of matches. Never proposition the Court Jester unless you were willing to risk getting burned.

Sometimes in a good way. Sometimes not.

Poet regarded the man with a remote expression. Or perhaps he was more invested than he looked and was merely considering the nobleman's offer.

The sensations piled in hot clumps. My stomach cramped. Heat incinerated my retinas. Everything stung like flying cinders.

Amid contemplation, the jester turned his head. And his eyes landed on me.

As we stared, a dislocated type of feeling overwhelmed the combustion of other sensations, as though something had been wrenched out of place.

A princess always shows restraint and resilience.

Mustering every ounce of dignity I possessed, I turned and strode into a connecting passage. The moment I was out of range, I halted in a colonnade. Arrested there, I squeezed my palm around a railing and endeavored to staunch my rapid outtakes.

Later in the library, sunlight leaked through the windows, the light contrasting with the black shelves that held books and overflowing cords of ivy. Unlike the wainscoting, tidy built-ins, compact study alcoves, and central mezzanine of Autumn's repository, this collection was spacious and high. The shelves towered, statuesque and narrow rather than short and wide. Additionally, they were arranged into aisles instead of embedded into the walls, like mobile ornamentations rather than permanent fixtures.

Regardless, the scents of old parchment and vellum remained the same. They never changed, no matter the Season.

I needed this. I needed this old-book fragrance wafting through the library and a satisfying hour of productivity. After locating a corner desk, I threw myself into work and poured over tidings from home until my fingers blotted with ink and my wrist ached.

All the while, I did not think about him with that man. I did not bother speculating what they were doing, that Poet had assured me he wouldn't flaunt his liaisons for the sake of Eliot.

I did not imagine them whispering or touching. I did not imagine them wanting more, taking more. I did not imagine them retreating to Poet's room, peeling off clothes, and sweeping their tongues together. I did not imagine them in bed, nor who would be on top. I did not imagine them tearing apart the sheets, the mattress rocking, or the sounds the men would make.

I did no such thing. It was none of my business.

My eyebrows didn't crinkle. My chest didn't hollow.

I didn't feel bereft of things I couldn't name. I didn't feel the sting of disappointment or the embers of jealousy.

I couldn't. I would *not* let those things happen to me.

While composing another letter, the sharp tip of my quill scraped across the parchment. At the bottom of the page, I pressed too hard. Ink squirted from my quill and puddled like tar across the leaflet.

I gaped at the mess, then left to find a cloth. When I returned to the desk, a sheet peeked from inside one of the manuscripts. To anyone else, it would look like mere stationery, like the rest of my notes.

My pulse skittered. I plucked the missive, unfolded it, and scanned the contents. Two words looped across the paper in fluid cursive.

Nothing happened.

In the great hall, he played with his audience. He juggled coins, flung them to the ceiling, and then hurled them toward his spectators. Everyone bleated and hooted as they tried to catch the golden pieces.

A fitted leather doublet with a sapphire diamond pattern hugged Poet's frame while he strolled past a know-it-all who claimed to have eyes in the back of his skull. In a sequence of moves behind him, Poet switched the order of the man's cutlery, the feat effortless and quick, to the guests' hilarity but with his target none the wiser.

In Queen Fatima's opinion, a third chalice of wine was one too many for her husband. Poet convinced her to let the monarch drain four, to which King Basil nearly knighted the jester on the spot.

Another day, at the lotus ponds, the jester recited poetry to his admirers. As he sauntered across wooden bridges intersecting over the water, words such as *covet* and *provoke* rippled like satin from his tongue.

The jester and his troupe entertained revelers on a lawn checkered in tulips. They pitched themselves into the air and vaulted across the ground. He moved like liquid. And when he finished with an elegant inclination of his head, those eyes slid toward me and discovered he wasn't the only one out of breath.

I sat in a chair amid the wisteria arbors, engaged in conversation with the Queens of Winter. At which point, a hand balancing a candle broke us apart. The jester presented the flickering taper he'd once denied me, his gesture hushing the crowd.

My heart gave a violent kick. I accepted the gift, our fingers brushing. His lacquered nails grazed my knuckles, and my smooth fingers clashed with his calloused ones.

The exchange invited murmurs. In fact, I knew of seven notable jaws that dropped.

Poet dipped his head, then magnified his voice for everyone to hear. "Your Highness. This is overdue, for the leenix was no match for you. What an honor to be saved by Autumn. And so, I thank you."

"You're welcome," sprang from my tongue. "I—rescue men all the time."

Amusement glinted in his pupils, the vision so angelically devious. Black and white paint swept across his temples in whorls, the design curling outward at the ends.

After a prolonged moment, Poet nodded to Winter and my heedful mother, then pivoted on his heel.

As he strolled away, Cadence grimaced at me and took a resentful swig of her wine. Posy and Vale cast intrigued glances my way.

The rest decided to get vocal. Questa mouthed, "Jester's pet," which earned stifled chortles from Freya, Lisette, and Rhiannon.

Although she'd been discreet so the Royals wouldn't hear, my head sliced in the female's direction. At the same time, Poet's boots stalled in place. With the slowness of a predator, his face cut a mercenary line toward the ladies.

Their mirth disintegrated, swallowed whole as he prowled their way. A bowl of apricot slices balanced on Questa's lap, and her fork sat arrested between her fingers.

In a rapid succession of movements, Poet bumped the silverware's hilt from her frozen grasp, sent it flipping into the air, and caught it in the opposite hand—all while keeping his face tacked to hers. He squatted, placed himself level with the bowl wobbling atop the lady's thighs, and gazed at her. "The only person who gets to laugh at the princess—" his voice dripped with venom, "—is herself."

Even though he sank the prongs carefully into a wedge of apricot, Questa jumped as if he'd rammed the utensil into a hard surface. Poet lifted the morsel to his lips. He squished it between his teeth, took his time chewing, and devoured the fruit while watching her.

My thoughts scattered. I didn't want him to humiliate the lady, but my mouth hung ajar like a broken padlock.

Questa nodded vigorously, conveying her understanding. Satisfied,

Poet set the fork in her bowl, winked at the other gaping ladies, and strode from the lawn.

That same evening before a performance, I found the door to his dressing chamber. Eliot had informed me the artists were granted such a space, abreast of the great hall and connected by an inlaid passage. I wove around several dancers who curtsied and pranced off.

I knocked. The gentle percussion of my knuckles echoed the pounding in my sternum, the drumming so heavy it felt disproportionate to my size. How was it possible for my body to contain this much sound?

Because the inner latch wasn't bolted, the door craned open under my hand. I peeked between the crease, my gaze stumbling across the expanse of Poet's back. He sat before a mirror, clad in an open robe of dusty pink, the satin falling over a pair of tight-fitting ebony pants. In his reflection, he drew a path of kohl beneath his eyelids and smudged the pleat with his thumb.

My fingers tingled with the urge to finish the job. The embellishment altered his features from impish to devilish. Transfixed, I watched him apply the makeup.

Poet's hand froze. His pupils halted on something in the mirror. I'd been so focused that I hadn't noticed my reflection inching into his periphery.

While staring at me, he set down the eye brush and waited. Dozens of options crowded my tongue.

I can defend myself. I don't need your protection.

"Jester," I began, the formality tasting bland on my tongue. "It's my turn to thank you."

Poet rose and faced me. The robe parted and hung off the brackets of his shoulders, the panels gaping around his torso. He took measured steps, the look on his face electrifying every pulse point I possessed.

Pausing in the doorway, the jester braced his elbow on the frame. In a low register that leaked steam, he said, "No need, Highness."

The reply grazed my throat like the tip of a plume. It wasn't a suggestion as much as an insistence—cursive engraved into stone.

Beneath my canopy an hour later, I replayed each moment, from his praise to his shadow draping over me in the doorway like an ornate dagger—lavish and lethal.

The recollections brought our kiss to the surface, the hard pump of his tongue, the hectic pace of his mouth, and his possessive grip on my backside. I thought of his fingers hooking around my knee and pitching me into him, splitting my thighs open around him and fitting us like missing pieces. While our hips were beating together, his mouth had enacted the same rhythm as his cock, his tongue probing me so deeply I'd felt it to my soles.

If his lips could do that to mine, what could they do to the rest of me?

The question urged my fingers down my stomach, then further to my navel, hips, and thighs. I swallowed, the sound audible in the cloaked room. My hand descended, sneaking toward a place that caused my cheeks to bake.

Embarrassment, curiosity, and need drew my touch beneath the nightgown. I glanced sideways at the chamber door, then swerved my head to the ceiling. My thighs steepled, the flimsy garment slipping down the inclines of my legs until the hem puddled around my hips.

Beneath the covers, the open gown exposed the naked crux of my body and accommodated my wandering hand, bidding it entrance. My teeth sank into my lower lip. The illicitness of it slowed my ministrations. Yet a warm throb lured my fingers nearer, and nearer, and nearer still.

My digits brushed the patch of hair springing from my center. A small noise quivered from my throat, and a new disturbance sprinted through my core. The throbbing built in intensity, accompanied by a terrible ache that caused my walls dampen.

I needed to feel more, know more, seek out more. My hand swooped in and cupped my private flesh—and I gasped.

A disjointed "Oh" fell from my tongue as I added more pressure, my palm massaging the cleft. Somehow, my body knew what to do. I undulated my hips slowly, riding the friction at an experimental pace.

Disorientating sensations gathered where I rubbed myself. Tingles bolted up my spine. Hot fluid poured from my walls. But instead of staunching these feelings, every stroke elevated them, disturbing and frustrating me to the point where they weren't enough. My flesh crackled as though lava flowed through my veins.

Briefly, I had known rapture in Spring's forest. I'd sampled it, been granted an introduction. And while I knew women could reach the same heights on their own, that they could do this to themselves, I hadn't imagined it could be this profound.

This spurred me deeper. As my fingers traced the slot of my thighs, a tiny whimper escaped my lips. And then I entered myself, my finger slipping between the sprigs of hair and through the soft, wet seam.

The excruciating warmth had my body sizzling. My mouth fell open on a silent moan, the shock of stimulation draining my thoughts.

My insides fluttered apart, the channel spreading and then sealing around my finger as it probed. I stroked in, penetrating myself and then withdrawing, the abrasion breathtaking.

With my palm bracing the mound of flesh and my finger plying between the folds, I began a steady rhythm. I followed the sensation, each pass depleting me of oxygen and coaxing more slickness from my core. My thighs parted wider, my soles planted on the mattress, and my toes curled into the sheets.

Then I added a second finger.

The cry I'd been withholding broke from my mouth, the noise fracturing as I filled myself to the brim. Liquid coated my fingers as I pumped into the recess, and streaks of pleasure jolted up my limbs.

Using my feet for leverage, I bucked against my hand like a wanton. My wrist ground into my core, and my fingers pitched inside over and over, working myself, soaking myself.

The pleasure accumulated until I was drenched. Inarticulate noises threatened to rend from my lips, yet I kept them in. I panted under my breath as I searched with each lurch of my fingers, chasing something continuously out of reach.

And then I imagined him.

I remembered the way his body moved on the training field, when he hefted himself up and down from that branch, how his torso contracted, all skin and sinew. His athletic buttocks had clenched the way it might while snapping between a lover's splayed legs. Heavy, thick outtakes had thrust from his lungs, matching the tempo of my hand as it siphoned in and out of my entrance.

Him, sinking his teeth into that apricot. Him, drawing a string of black across his lower lashes. Him, in those ebony pants and silk robe.

The visions scorched me, so that I melted onto my hand. As I prodded myself faster, my thumb found the swollen kernel of nerves rising from my center and pressed against it.

Sparks burst from that place. A gravely cry jumped from my throat before I could catch it.

More uncivilized noises ruptured from my lips as I skimmed my clitoris until it pulsated. The tendrils compiled and expanded, all semblance of discretion fleeing my mind. Instead, mortification transformed into something more potent, more powerful.

All the pieces worked in tandem. My hips rocked against my fingers. Two digits plunged while the other grazed my nub. My mouth was no longer in control of itself.

I pictured his face above me. The shadows sketched his features as he watched me do this to myself, as he watched me go wild. I envisioned those eyes glossed in erotic green, those lashes lined in sinful black.

I thought of him touching me this way. I thought of his fingers flexing into that intimate spot, his hand spreading me, opening me for him.

My tempo became his tempo. My fingers became his fingers inside me, flexing hard and high between my folds.

I thought of his strong hands, their width and length, which transformed into another part of him, another appendage that could do all this.

All this, and more.

I thought of his expression slack with lust as he whipped his cock into my sensitive flesh. I thought of his crown punting against my clitoris. I thought of him teasing me, tempting me, taking me.

Most of all, I replayed his words. Every decadent thing he'd ever said rekindled. I fantasized about him whispering, that silken voice slipping into my ear.

My hand sped faster, plied deeper. Plaintive noises sprinted up my throat.

Have you had your fill? Or would you like more?

My spine snapped off the mattress. Abruptly, my walls convulsed, a profusion of heat surging from my body. Spots of light exploded in my vision. I twisted my face into the pillow, muffling my fractured cries as they struck the down.

It wasn't enough. My teeth sank into the fabric, the uproar of my climax blasting into the cushion.

All the while, his words echoed. All the while, I unraveled like a spool of ribbon.

For once, I could not help Eliot. I could not torment him with my awful ballad lyrics to make him laugh, nor cheer him up with an offering of hard cider brought from Autumn. I could not beg Poet to alter his feelings and make Eliot happy, however much I wanted to.

The jester had delayed for five days before breaking my best friend's heart.

We sat against the wall in the ruins. Silence overwhelmed the enclosure as a raven flitted between the crumbling monoliths.

"I'm sorry," I said, then hazarded, "Do you want to talk about it?"

Eliot's legs pitched in front of him, his wrists dangled off his knees, and the back of his skull rested against the jagged stone wall. Slowly, he shook his head while staring with red-rimmed eyes at the grass. "If you don't mind," he said quietly, "I'd like to be alone."

I winced. I had never met this brittle version of my friend, and I had never lacked the means to console him, to alleviate his pain.

I heeded his request and crept from the ruins, doing my best to stonewall the pang. Part of me understood his unrequited affections. Yet another part of me felt something worse.

Something permanent.

In the underground hells, people lived in chains. Down there, instruments of punishment and torture designed by Winter were stored within wielding distance, in the event a prisoner became violent, or a convicted assassin withheld vital information. Whenever this happened, Spring had no qualms about using the tongs, pinchers, spikes, harnesses, and blades supplied to them by the continent's most inventive and deadpan Season.

In Winter, doctors and scientists were members of an oftentimes desensitized culture, the majority ruthlessly glacial and rarely moved by displays of suffering. Despite Silvia and Doria's refined nature, their grandnephew and appointed heir was reputed to be as icy and cruel as their subjects.

If this was true, what kind of ruler would the Winter Prince become? Coldhearted, unlike his reigning grandaunts? Only time would tell.

In any case, criminals weren't the only jailed souls languishing multiple levels beneath the earth. Spring's mad were ensconced in a separate wing of the dungeon. I wanted to see if their living conditions—if it could remotely be called living—differed from Autumn. It shamed me to realize I had no idea.

Poet would know how each Season compared. He would have made the effort to know.

I got as far as the top of the stairway, which disappeared into a void. It wasn't the darkness, nor the mucus-colored walls, nor the odor of urine and decay that had me gripping the banister. Rather, it was the solitary groan reaching out from those depths.

It was the feeble sound a person made when they were about to wilt. My father had produced that same noise when he died, when the Spring forest had gone still for the slightest moment, long enough to acknowledge his last breath. I'd tried to bury that moment under countless sunrises and sunsets.

Likewise, such a din was the reason I had avoided the dungeon back in Autumn. I'd let Mother handle the gruesome affairs and averted my eyes as guilty prisoners met their seasonal maker on the scaffold. Dealing with those horrors would be forthcoming, but I hadn't planned to endure them until forced to.

Do not let that subdue you. Have courage.

You are tougher than you imagine.

My impulse said so. Be that as it may, misgivings slithered in like a serpent, telling me I was not prepared for this.

Crimson stained the railing, streaked as if blood permeated the guards' hands often. Iron manacles rattled, the noise rippling up the stairway. Someone whimpered—then shrieked in agony, the sound lashing through the distance.

Like a coward, I fled. Tail tucked, I bolted down hallways, pushed past doors, and rushed through a winding passage. I didn't care where I headed or who saw me. In my dazed state, I knocked into a shoulder, ignoring the startled exclamations of witnesses.

Accusations pricked my mind. The people's needs mattered more than my timidity. If I couldn't face the gruesome, I hadn't a prayer of becoming a stalwart ruler for my people.

My stitches had been removed yesterday, so I grasped my skirt and sprinted without taxing my leg. Noontide drowned me in pale blue as I barreled through a gate. The partition flew open like a maw—and I smacked into Poet's chest.

"What the fuck—," he uttered, reeling back.

I scurried from him, and my hip crashed into an urn. The pot hit the ground and cracked open like an egg, scattering chunks of ceramic. Poet's hands lashed out and snatched my waist, saving me from going down with the mess.

My shaky hand clutched my stomach. "Oh," I trilled. "My apologies."

Recognition flashed across Poet's face. His eyebrows stitched together as his attention shifted between the urn and me. "Never mind that, sweeting. People throw themselves in my direction all the time."

We stood in a courtyard overlooking an herb plot twenty paces away. A fleet of clouds sailed overhead, their edges frayed and shredded like gauze. Beneath the neighboring archway, water slid down three grades of flat rock and trickled into a shallow pool.

He wore a jacket adorned in copper chains. Beneath each eye, the same metallic paint tapered into four points like webbed fingers, each one ending in dots. Those decorated orbs trained on me, tapering in concern. "Briar—"

"I'm fine," I muttered.

Recollections diced through my mind. The scrape of the manacles. The prisoner's desolate, pleading whine. The scream that followed.

Poet surveyed me. After scanning the courtyard, he guided me beneath the archway. Tucked away there, no one would see us. No one would see him ignore my protest, pull me close, and nestle my head against his sternum.

I told Poet what had happened, my lips moving against his jacket, my exhalations skating across his pulse. The more I drained myself, the more I burrowed into him.

He caressed my ear, rubbing the lobe with the pad of his thumb. After I finished, he waited a moment before responding.

"It took me longer to brave those stairs than it took you," he confided. "In my humble fool's opinion, you don't know your own strength. For pity's sake, look at what you did to the urn. Loutish princess."

Humor broke through my distress. I let out an affronted laugh, a sound that reached Poet's ears and caused his visage to soften.

"Much better," he intoned. "Humor has its merits, after all."

His soothing timbre did the opposite of what it should. Renewed agitation stirred up like debris inside me. My voice and fingers continued to quiver, no longer from sorrow but from something highly improper yet instinctual.

"With you, I think one thing. Then I say and do another," I admitted.

"That's called being human," Poet reminded me. "You're not alone there."

Perhaps. This jester didn't owe me anything. Other than with Royals and lovelorn minstrels, he had a right to do as he pleased, with whomever he pleased.

Yet after I saw him with that lusty nobleman, the jester felt compelled to explain in a note that nothing untoward had occurred.

Because of me? Or because of Eliot's feelings?

Did I hope for the latter or for both?

Except for that incident, Poet hadn't put his lovers on display. Since rejecting my friend, he had refrained from having public flings.

He cared about Eliot. He cared about me, too.

I thought of what I'd done to myself in bed the other night, how violently I'd brought myself to orgasm. The memory thrust heat into my face. Poet would never be able to guess the source. Yet I felt unmasked, as if he might see a candid difference in my features, as if he might discover I'd climaxed to fantasies of him.

Poet.

I shouldn't.

I can't do this.

So stop me.

Please, just stop me.

I squirmed, got my bearings, and disentangled myself from his arms. "Good day, jester. Thank you for your assistance."

For the second time, I fled. Only this time, I did not run.

I couldn't sleep. Beyond the window, a thicket of clouds bunched together, and a nightingale sang. Sadly, the lullaby failed to sedate me.

Moonlight speckled my duvet as I twisted in frustration. The fabric chafed my limbs, the mattress felt too hot, and the room seemed smaller.

When my father was alive, he used to pluck me from my suite at night and take me exploring. His hand would cradle mine as we ghosted through the network of Autumn's towers. We'd hunt through the weavers' workroom and investigate a vault brimming with relics of old. I'd play hiding games with Father, believing us invincible and that no harm would ever come to our family.

It had been years since I had explored a place. Never without him.

I had fled from Spring's dungeon—this time. I would not allow myself to do that again, to quail from the darkness or the cries of its inhabitants. Until then, I could pace my wits and seek out other uncharted spaces.

But why wait?

I lurched up and swept aside the covers, refusing to analyze this. My feet hit the floor and carried me across the chamber to my wardrobe.

22

Briar

With my suite patrolled by night sentinels, I would have to get sneaky. I dressed in a rosemary cashmere gown with capped sleeves and a matching cloak, then plaited my hair into a loose bun at the nape. After pushing through the camouflaged wall panel, I slinked into the private passage and ventured down the chilly artery, letting my appetite for space and freedom guide me.

I traveled at a fixed pace, having memorized my usual routes. Normally, I'd take the path to the garden ruins. But a series of turns later, I exited through a different partition, still in the Royal wing but far enough to have bypassed my guards.

I emerged into a vacant lounge filled with push seating and giant lupine pots. The absence of noise in the south corridor seemed promising, so I stepped in that direction.

"May I help you, Your Highness?" inquired a male baritone.

I whirled, my cloak dashing around my limbs. A strapping watchman of possibly forty, with maroon irises and a hoop piercing his lower lip, stood post at the hall's archway. Steel panels rode his shoulders, and he looked to be made of rocks beneath his breastplate.

In contrast to the armor, his obliging expression and dimples settled my nerves. When Father and I had romped through Autumn at night, we had done it candidly, because we'd reigned over those halls. As Royals, we had that liberty. Demonstrating otherwise—with a ducked head or a hesitant gait—would have given the residents pause.

Although flippant Spring wasn't the type of court that spurned adventure, the world nevertheless credited the Princess of Autumn for being straitlaced. A female with a reputation as pure as cream, a disposition as dry as flint, and not a daredevil bone in her body. Being caught roaming without an escort was out of character for me, and that would cause talk. Oftentimes, Spring liked to invent stories rather than settle for the truth.

Potential falsehoods cluttered my tongue until I remembered this was still the Royal wing. Fortunately, we weren't far from my mother's room.

With that arsenal at my disposal, I conjured the most appropriate alibi, then furnished the man with a humble smile. "I confess, you've caught me. It is rather childish, but I find myself unable to rest. I seek the company of my mother."

The watchman frowned, drew the obvious conclusion, and smirked like a Spring native would. "You seem to have misplaced your guards."

"Nonsense," I replied. "To the contrary, I gave them no choice."

"Shall I escort you?" he offered, stepping forward.

Condemnation. "Thank you, but if there's one route I've committed to memory, it's the one to my mother's suite. If anything, so that I might avoid it when she's vexed with me. As for night prowlers, legend says I have a face sharper than a sword—" or a thorn, I thought, "—and I need only to scowl to bring the enemy to his knees. You wouldn't deprive me of such a triumph, would you?"

A chuckle rumbled from his chest. Without further ado, the watchman stepped aside. "Your Highness."

Humor has its merits, after all.

Confidence bolstered, I glided past him, aware of his eyes following me. Around the first bend, my footfalls lightened, and a weight rose from my shoulders.

Instead of venturing to my mother's room like an honest princess, I veered in the opposite direction. More distance grew between myself and the Royal wing until I abandoned that area. Renewed energy flowed through my veins. My limbs quickened and darted through the channels. I gripped a column, looped myself around it, spilled into another outlet—and skittered to a halt.

In one of the coves, Posy and Vale moaned and ground their bodies together while plastered against a wall. The former lady had one thigh hooked over Vale's waist. Their mouths clutched, and their bodies rutted in tandem to the kiss.

It lasted half a second before they registered me. Their glazed eyes flew open, and they sprang apart.

"Your Highness," they peeped.

"Seasons," I exclaimed. "I'm so sorry."

Blood raced up their complexions, less from embarrassment and more from arousal. The assignation had left their garments in shambles. The porcelain laces of Vale's bodice swung open, revealing the crescent of a dark breast.

They made a show of restoring their appearance, fiddling with white linen and gilded silk. Vale tucked her left breast with its dusky nipple back into the bodice, then combed through her mussed hair.

I caught myself gawking. Belatedly, I spun away to give them a moment. While they put themselves to rights, I feigned interest in a stained glass representation of the castle's checkered tulip lawn, the design embedded into a nearby window. I had witnessed their coy touches before, but I'd had no idea it went beyond that.

They came from the same background and kingdom, so they had no cause to hide their affections. I'd happened upon an accepted dalliance, not a taboo indiscretion.

I reinspected the shell in which they'd concealed themselves and wondered what it was like to be so bold at court. To meet someone there—in a different manner from the way I met Eliot—and fling myself into the shadows with him. I'd done so in the forest, except this was much closer to prying eyes.

When the ladies were finished, I faced them and cleared my throat. "I-I beg your pardon. I did not mean to—"

"Our apologies," Vale professed.

"I'm disturbing you."

"Hardly," Posy lied, still fighting to catch her breath. "Are you lost, Your Highness?"

I wavered. Typical Briar would have replied that it was none of their concern. Typical Briar wouldn't have been caught, because she would be in her suite, having never left.

My presence surprised them. And what had years of acquaintance taught us about one another?

My efforts to know these ladies had not exceeded the surface. Vale's overbite and her burgundy irises and hair. Posy's diminutive nose, the blossoms inked along her collarbone, and her enviably curvaceous form. Their flirtatious innuendos and buoyant kinships. Their hair decorated with floral buds that eventually went lopsided due to a constant habit of throwing their heads back in laughter. It was hardly an omniscient impression of who they were.

I confessed, "I'm exploring."

Posy's face alighted. "Truly?"

"You?" Vale questioned, her disbelief reflecting Posy's.

"Me," I answered. "Would you ... that is ..." I folded my hands behind my back. "I would like some company, if you'd care to join me."

I expected gaping. I predicted they would make their excuses and scuttle off to a place where they could properly mock me. Either that, or they would mumble their acceptance out of duty.

The ladies did neither. Instead, they traded glances, a silent exchange occurring between them. Then they sprouted from their hiding place and eagerly looped their arms with mine.

Relief swept through me. Our skirts flounced together, veils of fabric rustling as we embarked through the passages.

Posy and Vale proved knowledgeable companions, having acquainted themselves with the accessible corners of Spring. The tailor's room, where bolts of cloth and spools of thread flushed under the glow of moonlight. The perfumer's laboratory crammed with oils, essences, and dried flowers. The frosty cellar containing barrels of Spring wine, all corked and sealed and clinking when we touched them.

Posy complained about having stiff nipples. Vale crooned a saucy comment about that, which made her lover grin, then she looted a bottle of merlot for our jaunt.

Lastly, we entered a repository lined in black velvet walls. My feet slowed as I frowned at the mounted harnesses, bridles, and rods. "What ..."

But after another leery step, I didn't need to finish the question. My hands bunched in front of me, and I struggled to quell my features. Metallic designs inlaid the collection of straps and belts. The rods were as thin as reeds and propped on a display rack, and several open cabinets showcased fringed items, as well as ropes and silk eye cloths and masquerade masks.

Posy and Vale trotted inside while tossing me sprightly expressions. Noticing something, they halted and rounded on me. Disquiet must be squatting on my face, because sudden uncertainty crossed their features.

"So it's true," Vale mused. "Autumn is indeed as modest as they say."

"Sorry, Highness," Posy hastened. "Perhaps we got carried away. Is it too much?"

I swallowed, not wishing to offend them. "We have our private preferences, as everyone does. I was just startled."

"Never seen a pleasure vault, then?" Vale inquired without judgement.

Quite the contrary. I had never seen anything like this, but I'd discovered not long ago several similar apparatuses in someone's wardrobe. Not that I would confess about that.

Posy took my hand and escorted me. "Are you not curious?"

No, I was not. The objects seemed either frivolous, aggressive, or highly complicated. Although I knew what Poet kept in his closet, nothing in his collection had been arduous or convoluted, though I had seen a few softly assertive options.

My scalp prickled. Perhaps I was a little curious.

Posy and Vale gave me a tour, their voices teetering between naughty and regal. According to the ladies, this vault was open to anyone in the mood to energize the ambience in their bedchambers.

I questioned whether that could possibly be sanitary until the females pointed to the shelves holding pearlescent liquid, compliments of Winter. The mixtures presumably took care of cleaning the accessories, restoring them as if they'd never been used.

Posy and Vale retreated to admire a variety of feather wands filling a vase, whereas apprehension delayed me from continuing by myself. Electing to keep an open mind, I maneuvered through the repository and pretended it was research. Clasping my hands in front of me, I viewed each instrument as if I were in a museum.

Despite the nature of these devices, the craftsmanship was beautiful. Dark colors. Eloquent patterns. The space itself was organized, streamlined yet lushly decorated with a miniature chandelier bolted to the ceiling.

I approached a chain dangling from above, which held an assortment of satin ribbons. My fingers glided over a thick one trimmed in lace, my skin pebbling as it glided over my wrist like a bracelet.

I blinked and drew my hand away. Vale and Posy debated whether to borrow one of the feather wands, then forgot to decide once they uncorked the merlot bottle.

From what I'd seen wine do to otherwise sane people, it appealed to me as much as spittle. But this was not my kingdom. Besides, the Seven pounded their spirits and kept them down better than most warriors. Tipsy or sober scarcely made a dent in their behavior.

They passed the merlot back and forth. I declined more than a sip.

"I'm impressed, Your Highness," a feminine voice intruded, this one sounding like a cut gem—fair but glaring.

Our trio startled. We spun toward Cadence as she sidled into the room wearing a gown of chartreuse silk, the pigment clashing with her evergreen tresses.

The lady gestured at the surroundings, then to Posy and Vale, then to the vessel in my hand. "Very impressed," she underscored. "To lower yourself to this level. I wouldn't have guessed."

That I would spend my precious hours with two of the Seven. That I would set foot in a pleasure vault. That my prim lips would take a drink.

I wouldn't have predicted it, either. Still, I did not care for her tone. As the most indiscreet of the Seven, Cadence also proved herself the brashest. Perhaps she believed her long-legged, razor-cheeked beauty could get away with having a cobra for a tongue.

"What a pleasant surprise," I said trimly, then quirked a brow, waiting for her to do as her station required.

With a barely contained huff, she curtsied and straightened. "Anything catch your eye, Highness?"

She dropped the question at my feet like a grenade.

My mind tripped back to the array of ribbons, though none had been dyed red. Prudently, I did not respond to her query.

Posy and Vale beamed, heartened to see her. They sounded apologetic, because as they spoke with her, it became apparent that Cadence had been roaming with them before the group accidentally got separated. Instead of searching for their companion, Posy and Vale had soaked up an intimate moment and then joined me.

They had accompanied me and forgotten their friend. Although I empathized with Cadence, I couldn't help reveling in being chosen. Especially while recalling how her eyes had feasted on Poet that first day, or how they'd traded familiar glances in the orchid garden.

According to Cadence, Vale had mentioned exploring this vault earlier. That was how she'd found us.

"We didn't mean to leave you," Posy said.

"You did what you had to do," Cadence dismissed.

Because I was a princess. Because they were obligated to indulge me—to like me.

Cadence's snide response spoiled my fantasy about being the

preferred company. If I wanted to give this snob the benefit of the doubt, she had officially talked me out of it. Now that she was here, only courtesy forced me to invite Cadence on our excursion.

In her language, that meant dominating the flock. "Lisette, Questa, Rhiannon, and Freya should come, too. We can't possibly do a thing without them." Her neck extended as she slurped the remainder of the wine, then licked her lips. "No one left behind. Wouldn't Your Esteemed Highness agree?"

"No, I would not," I replied. "This is not a getaway. It's a tour. Freya, Lisette, Questa, and Rhiannon—" deliberately, I listed them in alphabetical order, "—will live to partake in another one. Also, that's too many people and will cause a racket."

Wisely, Cadence elected not to browbeat the issue. Though, I would bet my coronation necklace that she rarely squatted over a latrine without her cliquey gang.

We exited the repository. After taking a random passage, we wandered into the artist wing, having come from an unfamiliar channel, despite my being in this area before. Torches stroked the walls and rugs in muted orange light. Most of the rooms were split by cul-de-sacs. The doors exhibited gilded nameplates, and the scent of herbs— charred yet sweet—lingered in the air.

My mind rioted at the prospect of loitering here. "Let's go," I hastened. "These are dull quarters."

Unfortunately, the alcohol had long since fattened my companions' pupils with impulsiveness. The courtiers traded an inspired look that scraped at my nerves, because it could mean only one thing.

One person.

They darted to Poet's door in a fit of cackles, then knocked while remarking under their mirthful breaths about his pretentious plaque. They did so with admiration, as if he were the most amusing man on this damned continent.

An unpleasant fact dawned. They'd located his chambers without having to search. For unwelcome reasons, the notion triggered a vile side of me and raised my combative hackles.

I hustled after the ladies. My hiss of "Not him" came too late.

The door opened. Poet materialized, the sight of him plaguing me with impure thoughts. He wore a pair of bed hose that hung low off his waist and accentuated the slopes of his hipbones. Light from the nearby flames traced the expanse of skin, brought his taut pectorals into disturbing relief, and highlighted his tousled hair.

He hadn't been sleeping. That much was clear from the lucid yet casual expression on his face. A husky noise resounded from his lungs, more from relaxation than exhaustion. And his eyes glittered with intrigue less than a second after answering the door.

I glowered at that insufferable rack of muscles, then at the hands he slowly propped on either side of the frame. This caused the ridges along his biceps to inflate, revealing a pair of arms that had the strength to bare his weight as he did pull-ups from a tree branch.

Apparently, a gardener must have clipped off Vale, Posy, and Cadence's tongues. They ogled him in silence, unabashed and uninhibited.

Because I lingered apart from the courtiers, the jester's attention settled on the ladies first. An indentation dug into the corner of his lips. His fingers tapped the doorway, his short nails smeared with onyx paint. "Well, now. Aren't you three a trilogy."

"Count again," I advised.

Green eyes clicked toward me. They flashed, then gleamed with elation. I wanted to tuck that visual in a box for safekeeping, to gaze at whenever I felt like it.

"We have a mission for you, sir," Vale said.

"We've been searching the high seas for you," Posy improvised.

"I'd expect nothing short of it," Poet quipped while studying me. "What can I do for you lovelies that I haven't done thus far?"

"I can name a few things," Cadence purred. "I thought jesters had a reputation for finishing what they start."

The implication crawled across my ribcage. Poet's eyes swerved toward her, their wordless exchange hinting at a previous rendezvous. Perhaps she had been a guest in his chambers before. It would explain her death glare when Poet offered me a candle at the wisteria arbors, not to mention her impertinent attitude tonight.

"The princess wishes to explore," Vale announced.

Shifting his attention and challenging me to a face-off, Poet inquired, "She's developed a case of the naughties, has she?"

"I would not go that far," I declared.

"You'll never guess where I found her," Cadence said, dismissing my wide eyes. "She was in the pleasu—"

"Wine cellar," Posy cut in, registering the mayhem on my face. "With me and Vale."

Truthfully, she should have stopped at *wine cellar*. Giving superfluous information never sounded honest. Moreover, the jester was a master of deception, able to sift through wordplay with the perception of a bloodhound.

His shrewd features contorted. His eyes ticked over to Posy, then slid back to me. He knew these ladies, as he surely knew about the vault's existence, since he possessed such comparable items. Also, he'd understood the words Cadence had been about to voice.

I folded my hands in front of me and weathered his scrutiny, though my nostrils flared.

Something keen—and aware—ignited his visage. Damn him.

I couldn't decide whether to be grateful or annoyed as Cadence's voice leaked into the silence. "We need a man to protect us," she flirted, her words oozing like sap. "You know, from the ghouls and incubi who roam these hallways, intent on stealing a virgin's maidenhead."

"As if you need to worry about that," Vale quipped.

"Whose maidenhead?" another voice yawned.

I clenched my eyes shut. This could not be happening.

Eliot shuffled toward us while scratching through his mussed blond waves and blinking in drowsy astonishment at our group. Presumably, our stupidity had woken him up.

My friend halted upon seeing me. "Br—Your Highness."

"Forgive us if we woke you," I murmured.

He hadn't spoken to me since Poet rejected him. Unaccustomed to Eliot's withdrawal, I had missed him and worried how he was faring. Even now, meeting his gaze caused my stomach to clench with guilt and longing.

Speaking of Poet, Eliot's eyes darted the jester's way and plummeted into misery.

Cadence noticed—*everyone* noticed the minstrel and jester watching one another warily. I swore, if this woman commented on it, the consequences would involve my fist and a trip to the infirmary.

The web tightened before my eyes. Eliot, in love with Poet but thinking the jester was in love with the Seven. Cadence, in love with Poet but thinking the jester was in love with Eliot. Posy and Vale, in love with each other—and with Cadence. Me, in love with nobody. And Poet, in love with himself.

Despite Eliot overhearing us, the remote location of Poet's room gave us an advantage. We bickered freely. Posy and Vale nagged a queasy Eliot to come exploring with us. In turn, Eliot rambled excuses. Cadence ordered him to go to bed if he was going to be a killjoy. I told her there was no need to be rude, to which Eliot told me—as formally as possible—that he didn't need a defender.

Defiantly, he changed his mind and accepted the invitation. He and the trio of ladies piped over where to go next. I attempted to fence in the argument by shushing their overlapping whispers.

Poet snapped his fingers. The sound cracked through the hall.

Everyone stopped. Witnessing their reaction, my jaw tensed.

I hated him. I hated that he achieved what I could not. I hated that he hurt Eliot and enabled Cadence.

Most of all, I hated the multitude of catastrophic emotions he made me feel.

"Now, now," Poet vouched. "There's plenty of me to go around, however I believe the princess is in charge." He glanced my way. "Your Highness, fresh air shall do this whiny troop wonders. I propose we explore the fabled labyrinth. Would that please you?"

Season lore had convinced the court's residents into believing the labyrinth's central well granted wishes to its visitors. It was also an attractive place to lose oneself. Poet seemed confident on how to get there without detection. I suspected he knew this castle more thoroughly than he let on. I wanted to see how much.

"Lead the way," I commanded.

"As you like," he said. "Allow me to dress first."

"Must you?" Cadence lamented.

"Yes," Eliot and I snapped at her.

In under five minutes, Poet returned looking ridiculous. He'd outfitted himself in a shirt the color of nightfall, which matched his dark pants and complemented a pair of high bronze boots. Though, that wasn't the ridiculous part.

It was the shirt's transparency that struck me dumb.

The sheer garment provided an unhampered view of his naked chest underneath. That broad, flexible torso filled out the material. Neither loose, nor tight, the transparent fabric draped down his frame like a tease.

The devious scoundrel hadn't been lying about getting dressed. It managed to cover him while leaving nothing to the imagination.

Only he could manage to look both dangerous and enticing in such a fashion. Only this jester could make the ensemble work to his benefit, technically meeting everyone's requirements for attire.

Especially his own.

Ignoring the insolent dash of my pulse, I squinted at him. *I suppose you think you're clever.*

His mouth twitched as he stared back. *I suppose you think you're right.*

Aside from the bronze crescent and black flecks decorating the corner of his right eye, he wore the scarlet bracelet, an accessory only I knew the truth about.

Every knot of tension thawed as I glimpsed the band of fabric.

The jester inclined his head. I mirrored the action, giving him leave to transport us. While Poet locked his door, I mouthed to Eliot that he should retrieve his lute. My bidding had the desired effect. He grinned, and my heart rejoiced.

As soon as Eliot reappeared from his room with the instrument strapped to his back, Poet instructed our group to clasp hands so that we formed a garland. Him at one end, me at the other.

"Come along, children," he purred.

His request leached the surliness from us and spurred awkward chuckles that we struggled to tamp down. It proved difficult as he tugged us with him.

We passed through hallways, a gallery of stained glass art, and private rooms. No surprise, Poet knew which passages to cross without being seen by the night watch. Though, there were fewer sentinels in this wing of the palace.

At a compact walkway leading to a dead end, the jester paused. Promptly, the rest of us idled. We watched as Poet ran his palm along the smooth wall and spoke in low tones.

"They say, as people will say, that Spring is a curious thing, for it has much to say. Take a chance, a second glance. And according to lore, you might find a door."

He craned his head at us and grinned like a demon. *"And who knows what more."*

His hand flattened against the wall and pushed. This revealed a hidden seam in the facade, another one of the castle's many private conduits. The masked entrance swung inward, and down its shaft we went.

Because this channel lacked torches, we funneled into a black well, with Poet's voice shepherding the way. We clamped hands, making sure to keep a tight hold. Free of witnesses, something contagious took over and snipped the cord of tension. At the shaft's landing and then along a tunnel, we unleashed and raced into the channel.

Farther into the unknown, the group became louder. The ladies and Eliot howled into the burrows, and I laughed. As for Poet, he remained so quiet, I wondered which of us he was listening to, which person made the noise that caught his attention.

We mounted another staircase and burst aboveground at the hem of the labyrinth, a coiling hedge maze that scrolled across the expanse.

Its location aided us. Guards standing post along the parapets would not discover our clamor from this distance.

The first person to find the center would win a kiss of their choice. We scattered like nocturnal creatures, our speed kicking up gravel. I thought of Nicu, who would never be able to find his way out of here. I thought of Poet thinking of Nicu. I thought to rinse myself of history and tradition for this hour. I outran law, searching for *more*, for *different*.

For someday.

This day.

Constellations bit into the sky. I sprinted, my arms pumping and my skirt whisking around my legs. I thought, *Hurry*. Make haste to the center, to that little girl I used to be, that child who waited.

Hurry. Find me.

He found me. I found him.

We swerved around the corners of parallel hedges. Our gazes slammed into each other, winded and breathless and a little bit ruined. We'd emerged on opposite sides of the labyrinth's central water well.

Poet stared at me in a way that bordered on feral. His eyes glinted through the shadows, the shameless green darker than usual. That gaze pumped blood into my veins, so that I couldn't look away.

From other lanes, we heard the females' "Boo!" and Eliot's yelp. I pictured him jumping a foot off the ground, spoiling those ladies with hysterics. Audibly, they jostled him in what sounded like good-natured fun.

My winsome heart relished his laugh, the sound unclogging my lungs.

Some type of immoral intent crossed like a shadow through Poet's face. The visual sent an ambitious tremble down my spine. With cautious steps, we stalked around the well, which held thousands of fantasies—some innocent, some not.

We prowled and circuited the stones at a slow pace, waiting to see who would break first. It would be easy for me to volunteer. It would be easy to stop and wait for him, to allow this sinner to reach me, to let him hoist me onto the well, so that my legs spread around his waist and my skirt rucked to my hips. The prospect was so tempting, that it physically hurt.

Poet must have seen something cleave through my face, because he paused. From across the rim, he raised his brows in nefarious inquiry. It felt wrong to shake my head, but I did.

All the while, I gripped the ledge, to prevent myself from grabbing him. And all the while, his own fingers curled, nails digging into the stones until his veins rose.

"No kisses, no wishes," he rhymed soberly.

"No winners, no losers," I agreed in a whisper.

Posy trampled into the scene, pursued by Vale, then Eliot, then Cadence. Poet and I sacrificed our win and gave Posy the honors. At Vale's encouragement, Posy grabbed Eliot's face and fit her mouth to his. And after the shock drained from his face, my friend responded and met her lips with an enthusiasm that caused my jaw to drop.

As I watched, I felt a pair of eyes on me. They breached the distance like a physical touch, skimming over my profile until my flesh prickled.

Carefree but still devoted to males, Eliot relinquished Posy to Vale. The group tossed petals into the well, offering them in exchange for wishes.

"I'd fancy the luxury of growing old," Eliot said. "And to compose a single perfect song that would be shared across the continent."

"I want to know what snow feels like," Vale confided. "I'd love to run through a forest caked in it, see my own puffs of breath, and curl up with a warm drink afterward." Then she chortled at herself, compensating as though she was being too maudlin for a Spring native. "And I wouldn't mind having the ability to climax more than twice in succession."

"Poet?" Cadence volunteered. "Care to help my lady with her orgasm aspirations?"

The jester checked Eliot's reaction, confirming my friend's jovial mood before theatrically pretending to give the matter due thought. "By all means, if I were your friend's type," he replied smoothly. "Otherwise, your wish wouldn't be limited to a mere number. For with me, you'd lose count of how often you came, sweeting."

The ladies chuckled. Eliot shook his head in wry humor. Thankfully, their reception rang loudly enough to conceal the hitch in my breath, even as I feigned indifference to Poet's degree of experience. And that Cadence knew so much about it.

As for the female, she wanted to see Summer's ocean someday and find a lover with stamina there. "Ideally someone who prefers going down on me. And maybe ..." Cadence hesitated as everyone grew quiet, listening. "Maybe it would be nice if he enjoyed holding my hand, too." She shrugged flippantly. "I have standards. What about you, Posy?"

The female frowned into the well. "I want my pregnant sister to give birth to a normal child."

Silence descended on the group. She could have said healthy. But like everyone in society, the lady worried about the possibility of conceiving a born soul.

Every vertebra in my spine went rigid. My eyes ticked over to Poet, whose relaxed face didn't match the flash in his eyes.

"And you, sexy?" Cadence asked him. "Care to confess your deepest desire?"

I marveled that he was able to do it, to contain himself from debasing Posy. Myself, I bit my tongue so hard I expected it to bleed.

"Hmm. My deepest desire," Poet repeated in a suave tone that I didn't believe in the slightest. "Oh, but my wish is too sacred to share."

I knew that wish. I'd met that child.

I wanted to confront what the ladies thought of born souls and whether these courtiers stood with the majority. But not tonight. As Poet had said, such conflicts required tact and pacing. And as a future sovereign, I understood this.

That didn't make it any less difficult to keep quiet. Warily, I unwound my shoulders and let it go for now.

The group excused Poet for his evasiveness. However, the biased traitors ganged up on me when I tried to skip my turn, too. I peered into the well's pupil and issued a modest hope. "I wish for each of you to get what you want."

Eliot grinned. Posy and Vale seemed moved by my gesture. Predictably, Cadence pruned her lips, all but calling me a show-off.

Meanwhile, Poet's brows knitted. He watched me in dissatisfaction, possibly even suspicion, as if I'd given an unsavory answer.

We sat around the well, with our backs propped against the gritty stones and our legs fanning out. To my detriment and happiness, Poet and Eliot sat on either side of me. I kept them apart, as they boxed me in.

Their nearness uprooted multiple sensations. A stab of longing. A pang of remorse. I squirmed, unclear which male produced which reaction and willed myself not to lean in any partial direction.

Except Poet complicated the matter. Shrouded from view, his hand lingered by my knee, the proximity turning me into a star—a white-hot, pulsating flash.

I slid my leg nearer, bumping his wrist. His fingers spasmed in place. Indecision stilled him, or perhaps surprise.

Then his digits flexed and slid over me. The heat of his palm seared my skin to the point where I thought he might feel it, might feel everything turning molten inside me. All this upheaval from a simple touch. It ignited the rift between my legs, streaks bolting from his fingers to the private notch at my center.

Now that he'd made contact, Poet held onto my knee, caught me in his grip. His hold grew firm lest I should retreat—away from him, out of the labyrinth, or into the wild. Who knew where or how far I'd have to go to wedge enough distance between us.

After another moment, a single thumb stroked my flesh. It swayed back and forth in a languid, titillating caress.

Sensual intoxication liberated my tongue. "Why are we different? What makes us that way?"

"The Seasons," Posy volunteered.

"Our ranks," Vale added.

"Obviously, that's not what Her Highness meant," Cadence said, surprising me.

"She meant beyond those things," Eliot supplied. "Titles and bloodlines, Seasons and breeding didn't stop us from coming here. Not that those things disappeared in this labyrinth, but she's talking about the rest of it—engaging with each other, confessing our desires, sitting here without regret. Not yet, at least. The night isn't over, but that it started in the first place proves we've underestimated ourselves. That's what she means."

As my limbs relaxed, Poet's hand drew higher. It burned a path from my knee to my upper thigh—lightly, slowly, intently. My exhalations hitched, as if caught in a hook. The world narrowed to that place where his fingers glided, pushing up my skirt until it rumpled around the gulf of my legs.

Cool air stole under the cashmere dress and rushed against my open thighs. My throat bobbed. The disarray of my clothing could be seen in daylight, but in the dark I sat unveiled without anyone realizing it, like a secret hidden in plain sight.

Simultaneously, I wanted to clench my thighs shut and spread them wide. I nudged my limb closer, giving him better access as my breathing tapered. I might have detected Poet's own outtakes accelerate.

He spoke with nonchalance, even while his tone deepened. "I've heard the word *different* tossed around too many times to make it count. 'Tis bullshit, sweetings. You need to define *different* further. Tastes, manners, looks, smarts. I'll play the devil's advocate."

"Naturally," Eliot remarked.

"Can you blame him?" Posy joked. "He does it so well."

"We're different for endless reasons and the same for just as many," Poet continued. "Therein lies the incandescence. There's the true harmony."

"Because there's more to discover," I summarized, trying to keep my voice steady.

"More to savor," Eliot finished.

I flopped my head toward him. Eliot rested his brow against mine and smiled, unaware of the boundaries I straddled. His touch and the jester's touch were obscured from one another.

I grinned back, grateful for them both, giving myself equally to them, if only in this spot.

Poet bunched the fabric of my dress in his fist, crushing the cashmere in his grip. I couldn't tell if he was stopping himself, tormenting us both, or waiting for me to decide.

Either way, deprivation and temptation clashed.

At last, he released the skirt and sketch his palm over my inner thigh. His index finger brushed the skin from side to side, the pattern melting my core like wax.

Then he sank further in. Approaching the crook where my leg abutted the seam of my body, he grazed a single fingernail over the sensitive flesh.

Oh, my Seasons.

My mouth parted, though no sound came out, because I couldn't let it. Yet that didn't matter. Everything loud occurred within me as Poet's hand scorched my flesh.

While everyone rambled, their words blurred, fraying at the edges. The jester's hand rose higher, higher still to the heat emanating from the fabric under my skirt. He stalled mere inches from my undergarments, where the slit would give him access to me.

To my wetness.

As though aware of the temperature rising from there, those dexterous fingers pinched the material and skated across the lace trim, rowing back and forth. My head rolled from Eliot's and craned toward the dark abyss sprawled above. My hips begged to move, to squirm, to do *something*. I dug my fingers into the ground, my knuckles bending.

Too many frustrating desires thrashed inside me at once. I shifted my backside, unsure whether my hips wanted to nudge away or shove themselves closer to him.

Poet paused near the slot cutting through the intimate fabric.

His fingers idled like a torment, so close to the liquid slickening in my crease.

He could spread the textile like a curtain. He could slip those fingers inside me right here, right now. He could do to me what I'd done to myself while thinking about him. He could fill the root of my body so smoothly, so easily.

The possibility of him whipping his finger in and out of me, with everyone none the wiser, was so tangible I felt its penetration. I milled my backside into the floor, which prompted his hand nearer. Purposefully, Poet circled his finger around the slit, outlining its shape, tracing the oval as if it were my core. He did this repeatedly, then switched direction, on the brink of slipping through the panel.

My teeth fanged into my lower lip, trapping a painful moan inside. I gushed between my thighs, so evident his tracing finger could discern the wetness. The point of his digit rolled over the damp edge, as if attempting to coat itself in me.

My eyes tipped to the back of my head. That shackled moan pushed against the roof of my mouth.

The conversation ceased. The absence of voices hit me like a splash of frigid water.

Movements broke us from the trance, snapping the moment in half. As everyone shuffled to get up, Poet withdrew his hand from the juncture of my thighs and dragged the skirt down my limbs slowly, as though he was moving through tar.

My lungs emptied, yet my body continued to ache. Fortunately, a cool breeze buffeted my face.

Disappointment and relief flowed together, until it was impossible to tell the reactions apart. Nonetheless, my joints unlocked, allowing new impulses to spring free.

We helped one another to our feet. Eliot strummed a melody on his lute while Vale and Posy flanked him, the sultry trio swaying in tandem. Cadence urged me into the maelstrom by yanking on my wrist, then let me go and joined Poet.

More to discover. More to savor.

The moon's reflection bathed my skin. I raised my arms and spun. I didn't care if I tripped. Because if I did fall, I would simply pick myself up.

Poet and I kept apart. But from the place where he twirled Cadence, he watched my ungainly movements. Fascination gripped his face as he stared at me, through me, into me.

Hyperaware of my body, I whirled faster, my breasts and hips out of reach and but visible to his dark gaze. Under the wild sky, I threw back my head, my skirt pinwheeling.

That I was fully clothed didn't matter. The jester had an imagination.

That same imagination had nearly led his fingers inside me, and at my invitation. Public discretion be damned. If he had succeeded in breaching that silken place, I couldn't say if I would have changed my mind and stopped him.

23

Poet

 any things happened to us that night.
Many things I never saw coming ...

She spun, losing herself in the haze and this maze. I took her in, mesmerized and memorizing. At the stroke of dawn, Briar would change and cast herself into the role of an expensive Royal, pissing me off with her reserve.

So be it. We had our parts to play.

Many found her wanting for looks. She had no admirers outside of crown chasers. In short, the people were ignorant. I wanted to pull this female from the roots, expose her for the goddess, warrior, and ruler she truly was.

When the princess didn't restrain herself, she still moved with a clunky lack of rhythm, but her awful coordination hardly mattered. For the dancing made her happy, and that happiness made her the brightest fucking thing in this garden.

Enthralling woman.

Hypnotized jester.

Me, the renowned trickster who terrified and seduced everyone. Me, who got hypnotized by no one.

Wicked hell. One more twist of her hips, and I'd be scooping my tongue off the floor. To say nothing of how my cock would react, for the cursed appendage couldn't be trusted in Briar's presence. Really, Cadence should have counted herself lucky I didn't veer her into one of the hedges, so thoroughly did that Royal of Autumn enthrall me.

Eliot's playing tripped as his head swung from me to her. It happened merely for a single note, but shit. I needed to be more careful. Enduring his crestfallen face as I'd made my feelings clear had been an awkward torment for us both. Having my attention linger on others would reopen the wound.

Yet. Still. Her.

Damn her. Now she had me thinking in fragments instead of prose. I drew the line there. My voice would not be tampered with. She'd already compromised the infamous regions below my waist by encouraging me to fondle the filmy, wet trimmings under the dress.

Fuck almighty. Such a pleasant surprise, this princess. Briar's limbs had yielded open like the pages of a spicy novel, her flesh had sweltered under my touch, and her thighs had fallen wider. That divine reality had driven me to the brink.

My hand had continued to move like a troublemaker, inevitable where she was concerned. My touch had ascended that lovely thigh toward the pleat between them. And there, an enthralling heat had pumped from under the skirt, from inside the slot of her rather short drawers, which barely covered her ass. I'd almost swallowed my tongue, to say nothing of the damage this did to my cock.

The precious fabric concealing her pussy had been soft, thin, rippable. My fingers had all but itched to slip through the gap, to dip into the slickness hiding there, to fill her cunt to my knuckles. I still tingled with the urge to fit them inside her. It had been agony, wanting to pump between the walls of her pussy, to see how resilient her moans were, to feel her squeezing me. She would have had to work diligently, fighting to be quiet whilst coming hard around my fingers.

I would have done her moans justice, were it not for our companions. How I had wanted to throw them out of the labyrinth at that moment.

After dancing, the ladies begged me for an exclusive diversion. Scarcely recovering from the princess, I stumbled through a lukewarm string of verse, in which I projected them as characters, to their whooping delight.

Flushed from the moonlit cast and a healthy dose of rebellion, Her Highness clapped for me. As I bowed, I slanted my head and thanked her with a fiendish grin. Oh, but I loved what that did to her applause, how my attention and unspoken thoughts snagged on her wrists like a rope, causing her hands to falter.

The route to the castle proved tamer, the end of an era as we traveled a path back to ranks and precedents. We filtered through the tunnel and mounted the stairway. Vale and Posy whispered sweet nothings to each other, Eliot conversed with the princess whilst maintaining a formal front, and Cadence suctioned herself to my side.

"The evening is young," she cooed. "And so are we."

"Are we, now?" I inquired but added nothing more.

I'd been in her room before. She hoped for an encore.

The princess's bated breath rustled from behind. She had overheard Cadence proposition me.

True, I needed to work off the tension—or for someone to release the tension with a few substantial tugs or a mouthful. Indeed, I might have accepted the lady's offer of a tongue lashing. It would have sent a lucid message to Autumn, reminding her of our agreement.

I might have if Eliot weren't there.

And if there was another reason I intended to decline Cadence's offer, I'd rather not dwell on it. And if that reason had to do with a certain redhead to whom no one could compare, who I couldn't evict from my head, and whose skin I craved like a drug, I certainly wasn't in the mood to analyze it.

Thereupon, I prepared an excuse about needing my beauty sleep, but the guards newly stationed outside the hidden shaft spared me the chore. My hand gripped the wall as their voices drifted through the crack. I held my free palm behind me to the halt the group, who clammed up, freezing like deer caught in the scope of a crossbow. By angling my head and listening to the guards' banter, I estimated them to be around the corner.

An eclectic band led by the Court Jester wouldn't usually ruffle feathers—if it weren't for two things. One, only certain areas of this fortress were open for all-nighters, most of which didn't include the gardens. Two, a certain member of this group wore a crown.

I didn't have to turn to know Briar's eyes bulged from their sockets. Ladies-in-waiting were acceptable company but not the minstrel, and especially not the Court Jester. It would seem more suspect now that she'd spent four nights and three days—ample time to get acquainted—in the woods with me. That meant Basil and Fatima would submit us to a tedious interrogation, which would drag on for at least an hour. Thereafter, Briar's pristine reputation would walk a tightrope.

A fool's work was never done. I hand-signaled to my companions. I would distract the watch whilst they crept back to their chambers.

I sauntered into the hall, my appearance startling the night watch, which included a woman and the same guard who'd summoned me the morning after I first met Briar. The pair jolted around, clasping the hilts of their swords.

"Evening, sweetings," I charmed, gesturing to their armor. "You didn't have to get dressed up for me."

It worked. With a bit of subtle pleasantries, I got them to turn their backs on my companions, who spilled out from behind the panel. One by one, the small group detached themselves from the black slash of shadow and skulked down the corridor.

My Autumn Princess was the last to go.

I bade the guards a productive alpha-worthy night and left. The route to her suite necessitated using one of two passages from the artist wing, which meant she had to pass my chambers no matter which one she chose. This made little difference to me until I heard the guards from their post.

"Wait. Who the hell was that?"

"That was Poet, you idiot. We just spoke with—"

"Not him. That other one."

Fuck. I caught up to the Royal, stole her hand, dragged her to my door, wrenched it ajar, and wheeled her inside.

Actually, I may have twirled her under my arm when I did it.

Briar yanked her hand from mine. "What's the meaning of this?"

I bolted the latch. "Hush."

"Don't *hush* me—"

"Briar," I hissed. "Shut. Up."

Either they suspected an intruder or someone pursuing me, or they merely needed to go through the motions of checking. They hadn't recognized Briar. However, if they found her, they'd want to know what she was doing in this wing alone.

Or not alone. Patrol guards could be entirely and ironically useless outside of invasions and assassins. But only during the quieter and smaller moments did they overlook roaming shadows.

And come, the night watch weren't negligent. It would seem too much of a coincidence to find Briar shortly after they'd spoken with me. Either that, or I was being paranoid.

By now, the fire in my grate had gone cold. Only moonlight from the window bled through, indigo puddling across the rug.

Boots pounded toward my door. The princess paled, color draining from her face. On second thought, of all the places to get caught, in my debauched abode might be the worst.

So be it. I never said I was right all the time.

I snatched Briar's fingers, hauled her across the room, and climbed onto my bed, where I started to bounce. Not my finest hour, but I'd been left with little choice.

I curled my palms at her. "Don't squint at me. Jump."

Briar balked. "You've lost your sense."

"I'll lose my valuable testes, and you'll lose your virtuous prestige, if they find you here. Now jump and moan."

"I beg your pardon?"

Clearing my throat, I demonstrated. A stream of lusty groans projected from my throat, in tempo with the headboard rapping against the wall, both loud enough for the guards to hear.

They paused outside my chambers and gave a tentative knock.

I mouthed to Her Highness, repeating my instructions. After a moment's hesitation, she did as I'd asked, bobbing feebly on the mattress. Unfortunately, she cawed like a frustrated crow instead of replicating a female in the throes of a climax.

Another knock. "Be gone," I called.

"Poet?" the male stuttered.

I couldn't have sprinted from our chat and directly into the arms of a paramour that quickly, much less shoved my pants down far enough to get the job done. Ultimately, I trusted they wouldn't calculate those details. The point was they believed I had company, likely with the person they'd noticed, likely a courtier on a mission to get fucked by the Court Jester. They wouldn't ask me to admit them if it meant threatening an impending orgasm.

Aye. Indeed, I could have answered whilst the princess kept out of sight. This charade could be overly theatrical on my part.

"We're searching the hall for a possible lurker who might have come this way," the male guard said. "Did you happen to see anything untoward?"

The bed springs squealed. I jerked my arms, instructing the princess to amplify herself.

Briar purpled but bounced harder and yelped as though I'd fatally stabbed her.

Defeated, I dropped my head into my hands—and bounded so high, the top of my skull smacked against the fucking ceiling.

Her yelps dissolved into laughter. Slapping her palms over her mouth, Briar convulsed into hysterics, tears springing to her eyes at my expense. The scene became so comically atrocious that I burst into quiet chuckles with her.

Ironically, Briar improved. She guffawed and moaned in unison. Sensibly, she altered her voice.

"Well, keep your door locked. And let us know if you hear anything suspicious."

"Ayyyye!" I howled.

They marched away, sniggering. We waited a full minute before collapsing onto the bed, keeling over and choking with laughter.

"You're a terrible actress—"

"You're a d-dreadful lover—"

Petulant, I pointed to my head. "Look what you did. I'm going to have a bump."

"Serves you right. You should have s-seen your f-face."

Exhausted, Briar flopped onto the pillows. I landed next to her and rubbed my scalp. Our chuckles ebbed, then faded. Realization crossed Briar's face as it became clear. We were in my chambers, on my bed, fun-drunk, and masked in darkness.

As we gazed at the ceiling, Briar bit her lower lip. I saw it in my periphery, witnessed her incisors sinking in.

Her fingers stole out to drag against my knuckles. 'Twas a straight shot of adrenaline to my cock, along with another organ pounding in my chest.

Not long ago, I was the one who had targeted her. Before that, I'd always been the one to seduce, to claim whatever conquest suited my fancy. I was the merciless jester whose tongue everyone feared, envied, and coveted.

But none had ever dominated me the way she had.

Neither of us pulled away. Absently, intentionally, we let those caresses slide through the precarious cracks. Her pinky rode my knuckles. My thumb stroked her wrist. We threaded, in and out, over and under.

When Briar found my stack of bracelets, the hairs along my arms sprang to life, not to mention a certain agitator between my hipbones, which went rogue and twitched in response.

Originally, my ribbon had been a marker for her ridicule. Tonight,

I imagined using it in other ways—dragging the strip across her lips and down her body, sweeping it over her pretty nipples, brushing it between her thighs, and tightening it around both wrists, among other techniques.

"Life is not purely rational," she whispered.

"Nor purely amusing," I replied. "That's hardly an epiphany for us."

"But we needed reminding."

"At the well, you would have wished for something greedy if you'd been alone."

"And you would have revealed your wish. And you would have said yes to Cadence if Eliot hadn't been there."

"Debatable. She doesn't hold a candle to you, although I can have her."

"You trifle with me. You can have anyone. And she's beautiful."

"She's typical," I corrected. "You're a thorn in my side. Also, you're loyal, courageous, and compassionate. What's more, brunettes are the soil, blondes the sun. You're a redhead—every fiery, inflaming thing in between. You're sheer magnificence."

My sidelong glance met her furrowed brows. "What's that look for?"

Briar shook her head, confounded. "Why do you share yourself when you've learned what can happen?"

Irritated, I dropped her hand and narrowed my eyes. "Likewise, you're unable to take a compliment."

"Calling me a thorn in your side was a compliment?"

"I meant it affectionately. Indeed, a careless shag rewarded me with a son, yet I still satisfy my needs like it can't happen again. You think casual sex makes me a whore."

"I never said that," Briar argued.

"You didn't have to, sweeting. You believe chastity makes you more honorable than any native of Spring. I've seen how you judge the courtiers. I saw how you scowled at Cadence. And I've seen that look plenty of times when your eyes are on me in a crowded room. You're so eager to slut-shame people for yearnings you have no experience with, for indulging in the basics of human nature, which you would call voracious and trivial. Except what else did you once tell me? That our kiss was meaningless?"

The princess was off the bed and on her feet before I could prevent it. "I'm not talking about other people," she protested from the mattress's edge. "I'm talking about you. I'm saying you should stop doing what you do with people."

I swung my limbs over the opposite side, then stood and sauntered toward her across the dais. "And what is that exactly, sweeting?" I drew out, murmuring low. "Tell me."

"I do not mean to imply there's anything wrong with having relations."

"Oh? Why the change of heart?"

"I'm merely suggesting discretion and safety." Briar stood her ground. "You're a father. And you're worth more than a series of half-hearted affairs."

"Very wise, Your Highness. I should be setting my sights higher. Mayhap the King of Summer will drop dead from stupidity, and I'll have a chance to replace him. His wife is gorgeous and rumored to enjoy certain vagaries."

Briar strode away whilst tossing over her shoulder, "Fine. That was invasive of me. I-I don't know why I'm here."

I faltered. I'd hurt her.

She got halfway across the room, but I was faster. I broke from my stance and slid in front of her to block the exit. Briar's feet skidded in place, a whittled intake slipping from her mouth as I moved in, breaching every slice of space that remained.

In the shadows, I stared down at her. Shafts of midnight traced her freckles and accentuated the rise and fall of her chest. Despite the darkness, her hair burned through the murk, hot red with filaments of gold.

If I hadn't been so riled up, I would have seen it. Briar hadn't been criticizing me for enjoying sex. She'd been worried for me.

"Court is a lonely place, sweeting," I confided. "I've engaged myself with others, mostly men. They're safer. As for the rest, I'm cautious and creative. Bodies—hands and tongues and props—can work around the obvious, achieving heights whilst still partially dressed. There are plenty of ways to know pleasure without it amounting to fucking. And there's rapture in restraint."

"Does that include Cadence?" Briar demanded, the name kindling on her tongue, a flammable thing.

My tone gentled. "It happened, but it didn't go as far as you expect. My fingers were the culprits, not my cock. We've never shared anything more."

"Not even to use one of the objects in your wardrobe?"

Although I had already drawn the conclusion, until now Briar had never verified what she'd seen whilst sneaking into my chambers. If I were with anyone else, my lips would have uttered a coltish reply. But with her, I had never felt more serious.

"You mean like the ones in the pleasure vault?" I inquired.

Contrite mortification flittered across her features. I knew she had been there with the ladies. Posy tried to conceal this fact, but Cadence's remark outside my door had been impossible to misinterpret.

"It wasn't my idea," she defended, as if her actions even need defending.

"Yet you stayed," I presumed.

"I didn't want to offend them."

"Did you feel compelled to explore, the way you did in my closet?"

She made no reply, and she didn't need to. More than in the vault, the thought of Briar's eyes perusing the items in my wardrobe turned my blood into a vortex.

"To answer your original question, nay," I husked. "I'm less casual about pleasure trinkets."

"Why do you need to use anything?"

"Because it's sensuous." My voice unfurled. "Because it feels good."

She didn't seem repulsed, only confused, frustrated as if she couldn't fathom why such items would be necessary. Days ago, she might have viewed them as tawdry. Now she only appeared baffled by their functionality.

And yet. She licked her lips, a sprinkle of curiosity dashing across her face before she endeavored to conceal it.

The crinkle in her chin relaxed only marginally. "And who else?"

"You want me to recite a list?" I asked. "That will take a while."

"Surrounded by the court, I cannot tell which of your admirers has shared intimacies with you. They all look at you the same way."

I stepped nearer. "There's only one person at this court I want looking at me, Briar. There's only one stare that matters. There's only one I care about."

Her exhalations quickened. "I refuse to be a conquest. You've had scores of visitors here."

"They have their own chambers to welcome me. That's not to say I've bedded anyone since our return, because I haven't. Believe this: I've tried to accept sexual advances of late, to find someone tempting, yet I've failed pathetically. You saw me with a man, but my note made it clear I didn't take up his offer for an exchange of oral pleasantries. Why, you wonder? That's easy. For the life of me, I can't stop thinking about you."

Briar's throat worked like a pump. My eyes tracked the contortion before trailing back to her face. "I've never had anyone else in this room."

Stunned, she reexamined the space, her eyes tripping across every furnishing. Every pot of color, every textile. Flamboyance be damned, I coveted my privacy. Having this woman here peeled another layer from me. For devil's sake, I shuffled my feet like an antsy juvenile.

I begged like one, too.

"Stay," I said, the word raw on my tongue.

Briar shook her head and pleaded, "Why are you doing this?"

"Because I lack the strength not to."

"Poet—"

"I see you. I see your resilience and strength of will. I see your determination and tenacity. I see your desire for control and your longing to dance. I see your integrity and daring, even when every other fool in a packed room fails to. I see it all, and I want it all, for you've bewitched me out of my wicked fucking mind."

"Poet," she implored. "You mustn't."

"What would have happened in the labyrinth if we had been alone?"

The memory surfaced like steam. Her legs opening, inviting me in. My hands inches from her, stroking the slit of her drawers. That dear pussy so close to the tips of my fingers.

Answering my question wasn't necessary. I already knew.

"You broke my rules," I said. "Now you're in my head like a verse and a curse. You're a plague and a fantasy. You're there when I'm tossing and turning in bed, twisting the sheets into a heated mess. It's you who I picture moaning beneath me, above me, in front of me. I've pumped my cock to those desires, and I'll keep doing so until long after you leave this place. I won't stop until you've drained me dry." The humid words rose from my mouth. "I won't stop until I'm so lost in your memory, your hand will tingle whilst I come."

A strangled noise squeezed from Briar's lips.

"You're the one targeting me now," I confessed. "You're every bitter and euphoric feeling I have. You're in every word I speak, every move I make. All of it is you. Whatever happens from now on, you will be my ecstasy and my downfall.

"And that face of yours. How I'd like to twist it in a thousand ways, in the ink of this room. My body wants to tear your body apart, to make you sing and sigh, to fill you with incoherent noises." On a sweetly erotic impulse, I took her hand and kissed the inside of her palm. "Say you want that, as much as I want to give it to you. Either that—" I lifted my head, leaned in, and husked against her trembling mouth, "—or stop me."

Briar shut her eyes. "This is wrong."

Because of my son, her minstrel, and the monarchs who reigned over this land. Most of all, every decision I made placed Nicu at the forefront. The more I shared with this Royal, the more she would know about him.

But she already knew the crucial parts. She was steadfast and didn't look at my son the way others would. She cared about him, committed treason for him with her silence. What we did here wouldn't change that.

And whilst this may be wrong, when has that ever stopped me?

We weren't in a forest anymore, where provocative temptations filled its recesses. Even there, with our mouths and bodies going wild in the dirt, the feelings had been stoked long before that.

As for the rest, alas. I didn't give a shit.

I moved nearer, fusing us together, my pulse on hers. "Dance with me."

Her gaze clung to mine, anchoring there. "We already did."

"Nay, sweeting. We haven't."

Not the way I intended.

She kept still, trembling as if on a precipice, expecting to be caught. And oh, but I would catch her. This woman didn't know the half of it.

We waited until the other was ready to move, and move we did. Our arms and hands reached with prolonged urgency, the backs of my knuckles gliding down her arms and landing on her hips, where I clutched Briar—and yanked her into me.

She gasped, mouth ajar. Her eyelids hooded, the pupils flashing as our groins met, the heat between her legs brimming against my cock.

Briar clamped onto my forearms as I guided her waist, swaying it from side to side in a languid tempo, as if a stringed instrument strained through the room. With serpentine motions, I jutted us together, our foreheads bent and brushing.

At length, her fingers relaxed and scaled my biceps. I rolled us into a single form, rotating our pelvises into a gentle grind. A mesmerizing flush unfurled across her lips, yet her figure went shamelessly slack, molding with mine.

With each lazy beat of my waist, she followed. No sequence of steps. No structure. Only instinct and reflexes as my fingers descended to her ass, cupping the swells.

A small whimper eased from her mouth, as thin as a tendril. And I swore, it took everything in me not to drive my lips against hers and claim that sound.

I prowled after her in a different way. Twisting her hips, I whirled Briar around, her back sliding against my ribs, her spine aligning with my torso. As I did this, my quick fingers unhooked her cloak in one seamless gesture that blended with the dance.

The mantle spilled to the floor. Like this, I captured her middle and pinned her to my front whilst continuing the sinuous movements.

Briar's profile turned, as if yearning to glimpse me over her shoulder. Yet her eyes didn't make it that far, straying instead to ground. Her skin hummed beneath my touch, and her fingers moved of their own volition, reaching behind on instinct to clutch my nape.

I snaked my fingers over her navel and whisked us into a leisurely, sultry tempo. Her head lolled on my shoulder as I tilted my jaw and nipped her earlobe.

My sweet thorn shivered. The noise was like a spike of adrenaline, inciting a hot spike below my waist.

The dance intensified, as though rising in temperature. We held tighter, our movements growing more exaggerated, each of us tugging on the other.

I spun her toward me again, and before we'd finished the full rotation, her hands drew the sheer shirt from the waistband of my pants. But before she could peel it over my head, I prolonged the frustration. Looping one arm around Briar's lower back, I gave her no warning, dipping her into an arc.

Briar's intakes hitched. Yet she stretched into it, trusting me as I unspooled her backward, my free digits plucking the upper clasps of her bodice open. The fabric eased halfway down her stomach, a riot of freckles and her embroidered breastband peeking from the neckline, the tops of those precious tits pushing upward.

I could drag the undergarment lower, strap my mouth around a pert, rough nipple, and listen to a moan crack from her lips. The thought watered my tongue. By the time we were finished with each other, I would do that and more.

But not yet. This jester would draw out the pleasure until it devastated her.

Summoning my willpower, I reeled Briar upright. Along the way, my mouth skated up the vent of her bodice, between those vicious breasts and to her neck, where I sucked the skin between my teeth. She whined, the fluted sound rippling into the air.

My low growl muffled into her throat. In a slick maneuver as she careened upright, I grabbed the backs of her thighs and hoisted her off the ground. The skirt flared over her knees, and her legs twined around my hips, ankles linking above my ass.

I swerved us toward the nearest wall. Her back hit the facade, my waist pinning her as we panted and coiled into movement, fluctuating against the wood paneling, swiveling heavily against it. One capped sleeve flopped down her shoulder. Her breasts swept across my chest, the thin breastband grazing my transparent shirt and creating anarchy against my flesh.

I traced my lips along her jaw. She bowed into me.

As if part of the dance, her hands snatched the hem of my shirt and lifted. Except I caught Briar's wrists and nailed her arms above her head. We undulated into the wall, churning whilst I gripped her.

That heady gaze sparked, my denial enticing and irritating the princess.

Good. Very good.

To atone for that, my fingers opened, eventually releasing her wrists. Every time Briar attempted to pare the shirt from me, I twirled and switched our positions. Me, against the wall. Then her again. Then me once more. It became a game, a tease. And eventually, her mouth quirked into a faint grin, which I mirrored with a smirk.

That's it, Princess. Work for this. Savor it.

How I love the way you dance.

I rolled Briar into the paneling one final time. Her drooping sleeve plunged lower to reveal more of her freckled cleavage and stomach. Heat radiated between her spread thighs, which flanked my waist like a sexy torture device, the warmth of her cunt abrading my upright cock.

We ebbed to a halt. Our mouths skated together, breathing hectically.

Unlike the mayhem of our first kiss, this one took its melting time. Her palms fastened at my nape, my arm banded around her waist, and my free hand climbed up the back of her head to lock her in place.

I tilted my head, braced my mouth against hers, and feasted on the rickety air gusting from her. My lips slid with Briar's, each electrified caress saying *this* and *there* and *now*, because *I can't stand this anymore* and *I won't anymore*.

I sketched her and grunted as she sketched me back, this barely-kiss igniting every frenzied impulse. It took an immortal amount of restraint not to crush her to me and seize that righteous mouth. But how I loved the bow of her lower lip quivering when my tongue rushed across its width.

It kept going like this, a flick along the down of her lips, my teeth coming out to play. She responded like a virgin and a ruler, a combination of innocence and domination. Seasons help me, I felt like the one being seduced. Briar followed me without hesitation, curling herself into my body whilst I hummed from the deep well of my throat.

We broke apart, changed the angles of our heads, and locked eyes. Then we surged into each other.

Ravenous, I groaned and sank my lips into hers. Briar whimpered, her mouth sealing with mine, splaying beneath me. My tongue pierced her lips apart and stroked into a wet envelope of heat.

Our lips slanted and clutched, opening and rowing together. My rhythmic tongue flexed between the seam and rocked against hers. I swatted into that hot channel, flicking against the flat of her own tongue.

As I licked into Briar, she sighed and gave in return, lapping against me. The divine taste of her drizzled across my palate.

My free palm dashed down her back to span her ass, grasping those ovals as I took her mouth. The kiss mounted to the point of aggravation. It didn't feel gratifying, the sort of liplocks of interludes past, the congratulatory conceit of a fine performance. Nay, I didn't reap the carnal rewards of an admirer.

It was more. This woman's kiss and bliss.

I ran my tongue along the roof of Briar's mouth. Her moan shattered between my open lips and chipped my soul to pieces.

Aye, there was that. That, and beyond.

It could be rebellion, the dumb rush of the forbidden, except for the hitch in my chest and the pained grooves across my forehead. For this desire felt honest and difficult, this privilege temporary. It stripped away what I'd previously known of seduction.

This was me, the jester. This was me, wanting her.

This was *wanting*.

I ripped my mouth from Briar's and broke from the wall. With my lips raging against hers, I stalked us to the fireplace, where a thick rug reclined in front of the grate.

Hunkering to the ground, I unfurled her across the rug before the mouth of the unlit hearth. As she crawled backward, I crawled forward, our movements in sync, our gazes latched. When I ran my palm up her shoulder and urged it toward the floor, she reclined beneath me.

In the darkness, she sprawled there. The skirt lay rumpled around her legs, and her bodice was spread open to the navel, exhibiting a pair of nipples poking through the breastband. Her complexion suffused with a deliciously ruddy tint.

I was done for.

Hefting myself onto my knees, I reached back and peeled the shirt from my head. The material slumped around one wrist. She grasped the damn thing and launched it to the side, then tracked her gaze across my hands, forearms, and bare abs.

Shallow pants siphoned from her lungs. Those eyes slid over my pecs and finally leveled with mine—willing, waiting.

I slithered over Briar. Half of my weight suspended above her, and my knees bent between her parted ones. Poised above her, I draped my index finger atop her neck and then stroked the tip over the valley in her split bodice.

Briar released a thin cord of breath, the remnants of our kiss a streak of condensation across her lips. I raked over the sight of this princess. Her jaw slackened, and the braided crown of her hair strained to be set free.

I leaned down and seethed against her mouth. "May I touch you, Princess?"

24

Briar

Yes. Touch me.

Here. Now. Please.

My delirious body said this. Not my head—that had stopped working long ago.

Poet's request fermented, the words hot and heavy as his mouth grazed mine. Slowly, I nodded, the motion scraping my lips against his.

He inched back. Those green eyes flashed like scythes, his weight a hovering shadow.

Unsteady exhalations leaked into the air. My pulse beat out a hysterical rhythm, the ripple effect coursing through my limbs. I inhaled the scents of amber and vetiver. Every sensation magnified, from the slick warmth between my legs, to the rug caressing my nape, to the blistering intensity of his stare.

The Court Jester had me splayed under him.

In his chamber. In the dark.

The broad span of him radiated heat as my thighs flanked his waist, my legs pitching on either side. I'd never experienced such prohibited bliss, such illicit anticipation. I felt the entirety of this moment in the crux of my body. With him braced above, a forbidden thrill spiked through me.

Quickly, he twisted toward the grate, snatched a few logs and kindling from the neighboring rack, and threw them into the mouth of the fireplace. With fluid movements, he drove flint against steel. Flames scorched to life and ricocheted across the timbers, blasting the giant well with restless light.

With the blaze smoldering, Poet turned back to me. Amber pulsated across the floor. It laminated the grid of his torso, the dark pants that hung low, and the bronze crescent and black flecks painting the corner of his right eye.

Impatience must have wormed its way across my face, because the jester chuckled and snaked down to me again. As he did, one sly palm slid up my calf, taking the skirt with it. I spread myself wider and rested my hand over his, both of us gliding the material higher until it bunched around my upper thighs.

Still amused, he planted a sweltering kiss on my lips while fisting my skirt. Not wanting to miss the feel of his mirth, I sloped my fingers over his smooth abdomen, charting the heady vibrations.

My touch cut his humor short. Emboldened by this, I flicked out my tongue, licking the tip of his snaggletooth.

Victory. Poet hissed. The sound came out feral, as though he'd felt the sensation much lower.

His pupils inflated, eclipsing the irises. The ribbons encircling his wrist shone in the firelight as the pad of his thumb dragged across my lower lip, his touch searing a path along my skin. "How I'd love taste your pussy and fuck you tenderly."

My navel fluttered. Only he could make such words echo like rustling silk. His wish pounded into my folds, dampening the cleft.

I wanted him. I wanted him to take me. I wanted that long, hard part of him inside me, so deep that I would feel every forbidden inch.

Yet a strange hesitancy crept through my mind. It clashed with everything that was happening.

The jester saw that. In the next moment, his aim became clearer. "Nay, I won't tonight," he prefaced. "Instead, I'm going to toy with you, make you feel good in another way. May I?"

I licked my lips. "I demand an equal share."

"By all means, Highness. Though, I'll stop when you tell me to. You only need to say the word."

"I thought I was your target."

Poet leaned down and scraped his incisors along my ear. "You still are." Then his mouth blew into the shell. "Every. Single. Part."

I shivered and strapped my hands around the dip in his back. But Poet shook his head.

"That won't do, sweeting," he murmured, then guided my hands to his buttocks. They were tight and sculpted, with indentations in the sides. As they flexed under my palms, heat eddied through my walls.

"Hold on," he crooned.

A nervous chortle tripped off my tongue. How effortlessly he made me quiver with need, then laugh without fear. It drained my lingering shyness, so that we stopped talking, ceased thinking, because thoughts could be destructive.

Some type of feverish intent incinerated his gaze. He hunched over and claimed my lips, roping them into another sensual kiss, and then another, and another. Each one was swift and scalding, a series of taunts that drew whines from me. Over and over, his mouth stroked mine, teasing mercilessly.

Not enough. Every time the jester's conniving lips made contact, I wanted them deeper and for longer. And I wanted them everywhere.

My steepled knees tried to trap him, to clamp him to me. But the jester held himself aloft, as though baiting me to break my own barriers, to tear free of invisible bonds.

It stoked the flames. With a frustrated grunt, I gripped his buttocks harder, the action an entreaty for more.

A shudder tracked down his body. That's when I felt the firm ridge stretching between us. His cock thickened, straining in the tight wedge of space between my core and his hips. It rose high, like

274

it had in the meadow and as we'd been dancing.

I felt every inch of his erection, from the solid base to the rounded head. He'd been like this for a while, I realized.

Encouraged, I used one of his moves against him. I licked the pleat of his mouth, my tongue swiping across the fine slit and tasting something tangy.

With a throaty hum, he dove in. His chiseled body covered me, and his inflamed mouth crushed to mine, sucking the air from my lungs.

On a gasp, I yielded my lips under his. We seized each other's faces, angling the kiss to deeper effect, our tongues flaying one another.

I should be flustered by the broad length straining between us. Instead, my head fogged, and my inner flesh ached. As with our first kiss, I shocked myself by arching into his cock, grinding into the shape and tension of it.

Poet growled. His tongue pitched into my mouth, the motion punctuated with a nudge of his waist, knowing what I yearned for and offering a sample. In that very spot, static bolts lanced through me. Seasons, it felt so good.

Everything below my navel dissolved. I melted, my folds soaking the undergarments beneath my skirt. Yet I didn't care.

More. Please, more.

I told him this with my legs, which gripped his hips. I told him this with my lips, which fused with his.

And he listened. Without pause, Poet descended along my throat, his lips grazing the column. He nuzzled the crook between my neck and shoulder, then sucked deeply. The destructive effect charged between my thighs, so that I felt the tempo of his mouth there, too.

I whimpered. My nails clawed through his hair, which only made him pull on my skin more, more, more.

Humming, Poet snatched my wrists and stamped them to the rug while continuing his onslaught. He alternated between suckling and tracing his tongue along my throat, swiping between my clavicles and skating across the underside of my jaw.

An outburst of sensation ratcheted down my spine and accumulated in my pelvis. My head bowed backward into the floor, and inconsolable moans jumped from my lips.

My breasts came next. His lips sank and tugged at the flesh rising from my breastband, the wet strokes of his mouth stirring my blood into a frenzy. The skin of my nipples toughened, the tips poking through the material. I wanted his mouth there, his tongue drawing circles around the bare shells until they darkened, his lips folding over the exposed crests until they were raw.

Instead of ushering the material low, that notorious mouth clamped onto one breast over the fabric. And then he sucked me into him, claiming the nipple through the embroidery. Intoxicating pressure encased the stud, the flat of his tongue swept over the peak, and the heat of it seeped into the garment.

The force of his mouth lured inarticulate moans from my lips. All the while, his broad erection plied between my parted thighs. My waist lifted, hooking over his hips to catch the sinuous lashes. The skirt fell around my stomach, revealed my drawers as I rowed my pelvis against his. Dear Seasons, the bridge of his cock skidded against the crease in my legs, throwing shocks of pleasure through my walls.

My head snapped back, and my mouth gaped. "Oh."

Poet dragged his lips to my ear. "What is it, sweeting? Do you like that? Does it make your lovely cunt feel good?"

No, I didn't like it. And it didn't feel good.

It was bad. So very bad.

"Yes," I moaned.

Taking that as a sign, Poet removed one hand from my wrist and snaked it between us, his fingers maneuvering against the clasps of his pants. The fabric shifted and slumped open.

Poet returned his grip to my wrist and sank his hips deeper into me, which sprawled my thighs farther. My thoughts misted, eclipsed by a haze of stimulation and need. He wouldn't enter me, but he was about to do something else.

I'm going to toy with you, make you feel good in another way.

I bit my lower lip to stifle another moan, but the noise came out regardless.

Poet heard it. He broke away, those pupils bloated fully now, black swallowing the green. The jester poised himself against the aperture in my undergarments. His gaze locked on mine, and with languid motions, he slung his waist forward.

And my body sang. The naked bridge of his cock slid between the crevice in my drawers, brushed through the curls, and rode up the groove in my core. I cried out, embers flying through the place where his unclad erection plied my bare flesh.

Poet's mouth fell open at the contact. His eyes hooded.

While fixating on me, he followed the sounds I made, translated every response, and gave me what I wanted. He arched his backside, sweeping his cock back down, exiting the slit in my drawers, then slowly reeled through the barrier again. This time, the pommel of his erection angled, sketching along the rift in my folds.

The jester continued this. His flicked his hips between my spread legs, passing in and out of the furrow in my undergarments and skating his bare cock over the split of my walls. As he did, plaintive sounds tripped from my lungs, and I arched beneath him.

Dear Seasons. Our nude flesh pressed, aligned, and swiped against one another. So very near to my entrance, so close to sealing him inside me.

My core throbbed like a pulse, hectic and uncontrollable. A shameless rush of arousal leaked from my body and smeared his erection from base to roof as it swayed back and forth against me. Each movement rubbed us together, his arousal skimming my center, the traction stunning.

Poet groaned in tempo to our motions. His hips rolled, his thrusts shallow and measured. I felt the circumference of him, the shape and mass of his cock, topped by a broad crown. The hard line of his body massaged my wet cleft, the rhythm even and patient, the result overwhelming.

We rocked together, the temperature building. I moaned, clenching my thighs around his roving buttocks. Each intimate muscle inside me compressed, coils winding in too many areas to heed.

Yet it didn't suffice. I needed it deeper, faster. Either that, or I'd surely burst into pieces.

I wasn't alone in my torment. Poet shook as if holding himself back, as if struggling for control.

The need to do something, *anything*, overtook me. Mindless, I tasted him. My lips snatched his ear and drew on the lobe, my tongue curling over the patch of skin.

He rasped, the guttural sound amplifying. And the more I traced him, the rougher he crooned. The rougher he crooned, the deeper his hips ground into my core.

The kernel of nerves at my center throbbed. My clitoris prickled with stimulation, the stiff glide of his erection wrecking me, soaking me. I pictured its shape, the flush of its head, the skin coated in my slickness.

With gentle lurches of his hips, he breached the slit of my drawers. The distended length of his body raced across my drenched folds and pressed into the kernel. The spike of sensation uprooted a shriek from me.

A haggard sound emptied from Poet's chest. "Seasons almighty, Briar."

He must have felt it, because his cock hardened even more. On a growl, he snatched my mouth and rocked his tongue into me. Every undulating flex of his waist matched his kiss and roused a sequence of chants from my lips, which Poet swallowed hungrily.

My head swirled. Sparkles crackled across my flesh. It felt like touching myself, except a thousand times more agonizing.

I swiveled my hips against his, my cleft so wet and wanting. Fluid poured from me and dripped onto the ridge of his cock.

Poet pulled back again to watch me. His features cinched—harsh, pained, possessive.

I was doing that to him. No one else.

The notion fueled me with pride and power, as intoxicating as the press of his cock. Every fiber sprung to life. I was so slippery against him. I clung to the jester, reeling myself with his waist, chasing the hot pressure that washed up my legs and swirled in my crease.

My moans thinned into cries. "I'm ... I'm ..."

"Aye, my thorn," he grated, kissing my unhinged mouth. "That is precisely what you're going to do."

And so I did. Pleasure spiraled through my folds, whirling quicker and quicker. My joints tensed as the sensation surged between my thighs, seized the tip of my clitoris, and finally broke apart. I spasmed in his arms. The force of it ruptured through me, shoving incoherent noises from my tongue.

Blackness flooded my vision as I bowed into him. I cried and cried as his mouth swooped against mine, consuming the wild noise while his cock swayed in the gap of my thighs, rubbing me, stroking me. His lips muffled the noise from traveling, kissing me through the climax, kissing me so deeply. My walls convulsed against his cock, the flanks shuddering repeatedly, my pleasure spilling onto him.

At last, I sagged onto the rug. With a contented hum, Poet pried his mouth from mine.

Soft pants dropped from my mouth. My eyes floated open to find him looming. His orbs hooded in satisfaction.

Spent, I reached up to hold his jaw. And at once, he slowed his movements, his waist and cock ebbing to a halt.

A disgruntled sigh fell from my lips, but the protest was short-lived as Poet just stared at me. The kohl under his lashes crimped. Those eyes flared through the half-light. Whatever he saw, felt, or thought, I couldn't say. But something in his expression transformed as he watched me coast back to earth.

Something else took over. Something dynamic, unprecedented, and tender.

My erratic breathing resounded through the room, refusing to be silenced. While absorbing the sound, Poet ran the backs of his black fingernails down my cheekbone.

Despite what we'd done, he touched me in a different way now—obsessed, entranced, almost uncertain. With our groins still pressed together, his hands sketched my knees, climbed my waist, and trailed over my ribs.

My capped sleeve sagged, splitting the bodice completely. Yet the cashmere dress stuck to me, too restrictive. I wanted it off, gone, never to return.

Every spot Poet caressed brought a shiver to the surface. The whole time, he studied me, and I studied him. Somehow, the staring felt even more intimate, more penetrating than what his body had done to me.

Invigorated, I traced the mantels of his shoulders, encircled his strong wrists, and pinched the scarlet bracelet, giving it a light tug.

A deviant grin slid across his lips before dissolving once more into fascination, so much that I doubted he'd ever gone at an exploratory pace with anyone.

We made it into a provocative game, swapping touches. Enthralled, he thumbed my lower lip, the pulse in my temple, the errant strand of hair that came loose from my braid. He tucked that piece safely behind my ear and sketched the weave in my braid.

I skimmed the ledge of his jaw. His index finger etched a line down my neck, and I dipped my palms to the upper slopes of his buttocks. He stroked under my calf, turning it to liquid. And as I descended to clutch the divots of his backside, his sharp intake tingled in my ear.

With the jester, the world receded. I became someone else—someone impulsive.

Then I realized something with a measure of disappointment. He hadn't orgasmed with me. At some point, my legs had fallen from around Poet, but I moved to encircle him once more, to give back what he gave. As I started to wiggle my sodden core against his cock, Poet's hoarse groan accompanied the shake of his head.

"Nay, sweeting," he whispered. "Just you."

Then he ground his lips to mine. He claimed me with another shattering kiss, his palms clamping onto the back of my scalp, angling my head to meet his urgent mouth.

Our desperate lips sealed. My tongue swayed against his, inundated with plenty to say but less will to say it.

This happened. I had no excuse.

25

Briar

easons help us, it kept happening.

From behind a hallway tapestry, an arm shot out as I walked by. It snatched my wrist and hauled me into an alcove of shadows. I gasped as a shaft of darkness surrounded me, and a set of hands gripped my waist.

My fists balled, about to smash into the assailant. But then I recognized his scent, the shape of his body, and the strength of his hold.

Glancing up, my gaze collided with a pair of verdant eyes smudged in black. It looked as though he hadn't remembered to remove the kohl the night before. More than that, it appeared as if he hadn't slept—like someone had torn through his dreams and ripped them asunder.

I opened my mouth to speak. However, the words died as his gaze torched a path across my face. The jester gave me less than a second to process before he mashed me against him, and his lips crushed over mine.

The hot clutch of his mouth tugged me into a frenzy, his tongue plying through and tracing my own. I moaned against that tongue, the sound tracking down his throat. To my ears, the noise was less brittle, more sustaining. While my toes curled into my heels, the rest of my body felt reinforced, secure.

I cleaved through his hair and seized that mouth, kissing him back. His firm body encased me like a shield. My fingers dashed through his roots like thorn vines. The instant the tip of my tongue flicked against his, a deep rumble scrolled from Poet's chest.

The world spun as he twisted me to the nearest wall. My spine thudded into the stone facade. His lips rushed across on mine, consuming me. Our tongues swatted at a rampant pace because time was of the essence.

He looped my thigh beneath his arm, hiked it to his hip, and plowed mouth into me. The flat of his tongue flexed sharply against mine until my thoughts evaporated. His hard body splayed me against the wall, and his lips crawled from my own to the basin of my clavicles, where he sucked hard.

With a brittle yelp, I bowed into the stones. As I fractured into pieces, he lifted his drugged face back to me and devoured the noises I made.

But it wasn't until I released his hair, raced my fingers along his shoulders, and skated a trembling digit down his spine that I dominated him. Poet's mouth shook. He sucked in a harsh gust of air, and his frame shuddered against me.

How I loved wiping that mouth clean of mockery. How I enjoyed that my touch could do him this harm.

I could rule a nation. And I could do this to him. Yet I could not say which felt more powerful.

We ransacked time. Every encounter was fraught with risk, every tiptoe a hurricane resounding in the halls. That made the quickness necessary. And that fueled us.

He was impulsive. I was calculative. We were careful.

Poet was a sly one, for certain. Whenever he wanted me, messages would turn up in my room without any indication of how they'd gotten there. Usually they would contain verse, riddles, or blatant flirtations.

Either that, or I'd find a ribbon affixed to a blossom in one of the gardens, the clue located beside a path that guided me in the right direction. Always, the signs arrived at dawn or dusk, when it was easier to skulk through the passage leading from my suite.

Every time, a terrible thrill raced through me. Upon finding the envelopes or bands of fabric, my grin became increasingly difficult to suppress.

It had to be a violation of nature, these turbulent sensations. I didn't recognize myself. It was like awakening to nightfall instead of daybreak.

It was effortless, elemental. My body knew what to do and how to do it. When he got his hands on me, I turned into a nymph of the highest order—daring, liberated, wild.

I savored how he held me. More than that, I relished how I held him back.

In the interims, the trepidation, remorse, and exhaustion surfaced. Constantly, I glanced over my shoulder, anticipating shrewd gazes or watchful eyes.

Poet tucked my back against his chest. His limbs flanked me across the oversized chair in front of his roaring fireplace, one foot propped on the cushion, the other stretching out lazily. Midnight poured deep blue across the room, and the flames lapped at the shadows.

Absently and repeatedly, he massaged my shoulders, rolling his thumbs into me and easing my tension while I vented. Frustration over my exclusion from the Peace Talks had gotten the better of me. He listened, challenging my rant with sarcasm and frankness.

Afterward, I listened to his stories about raising Nicu. My favorite was how when the child first began to crawl, he became obsessed with hunting windblown leaves across the grass.

The circumstances also held their share of grimness. The confessions poured out as if from a tap, as if Poet had grown sick of holding back. His features warped while he admitted how petrifying it was, panicking about Nicu wandering beyond the cottage to where someone could discover him.

Worrying about his son's fate wore Poet out, to the point where he yearned to scream. Once, he fled to the woods and unleashed there.

I listened, then whispered comforts and encouragements. I reminded him about the progress he was making with the monarchy, reassured him of how much effect he was having on Spring's Royals.

Often, I could not wait to share whatever ideas or random thoughts consumed my mind. After that, I would offer objective feedback on an epic verse he'd been working on.

We debated and mused. We argued and confessed. We murmured about the day and the people who had filled it.

I kept thoughts of Mother and Father to myself. Not because I didn't want to share, but because I suspected Poet would see through me, hear the parts I omitted, the fears that came with them.

Mother and I strolled through the corridors with a band of guards. From the opposite end of the hall, Poet appeared.

My pulse turned into a violent, thrashing thing as he sauntered toward me, surrounded by an entourage of performers. The dancers, aerialists, acrobats, and musicians walked on either side of him, some as toned as marble and lithe as flower stems, others lush and curvy.

Eliot walked with them, his golden features and affable smile dousing the space with light. As we crossed paths, I flashed my friend a quick smile.

By contrast, the jester and I did not acknowledge one another.

We waltzed by as if the encounter bore no consequence, was hardly worth our notice.

Inside, my body screamed.

I need you. I resent you. I envy you. I crave you. I miss you. I want you.

Just before we passed one another, our fingers stole out to brush. For a second, they made contact, faint and fleeting.

Poet accompanied the seven monarchs and me on a tour of the greenhouses. With his hands behind his back, the jester sauntered by each person and muttered comments that amused them. To his deceptive credit, the ruse made it seem like no strange occurrence when my turn came.

I'd been drinking from a chalice when his silhouette halted beside me. Then he leaned his chin over my shoulder and blew insolence into my ear. "Ten minutes hereafter, I shall have you moaning."

I almost choked on the nectar.

And *ten minutes hereafter*, ensconced in a shrouded hollow, my head slumped back as Poet feasted on the curve of my neck, his tongue lashing my skin raw. One arm banded around my middle, fastening my spine to his chest, while the other hand dipped under my raised skirt and cupped my damp center.

His wrist pressed into my clitoris, and his fingers sketched the outlines of my folds over the drawers. The contact hurled sparks through my bloodstream. My arm reached up and back, so that my fingers clamped the nape of his neck for balance. I needed, wanted, demanded.

Poet obliged. He sucked on my flesh and rolled my clit with his wrist, teasing it into a frenzy. Then he palmed my mouth to quell the moans.

Someone was following me.

As my heels clicked against the polished floor, my spine chilled.

A blot of color flitted in my periphery but made no sound. I halted several feet from the archive library door, then swerved around. My eyes skipped across the corridor but found only iron chandeliers and lupine pots.

I must have been wrong. It was the middle of the day, and I was exactly where people expected me to be. Clearly, I was overreacting.

Atop an unmanned turret beneath the evening sky, the jester's hands scorched my flesh. My nipples studded, pushing firmly through my bodice. The crests became so tight, I squirmed for relief, aching for the enclosure of his mouth. Modesty fled me, that need baring itself to his perceptive eyes, which simmered in response.

Poet waited for me to change my mind, made sure that I meant it. While holding my gaze, he unlaced me. Every thread fell limp under his fingers, every tug pulling at my sanity. The cumbersome chore had us panting until the dress loosened.

My breasts quivered free as the fabric drooped, barely concealing me now. Unbidden, my sheepishness took over. Despite all we'd done, my clothes had always stayed on.

I moved to cover the slumped neckline, to brace it higher. But Poet cupped my chin and framed my profile with his free hand. "Look at me, sweet thorn." And when I did, his expression halted my fingers. "I want to see your body. I want every beguiling part of you on my mouth. But most of all …" His breath sailed across my lips. "I want to see every truth about you—everything raw and real. I want you to destroy me." He ducked his head and met my gaze. "Show me those lovely secrets, and I promise, I'll honor them."

The words brushed my skin like feathers. My arms fell to my sides.

Fastening his gaze to mine, Poet draped a single finger down the bodice's center, slowly peeling the material from my body. The panels flapped apart, and the laces spread.

My breasts pushed from the fabric and spilled into the night. The air rushed at them, brushing the taut skin.

Poet's eyes dragged from my face to my breasts. They pitched out between us, small and capped in points, which darkened from his attention. Those irises flickered like burning wicks, heat and reverence consuming his gaze.

He cupped my breasts, the sensation of his hands balancing their weight swiping the oxygen from my lungs. A moan wrung from my mouth as his thumbs circled wide and then narrowed to the centers. He sketched the mounds, swept across my nipples, and pinched the hard nubs, turning me into a quivering mess.

Poet shook his head and muttered, "Wicked fucking hell."

Life exploded as he bent his head. The first breast strained into the hot cavern of his mouth, his tongue curling around the pellet, lashing it delicately. I cried out and arched into him, my digits spearing through his hair. He lapped at me, sucked on me, his tongue plying my nipple with streaks of pleasure.

When I could barely utter a coherent word, he switched to the other breast. His kisses covered each inch of flesh, the damp heat of his lips taking me in. On a hum, his mouth cinched around the bud and licked, and I made every raw and real sound possible.

While waiting for Poet in one of the gardens, I wandered into an iron rotunda, its gate having been left open. Rose bushes threaded through the area. Thorns barbed the stems, in sharp contrast to the soft petals.

Spring bred the greenest trees on our continent, as well as the most fragrant blooms. Their perfume saturated the enclosure, wiping out any other scent in the vicinity.

Caught in the aroma, I stepped nearer. The pad of my finger extended toward one of the rose spikes.

A hand shot out and clamped around mine. Glancing sideways, my gaze hooked onto Poet's, our fingers halting less than an inch from the thorn. Mayhem and protectiveness flashed across the jester's features, silently warning me that I'd been close to making a grave mistake. I had forgotten what the flowers in this Season could do to people.

"Ah, ah, ah." Poet lifted my knuckles to his lips, then spoke against them while staring at me. "Never those."

If I wanted to explore the outer reaches of intimacy without being inebriated by thorns, there were other ways.

Poet demonstrated by draping me across his mattress. Flattening one hand beside my head, he leaned over and whispered, "Do you trust me, my thorn?"

When I nodded, he reached toward the headboard. Something clicked like the fastening to a compartment, and the frame trembled.

Pulling back, Poet held a ribbon, which dangled off the plank of his finger. "Close your eyes."

At this point, my gown was a velvet puddle on the ground beside his door. Tonight, we had barely made it into the room. Though, he was still fully clothed.

My thin shift remained the only vestment concealing me from him. He would not remove it unless I asked him to. While he had seen and felt a great deal of me, it had occurred in batches, the layers peeled back at their own pace.

I did not feel ready to bare myself completely. So he penetrated me in yet another new way.

Curiosity and yearning encouraged me to do as he bade.

"Hands behind the pillow," he murmured.

Butterflies flapped in my stomach. I snuck my fingers under the mound cushioning my head.

The moment darkness enveloped me, his voice sailed into my ear. "Now then." His lips tugged on mine, the kiss far too brief. "Let us see what you're made of, hmm?"

The bed shifted with his weight as he climbed over me. My skin tingled, discerning another presence getting nearer.

Then the narrow strip of material slid across my mouth. I gasped, my breath puffing against the ribbon as it traced the margins of my lips. Like a tongue, it licked across my cheek, buffeted the outer curve of my ear, and stroked down the side of my neck.

Shivers followed the band's path. Each one shimmied over my flesh.

The ribbon feathered over the crook of my neck and shoulder, then prickled along my collarbones. I squirmed, a small pant lifting into the air. I heard him breathing, too, steadily and thickly.

The fabric pursued every corner and crevice. Light as the tip of a brush, it circled each of my breasts, then coasted over the nipples.

I jolted, awash in a flurry of stimulation. Effervescence danced across my skin wherever the ribbon made contact. From one arm to the underside of my palm, to the back of my wrist.

He ghosted over my navel, tickled my kneecaps, and brushed my toes. Something akin to a giggle and a sigh sprung from me. Each part of my being grew hyperaware, so acutely attuned.

The ribbon disappeared. I grunted, only to be rewarded with his low chuckle. An instant later, the band trailed my hips, rolling from one to the other, constantly bypassing my core.

The nexus of my body clenched. My waist bucked, imploring the ribbon to slip under the shift. But Poet only resumed taunting the rest of me until my teeth burrowed into my lower lip, and I arched.

Every place vibrated like the strings of an instrument. Finally, that strip of cloth slithered up my inner thigh.

I parted my legs, welcoming the disorder.

Despite my undergarments, the ribbon skimmed over the fabric and grazed the opening. It glided along my slit just once. It was barely a touch, yet every nerve jumped. It charged through me and coaxed a tremulous noise from my mouth.

Then the ribbon swam over the projected shape of my clitoris. I gulped, and the apex buzzed. The band's tip swished atop my peak, fluctuating from side to side. Each centimeter thrummed and percolated, my center stirring up its own commotion.

My hips lifted for more. The strip responded, circling and patting my clit like a quill. I whined and bounded my lower half against it, the contact too light when I needed it firmer. The frustration became its own sensation, which mounted with every swab, so that my respirations stuttered.

Moaning, I bolted my core upward, meeting the fabric's ministrations over the bud. The nebulous touches made my thighs clench and drew arousal from their juncture. Still, I hefted myself toward the evasive cord as it wiped against me, the collision as impactful as a thrust.

I grasped the pillows and stabbed my fingernails into the down. My clit tightened, and my folds cramped. The titillation became so much, too much, until my flesh surrendered.

I opened my mouth, and a hard cry surged out. Each joint and muscle contracted as my core released itself. The ribbon beat gently onto the crest of nerves, as if mopping the fluid that drained from me.

My bones rattled. A string of moans quaked off my lips.

In the midst of that, Poet husked, "Beautiful."

Being lost in this oblivion should feel vulnerable, but knowing Poet watched me only magnified the feelings. Even with my vision shrouded in darkness, I sensed him there with me. The ribbon tethered us, so that I wasn't the only one affected.

This needed to stop. I had to compose myself, restrain myself, deny myself. We needed to regain control for the sake of his cause and both of our heads.

Tonight, I would disengage. I'd end this before it went too far. It would be better this way, safer and easier.

We would get over this.

In the great hall, the jester danced with daggers. His bare chest contorted, the cobbled muscles rippling as he flipped the weapons in his grip—upside down, right side up.

Without pausing to properly aim, Poet spun into a half circle. In one agile movement, his arm lashed out and executed a backhanded toss. The blade flew and struck a moving wooden board shaped like a shield and held aloft by a female who danced through the room. Costumed in a corset and slitted skirt, the dancer pirouetted on bare olive feet without flinching as the weapon hit its mark.

Poet jumped, his limbs scissoring the air. When he landed, another dagger punctured the center just before his partner twisted. Their movements flowed in sync, reflecting countless hours of training and trust.

The jester monopolized the attention of every living creature in the room. Their ravenous eyes sketched his form while those elastic abs stretched.

From my seat on the dais, I squeezed my drink. My chest burned with desire, teemed with pride, and stung with envy. Others wanted him, but this jester was mine.

For now, at least.

Once he'd deployed all his blades, Poet straightened and stepped back to a thunderous ovation. He swung his arm toward the female, giving her the spotlight as she curtsied like a gazelle, graceful and limber. Then he took her fingers, held them aloft, and inclined his head while they bowed in unison.

Afterward, Poet shrugged into a dark jacket trimmed in silver, which framed the brackets of his shoulders and hung open to exhibit his bare chest. Flushed and catching his breath, he toured the room, greeted me on the platform, and wordlessly raised a tankard in my direction.

Keeping my expression neutral, I inclined my head, which he took as an invitation to move on. Yet the sudden mood to provoke struck me with a vengeance.

"Wait a moment, Court Jester," I called.

Poet halted, then rotated. "At your service, Princess."

"Proper decorum requires you to bestow a few parting words."

"And that would be?"

I took advantage of my status and prissy reputation. "You haven't yet wished your superior a pleasant night."

He raised a brow, then spread his arms in a show of mockery. "Have a pleasant night."

My mouth crooked as he turned away once more. "Wait a moment."

Slower this time, Poet rounded on me again. His visage reflected both intrigue and impatience.

I chose this moment carefully while everyone preoccupied themselves with racks of lamb and lively conversation. But although there was nothing amiss about this exchange, I sensed an exception—the flicker of someone's attention on us.

Outwardly, I wasn't flirting as others did with him. The best course of action was to ride out the scene as if I had nothing to apologize for.

"Inferiors also bow to their sovereigns before departing," I stated with all the pretense of placid snobbery.

Those sinful lips twitched. With exaggerated finesse, Poet obliged me and then turned yet again.

"In addition—" my voice forced his booted feet to stall and his fingers to clamp around the tankard's handle, "—I should like inferiors to observe standard protocol and to acknowledge me as a princess. *Your Highness*, as is customary. I'm not unreasonable in expecting you to address me thusly."

With the pacing of a lion, Poet reeled toward me. A single, slender diamond cut through his left eye, the design shifting as his features transcended from accommodating to threatening.

He stalked to the dais, his measured steps drawing several pairs of eyes until he loomed over me, his shadow colliding with mine across the table. "Have a pleasant night, Your Highness," he said while simultaneously falling into another bow.

For the rest of the evening, we moved in separate circles and barely cast one another glances. That lasted until midnight when the castle bell tolled, and the candelabras had melted to their bases. I rose from my chair and tipped a chalice to my lips, about to take a final sip before retiring.

That's when I felt his approach. The Court Jester stalked my way amid the crowded hall.

As he passed behind me, his silken voice brushed my ear. "Leave your chamber unlocked tonight."

His finger grazed the edge of my crown before he vanished through the room like smoke. The chalice trembled in my fingers, about to crash to the ground. At the last moment, I tightened my grip on the stem.

Hours later, I shut the door to my suite, whirled toward the facade, and pressed my forehead to the panel. Flames crackled from the tall mouth of the fireplace, its heat stroking my back. Because the maid always prepared my rooms, marigold light from a dozen candles trickled through the space. Though these small comforts did nothing to alleviate the tension, nor to relax my fingers as they choked the doorknob.

I shouldn't let him in. I couldn't.

My behavior tonight had been indiscreet. If I knew better, I would not run rampant like that again.

This wasn't a game. This court wasn't our playground.

Wanting him was treasonous. Touching him was calamitous.

Sooner rather than later, the consequences would catch up to us.

My body slumped toward the door. A desperate flurry of air blew from my lips—then froze at the rustle of movement that resounded in the space.

From behind, a masculine timbre slid through the darkness. "Come here."

26

Briar

I whipped around. Beyond the antechamber, the Court Jester rose from a chair in the corner of my bedroom, his figure partially cloaked in firelight and candlelight. The black diamond slashed through his left eye, and his body was still clad in that dark costume, the trimmed jacket slung open and his leather pants clinging to his hips.

My heart did its worse, ramming into my breast like a caged raptor. The jester was in my room, looking as if he belonged here.

This was getting out of hand. I had nudged, and he'd nudged back, but it could not go on this way. Inevitably, we would find ourselves in fatal trouble.

I released the knob but pressed my spine against the door. "What are we doing?" I asked, helpless. "What's happening between us? Are we fools?"

Poet halted beside the restless blaze, his pupils reflecting a single slash of flame. "Aye." After another second, he pushed the words out. "But how much does it matter?"

At this point, very little. Yet I couldn't admit that. Not that I needed to with this man, when everything always felt as candid and exposed as a wound.

I took tentative steps forward. "You're dismantling all my assumptions."

"Aye," he agreed again, prowling my way. "And you're ruining all my plans."

"Breaking down the walls."

"Burning them to cinders."

The jester paused once more and watched the emotions trail across my face. Then he curled his fingers, softened his voice, and repeated, "Come. Here. Briar."

I did not *come here*. I lunged.

I kicked off my heels, hurled off my crown, dashed across the room, and flung myself at him. Poet grabbed the backs of my thighs and lifted, hefting me off the ground. I strapped my limbs around his waist. One of his hands braced my buttocks, and the other clasped the back of my skull, holding my head in place as his mouth tore into mine.

I moaned into his lips, which clamped onto me and flexed in, drawing me into the deepest kiss I'd ever known. Seasons help me, he tasted of wine and chocolate. His tongue caught my own, hooking and retreating, each lick dissolving my doubts. The sensuous force of his mouth brought out the ambitious in me, so that I clutched my lips with his and fought him for dominance, putting my whole being into it.

Poet groaned into my mouth. The sound emboldened me, encouraged me to nip his upper lip and enjoy his muffled growl.

Releasing sharp gales of air, our lips surged together once more. His mouth rocked against mine, grinding us into an even deeper kiss.

Upright and secured in his arms, I rose higher and came down hard on his lips. Kissing him felt reckless, scary, invigorating. My tongue swiped his as I adhered myself to him.

His naked chest pushed through the open jacket and abraded my bodice. It reminded me of his whipcord frame rippling as it had whisked those daggers. My nails clawed at the garment, fumbling to get it off his shoulders.

Yes, this had to end sometime. But perhaps I could mark him first.

Poet must have sensed what I wanted, because the room shifted as he strode across the rug to the bed. He laid me atop the pillows, hovered like a specter, and muttered into my mouth, "Too easy, sweeting."

His denial caused a torrent between my legs. True, ridding him of the vestment wasn't necessary. Instead, my fingers dashed between the panels, my touch sliding over the ridges of skin.

The fireplace burnished his pectorals in a hot gleam. I swallowed, prideful. However much they feared being the target of his sharp tongue, every person at court wanted the jester like this, looking at them with a frenetic light that bordered on possessive.

He soaked in my features, as if waiting for my approval. The vision sent eddies of pleasure through me.

That look was mine. *He* was mine.

We had done so much, but his gaze told me we weren't even close. Nowhere near so.

Poet crawled on all fours, moving as he always did. Like a vapor, fluid and lithe.

I met him halfway, rising enough to grab his face and seal my mouth with his. That forbidden tongue struck mine, the tempo spine-tingling.

My stomach flipped as he folded himself over me. I dissolved onto the mattress, and my legs split around his waist, which settled in the gap of my thighs. His frame covered my body, the weight of his hips decadent, spurring me to bend my knees high.

The jester inched backward, his arms bracketing on either side of my head. His pupils bloated as he studied my countenance. "Are you wet?"

The request whispered like satin up my limbs and reached their nexus. So much arousal gushed from my walls that I felt myself blush, yet I spoke without wavering. "I am."

"How wet, my thorn?"

"I don't know."

"Then may I find out?"

"Yes," I heaved.

Like this, his touch slipped under my skirt, coasted along my legs, and gathered the dress's hem in his fist. He rucked the material to my waist. With the garment bunched around my hips, coolness prickled my limbs.

In stark contrast, I felt the heat of his hand even before it stole into the slot of my undergarments. The temperature there rose, considerable degrees warmer than the rest of me, and it set my walls to throbbing. I squirmed, that intimate place needing, wanting, aching.

"Open them wider, sweeting," he instructed, his voice gravely.

My thighs broadened, parting and allowing his arm to sink into the vent.

His digits brushed through the curls, a gentle scrape that drew a gasp from me. Poet's eyes flared as he traced my core, fingers skimming like quills.

I bit my lip, stunned by a profusion of bliss and anguish. My backside rutted into the mattress as he etched the delicate folds, wetting me more, coaxing dampness onto his hand.

Then he cupped me, his palm bracing over my bare cleft. My mouth dropped open on a silent moan, and I leaked onto him.

Poet leaned in to kiss my cheek, then strummed his mouth against my gaping lips. As he did, his hand pressed firmer, burrowing onto my core. The pressure incited a maelstrom, and my body smeared his hand.

Against his skin, my clitoris thrummed. The bud at my center pounded.

"Wicked fuck," he rasped. "Feel that?"

The intimate pulse of my clitoris thumped against his wrist. Yes, I felt it so much. But I whimpered, unable to answer him.

We concentrated on the steady drum coming from me, the slickness that welled from the rift in my thighs. Fully clothed, I couldn't have felt more naked, more riveted, more alive.

"Tell me," he intoned. "What am I doing?"

I panted so hard it was difficult to speak around the shallow mouthfuls of air. "You're holding me."

"What am I holding?"

"Oh, Seasons. I ..."

"Share it with me, Briar."

"My core," I answered. "You're holding my core."

"Indeed, Princess." Poet lulled while his fingers slid lazily up and down my crease. "What else?"

My head flapped from side to side. "The words are crude. They're too vulgar."

"No," he uttered. "Not from your mouth, nor from your body. They're sexy, as is the feel of your arousal against my hand. The words are real, and they're exquisite. 'Tis a blissful torment." He kissed my chin. "Now again. Tell me what I'm holding."

"My pussy," I whispered finally, the answer sleek on my tongue, passionate rather than crass. "You're touching my pussy."

"That, I am," Poet crooned, his digits grazing through the sprigs of hair at my juncture, then circling the entrance and swirling my wetness. "And what does it feel like? What is it doing to you?"

"My pussy is aching and ... and it's wetting your palm."

"That, it is," he murmured. "And have you ever touched this delicate pussy before?"

The confession dripped from my tongue. "I have."

A hiss escaped him. "Did you make yourself come?" My face detonated with heat, but when I inclined my head, Poet asked, "How did it make you feel?"

"Strong," I blustered. "Invincible."

"That's right." And this time instead of asking, he whispered, "I'm going to touch you now."

"You are touching me."

"Nay, Briar. I haven't begun yet."

My insides jumped, adrenaline teeming through me. I nodded, and my hips rose off the bed, thrusting tenderly into his palm.

Poet husked, caressed my lips with his, and obliged. Though, not as anticipated.

Not with his hand.

I growled in aggravation when he released my core. Small pants rattled from my lungs as Poet kissed a searing path down my neckline where the tops of my breasts inflated, and then he slid to my quavering stomach. On the way, his nails grazed my hips, the motion plying me with goosebumps.

In burning light of flames and candles, the jester coasted off the bed and lowered himself to his knees. My breath hitched. Somehow, my fitful body drew its own conclusion about what was going to happen.

Poet's fingers glided under the skirt and massaged my inner thighs until they relaxed. Then he teased the lace trim of my undergarments before rustling them in his grip. The dainty cloth slipped past my hips and knees, the fabric running over my flesh, tickling my calves, and vanishing past my toes.

The material dangled from the tips of his fingers before the jester dropped it to the ground. He strapped his hands around my ankles. And in one firm tug, he slid me to the mattress's edge.

My limbs steepled, my soles planted on the rim, and my body spread. The pads of his digits smoothed across my heels, up my shins, and behind my knees. Hooking my limbs over his shoulders, he scooped and lifted my backside. Those cunning eyes descended to stare at the cleft between my legs, the bright flash of his gaze making the ache worse, the slit wetter.

Never had I been stripped bare and splayed apart like this, yet the moment felt instinctual, the force intrinsic. I wanted this. My chest rose and fell in rapid succession as Poet took in the sight of my exposed core—my pussy—every flushed part visible to him.

His molten gaze caused liquid heat to flood my insides. "There we go, Princess," he exalted. "Such a lovely cunt. So very open and pretty."

"Poet," I entreated. "Please."

Done with words then, the jester pressed a finger to his lips. *Hush.* Or someone might hear us.

He vanished between my legs, so that only pure sensations remained in his wake. His hair swished against my skin. The blanket shifted with his movements. I rested on my back, my eyes surging to the canopy. My expectant body tensed, then loosened into the mattress when his warm lips pressed against the leenix scar, kissing it gently. From that alone, something new blossomed within me, elevating the desire.

Poet grasped my naked buttocks, securing me in place. His weight drew nearer to my center, his head nudging into that delicate space. The temperature of his exhales met my own heat, causing my eyelids to flutter.

There was a pause, followed by Poet's groan. The noise came out ragged, equally carnal and reverential.

Then I felt it—a short, wet lick up the pleat of my body.

My spine snapped off the bed, and a whine leaped from my mouth.

And he did it again. His tongue flicked over the slick crease, dragging the tip slowly. Then again, and again. He dabbed that place softly, as if collecting the wetness, as if to consume it. Tremors rippled from that spot, the likes of which I'd never known.

So it began. One pass after another, he swiped his tongue along my core, over the split of my entrance. Poet lapped at me, deep hums echoing from his throat. He sketched my opening, tracing its shape with deft strokes and teasing a series of stuttered noises from me.

The drastic sounds grew in pace and octave, until I could barely recognize them. My moans fractured with every swift lash. I raised my hips to his face, and the dress hem bundled higher, exhibiting me completely from the navel down. With my lower half suspended and straining closer to his mouth, I beseeched him for more of this, more of whatever he was doing.

But he pinned me, his glossy black fingernails spanning my hipbones. I had no choice but to whip my head back and forth, unable to keep still. It felt so good, too good. This had to be forbidden, this savage pleasure, this loss of composure.

Lazily, the flat of Poet's tongue roved up and down my pussy. My walls soaked his tongue, and my hands seized his bent head, now visible to my gaze. I pressed him into me, urging him to keep going, don't stop.

Dear Seasons.

Do. *Not*. Stop.

He licked my folds, then did something outrageous. Draping his tongue over the gap in my body, he glided upward in one long pass, reaching the pert nub rising from my core.

And he licked there, too.

I sprang apart. "Oh, gods."

Poet rasped and flexed his tongue over the crest. My mind emptied, everything I felt reduced to that cinched bit of flesh, that one small peak. With every lick, the nib swelled further. He patted it rhythmically, each hot sweep sending bolts through my walls.

My eyes rolled back. I gripped his head harder with one hand and seized the nearest pillow with the other. I sunk my teeth into the down, muffling the broken moans. The jester charged at me then, strapping his lips around my clitoris and sucking it into his mouth.

My moans splintered into sobs. Poet latched onto the bud, all the while flitting the tip with his tongue just so. With each nudge, another shocked convulsion lurched from my mouth, the cries in tempo to his steady licks.

I released the pillow and fisted the sheets. My hips bucked against his relentless mouth, my arousal melting like a candle and pouring on his tongue. He worked that tender knot of heat, plaguing me into a near swoon as my body lost control against his lips.

Yet Poet wasn't done. His mouth pulled away from my clitoris, slid between my folds, and probed them open. Like that, he curled his tongue inside me, slowly so that I felt its entire length.

The sounds I made became guttural, welling from a place so deep, so buried. Poet moaned, the vibration palpable against my inner flesh. He tasted me this way, his tongue pushing in and out, the motions patient and attentive to my sobs. The penetration was smooth, fluid, and breathtaking.

The lithe pumping of his tongue increased my moans. As they did, he licked into my folds faster, levered deeper, then withdrew and captured my nub again. The agony tripled as he alternated between sucking the pellet of flesh and siphoning inside me.

The sodden walls of my pussy contorted. Fissures of pleasure crested, heading toward a breaking point. I reached back and grabbed the mattress's edge. Using that for leverage, I ground my waist, swatting myself against Poet's mouth, riding his tongue.

A pleasured growl skated from his throat. He doubled his efforts, whisking his tongue into me, prying himself away to suction my bud, then striking back in. My mouth fell ajar, the cries fraying into silent shouts, because if I let it out, the whole castle would hear me.

The same rapture mounted from when I'd touched myself, then when he ground his cock against me on the floor, only this was magnified and infinitely more destructive. Poet's tongue cast into my pussy quicker. He hit a tapered spot that had me arching, which prompted my legs to fall far apart and a wet influx to pour from my slit.

The jester's lips swooped to my peak and snatched it once more, sealing his mouth around the distended skin and wrapping me in tight warmth. His body moved. His frame jutted forward, head bobbing, lips thrusting around my clitoris, which intensified the force of his ministrations. The feelings escalated, and the sensations climbed.

Oxygen drained from me, and my bones locked. I teetered on a precipice, helpless and on the verge of screaming.

And all at once, everything shattered.

A torrent of pleasure burst from my clit, from the place where Poet's mouth clung to me. The upheaval spread through my being. My folds pulsated against his tongue. I hovered off the bed, and my mouth flew open, a long holler shuddering from my lips.

Poet kept brushing his tongue over me, caressing my pussy with gentle licks until I slumped, wheezing and incoherent.

Never before.

Never until him.

When I regained some presence of mind, I glanced down. The jester still knelt before me, with his arms looped around my hips.

He planted a soft kiss on the tip of my clitoris and then stared back, his cheek resting on my shaky thighs, which had fallen off his shoulders a while ago.

My climax glistened on his mouth, the vision enticing rather than embarrassing. I watched as he deliberately licked his lips clean. Those eyes hooded. The irises brightened as my fingers flitted through his hair, as we gazed at one another.

Hush.

Too late. I couldn't have obeyed if I'd tried.

27

Poet

I still taste her. I remember the breathtaking flutter of her pussy against my tongue, the wet ecstasy when she came hard and sweet on my mouth, the feel of her body clenching and then going limp from the spasms. I recall the aftermath of her gaze, peach with delirium and hazy around the eyes as she stared at me. Even now, I feel her limbs splayed around my head, the heat radiating from her beautiful cunt driving me to madness.

Seasons almighty. That sort of kneeling, I don't mind. Ever.

It had elated me to discover that she was a loud minx, the flex of my tongue penetrating the impenetrable Royal and making her seep with pleasure. I'd dipped under her skirt and given her euphoria.

I could have talked her into anything then. The feeling had been mutual.

I would have stayed for as long as Briar had wanted. Alas, lingering for too long would have endangered her. So I tucked her in, kissed her nose, and slipped through the suite's hidden panel. In fact, I marveled the guards hadn't overhead, and whilst I could have covered her mouth and plagued her with pleasure all night long, I wasn't about to risk it.

Yet fuck …

The second I blasted into my chambers, I took care of the after-effects. I'd barely made it inside the room before ramming my back against the door and tearing through the clasps of my pants. My cock pitched from the fabric. The stem rose thickly, its sheath flushed a dark shade, and the crown enlarged.

Slickness beaded from the slit, proof that her pleasure had burrowed skin-deep.

I used my arousal to coat myself, then grasped that hellish, stiffened problem in my hand and began to pump. From the seat to the head, the weight of my cock broadened, pulsing with every firm stroke.

My head dropped against the door, a sequence of gritty noises fleeing my lungs. Briar's wild cries rooted into my mind.

Bewitched, obsessed, and in over my head, I seized the throbbing erection and jutted up and down. My hips lurched, my aching prick slinging in and out of my palm. I rode my hand, casting my body toward it with such abandon that my wrist threatened to snap.

My skull thudded against the foundation. Heat vaulted from my sac to the roof of my cock. And as I licked my lips to preserve the sweet tang of her body, my soul detonated.

With the luxurious taste of her pussy on my tongue and the memory of her moaning my name, I pounded my waist toward my hand. And I came—hot, heavy, and heavenly. On a fractured groan, I granted myself a long-suffering release, warmth spilling from the crown.

Muscles straining, I groped my cock until I nearly bit my tongue in half from the climax, draining myself to the last drop. Then I slumped, my breath racing to catch up. Her own name dangled from my tongue, but I kept it in, kept it close, because she was mine.

And I was hers.

All hers.

Peeling my body from the door, I cleaned myself in the bathroom before returning to the bedchamber. Tipsy on the princess, I dropped face-first onto my bed.

Very well. I was destined for hell.

The Royal thorn had slayed me to the besotted edge of lunacy. During the banquet dinner, I'd somehow managed to strike that block of wood with my daggers, flipping them in my hands without cleaving my fucking pinky.

If she were a courtier, I could have stayed in her bed. I would have recovered in the valley of her legs, with my head on her navel, our bodies in a position to go another deep round once she recuperated. We would have been naked, coated in sweat, and shouting by that point.

I would have placed myself at her mercy, breaching that small, ripe barrier inside her. After that, I would have made love to her leisurely, then harder. If she fancied, I'd have used one of my nifty little trinkets on her. If she wished, I would have shown her passion from every angle, every position.

Oh, but I longed to fuck her sweetly.

This week of lusting in fits and starts whilst partially dressed had been a torment. I had been a wreck for days, with no comprehension of a single cursed thing that occurred outside those slivers of time with Briar. With my brain and body preoccupied, who knew what sloppy counsel I'd offered the Crown at the Peace Talks.

Yet it was more than that. I wanted to make her happy.

Tossing amateurish, uninspired, and frankly maudlin options like baubles and bouquets out the window—hardly Briar's style or remotely what she cared about—I seized on the one gesture besides the physical that I could offer. She'd griped to me about heirs and heiresses being banned from the Peace Talks. Tradition for tradition's sake, etcetera, etcetera.

She had tried not to let the implication show. Yet however blunted, I had noted several times the envy in Briar's voice, all directed toward me for being allowed to join the Talks.

But had she, or any previous offspring in history, ever tried to debate the matter? Nay. Briar lamented, but she tolerated the rules out of a stale notion of custom and respect. In which case, compliance wouldn't change a thing.

The next morning, I strode into Basil and Fatima's antechamber unannounced and requested an audience. The subject was a tricky affair. I couldn't show my true intent without rousing speculation that I favored Her Royal Highness.

Instead, I arrived on the pretense of discussing the Lark's Night carnival. Since I'd plotted the discussion in advance, the topic unfolded as if by accident. My point of attack involved playing dumb and stacking innocent questions at their feet.

Did a doctrine exist stating Royal successors couldn't attend the Peace Talks until coronated? Did Spring not pride itself on being a progressive kingdom? Did the elder Royals suppose they had nothing wise to offer, nothing their offspring wouldn't eventually learn on their own?

Would the Royals say these Peace Talks inspired their heirs and heiresses? In what capacity? Do tell.

'Tis a shame Winter and Summer felt less compelled to bring their heirs to Spring, was it not? One would think they considered it unimportant, that if their colts weren't allowed to view the Talks as part of their breeding, why bother honoring this court with their presence at all?

However, Autumn had brought its daughter. At least one Season understood the magnitude of these events. Too bad the others hadn't set the same example.

It might show goodwill to reward Autumn for such fealty. It might influence the others next time, would it not? But naturally, I had no suggestions on the matter. What did I know of princesses?

By the way, wasn't tonight the final meeting? The one dealing with the least vital matters? Not so heavy-handed as to keep sacred, surely.

On that note, I wondered whether there was an exemplary way to provide closure to the Talks—something in addition to the final speeches, not altering tradition but adding to it.

What could that be, oh knowledgeable Crowns?

In the interim, I may have imagined Briar's face twisting in ecstasy whilst I sucked on her clit. I'd needed a visual to keep me motivated.

It took two hours, three flagons, and a dozen of my wittiest puns to manipulate the Spring Crown. They drew the conclusion I'd hoped they would, and I praised their wisdom.

What an excellent idea they had, inviting the Princess of Autumn to participate in the final Talk. However did they come up with it?

Dusting myself off, I strutted from the antechamber and headed for the first place I suspected to find her.

Low murmurs resounded from the archive library. At this hour, fewer visitors lingered, which was likely why she'd chosen to be here now. I slipped between the statuesque black shelves overflowing with ivy, disappeared into the recesses, and located her.

She faced one of the stacks, with those red tresses lazily bound at her nape. A high-collared hickory jacket hugged her frame, and a skirt flounced beneath, both pieces woven of tapestry. Like this, she resembled a proper university scholar—upright, studious, and corruptable.

When I'd sidled through the library and slipped that note onto Briar's desk after she saw me with the nobleman, it had been easy to pinpoint her. Reputably, she'd been spending quite some afternoons here.

Between the tall rows, the princess rifled through a shelf of tomes and tubular cases holding rolled documents. As I tiptoed behind her, my shadow bled across the gold-leaf spines. The instant my silhouette darkened the shelves, Briar straightened.

My arm snaked past her shoulders, and my fingernails flashed as I plucked an encased scroll from the shelf. I tilted my head, my lips brushing her earlobe and producing an enticing ripple across her flesh.

Low and lush, I murmured, "Read this one."

She quivered and whispered, "Why?"

"It chronicles a smutty, forbidden love story."

"Actually, it's a Spring ordinance against excessive public drunkenness."

"Pity. I feel so deceived by the fancy casing."

"That will teach you not to judge a scroll by its tube."

"The mouth on you," I flirted. "Are we still talking about paper?"

Pink stained her ears. "You are an unrepentant rake."

How tempting, the way Briar struggled to preserve a semblance of formality, despite the tremor in her voice. I was a glutton for this reaction. Her struggle to remain calm sent my blood racing.

Tart apples and fresh parchment wafted off her skin, inciting a myriad of immoral thoughts, all of which involved Briar plastered against the books and her wrists tacked above her head whilst I snapped my hips between her thighs. I pictured her moans hitting a volume that flooded the library.

My greedy fingers itched to grab. The gush of blood plummeted to my cock. If things kept on like this, my prick would be stuck in this position for the rest of its life. That would make it difficult to juggle.

It took far too much stamina to behave myself. The thought brought a smirk to my face.

"Astute, as ever," I intoned against the crook of her neck. "I imagine you would have a lot more to teach me." I returned the scroll to the shelf, then lowered my voice to a wily timbre. "Turn around."

Her voice came out as straight as a ruler. "We will be caught."

"Perish the thought," I rhymed, grabbing her hips and walking her backward into the aisle.

The princess smacked my wrists, trying to admonish me into letting her go—until my mouth latched onto the side of her neck. She gasped, and the back of her head dropped onto my shoulder.

Humming, I greeted her properly and deeply. My lips drew on her skin, and my tongue plied the sensitive flesh. Briar's mouth fell open, and her eyelids fanned like moth wings. The best part occurred when she threaded our fingers together over her hips and squeezed.

"Oh," she sighed. "Seasons. You are so disrespectful."

The crook of her throat muffled my devious laugh. Like that, I pulled her into the shadows. In the quiet, Briar's shaky pants and my low rumble filled the space.

Reaching a safe distance from the cataloger's desk, I dragged her behind the last row, towed my lips from that delectable pulse point, and spun her to face me. Our foreheads skidded together, our open mouths hovering closely. It took supreme effort to contain the pubescent grin threatening to ruin my devilish one.

A blush splashed across her face. I knew why. This was our first encounter since I left her bed last night.

Intent on darkening that blush, I descended and crushed my mouth to hers. My tongue split open Briar's lips, probing and mimicking a rather naked act. Her mouth folded under me, lips clutching and radiating moist heat. As I licked into the princess, a small appreciative noise curled from her chest and traveled to mine.

Damnation.

The instant my mouth peeled away from Briar, a puff of air blew from her swollen lips. "Poet," she breathed.

My response came out drugged. "Aye, Your Highness?"

"I wish you did not have to call me that."

"Aye, My Thorn?"

"If someone sees, I shall tell them you abducted me."

"Be my guest," I encouraged. "Now then, what are you meddling in down here? Tell me or I'll continue to violate you."

"Are you always this insolent?"

"Do I need to answer that?"

She withheld an aroused chuckle, then cleared her throat, a red splotch developing there. "I was ..."

"Hmm," I cooed. "Something amiss, Highness? You look flushed. Did someone fondle you inappropriately? Tell this jester at once, and the perpetrator shall endure a slow and agonizing castration."

Briar folded in her lips and whacked my arm. "If you can refrain from talking for more than a minute, I shall answer your original question."

Obediently, I waited with my arms banded around her.

Satisfied, she cleared her throat. "I was hoping to find documentation on the treatment of born souls. Perhaps a particular record of the past that might help when you approach the Crown. Something I might be able to use as well, to propose that Mother also reconsider the law in Autumn."

I leaned back. "That's what you've been doing?"

"During a few visits, yes. Whenever I have a free moment."

Briar spoke as though this were an obvious step for her to take. Yet for once in my infamous life, my tongue stalled. I gazed at her, warmth flooding my chest.

She wanted to help.

We stood in the heart of the mightiest weapon of all, a place of learning and knowledge, yet I'd poured through these archives before. I tried not to get my hopes up that she would find anything beyond the details of the law itself. That, and soulless logs listing the names and conditions of each prisoner who'd ever been swallowed whole by that law.

Seasons almighty. At this rate, the woman would slay me.

When I asked if she had made progress, her eyebrows crinkled in frustration. That expression testified she wasn't making as much headway as she'd wanted. She had a pile of chronicles yet to go through.

In the meantime, Briar shared her ideas, solutions about how to treat the mad and possibilities for those like Nicu, who needed special care. We hunkered deeper into the stacks and debated in hushed tones. I told her the points I planned on making to the Crown, then deliberated the strengths and drawbacks with her.

Gleaning Briar's insights for the next hour boosted my mood, to the point where I started to feel naughty. My palms sank to her ass, and my thumbs slid across those delectable spots where the crescents met her thighs.

Briar's eyes bulged, and she suppressed a grin. "Pooooooet," she drew out, part chortle, part reproach.

"I could devour you senseless," I swore whilst drizzling a finger between her collarbones. "I could open you up, right here against these books."

"Don't you dare. You'll ruin my concentration."

"Is that so? Though I'd relish the challenge, I can't imagine it's that easy."

"It wasn't until you existed."

"Mmm. Does that mean you enjoyed what my mouth did to you last night?"

She squirmed, my words reaching the right places under her skirt. The deep, damp, honeyed places that I still felt melting on my palate.

Another peachy flush consumed her cheeks. "Very much. I've never felt so ..."

My lips quirked. "In that case, I have a confession. I've never felt *so*, either."

"Liar."

"Only if we're being literal, sweeting."

Despite Briar's teasing, genuine uncertainty crossed her features. "Aren't we?"

My voice took on a raw edge as I ducked my head. "Would you like to know how you taste?" When she shivered, I pressed her harder into the bookshelf, my chest flush with hers. "I still feel your beautiful pussy on my tongue, slick and tart as the rest of you. I still feel your pleasure throbbing on my lips. I still feel your release like it's my own pulse."

As Briar's breathing stuttered, I pulled back enough to relish her slack features. "Princess, I never wanted to kneel before a ruler so badly in my life. My mouth has been parched for you. It's never been that way with anyone."

Her dilated pupils clung to mine, seconds before she hissed conspiratorially, "I can't believe we're talking about this in a place of antiquity."

I chuckled like a deviant. "Such a daring princess. But shall we find out just how daring you are? Hmm? Because we can do more talking."

Temptation snuck across her features. "It would be wrong."

"Your breathing doesn't sound like it would be wrong."

Her respirations had quickened and turned shallow. They thinned into slices that I could have plucked like petals.

Briar was earnest, genuine. Despite her withdrawal from others, this woman meant what she said and didn't mince words. And she wasn't the type to procrastinate. My thorn checked her thoughts briskly, sifted deeply through her feelings, and made her choices willfully. She scarcely delayed her decisions, and once she had her mind fixed, she acted.

Hence, one of the countless strengths I admired about her.

Another thing? The idiots of this court called Briar of Autumn uptight, starchy, and austere—terms I had capsized against the people who'd dared utter a critical word about her. I had shut down those judgements swiftly and tactfully. Regardless of society's ignorance, this woman could outshine this court any day with her intensity of emotions. The Royal widely deemed as genteel, squeamish, and reserved was in truth ardent and genuine, with a respect for her principles as well as her body.

But once acknowledged, Briar didn't cower from her desires. Nay, she claimed them. This thorn was scrupulous but passionate. More so than anyone I'd ever met.

That she allowed me to see this, feel this, hear this. 'Twas an honor that oftentimes humbled me as much as it excited me.

It took Briar only several moments to decide. Those mercury irises glinted with a mixture of fervor and heedfulness. She glanced sideways, monitoring the activity beyond the bookstacks. But no one ever came to this section, which is why I'd chosen it.

I balanced my finger under her chin and steered her back to me. "No one shall see or hear us," I promised.

Briar prefaced, "We won't disrespect the library."

Her bookish sanctimony won me over. My lips crooked. "I couldn't agree more. On the contrary, we shall pay worship to it."

I sauntered closer, staking my arms on either side of her. Not to cage her in, but to shield her on the rare chance someone did happen upon us. My body would conceal that fiery hair.

The panels of my jacket rustled against the clasps of hers. She rested her palms on my hips and burrowed her fingers in, the action loaded with need and trust.

My breath met hers. "Allow me to explain what I would do to you if this library were vacant. Whilst I fill your head with ideas, you're going to react whichever way your body wants. Let's see what happens, shall we?"

The books behind her jostled as she nodded. "Leave nothing out."

The request hauled my cock upright. "It's dark in here," I began. "So dark you can barely read the titles on the book spines. You're not supposed to be in this sanctuary at night, but you've broken in, eager to have these tomes at your disposal, like they belong only to you. But as you wander through the stacks, running your fingers over the bindings, you feel a presence behind you."

Briar closed her eyes and curled into the shelves, listening to me narrate.

"He's there," I whispered, my words slithering up her ear. "Indeed, he's been waiting for you. The jester knew you'd come, and you knew he might be there, so you forgive him for the presumption. Thus, you make a game out of it. You shift between the rows whilst he trails behind, stalking you into the alcoves. And you wonder what shall happen if he catches you ... what he'll do."

Briar's teeth pinched her lower lip. One set of fingers abandoned my waist and glided over the spines behind her.

"You hear muffled footfalls, feel his weight. No matter where you turn, the signs never abate," I rhymed, because why not? "Until at last, you round a corner and stumble into a dead end, where the shelves loom, so tall they disappear into the rafters. Your finger reaches out to trace a gold-leaf title. And there, he finds you."

The other hand released my waist and draped across her stomach before sinking to her abdomen. Then it descended lower.

I tilted my head, speaking even harsher against her profile. "One arm snakes around you from behind. The other slides from your ass to the back of your thigh, which he raises off the ground."

A private sigh left Briar's mouth. She gripped one of the books whilst the other hand groped her skirt, lifting the hem to the apex of her body.

I mumbled, "With his arm bracing your leg, the jester plants your foot on one of the shelves, the toe of your boot nudging the titles. Like this, you feel a current of air stir under your skirt and dip into the cut of your undergarments. Then it strokes your crease like a tongue."

My eyes sank from her face to the groomed hand vanishing between her legs and—wicked hell—pivoting upward. The sight broadened my erection. I bent my fingers, nailing them into the bookcase to keep myself anchored.

The words charged at her. "The jester's own fingers follow the current and dive into the slit covering your pussy, which has become so very wet."

Briar yielded to a soft moan, which hit my lips. How I would like to bite that sound.

Instead, my eyes clung to the vision of her legs shuffling wider for access. One heel propped onto a lower shelf to splay her further. This bunched the skirt higher, revealing her hand as it jutted languidly between the plush folds of her pussy. She would be sleek, pliable, her walls consuming the delicate pump of her fingers.

Seasons help me. The image spurred my mouth, the descriptions rolling off my tongue in sharp pants. "You're pressed between the books and your lover's chest. With his arm securing you, his fingers nudge through your cunt and fill you to the brink. They start thrusting, slowly and so far into you, all the way out and then back in."

Briar's exhalations diced through the alcove. She arched into the books, and her hand swiveled, her fingers mimicking the fantasy. I caught sight of those glistening digits entering and retreating from the rift, sifting between her folds, pitching into the sweet oval that tightened around her.

As I spoke, my teeth ached, as did my cock. "He probes your pussy, fucking you gently with his hands, striking your cunt to the knuckles."

Briar's mouth hung open. Rapid puffs ejected from her, in pulsing tempo with her hand. From her clenched eyes and heaving chest, I saw how the slick flanks inside her started to constrict, clamping around her lunging fingers.

"You flatten your palms on the books," I murmured. "Your hips sway faster against the jester's hard fingers as they contort into that compact, intimate part of you."

The bookshelf trembled. One of the tomes lurched toward the edge, in danger of toppling over.

Briar keened, matching the movements. Her waist circled against my pelvis, her fingers bobbed into her soaked body, and her face crimped with building pleasure. She hastened after that bliss, joining both hands now and hoisting them into her.

Briar bore into herself, her body twitching from the impact. Her mouth hung and emitted rough but silent moans, in sync with the cadence of her wrists. She worked her cunt keenly, relentlessly.

At last. She was *there*.

I dragged the flat of my tongue across the seam of her lower lip. "And because his vicious touch makes your pussy feel magnificent ..." I leaned in, covered my palm over her mouth, and muttered quietly, "you cry out."

Briar tensed, then splintered apart. Her folds tremored, firing down her limbs so roughly I felt it against my own. Endless moans slammed into my hand, her bones rattled, and her frame jolted into me. With her spine bowing toward the ceiling, and her digits lodged between her thighs, Briar came long and low.

My other hand choked the shelf as I hunched into her, savoring the texture of her sobs. Less than a foot from where she pounded into herself, my cock twitched painfully. Seasons, the stem was so hard it could chop logs in half.

My train of thought staggered, held captive by the sight and sound of the princess with her eyes slammed shut and her orgasm striking my palm. Her pussy would be thrumming, inflated, and flushed.

Another moment, and I would have exploded with her. That, without so much as fondling a single phallic inch.

Briar heaved into my palm until the sounds ebbed into a fine mist. She crumbled against the bookcase, the weight finally knocking that one precarious tome from its perch. Wheezing, she opened her eyes to glance at the fallen title, clarity returning.

She withdrew her fingers from the crux of her thighs. The skirt flapped back into place.

Her attention floated to me. "How am I ... ever going to ... research now?"

An amused chuckle jumped from my chest. "Blame me, sweeting."

She laughed weakly. "I will, thank you."

"You're *very* welcome."

To that, Briar shook her head. "You are impossible."

I snatched her wrists, brought those glistening fingers to my lips, and sucked them into my mouth. Her release seeped onto my palate. Briar blushed, watching in fascination as I tasted what she'd done to herself.

What could I say? This besotted jester couldn't keep his hands off this magnetic princess. In an alternate reality, I would stay with her so we could take a victory lap, bring the fantasy to life for a second time. More innocent books would plummet. The entire library would quake off its hinges. And once we had our clothes back in order, she and I could investigate together.

In this reality, jesters and princesses thrived separately. Nonetheless, the desire to return her industrious efforts spurred me on. Of what was to come, I felt excitement.

Finally, our breathing evened out. We sank back to earth, echoes of the library drifting through the rows.

I kissed the tips of Briar's fingers, relinquished her hands, and cradled her face, my thumbs stroking her cheeks. "Be studious but spare some mental energy for tonight." When the space between her brows bunched in puzzlement, my mouth gave hers one more heated caress. "'Tis a surprise."

Poet

Are you still with me? Splendid.

Except you might regret it soon. For I certainly did …

That evening, I dressed to slay. In a dramatic mood, I chose black and white from my wardrobe. I polished it off with filaments of kohl around my eyelids and added a sickle-shaped thorn vine to the corner of my left eye.

Second-guessing myself, I checked my appearance three times in the mirror.

Primping aside, I got to the throne room early, where I poured myself a chalice from the trestle table laden with flagons of wine, carafes of nectar, and trenchers of pomes, grapes, meats, and cheeses. Ever the jester, I refused to wait for the Royals to assemble before drinking.

Mid-slosh, Briar entered the room with her mother. I glanced up—and my tongue cleaved to the roof of my mouth.

She wore an off-the-shoulder emerald dress with short sleeves and simple, clean lines that allowed the shade to flourish on its own. The style was classic, elegant, and confident. Not to mention, it allowed her flaming hair to explode with color. Her tresses hung partially down, the upper layers swept up loosely and threaded with tiny wildflowers.

Her wide eyes, a clear sky. Her freckles, a constellation.

She had the glow of someone recently and repeatedly licked, rubbed, and sated. Her jester did that. His tongue would do it a million times over, until his knees embedded into the floor.

Briar's gaze leaped across the room and landed on me. Visibly, she tried to remain placid, but it proved an evident chore. Her complexion warmed, and a grin fought to break through her lips. In the library, numerous moans had softened that mouth, and—

Fluid splashed onto my sleeve. I jolted as wine overflowed from the cup in my left hand, whilst the tipped flagon arrested in my right poured claret liquid all over the fucking place.

"Shit," I hissed, jerking the vessel upright and dropping it onto the table, where it teetered for a second before settling in place.

In my periphery, I caught the humorous flash of Briar's teeth. Two incisors dug into her lower lip, stifling her mirth.

Oh, I knew other ways to make those teeth sink into that lip. However, that was the bloody problem. I had been mentally stripping her to the point where I'd forgotten the vessel in my grasp, and now the page closest to me hastened to wipe the mess.

Impulsively, I reached for the cloth. "It was my fault. Let me."

The lad gawked. "It's my pleasure, Court Jester."

And it was his job. Denying him would insult, discredit, and mortify the servant.

I could flout the rules. I could take care of the spill myself on the pretense of arrogant pride, and it wouldn't shock the monarchy. But I couldn't invalidate the lad's position.

Only in moments like these did I feel the remorse of being pampered. There was nothing gratifying about watching someone prostrate themselves to clean my mistakes, as if I were an emperor and the servant a peon. Dammit, I couldn't even thank him audibly without causing controversary among the staff, who would hear about it and sneer at the lad.

Nevertheless, I inclined my head to the page. Then I turned and stumbled into the piercing gaze of Briar's mother. Based on her narrowed eyes, the Autumn Queen had seen my lapse.

As did the Spring King, who entered behind them, along with the remaining Royals. Though, Basil interpreted the cause differently. The man grinned like a happy asshole and ribbed, "Gracious, Poet. Intoxication and clumsiness entail drinking the wine first."

"Very wise advice, Sire," I answered with a phony slur, to everyone's amusement.

The Royals were in prime spirits at this final assembly, all of them eager to celebrate and then get the hell out of here. In addition to kinship, weeks of conference had produced its share of animosity and hissy fits.

The princess's throat bobbed. Her anxious gaze flitted my way and received the most imperceptible of nods from me.

Beguile them, Your Highness.

She nodded back. Henceforth, Autumn and I became invisible to one another. That was the impression we gave as the Royals took their seats. I leaned against a column and noted the princess's wistfulness as she settled into her late father's chair. As she did, Briar traded meaningful looks with her mother.

Basil and Fatima wiggled their rumps to get comfortable, then the king slammed his paddle palms together. His peers jumped in unison, as they always did.

"I declare this the final gathering of The Dark Seasons," he said. "And a novel occasion, for not only do we culminate these proceedings and go forth in peace once more, but we enhance tradition by having Autumn's heiress as our guest. A new branch of custom that my queen and I have proposed, and we Royals have agreed upon and hope to continue with the sum of our offspring over the years to come. From this day forth, our successors will be invited to attend the closure of the Peace Talks. Princess Briar, you are most welcome."

To their applause, she beamed.

To that beam, my chest warmed.

"A hasty overture," the Summer King grunted behind his flaccid whiskers. "But tolerable, I suppose. My queen and I will be pleased to have our son bred with this tradition. It's a misfortune that other proposals regarding appropriate attendants were denied this year."

I rolled my eyes. A travesty for him, indeed. I had made him snicker like the rest of them, yet this hypocrite—this ignoramus who wouldn't know a true fool if they pissed in the king's tankard, much less if I flashed a mirror in front of his face—remained set on banning me from the Talks.

"I must say," Fatima's rather spacious mouth bragged, "it behooved us to set such a precedent, but arguments were made in favor of it. It never entered our minds until a conference with Poet—"

My head whipped in her direction.

"—and somehow, the notion sprung into our heads."

Fucking. Shit.

For a second, my eyes clenched shut. The queen could have left me out of it, and things might have turned out differently. Because she didn't, it snuffed the mood like a candle.

Well, now I had to look.

Briar's smile vanished in a blast of smoke. A series of noxious emotions followed, namely confusion, disappointment, and finally indignation. The muscles in her face ticked. As they did, she wrestled with them, striving to appear neutral and unruffled.

Yet I saw the accusation in her eyes as they sliced over to me. Briar thought she had earned her seat here by being a flawless and respectable princess, when in essence I'd handed this opportunity to her.

I made this happen. She hadn't.

Had Briar assumed it a coincidence when I told her a surprise was coming and then, on the same day, an invitation to join the Talks arrived at her door? Apparently so.

Either that, or she had understood this was the surprise. Except she hadn't realized until this second that I played a role in orchestrating it.

Her nostrils flared. She snatched her chalice and drained the contents, her throat overextending itself. I had offended plenty of times, but I'd never vexed a woman to the point where I lacked a prolific means to fix it. My powers of perception deserted me, since I should have predicted this upheaval, that the Crown would reveal the details of our little chat.

From one topic to the next, the princess contributed her thoughts with tenacity, objectivity, and a private grudge. The whole infernal time, she ignored me. To my comments alone, she remained stiff and dry, all timber and no blaze.

Since I couldn't do it myself without rousing suspicion, I silently motioned to one of the servants, who headed toward Briar with a bowl of strawberries. She had once mentioned they were her favorite of Spring's fruit. 'Twas a subtle and gentle peace offering to start, until I could figure out how to atone more frankly later.

Unfortunately, His Royal Fart of a Summer Majesty had been drinking with aplomb. On the servant's way, the king took a break from his mead binge and toed the lad's calf with his boot, which caused the young man to stumble and nearly drop the bowl. This happened too quickly, before I could intercept.

Rhys had also done so without the Royals noticing, otherwise it would have insulted his hosts. Briar and I flung the prick identical glares. He hadn't hurt the lad, otherwise my fist would have found its way into King Rhys's face. However, his actions had discouraged the servant, so that he placed the bowl swiftly beside Briar without making eye contact.

The princess motioned to offer a kind word and conciliatory gesture, but the page walked away too fast. On his way back to the refreshment table, I cupped his shoulder and murmured reassurances, after which he retreated with a grateful expression. Still, my locked jaw took several seconds to smooth out.

To hell with this. We needed to appear impartial to each other, but I should have risked it and delivered the fruit myself instead of involving someone else.

Nonetheless, I had a hunch my offering went unappreciated. But out of respect for the servant, Briar chewed on the berries until the bowl was empty.

I rounded the table, hands bolted behind my back, and preceded to make points of my own. My mockery should have riled her. My reflections should have drawn her attention. Alas, to my annoyance, the princess consulted her peers without sparing me a glance.

"Moving on to the subject of fools," Basil announced.

My gaze whipped up, as did the princess's. Her eyes darted to me, silently questioning whether I expected this to be on the agenda.

Despite the collective monstrosity and the continental decree proclaiming born souls as Royal property, the specifics of their treatment were determined by the individual kingdoms. The methods used by each Season weren't unified concerns like import and export routes, neutral territories, pirates and smugglers, the codes of war, or migration between borders.

So nay. To put it mildly, I hadn't expected this.

At the right opportunity, I'd meant to coax new ideas about born souls into Spring's mind, to win them over slowly but surely. However, here was a bounty of Royals at my disposal. The laws wouldn't change today, but it could be a beginning. This might be an opportunity to put a dent in their bigotry on a grander scale.

Whether or not I fancied myself ready, I had to be.

The princess and I swapped another mutual look wrought from three days in a forest. It deemed this moment worthy of putting aside her wounded pride and my sly inducements. We hadn't planned for this, but we'd shared ideas in the archive library. That, and our ability to read one another, would have to suffice.

As a formality, Basil unrolled and recited from the Fools Decree. The document stated that whilst so-called *"born fools"* remained blood relations to their families, they became the property of the Crown. They were to be used either for labor if the tasks demanded *"little in the way of intellect,"* or entertainment if they were prone to *"clumsiness and comical behavior,"* or to be manacled as prisoners in dungeons if they were *"violent or useless."*

My retinas burned. As the Spring King reiterated this, I envisioned my son belonging to the alleged "simpleton" class, to be harassed at carnivals whenever he lost direction.

Basil dropped the scroll on the table. "Spring welcomes any arguments regarding a new trade amendment to be added to the Decree."

And now I understood.

In one of the earlier meetings, the Royals had briefly considered the option of trading born souls between the kingdoms. Nonetheless, they had agreed to postpone the discussion until next year. I'd been counting on that delay to prepare counterarguments. Yet evidently, these monarchs had changed their minds at some point during my absence, whilst I'd been confined with Briar in the wildflower forest.

Fatima quoted from a working draft, which stated, *"Fools, and all that they are, shall be bound to their new Season."*

Because each Season valued certain attributes in born souls, I harbored no illusions that this gathering wouldn't sign the amendment—another way for the vultures to turn slaves into easy pickings.

In Summer, child prisoners wove nets, working nonstop despite how it mutilated their hands.

The clumsier they were, the more amusing to Spring.

Thirsty for knowledge, Winter's scientists and physicians valued sedate captives. By the same token, the court's university scholars had been expressing an interest in researching born souls' varying behaviors—so I'd heard from my sovereigns.

And despite requiring more beguine tasks such as clearing orchards of rotted fruit, Autumn benefited chiefly from the able-bodied.

As for the mad, they decomposed in the Seasons' prisons. Yet the Royals considered this problematic not because it was barbaric, but only because they needed those spaces for criminals.

This applied to Summer most of all, having the greatest number of criminals. Sea breezes aside, humidity and mosquito bites tended to make its citizens irritable. Whoever deemed the ocean an invigo-rating place needed to reconsider the reality of sunburns, crashing waves, and sand wedged into places no one should have it.

Although none of the monarchs wished to house or tolerate them, the mad would be included in the amendment, in case an unforeseen change or opportunity arose. In the meantime, no doubt the Royals would be discussing alternatives of how to deal with the situation.

Rhys of Summer grumbled, though he'd be of more use to ev-eryone stuffing his mustache in his mouth. "I propose a collective dumping ground for the deranged and overly imbecilic," he said. "The ones who prove savage or impossible to utilize. We might establish an encampment on neutral soil—one of the islands, perhaps. There's a legendary but uncharted rainforest island our seafarers and sand drifters have been searching for. If we expand our efforts and locate it, that would be the perfect remote location. Like a leper colony."

My blood boiled. "Ignorance is more contagious than leprosy will ever be."

"Buffoonery is a hazard," Summer said. "The mad rant and rave and injure innocent people. If not useful, the naturally stupid are meddlesome and a burden. In and of themselves, those factors act as a contagion—a severe case of fleas."

Briar's eyebrows slammed together. "If you consider born souls such a trial, why not leave them to their families?"

"And allow the mutants to freely litter our kingdoms? That would complicate our plight, not solve it. It's bad enough that we must stock the unmanageable ones when we lack the cell space."

"Ah," I pounced. "May I offer a tip, then?"

"Over my rotting corpse, you may."

With relish, I added his dead carcass to my bucket list of ambi-tions, then moved forth. "I would suggest getting rid of assholes. Send them to this remote, mythical island of yours where starvation, dehydration, and basic survival will be a problem. I mean, nobody values the company of a piece-of-shit. That would provide extra room in the villages."

Rhys's head practically doubled in size. "I see your puny brain requires perspective. Why do we own idiots? Because they inhibit our citizens. One who doesn't have the wit to look after oneself is a waste of space. Families, both rich and especially poor, cannot afford the shame or inconvenience of looking after a fool. As sovereigns, we serve our people by shouldering the task, working the able fools and leashing the rest. It's our responsibility to oversee the unnatural."

"That doesn't extend to treating anyone with cruelty," the princess blurted out. "That's not our right, nor should it be."

The Royals stared at her. Their expressions couldn't be more transparent, nor more effortless to interpret: Since when had this become an issue of sympathy instead of practicality?

"You speak as though they're one of us, dear," Silvia of Winter said with concern.

King Rhys blew hot air. "You may come from the lenient land of Autumn, but don't be naïve, Your Highness. The mad are prone to explode at any moment. As for simpletons, if they're good for labor or humor, at least then they have a purpose."

"Spring's standards for humor could be higher," I suggested. "If Spring needs slapstick, my kind can perform that to greater effect."

"And you cost more to do it."

"In other words, you're cheap. Or you think Spring is penniless." I maneuvered between Basil and Fatima and draped my arms over the tops of their chairs. My hands dangled beside their heads as I leaned down. In turn, they regarded my words, their attention a crawlspace through which I implanted an idea. "I didn't realize that was the widespread impression you wanted to give, Your Majesties. 'Tis dawning on me. You may own born souls, but that any court would rely this desperately on unpaid service is inconsistent with the quality of your wine."

"For the mad, I propose a physician's facility on neutral ground," Briar announced, introducing one of the ideas we'd talked about in the library.

King Rhys stamped his fist on the table like a mallet. "An excellent recommendation. A tower for fools, where we could use them for medical research. Winter, your scientists and doctors will be pleased."

The princess bristled. "I meant a sanctuary. A place for rehabilitation. If something is amiss with the mind, it should be examined and cared for. In addition to physicians from *each* Season, Winter might devote a batch of its scholars to the cause."

"You cannot fix quicksand. It's an eternal peril."

"We don't know that. From our individual thrones, we could hold court and summon physicians to determine what conditions born souls live with and whether they pose a threat. If so, they will be sent to this sanctuary for healing and stability."

"Good grief, we'd be attending to them more than the rest of our people," King Rhys brayed. "And for no fucking reason."

I rose from my spot between Basil and Fatima, then rounded the table. "Improvement of society comes to mind," I said, as though the prospect just came to me. "Royals consider themselves regal and forward-thinking. If that's true, your actions should reflect that. There's hardly dignity to be found by relying purely on dungeons, oubliettes, and drunken guards.

"Imagine. If you have the talent to better comprehend the grips of insanity, the people will have unlimited faith in you. Think of the widespread awe. It will establish there's nothing the Seasons can't accomplish. That shall be quite the legacy."

Avalea of Autumn twisted toward her daughter. In a reasonable voice that made me tense in my tracks, the queen asked, "How many physicians would we require for this treatment, when so many of our other citizens need remedies daily? What manpower could we spare to build this facility? At whose expense? How much of our resources would go to it?"

Briar wavered. "Exactly. Those are details to be deliberated upon. As to the people who don't present a danger, they should remain with their families. Their fates should be a matter kept between them and their relatives."

Her eyes flitted to me. On cue, I swooped in. The vile terms being thrown about tasted rancid on my lips. But for this to work, we had to maintain that facade.

Whilst pacing beside the length of the table, I tapped my chin. "I wonder. Far be it from me, but granting families that liberty would establish even more loyalty and devotion to their Crown. Everyone longs for the power of choice in their life, no matter how insignificant. And come, 'tis not as though relatives of half-wits will want to keep their burden."

I would. Most wouldn't.

That was because I didn't consider it a "burden." Most did.

Nicu had a less taxing condition compared to others, so the devotion I expressed wouldn't be uttered by every relative. All the same, that didn't warrant clamping anyone in manacles. These were *people*, we were speaking of. The world needed to stop identifying what they called "born fools" as inhuman and worthless, with no strengths or souls of their own.

Though, it was too soon to voice that point. The denizens of these kingdoms had livelihoods to think about. If they weren't engaged in trades that already utilized their own blood relations with the Crown's permission, chances were slim those families would be attached. In that case, artists, fishermen, harvesters, and doctors across the Seasons weren't likely to lose their appointed slaves.

Hideous as I found it, this wouldn't create a major shift or influence anyone's attitude, but at least relinquishing born souls to their families and rightful homes would be a small beginning.

It would allow me to keep Nicu. That came first, before all else.

I leaned my hip against the table, directly across from Briar. "It's a minor risk that creates the illusion of choice. The people won't have their relatives taken from them, but rather be given the power to 'donate' them, should they wish. Hence, widespread love for the Crown will be further cemented."

"We'd be taking fools seriously," Silvia of Winter censured.

"And asking our people to do the same," Giselle of Summer revoked.

"This discussion is negating the entire amendment," her husband spat. "It's negating the entire Decree. That we've detoured this long is beyond disgraceful. Since when do freaks of nature deserve our compassion?"

Her Autumn Highness turned up her nose. "You could say avalanches and floods are freaks of nature."

"We can't control the elements. They are the divine forces of our world, and their power is the great mystery of the almighty Seasons. As for our society—*that* we can control."

"Every human on this continent—on this *earth*—was created by nature."

"And we Royals are ordained by The Dark Seasons to make decisions." The Summer King stabbed his finger onto the table and gritted out, "It's. Our. Duty."

"It's not our duty to abuse. It's our duty to assist."

"For insolence's sake!" he boomed. "They are not normal!"

Those four words erupted like a volcano through the room. The momentary silence that followed had an eerie, equally destructive quality.

"Mother?" Briar swerved toward Avalea, imploring, "You and Father always said ... You always showed me how we should try to ... If people need help ..."

The queen rested her palm over her daughter's, voicing her fellow monarchs' next thought. "How would the people feel about this in any kingdom? Yes, they may appreciate the choice of what to do about their relatives, without creating a notable reduction in service. But if some families *did* choose to keep their born relatives at home—for whatever reasons or beliefs they've kept hidden—there would be forced integration in the towns."

"But perhaps that's what we need. If that's what it takes—"

"Those families would be accused of sullying their communities and being sympathizers, a circumstance that could lead to civil tension and public aggression. Moreover, the kingdoms would see their rulers spend precious energy and reserves to assist the mad over the rest of the public. This, while also rejecting the possibility of widely supported trade. In the minds of many citizens, we would be favoring those viewed as …" She hedged, illustrating her own private dislike of the phrases so often used by our courts. "Well, we would be favoring the minority over the majority, who also require our aid. The latter would see it as an imbalance, a reduction of our support."

Briar shook her head. "But—"

"So how would they react to this change?"

"Precisely," seconded the Summer King, flinging out his arms and falling back into his chair.

Precisely, I thought with fury racing through my veins. Impartial Autumn, naughty Spring, and stoic Winter had their limits, their dark sides like wrathful Summer. And prejudice was a generations-old curse.

How *would* the public react?

They would riot. They would commit mass acts of violence. That was how.

Actually, that was the least of it. They'd do more than riot if they got their hands on born souls or anyone labeled as a sympathizer. Those farming pitchforks, blacksmith tools, and carpentry instruments weren't just good for practicing a trade.

Helpless, I watched the queen's rebuttal mobilize my princess to the Royals' side of the throne room. "You're not only proposing a monumental social change. You're proposing to question people's beliefs on a massive and sudden scale, thus risking upheaval. You're asking them to make sacrifices and to doubt you. What you're suggesting could take decades to achieve peacefully."

"We don't have decades!" Briar shouted.

She meant that I didn't have decades. Nicu didn't.

It got so quiet we could have heard a dust mote landing on the floor. The stunned expressions of Briar's mother and everyone seated extracted a blush from the princess. "That is," she stammered. "That is to say …"

After a moment, those eyes dulled, losing their defiant luster. Her gaze cast toward the windows. Then she took a deep, resigned breath. "Yes. It will take more time."

My mouth snapped out of its paralysis. "By my estimation, there are two more hours for this meeting. Entertain us with ideas."

Avalea narrowed her eyes at me. "This isn't something to be decided in one sitting, Court Jester."

That look sunk valleys-deep. It said, *Stay away from my daughter.*

Never mind that her daughter was a grown woman. Because she was also a future monarch.

And the queen *knew*. She knew I'd done everything graphic to the princess, short of burying my promiscuous cock inside her. She knew as Jinny had known, as mothers did.

As fathers did, too.

"Autumn is right. It could take years alone to reach a unified plan on this matter," Fatima agreed with reluctance, along with her husband.

"Assuming we all have the same goal, which we do not," Rhys nagged. "The topic is moot."

"Of course. I understand," the princess said. "It was untimely of me to suggest it."

I felt her words in my fists. Her speech drifted through this room and fled through its doors, where it surged beyond the palace and led to Jinny's cottage.

Briar glanced at me. An apology cracked her lips apart, trying to claw its way from her throat. But dear us, we were surrounded. We were on display and had made a display.

A vicious corner of me relished seeing the princess's mouth clamp shut, seeing her inwardly gag on her own guilt. Her remorse insulted us both, for that meant she'd accepted her blunder rather than rising above it and pushing this feud to its limit. Hence, I didn't want this woman's sorrowful eyes. Nay, I wanted a fucking retraction.

Fury scorched my tongue. "I wouldn't have anticipated you'd accept defeat easily, Your Highness," I sneered. "It's not a Royal's way. Rather disappointing."

Briar hardened into a bust of marble. "It is not defeat. It's diplomacy. If you were one of us, you would understand that."

"True. I'm not one of you." From the end of the table, I flattened my palms on the surface and leaned in. "And yet I'm here."

"You're here as a cohort, a darling of the Crown."

How she wished that were exclusively true. "Correction, Princess. My face might get me through plenty of doors, but it's my tongue that allows me to stay."

"Influential or not. You're a subject, not a sovereign. And my queen is right. This is a colossal undertaking, not to be pursued rashly but diplomatically."

"When you choose to shackle a topic—enslave, torture, and ridicule it—you're not confronting it or being *diplomatic*," I hissed. "You're only telling the world you're not equipped to solve it in any other creative or intelligent way. You're admitting that *you're* the fucking fool."

"Poet!" Basil railed.

Poet, indeed. I'd gotten us into this and blamed myself for not thinking quickly enough to shoot her down. I should have whipped up a word, a sentence, a fucking cough when I had the chance, instead of letting her walk us right to the precipice—then turn us right back around.

Apparently, I should have known better than to hope the princess wouldn't be swayed. Verbal parries with me didn't compare to debating with Royal elders.

Betraying this most tender of subjects hadn't been Briar's intention. If the regret in her eyes was any indication, her instincts had played little part in this.

But deliberate or not, her rationale made a choice and voiced it, jilting me in the process. How pitiful to think we could band together. I should have relied on myself, as I had been doing. I'd spent a year honing my power over this court; targeting others until they either feared me, respected me, or wanted me; and wheedling my way into Spring's trust. For that, I didn't need Autumn's help.

Nay. I had wanted it. Disillusioned, moonstruck me had wanted

333

her on my side. This woman—the one person who had backfired on me, who'd turned my motivations inside-out from the very beginning, who turned *me* into the target.

No more, and never again. Once more, me against them.

I must have been picking the princess apart with my eyes, because heads banked from me to her. The Queens of Winter blinked. Autumn's queen stared at the princess. Basil and Fatima festered in my direction. With a single verbal punch, I had offended every Royal at the table.

Under that horrendous mop of a mustache, the King of Summer gloated, taking black pleasure in watching my sovereigns reprimand me.

Aye. 'Twas a rare sight.

With my humor lost, I trod on thin ice. The princess and I both did, and from the perspectives of present company, over so paltry a topic.

If I persisted, I would dig a deeper grave. My temper would flare and override my cunning. It would lead me to spit things I'd regret later, possibly whilst I spent a day in the dungeon cooling my heels. Best-case scenario if I didn't outright expose myself as a sympathizer.

We may not have rallied each figurehead, but we'd had Spring. We'd had my sovereigns in our fucking grasps.

Basil and Fatima dismissed me from the throne room. The princess finally located her spine and had the nerve to object, which her mother quelled by clasping Briar's hand. Brilliant move, for my sweet thorn had done me enough favors today.

Inclining my head, I took measured steps to the door. Outside, I thundered down the corridor toward her suite, where I hid in a recess, waiting to ambush the shit out of her.

Two hours hence, she came.

Pausing in front of the door, Briar turned toward me at the same instant I turned away from her. I headed toward the first hidden panel available, thwacked my palm against it, and stalked inside. My pace forced her into a trot behind me. We cut into a tunnel and ascended a random stairway. I couldn't care less where the fuck it led.

We spiraled high, our shoes beating the stones. By the time we reached a solitary door at the landing, my joints burned. No matter, for I threw open the barrier and flung myself inside, listening as she closed the door behind us.

My eyes scrolled across the room. Ah, the bell tower.

Arched lookouts cut into the four walls, offering a panorama of Spring. In the room's center, a bloated instrument of song dangled, its girth promising a bloody death to one's eardrums if they happened to wander here on the hour.

I stood there, contemplating the massive bell. "'Tis a wonder the Crown doesn't use this room for torture," I mused. "Punishment by a dozen gong-lashes. The considerable effect of noise is underrated—not that I condone torture. The sight of blood makes me woozy."

"I realize you're angry," Briar defended from behind, her voice jabbing needles into my shoulder blades. "I did not expect the Decree to come up for discussion."

"Did you already know how you felt about the matter? I'm told having a solid point of view helps when you're taken off guard. By the way, I assume the Royals sanctioned the amendment and signed it. 'Tis splendid to know it's gone into immediate effect."

"A point of view needs backup, as in any debate," she argued. "You could have cautioned me in the library to prepare better. Perhaps I would have found something of substance had I known to look harder, but you threw me into this!"

"One, I've every faith that you did your best in the archives. I've tried myself to unearth information that would help my case, to no avail. That you didn't find anything isn't the problem.

"Two, whilst I do have access to privileged intel, the Peace Talks are another matter. I'm not privy to an advanced schedule of their theatrics, though I'm flattered by your assumption. Three, forgive the professional fool for thinking he was doing something special for you."

"I assumed you merely heard they were going to invite me—and *that* was the surprise," Briar defended, her presence a cannon at my back. "I didn't think you schemed them into it, but I should have. I should know you by now. Who are you to represent my business? Who are you to steer my fate? You undermined and mortified me!"

"Nay, I accomplished what you should have done for yourself," I seethed, whipping around. "That's what this is about. You're smart and self-sufficient, but you let tradition cheat you. Mayhap that's why we couldn't find a fucking thing in the archives—because when you cling to past ways and past documents, there's nothing *new* to say!" I punctured the word by slamming my palm against the bell. "You want things to change, Briar? Then change them!"

"It's complicated," she yelled back.

"So is having a son, but I manage."

"You're speaking about one child. I'm speaking about seven monarchs and the principles of four kingdoms. That's what I have against me."

"Against you?" I scathed. "Plague. Natural disasters. Traitors and assassins. A broken treaty and an unexpected war with another Season. Brush up on your princess skills, because if Mama Autumn hasn't warned you yet, devastation is a monarch's responsibility. A seat at the Peace Talks and a failed debate with the Royals might soon be the least of your challenges. If you can't handle that, then at least fake your gratitude when a person cares enough about you to help."

"I care about you, too!"

In an instant, I stood in front of Briar. My hot breath clashed with hers. "Tell me, then. Tell me what I am to you."

I scarcely entertained the illusion that our world would accept us. Yet my mind demanded to know. However daft, my pulse hammered to know.

Briar's eyes shimmered. Naturally, the answer I wanted didn't come.

Without noticing it, I'd let her too far into me.

"I'm Autumn. You're Spring," she said, helpless. "You're staying. I'm leaving."

"You're royalty. I'm not." My chuckle came out spiteful, as dry as soot. "It must have been titillating for you, having the sinful Court

Jester at your disposal, bringing your pretty-filthy secret to his knees—in so many ways."

Pink flooded Briar's cheeks. "It wasn't like that! You are—"

"Of course, whilst you were beating the shit out of my heart in the throne room, I would have appreciated you not crushing my agenda."

"They're my predecessors and have reigned for decades. They've done it while maintaining a peaceful alliance. I had to consider their arguments."

"You fickle, submissive twit! I've spent a year buttering up Spring, but in a single bite you chewed my efforts and spit them back out!"

"I hardly forced you to snarl at me in public." She flattened a palm on her stomach, the other extending toward me in a placating gesture. "Poet, I believe from the bottom of my heart in what you're doing. I'm on your side, but you're looking at this as a father. I must look at this as a Royal. I can't shirk what my ancestors put in place."

"You mean the dead and buried ones, sweeting?" I snarled. "Those ancestors?"

"Stop talking down to me, Poet. I'm not a lost child who will never grasp the difference between left and right. I'm not Nicu!"

Dead. Silence.

When I'd flung those daggers at that wooden board in the great hall last night, the impact vibrated the hilt. Her words were those daggers. I was the marker. She hit my center, cleaved into it.

I staggered back, one clumsy step, like a fool.

Like a *fool*.

If the bell wailed, I wouldn't hear it. Her voice hacked through me enough. If I'd been livid before, 'twas nothing compared to this.

This pain.

Briar's eyes widened as she registered her mistake. Her brows winged into her forehead, and her skin whitened in horror. "No," she pleaded, stricken. "No, Poet. I didn't mean …"

What she didn't mean was to cross that line. But she had.

This, after treating my son with kindness, after tricking me into thinking her above them.

Panic pushed her toward me. "Poet, I'm sor—"

My palm snapped up, halting her. With my jaw locked, I swatted my finger once, making it clear.

Not. Another. Word.

She could be sorry all she wanted. I was sure she would be, for losing a coveted jester was like losing a gilded sex toy—expensive and pleasurable, yet still a cheap thrill.

Indeed, she could be sorry. And so what? Sorry wasn't the whole story. When anger came out and drew words like swords, so did the truth.

So now I knew how she really felt.

Lost. That was what she thought of him.

I would concede. Sometimes the simplest words had the sharpest teeth.

Good riddance, for I strode past the woman and left her behind. We were done. So very, fucking done.

29

Briar

When my scribbled message to him went unanswered, desperation got the better of me. I declined a late celebratory meal with the Royals by feigning a headache to Mother, then dallied in my suite until the bell tolled the hour, the vibrations flooding the kingdom. My chin trembled at the memory of that tower, of what I'd said there.

Sans a candle or lantern, I took the secret passage and braved the route to the artist wing. His room was empty and dark, moonlight puddling on the floor and the scent of wax from the unlit tapers lingering. I longed for him so badly that I imposed myself on his bed, perching at the edge and drawing my legs into my chest. I wrapped my arms around my knees, curled into a ball, and waited.

He could be diverting the Royals while they supped. He might be keeping company with the one person it would pain me to see him with.

Soon enough, Mother might return to my rooms and check on me. If I didn't make it back in time, I would have to invent yet another lie. I had been shutting her out for ages. In becoming allies with the jester—and more than that with him—I'd deceived her.

Her and others. Though I would never regret what I shared with Poet, I hadn't forgiven myself for lying to those closest to me.

A princess does not forsake her kin. She does not wound them.

I had found nothing of substance in the archive library. I'd done Poet and Nicu no justice, and now the Seasons could trade born souls. I may not have signed the amendment, but my silence had contributed to its existence.

The door creaked. My head lifted. A sliver of firelight from the hall stretched across the floor, accentuating his tall shadow and unkempt hair.

At the sight of me, he startled. Then he glanced behind him, checked the corridor, and blinked my way again.

"Briar?" Eliot asked.

"Hello," I croaked.

"What are you doing here?"

"I know. I'm sorry."

Hearing the splinter in my voice, he sighed. It wasn't the supportive reception I had hoped for. In the past, he would have dashed over to me, insisted upon knowing what was amiss and how to help—as I would do for him without question.

Instead, my friend hesitated. We never met in his room. I'd been here before, but briefly and on the pretext of requesting a song for an event. The tension lining his face had nothing to do with the scandal of me being here when the piper, who bunked with him, could walk in at any second. His brusque tone hinted I was trespassing for other reasons.

Eliot crossed the floor and settled beside me. No arm around my shoulder, no hand squeezing mine. We hadn't seen one another since the labyrinth, yet something had shifted in my absence. When not with Mother, I had spent my secret hours with Poet, doing things that would break Eliot if he were to discover them. I had no right to be here. Horribly, self-indulgently, I had been neglecting my friend. I'd betrayed him.

But he didn't know that.

He wore a thinly knit azure sweater, woodsmoke and sage drifting from the fabric. Those aromas that had always made me feel at home in this fortress.

Eliot regarded his lute propped in the corner with cool detachment, the sort of expression that meant he wasn't feeling detached at all. He must have been upset that I'd taken this long to meet with him again. That would account for his uncharacteristic silence.

When we were fourteen, we wrote a song together. It was about horses ruling an animal kingdom. My contribution had been terrible, but he'd added to the lyrics anyway, because we were friends.

Because that was what friends did.

Except weren't children any longer.

My throat constricted. I would not cry.

"I was invited to the Peace Talks." I stared at my feet, realizing this was news to him. Not long ago, he would have been the first person to know about it. "I wanted to make a good impression and make Mother proud. I tried to speak about something very important to me. But I ruined it. I sat there while they all stared. I failed the people who trusted me to help, and I can't undo that."

"I'm surprised you'd tell me this," Eliot said after a terse moment. "I'm surprised you still value my opinion, being that you haven't asked for it lately. Not in the weeks since your return from the forest."

I flinched. "Your opinion always matters to me."

A dry laugh pushed out of him. "Bullshit."

"I beg your par—"

"But whatever. You're a busy woman, I know. Busier than you used to be, whereas I'm a lowly minstrel."

I grabbed his precious hand, clung to his long, musical fingers. "That's not true."

A muscle ticked in Eliot's jaw, which disturbed the lute tattoo inked down the side of his neck. The instrument shuddered along his skin as he pulled away. "Anyway, I'm just stumped why you'd confide in me now. Considering everything else you've been keeping from me."

The curtain slapped his windowsill. His words snatched the air from my lungs.

Eliot waited a beat, then cranked his head slowly toward me. "I saw you," he clipped, his grimace daring me to deny it.

My stomach dropped to the floor. Remorse clawed at my ribs, and fear strangled my throat. But I wouldn't lie to him any longer.

I licked my chapped lips. "Eliot, please."

"I saw you together."

"Let me explain."

"Last night when you taunted him to bow and wish you a pleasant evening. Long before that, I had a feeling when you both came back from the woods, but I ignored the looks between you. Like a loyal pet, I refused to believe you'd do that to me. But for Season's sake, you started wearing your hair loose and constantly acted like you wanted to apologize to me for something. Your chin crinkles when you're rattled, Briar."

"We didn't mean for it to happen."

His eyes slitted, a crawlspace impossible to get through. "We," he repeated, like I'd smeared the word on him, like he yearned to wipe off the residue.

"Eliot—"

"At dinner yesterday, I noticed how you favored one another. I followed him, watched him enter your suite. And when you got there, I waited. But you didn't throw him out." Eliot's face creased. "The door wasn't locked."

The ground bottomed out from under me. Mortification singed my cheeks.

In the great hall, I'd sensed someone observing us. I had teased Poet, then he'd stolen into my room, sank to his knees, slipped his head under my skirt, and pitched his tongue inside me.

Havoc must have shown on my face. The sight of it broke down Eliot's features, his visage collapsing, as if struck by a wrecking ball. "Spare me the details. Whatever the hell else you've done with Poet—or rather, whatever *he's* done to *you*—I don't want to know. After the kiss and that migration to your bed, I couldn't bear to watch any longer." He stood, putting his back to me. "You were my best friend, Briar."

I rose on jellied limbs. "I still am."

"Did you think of me? With Poet, did you once think about what this would do to me? How fucked up I'd feel?"

"Yes," I implored. "Of course, I did. Our friendship means everythi—"

"Don't." He swerved around, his eyes rimmed with fury and hurt. "Don't. You. Dare," he gritted out. "You might have denied it at first. Oh, I'm sure you lied to yourself plenty about that. But in the end, like everyone else in this court, you were antsy to fuck him. You let him seduce you."

"I didn't have sex with Poet."

"Dammit, I told you! I don't want to fucking know!"

And in hindsight, it was only partially true. Technically, Poet and I had done many things short of consummating.

And Seasons help me. I'd wanted that, too.

I still did. Since that afternoon in the meadow, I had wanted him inside me. I wanted to taste him, the same intimate way he'd tasted me. I wanted him above me and under me and behind me, naked and panting. I wanted to come in his arms, crying out with my legs strapped around his waist. I wanted every prohibited, passionate, and primal thing he awakened. I wanted that and more.

I wanted his heart. I wanted to give him mine.

It didn't take a mirror to know the desires broadcasted across my face.

Eliot saw the proof and shook his head. "You of all people, who wrinkles your nose at dalliances, who'd never been touched by man, and would rather eat salt than dance. But there you were, going rogue with a bunch of immodest Spring revelers in the labyrinth. The only other time I've seen you that carefree was when we met, during those few hours before your father died.

"I've treasured the person you've become, but I've always felt sad

343

for you, too, because you've never been completely yourself, never been happy. I knew that woman was inside you somewhere, and I've been seeing glimpses of her." He stared at me. "Now I know the reason why."

Yes and no. Poet had not brought out anything that wasn't already there. That woman had been buried within me, dormant beside my father, waiting to resurface. I had resurrected her just as much.

I released a jagged breath. "Poet's important to me. You know I wouldn't take the chance if he weren't."

Eliot spread his arms. "Briar, I haven't no damn clue what the hell you'd do anymore."

"Please, Eliot. I'm sorry. I'm so sorry," I begged. "I swear, I thought about you. I thought about you and Mother. But he became someone who didn't exist in the same way." My voice softened, and a pang cleaved through me. "It's over now. It wasn't going to last."

Eliot stared at me. "Do you love him?"

"Not like I love you."

"That's obvious."

"You're my best friend."

"I'm your only friend. And that's not an answer."

It was not. I recalled Poet's sorrow when I withheld what he meant to me, then his collapse when I insulted Nicu. In my tumultuous state, I had abandoned myself and offended his beautiful son. I'd uttered words I hadn't meant, would never mean. I couldn't punish myself enough for it.

Nicu had leaped into my heart.

And his father had stolen it.

Based on the anguished clench of Eliot's face, he guessed my feelings. He didn't know about Poet's history. He didn't know Poet's secrets. He didn't know Poet's worst fears, hidden demons, or greatest desires. But it didn't stop Eliot from wanting the jester, too.

Many would dismiss my friend's affection as irrational, misguided, and based solely on infatuated lust. Whereas others would consider it earnest and true, as I did. Because now I understood.

344

Eliot and Poet had developed their own bond. My friend might love Poet from a different angle, but it was still love.

All these years, not for a second had I feared an interloper would jeopardize our friendship. That didn't mean Eliot mattered any less to me. Whatever I felt for the jester made no difference there.

A sob slipped from my lips. "If I have to make a choice, I will always choose you."

"Do you honestly believe that?" And when I made no reply, Eliot crossed to the door, held it open, and spoke coldly to the floor. "Besides. What if I don't choose you?"

Memories of the ancient garden, our meeting spot where we'd whisper and laugh together. Stolen moments that we used to wrap ourselves in. They pierced my mind, the visions there and gone.

Seconds passed by in a montage, swift and intangible. Us, no longer young and innocent. Him, averting his gaze as though my avowal repelled him.

Me, silently begging him to look my way. My minstrel, silently begging me to leave.

My friend, closing the door behind me when I did.

The latch, clicking into place.

Lark's Night's annual sunset carnival lauded the end of the Peace Talks. It began in the early evening and lasted into the night, the revels spanning the rolling hills.

In the past, custom limited the event to Royals, the court, and selected performers—the resident troupe and Spring's traveling groups. But this year, Lark's Night welcomed all citizens, including servants and villagers.

The first hours would supply an array of richly dark diversions. Naked acrobats, uncensored musicians, knife-throwers, taboo storytellers, and master puppeteers. Instruments of play, such as blindfolds and batons.

Later, it would progress. Come twilight, the carnival would deepen into an event marked by shadows and bonfires. Heady music and erotic dancing. Intoxication and cloistered nooks where couples would either disappear or welcome anyone who'd like to watch them.

That was the nature of Spring—lively by day, wolfish by night. In many ways, this culture reminded me of faerie lore, of a society that enjoyed its own degree of coltishness and devilry.

Basil and Fatima anticipated the revels with glee. As the designated Masters of Mischief, the Crown elected someone to play the carnival's Fest Fool. Attendants would order the Fool to perform whatever inventive or humiliating feat the attendants fancied, then judge the Fool with either praise or scrutiny.

The Fool could be anyone, from a scullery maid, to an artist, to a Royal. The Crown planned to consult with Poet—presently on trial for his behavior in the throne room—and debate a list of candidates.

I had managed to convince the Royals that his outburst during the final Talk had done us no harm. Jesters were excitable after all, I'd claimed. And he hadn't offended us publicly, so making an example of him wasn't necessary.

However, Basil and Fatima had commanded Poet to kneel before us and apologize the next day. Because this was hardly a common occurrence, the Crown's discomfort was evident.

By contrast, Poet had complied brilliantly and with a monumental amount of hidden scorn. Mostly he aimed it toward me, but at least his obedience had spared him further retribution.

Now three days before the event, builders began outfitting the hill, erecting stages, ivy-strewn tents, and pavilions. Workers made of steel hammered poles into the soil, the repetitive thwack of wood resounding across the vista.

Both Queens of Winter and the Seven joined us. The elderly monarchs supervised the structures' interior arrangements and exterior layouts. The Seven gathered in a circle, threading garlands and leering at the craftsmen hewing, pounding, lifting, and sweating in the vicinity.

Mother and I volunteered to help. While balancing atop ladders, we fastened garlands—a red one and a gold one—to the top mast of a pavilion. By connecting all the venues that way, the cloths would sway from one structure to the next and form an attractive web one could see from a distance.

My chest gave a violent tug. The cords reminded me of Jinny's cottage, the ribbons dangling from the ceiling to guide Nicu.

Mother said something, shaking me out of my trance. Under the baking sun, her eyebrows knitted, and I noticed a thread coming loose from her linen dress.

"Sorry?" I inquired, turning back to my work.

But from my periphery, she continued to stare. "I said, are you all right?"

"Why do you ask?"

"You've untied and retied that garland several times."

I glanced at the red rope. "I'm a perfectionist."

"You're an overachiever." Mother knotted her gold cloth to the base of the tent's topper. "As a monarch, I'm proud. As a mother, I'm troubled."

"I'm well."

I had lost sleep. I had dreamed of him, thought about him, longed for him. I had wracked my soul for ways to atone, to convince him that he mattered. I'd searched for him in the halls. I'd considered going to him, fighting harder, not taking no for an answer. I longed to prove myself.

Sometimes *him* was Eliot. Sometimes he was someone else.

I drew in stinging gales of air through my nostrils.

A princess does not suffer in public.

Not unless the source of that suffering made an unexpected appearance.

The wind sighed. The tower bell rang.

Often, he arrived in a cacophony of sound. As far as I was concerned, the noises warned me too late. I sensed his bitterness before I mustered the courage to search for it. My eyes drifted across pennants draped limply across the grass, serrated tools, and bearded faces.

Then I tripped over a pair of venomous green irises. My gaze stalled along with my breath, both caught in the net of that stare.

Poet stood beside a partially raised tent, with a trio of performers who stretched absently and joked with each other. A shirt the chilled color of lead buffeted his form, the garment's sleeves rolled up his forearms to reveal not only the bracelets but his knuckles smudged with dirt. Until now, he must have been volunteering in a different part of the grounds.

His neckline slumped low, his clavicles glazed in a thin layer of condensation. With his face tight and his eyes laced in black, he resembled a scornful fae, providing one took those irises into account, the color as sharp and verdant as cut glass.

From the sidelines, one of the male construction workers noticed the jester and walked straight into a pole. Though, Poet didn't notice. Those orbs slid over me with contempt, then slid away—toward Eliot.

Standing among the group, my friend's wary gaze crept from me to the jester. Aware of the rift between us, Eliot seized the opportunity and reached out to touch Poet's arm.

A prolonged stroke from shoulder to wrist. A gesture meant to steal Poet's attention.

Their mutual ease proved that Eliot hadn't confronted Poet about me. But presently, Eliot said something, to which Poet glanced at the minstrel's fingers and then at him. The jester contemplated something within my friend's words.

Whatever Eliot had told him, it was working.

My fingers curled, suffocating the cord still resting in my hands. A glutton for punishment, I watched them. Every second their eyes remained locked, another one of my ribs cracked. I didn't know how to speak with this Eliot, nor with this Poet, now strangers who resented me to the point where I became insignificant.

They could be together without consequences. They had that luxury.

I wasn't like them. I wasn't born to have anyone I wanted, not if it conflicted with my station.

My kingdom owned me. My desires were the court's desires, the people's desires. My joys were their joys. My grief, their grief.

Yet for a few beautiful weeks, I had forgotten.

The world faded, reduced to blots of color and blurred voices. All that remained clear were Poet and Eliot as they settled into a pair of lawn chairs and shared a laugh, unconcerned whether I saw. Perhaps they even hoped I did.

It hurt, and I hated them for it, and I was sorry for it, and I understood it, and I didn't understand any of it, and I missed them, and I longed, and I craved, and I needed, yet I shouldn't, but I wished, and I wanted, but I couldn't, yet I felt, and I felt, and *felt*.

"Your Highness," Mother vented. "Listen to me when I'm speaking to you."

That voice carved through my consciousness. I twisted to Mother and snapped back, "I'm *listening*."

"Do not use that tone on me."

"I was preoccupied for one moment. Am I not allowed that? I've been listening to you for twenty years. Is it not enough?"

"Your eyes are shadowed. You've been sluggish. You caused an uproar at the Peace Talks. You are far from well. You're upset, and you won't tell me why."

"I won't tell you why because I'm an adult. Let me breathe."

"I am your mother and your queen," she fumed. "You will remember that. If you insist on doing otherwise, then you're not your father's daughter."

"If that will make it easier for you."

She sucked in a breath. The words had jumped out before I could stop them, airborne and resounding like something blown from a horn.

The hammering and conversations ceased. Presumably, it had gone quiet a while ago.

Our audience stared openly. The Queens of Winter balked. The workers and performers cast awkward glances our way. The seven ladies watched with varying degrees of astonishment, intrigue, and validation, as if this sort of buzz would keep them busy for hours.

Eliot's brows furrowed in concern.

From the corner of my eye, Poet reclined in his seat. His fingers were draped over his mouth as his eyes ticked between my mother and me.

Remorse wilted my insides. I shook my head. "Mother, I—"

But she swerved away and jerked on the ends of her garland, yanking it into a knot. "Get out of my sight."

I deserved that. Yet I blanched that she would dismiss me without a chance to apologize, that she'd brought Father into this at all, and that she had used his memory to flay me.

Raising my chin, I tore down the ladder, aware of Poet's gaze but refusing to acknowledge it. Within an hour, rumors would spread that Autumn had taken leave of its senses and quarreled in front of Winter, the Seven, the Court Jester, and a host of servants, builders, and artists.

And I did not care.

As I passed the ladies, Vale and Posy gave me sympathetic looks.

However, Cadence lowered her voice and snickered, "Who needs a carnival? Baiting a simpleton in the stocks can't be more fun than this."

Mother hadn't heard her. Cadence made sure of that.

But I'd heard. So had Poet.

His gaze sliced toward Cadence, unbridled wrath streaking across his pupils. If I had given him another second, he would have taken her down with a single flick of his tongue. I saw it, the way his eyes glinted with promise. He would say something to ridicule Cadence publicly, to put the chit in her place. He would do what he did best, what people loved and feared most about him. Everyone adored that skill, so long as it wasn't directed toward them.

Except I'd had enough. And truly, I didn't feel like giving him the chance.

Rage festered under my skin and climbed up my wrists. In a spasm of action, I whipped around, strode over to the female, and smacked her clear across the face. The crack of my palm against Cadence's flesh resounded like something launched from a cannon. Her head twisted on impact, and she yelped while clutching her blazing cheek.

Beside her, the clan of six stared, aghast.

"Briar!" Mother hissed.

"That was not funny," I gritted to Cadence through my teeth. "In case you were wondering, no one cares for your snide and petty remarks. They're about as valuable as your simpering, and I'm tired of hearing both. If you cannot say anything without due respect, then do your work, act like the lady you're supposed to be, and keep your bitchy mouth shut!"

Disregarding Mother's calls, I marched past the company. The weight of Poet's eyes pursued me as I stormed off.

My skirt snapped around my legs as I trekked down the hill. The second incline led to a private thoroughfare that bordered the lower town and ended at the citadel, where I stormed across the drawbridge and into the orchid garden.

While crossing the flora paths that provided a shortcut to my suite, I flexed my hand. My skin burned from the contact with Cadence's hateful sneer. Yes, the jolt of satisfaction I felt went against my principles. It defied how a Royal should conduct herself, especially the daughter of Autumn, known far and wide as a female composed to a fault.

Being upset was hardly justification. By striking one of Spring's ladies-in-waiting, I had disrespected Queen Fatima and dishonored my mother. I'd set a terrible example and would need to make amends before the court.

A smug grin wormed across my face.

A hand lashed out and yanked me into the nearest bush. I parted my lips to scream—until I noticed the silver hair, crinkled skin the texture of burlap, and frantic eyes.

"Jinny," I gasped, staggering into her.

The trembling woman clasped my elbows. Urgency scrawled

across her weathered face. "Briar. Thank Seasons, it's you."

"What is—how did you get here?"

"I can't find Poet. I searched, but I've never been here before. I got lost and ... oh, Seasons."

"He's helping set up for Lark's Night. What's happened?"

Jinny's features withered, and her eyes glistened. "I should have guessed. I-I wasn't thinking."

No, she was not. She was panicking.

Belatedly, I discovered an agitated critter scuttling around my heels. Tumble had burst from the shrubbery and was galloping between me and Jinny, a string of low, staccato hisses reverberating from his body.

"It's Nicu," Jinny rushed out. "I think it was the ribbons. The ones at the carnival. He must have seen them, and—I-I don't know."

"Tell me what's happened," I pressed.

"I think it was the ribbons. I hurried, I tried, but I was too late. They got to him."

"Jinny," I demanded, prying her hands from her face. "Focus. Who got to him?"

"The guards. The Crown." She swayed, then crumbled in my arms. "They have him. They took Nicu."

Briar

Father had described to me what chaos felt like. I had been five and already curious about it. In a castle, I'd been exposed to things other children hadn't, and my parents vowed to be truthful to me. They had treated me like a girl who'd come of age, even when I hadn't been one.

To endure, Father oftentimes went numb. His body ceased to function, all the resilience going straight to his head. The swarm of calm helped him think clearly during the upheaval, sharpened his mind into a weapon.

"But what about ruling with your heart?" I had asked.

"Love with your heart. Rule with your head," he'd answered.

"But maybe my head and heart can help each other. They can work together. Isn't that what they're for?"

Pensive, Father had stared at me. "Someday, if you find a way to use both, do advise me." He'd placed me on his shoulders and quipped, "In the meantime, your weight is much easier to bear."

My weight. The heft of a child had been easier to bear than the weight of a nation. Of course, it had.

Whenever problems plagued Autumn, I would watch Mother's head bow with indecision, then rise with resignation. Perhaps the numbness became a shield for her, like it had for Father.

And now for me.

Before Jinny's words could snake into the pit of my stomach, numbness swooped in like a raptor and snatched the terror in its talons. As it did, a single thought looped in my mind.

They took Nicu.

They took him.

Nicu.

Sick with worry and exhaustion, Jinny's limbs gave out. I caught her before she collapsed like a rag doll. Tumble shadowed me as I hooked my arm around the woman's waist, hefted her into the stronghold, and scowled at one of the baffled sentinels.

"Help me," I commanded, incredulous.

Tumble dashed out of range, the ferret's sly movements going undetected. But the sentinel's eyebrows tilted like ramps as he surveyed Jinny's cotton dress, the apron embroidered with sprigs of lavender yet stained with dirt, and the soil wedged under her fingernails. "Your Highness," the man cautioned, "wouldn't it be best if—"

"No, it would not," I commanded. "But I do recall telling you to help me."

The confused man scooped Jinny into his arms and followed me to my suite. I sensed him itching to question the matter, to suggest we deposit her at the physician's repository, to insist a mere peasant's swoon hardly warranted a trip to a Royal's chambers.

My glare ceased his objections. In my room, the sentinel draped Jinny on the bed while I perched at her side. "Send a maid," I ordered.

As the man left, Tumble snuck into the room, bolted around every corner as if searching for Nicu, and finally slid under a reading chair. He blinked from beneath the upholstery and kept hissing, likely emitting some type of alarmed noise.

Jinny struggled to sit upright. "I have to—we have to—"

I gently pushed the woman down and wrapped her in my duvet.

"We will," I promised. "We will get him back. First, tell me how you got here."

She panted at the canopy, her eyes jumping about in thought. "There are these herbs—they grow in a clearing off the main road. At our pace, it's a right trip there and back, but I've been suffering a pained head something severe. I told myself we'd be careful of strangers, then hitched our horse and wagon.

"I-I bundled Nicu into the cart so no one could see him, told him it was a game." Her wild gaze staggered across mine, and her features crimped with terror. "I told him it was a game," she confessed, haunted.

"It's all right," I murmured, gathering her hands in mine. "Then what?"

"I was busy harvesting with Tumble when Nicu disappeared. He must have taken the road to the palace and seen the carnival ribbons. He must have mistaken them for the ones in our home. When I realized he was gone, I ran. I ran so fast, and I saw him at the drawbridge with the sentinels." Tears rimmed her eyes, yet she didn't allow them to fall. Instead, her jaw hardened an instant later, rage replacing the fear. "They were taking him away. Those bastards were taking my wee boy away."

A growl scrolled from my throat. "Did they harm him?"

"Not a hair. If they had, I wouldn't be standing here in one piece. I'd have skinned them alive with my bare hands, but no. Seeing as they didn't hurt him, I knew intervening would only endanger Nicu more. He went with the guards willingly, probably thinking it was another game. Poet told him over and over not to pounce on strangers, but Nicu isn't a child who remembers everything he's told."

"Is your wagon still tethered where you left it?"

Jinny nodded, her wits slowly recovering. "You have something in mind, then?"

"A servant is coming. Don't say a word to her," I instructed. "You're ill. You don't know me. I'm simply being charitable to a stranger. Once you've rested, go home. Poet and I will get Nicu, but someone needs to be there when we return him."

"Tumble will make a loud fuss if we leave without Nicu. Usually, Poet can calm the critter down, but Tumble might not go with me. And he's right tough to snatch, must less keep ahold of when he's upset."

"Then let him be. He's safe here, and we'll bring him home later. The most crucial thing is for you to be waiting for Nicu."

Momentarily, her distress gave way. Despite the unshed tears, Jinny's pupils flickered with something like wry comprehension. "You're saying an old woman is going to slow you down."

"I'm saying I don't wish to risk you getting injured."

"Sounds dangerous."

"It does."

"So it's that kind of trouble you're planning, is it? I knew you didn't have red hair for nothing." As she inspected my features, whatever stared back reinforced the set of her jaw and resurrected her complexion. "No ruler can lead unless they're willing to. That's what he sees in you. There's fight in your soul, Briar of Autumn. I approve."

I swallowed around the knot in my throat. "I'm honored."

"You'd damn well better be. Now go get my boys. Both of them."

The maid scampered in. I tossed her instructions to look after Jinny. "If anyone enters—if my Mother enters—let her know I found this woman in the garden. She's here at my insistence and will recover with rest and drink. Allow her to leave once she's fit to do so. Understand?"

"Yes, Your Highness," the maid said, then set about pouring water and banking a fire.

"Rest now," I whispered to Jinny, leaning closer to her. "Afterward, you must get back to the cottage with the wagon. Can you make it?"

Jinny's chin rose. "Try and stop me."

In the corridor, torches combusted, their flames writhing. I hastened down the hallway, my skirt thrashing around my limbs.

Nicu could be cold. He could be hungry. He could be hurt.

I quickened my pace, ignoring the blur of faces greeting me from various corners. At the bottom of a winding stairwell, the Court Physician's door stood ajar. I spewed a lie to the man about needing a sleeping draught, trusting the shadows under my eyes were suitable proof of my troubles. The man's fingers lagged through cupboards laden with vials and tinctures. Glasses clinked, the noise pinching my patience.

For Season's sake, he moved slower than a sloth. I nearly shouted at him.

Armed with a tiny vessel of liquid, I left the room and headed for the dungeon, darting through passages and down a familiar stairway glazed in phlegm-colored slime. While stuffing the sleeping draught in my sleeve, I descended into the dank chill, undeterred by the waifish shadows, malnourished groans, scuttling roaches, and the rancid stench of vomit.

Below, torches illuminated a hulking man with mead breath, a grainy rind of facial skin, and a coarse beard nesting across his visage.

The guard set aside his poleax and rose from a bench. "Milady," he blurted out.

Disregarding his improper form of address, I stepped around the corner from his post. My eyes scanned dozens of cells and bars that whittled into the darkness. My gaze stumbled across the silhouettes of filthy rags, skeletal limbs, and scabbed bodies. Manacles and chains dragged over the stones, the commotion scraping through the murk.

Someone hacked. Someone else mumbled repeatedly to themself.

Then my ears discerned the patter of small feet.

I swung toward the third cell, where a faeish boy waddled from the shadows and clutched the bars. Upon recognizing me, his hopeful face poked through the gap. His green eyes shone with desperation and confusion, those orbs begging me to help him—to save him.

Deeper into the cavity, blood stained the floor. One wall displayed mounted weapons and instruments forged for baiting and torture, from knives to spiked tongs, shears, harnesses, and lances. The courts lived and reveled while these atrocities occurred only several levels below the ground.

Bile rushed up my throat. I swallowed it back down.

Each cubicle allowed scarcely enough space for a person to extend their arms. The guard hadn't squashed Nicu in with other prisoners, which otherwise seemed to be the case in majority of the cells, but how dare Spring behave so unmercifully to these people! Moreover, regal Autumn would never treat any child this way!

The numbness dissolved. My heart came back to life with a vengeance.

The guard hadn't even given Nicu a blanket.

The boy whimpered. Behind the sentinel's back, I pressed a finger to my lips. *Hush.*

He bit his lower lip. At which point, I more than crossed the boundaries of my jurisdiction. I outright trampled over them.

To the guard, I glanced over my shoulder and lifted an imperious brow. "I was informed that you held a child down here."

"The Crown's orders, milady. This urchin's a simpleton. He's to be shackled while His and Her Majesties make plans for him."

"He's hardly a physical threat. Surely there's a better place to detain him."

"The Crown's orders," the man and his jowls repeated.

"I wish to question him. Open the cell and leave us."

"Milady—"

I spun toward him. "Stop addressing me as a noble," I hissed, my voice hot enough to incinerate his flesh. "I am not a 'milady.' I am a Royal, the Princess of Autumn, and an honored guest of Spring. In other words, 'Your Highness.' I suspect this child may very well be the smuggled property of my nation. Your sovereigns have granted me leave to investigate the matter while my mother is otherwise occupied. Now I command you to *open the cell!*"

He fumbled with a ring of keys. Nicu scurried backward as the door winced on its hinges and swung wide.

Another thorny look at the guard sent him away. Muttering, he shut me inside and returned to his post in the alcove.

Just in case, I waited a beat. Then I dashed into the cubicle and dropped to the floor. With a low cry, I spread my arms at the same time Nicu flung himself at me.

His whole body quaked. His skin was ice cold, his fingers frosting over. I wanted to check him for bruises, for signs that he'd been mishandled, but I couldn't let go. I rocked him from side to side, encircling his waist and cupping the back of his head with my free hand.

He sniffled into my neck. "Briar Patch."

"Yes, it's me," I whispered. "I'm here. It's all right now. It's all right."

"I want my papa."

"I will get him for you. I promise."

"I met a king and queen, but they didn't want to be my friends. And the guard didn't want to play with me. He yelled mean things. He called me names."

Poet was going to murder the guard. I fantasized about it, too.

Jinny had said that Nicu went with the sentinels willingly. It did not take a genius to surmise why. He must have been thrilled to meet so many people. He must have believed everything was fine. Doubtless, that assumption had changed once they locked him in this horrific place.

Nicu launched into a peculiar story. I managed to pick through it and puzzle together the facts: Jinny, the herbs she'd been gathering, and how Nicu wandered off to explore.

At the woodland's fringes, he had seen the carnival ribbons in the distance. He'd thought of home and how he was supposed to follow the colors hanging from the ceiling. Tired and longing to sleep in his bed, he hurried toward the garlands, then got distracted by the looming spectacle of the castle, with its towers vaulting skyward. Because he'd never seen anything like it, Nicu changed his mind and hastened toward the stronghold.

Among a horde of citizens, the child hadn't known what to do with himself. He'd cavorted from one person to the next, bursting with hugs and questions.

At the gate, the statuesque guards in their shiny armor had made an impression. They were metal trees. Their poleaxes were giant toys. Nicu had tried to climb one of the soldier's legs, but the man kicked him away and then got a good look at the boy's face. That, plus a string of queer comments, had gotten Nicu into this mess.

He wept in my arms. Tears sliced through his muck-stained cheeks. He didn't understand what was happening or why.

I didn't understand it, either. No one should.

When I called for the guard and ordered him to bring milk, bread, and cheese, the man grunted. "He isn't right, Your Highness. Everyone knows a half-wit isn't right by nature. They can't fend for 'emselves. They grow up to be trouble what can't look out for their own. They're good for nothing, much less a Royal's mercy."

"Did I seek your counsel?" I snapped. "Bring me what I asked for. Now!"

The guard tossed Nicu a repellent look, then disappeared while uttering the words, "stupid half-wit" and "stupider cunt."

Nicu watched him go, then asked, "What's a half-wit?"

I framed his face. "Listen to me, Nicu—"

"Is it a monster? Is it going to eat me like thunder? Thunder eats the grass."

"Nothing is going to happen to you. I swear it. Thunder won't eat you because you're a fae. You have magic. Papa gave it to you."

Almost. He almost brightened, but then he jumped when a brittle creature two cells down shrieked, the prisoner's paper-thin voice ripping apart. "Alarm, alarm, alarm!"

Nicu shrank into my chest. "Don't leave me. I'm scared."

I hugged him tightly. "I'm not going anywhere."

"Papa goes."

"But he comes back. He comes back because he loves you. He loves you more than anything else."

"Love is the sun. You have a yellow sun in your tummy, like Papa and Jinny. Your hair is a red ribbon, and your brown dots—" he tapped the freckles on my nose, "—are stains from the rain. If you leave me, there will never ever be colors again. They will die."

"No," I said. "You're all the color in this world, not me. You're Spring and Summer and Autumn and Winter. Your eyes are good luck clovers."

"I don't want to be colorful without you, Briar Patch. You make me happy orange and Papa smitten pink."

"In truth, my name is just Briar."

"Just Briar," Nicu repeated in a remarkably accurate imitation of my voice.

He stared at me like I belonged to him, like he belonged to me, like we belonged to each other.

Like I made this dungeon safe. Like I made the world safe.

I'd held back for so long, despite Father's death, Mother's disappointment, Eliot's heartbreak, and Poet's passion. Nicu was the pin that burst me open. After weeks of resistance, two bloated tears popped and rushed down my face.

Nicu extended a finger and traced each wet path. "You're raining."

I'm crying because there's nothing I wouldn't do for you.

Perhaps this was how Mother felt about me, unconditional and absolute.

The solitary torchlight pulsed against the sooty walls. Our shadows formed a single body. I watched myself disappear into Nicu.

I loved this boy.

I loved his father for making him.

A servant balancing a plate trailed behind the guard, set the meal on the cell floor, and curtsied to me. Straightening, she crinkled her nose at the scent of excrement permeating the walls and darted upstairs.

Nicu gobbled the food, his lips smacking with each bite.

While he bent his head, I uncorked the sleeping draught. "Can you eat and drink all the treats in the world, Nicu? Is there anything that makes your throat and lips burn, or makes you sick?"

With a full mouth, he answered, "When Jinny eats nuts, she gets a duck mouth."

"Does anything do that to you?"

He shook his head. I laced his milk with the vial's contents and watched him guzzle it. Unclasping my wool cloak, I swaddled it around his shoulders and flopped the hood over his head. Within moments, he yawned. I guided him to a spot on the floor, sat against the wall, and gathered him onto my lap.

"Tell me a story," I urged. "When you're finished, Papa will be here."

Nicu's shaggy head lolled against me, and his ear pressed to my bodice. I covered his other ear to protect him from the noises surrounding us. Prisoners bellowed, cackled, or wept through the cage bars. Outlines bumped into walls, and hands slapped the grilles. Across the way, one hunched body said nothing, did nothing but rock in place.

A tale leaked out of Nicu about anthills and half-wit guards, which made less and less sense as the child drifted. At last, his words faded into sleep. When he next awoke, I prayed this place would be nothing but a bad dream.

I eased Nicu down and noticed a familiar red band peeking from his pocket. Dirt smudged the ribbon, the material identical to the one around his wrist.

A memory surged to the forefront. It yanked me back to a time when I'd tied a similar ribbon to a bush while chasing after Poet. My gut churned. I had an awful vision of Nicu finding it when he wandered from Jinny and ventured farther from the woods, expecting to see more strips, as he would have in the cottage.

Then the carnival and its garlands had come into view. Then the castle.

With all that had happened, I'd forgotten about that ribbon. If I hadn't, Nicu might not have ended up here. The possibility ran its awful course, the truth clenching my stomach.

I rolled the hood of my cloak into a pillow for Nicu, tucked the material snug around him, and kissed his cheek. "I'm sorry," I whispered, my throat made of straw, brittle and thin.

I swiped my sleeve across my eyes, ridding myself of the evidence that I'd been crying. I stood, crossed a thousand leagues to the cell door, and bade the guard to let me out. I had to do this. The sooner I left, the sooner I would return prepared.

If need be, I would reduce this pit to rubble.

And I wouldn't do it alone.

31

Poet

I knew it by then. For she taught it to me by then. Yet I was about to learn that lesson once again. A jester doesn't see everything that's coming ...

The artist wing was deserted when we reached the private hollow leading to my chambers. We walked without speaking, our footfalls echoing. Two motives split me in half, and the closer we got to my rooms, the more tangibly I felt that divide.

Eliot paused beside the door. An uncertain look crossed his face as he scratched the back of his neck. "Well, it's been a long day. I should go."

Indeed, no truer words could be spoken. He should leave, though not before I made something clear. Thusly, I jutted my head toward the entrance. "A word first?"

The minstrel blinked. "In there?"

My lips quirked. "If you wouldn't mind."

"Normally, I wouldn't. It's just that ..."

"Eliot, I might have a reputation for fuckery and mockery, but not when it comes to anyone who lives in this wing."

He laughed, nervous. "That wasn't what I meant."

"I didn't think so. Nevertheless, it warranted saying." I inclined my head toward the room. "'Tis only for a moment, for this can't be uttered in public."

"I ... yes, of course."

I stepped in after him and closed the door behind us, keenly aware of the motions. A fire crackled in the grate, spreading warmth through the room. It illuminated the rug, where I once draped Briar after we danced, where I lowered myself over her body and—

A muscle pounded in my temple. I wrenched my gaze from the rug.

Eliot glanced around with interest, having never been inside before. I motioned to the chairs standing before the flames, then reclined into one and waited as Eliot hedged.

So I wasn't the only one conflicted. I knew why on both our parts, and it was precisely for that same reason I needed to talk to him.

Apprehension cramped his features, along with the telltale slivers of yearning. He appeared visibly torn between the desire to sit and the guilt of wanting such a thing. I could say his ruddy complexion had everything to do with exertion after setting up the carnival, but I would be lying to myself.

I'd also be lying if I denied feeling borderline self-destructive. To thrill him gave me a genuine satisfaction I hadn't enjoyed since the archive library.

Nonetheless, this room was free of eavesdroppers. That proved vital for this conversation.

At last, the minstrel took his seat. In doing so, his eyes tripped across my forearms exposed by the rolled-up sleeves of my shirt. From there, his gaze ascended the garment's plunging neckline, which offered a peek. The ardent flash in his pupils reminded me I should have laced the cursed thing.

He caught himself and gestured wildly around the space. "These are extravagant chambers, more than any artist in residence can say about their own quarters. The richness of your sheets alone—I mean, not that I was staring at your bed for that long, but one can tell from a mere glimpse. The pillows are, um, fluffy. And to have a private bathroom rather than a common one must be a prize. Also, I've never seen these many candles outside of a Royal suite. You're fortunate the Crown values you."

In particular, I thought of one marvelous and merciless female. "Alas, most would say I'm spoiled."

"I doubt anyone would expect less for the Court Jester."

"That's because you haven't yet peeked at my wardrobe. Some would accuse me of being ostentatious."

"Ah, that. Yeah, I do know one person who would say as much." But Eliot's fond chuckle trailed off, and he glanced at the floor, sadness overwhelming his features. "Is this about what happened today? Is that why I'm here?"

"'Tis about several things," I told him. "But yes."

"What did she tell you?"

"What do you fear she told me? And why would you assume she'd betray your confidence? The last time I checked, you were friends."

The lute tattoo rippled down his neck as he swallowed. "I thought so once."

"Then stop thinking it—and *know* it." I couldn't help the way my tone grew firm, shielding, protective. By now, it had become a permanent reflex. "Don't discount her. You mean the world to Briar."

"Briar, is it?" Eliot swung his gaze my way. "First name terms with the princess?"

"As you pointed out, I'm the Court Jester. I don't play by the rules unless they suit me. I'm on first name terms with everyone."

"Still, you seem invested in someone you targeted for satire—at a crowded feast only weeks ago."

I lifted a brow. "She told you about the ribbon?"

Eliot stared at me. "She didn't have to."

So he figured it out, likely because he'd gotten hints.

Indeed, every part of me was invested in Briar. But I wouldn't entertain his remarks, wouldn't set foot on that trap.

Also, I saw no point in confirming. Based on the wounded way Eliot and Briar had looked at each other on the hill, he'd somehow found out about us. He hadn't said a thing to me in the interim, but he must have to her.

At the thought of him devastating Briar, another surge of protectiveness for her curled my knuckles. Only guilt, compassion, and lingering fondness toward Eliot stopped my fingernails from digging into the chair.

The minstrel felt deceived by Briar. The problem was, he blamed her and forgave me. That explained his undivided attention today and our banter in front of the princess. We'd wanted to punish her, and that goal had brought out the prick in me, yet all it did was make me feel like shit shoveled from a gutter. I doubted it made Eliot feel any better.

Aye. I had treated her that way because of Nicu, not the Peace Talks. I'd been too harsh with Briar about the latter, but the former ... I couldn't get her words out of my head.

I'm not a lost child who will never grasp the difference between left and right. I'm not Nicu!

Continuously, those words sawed through my fucking ribs. Yet the same agonizing, wrathful afflictions had consumed me on the hill, when Avalea had dismissed Briar in front of an audience. I had wanted to snarl at anyone who so much as looked at the princess with judgment or hostility, and I'd come close to acting on that.

Of course, my brave and willful thorn wouldn't have wanted me leaping to her defense. Moreover, she hadn't needed me to, for she had refused to wilt, to let Cadence's remarks go unpunished. Pride and an inconceivable need had rooted me to the spot, watching rage color Briar's skin as she slapped the lady off her pedestal.

How passionate.

How not enough. There was so much *not enough* that I'd lost direction from whence it came.

But because I'd helped put a rift in Briar's friendship with Eliot, I sought to mend the damage I had done. For that reason, I'd brought him here. I had told him already how my feelings didn't extend beyond friendship, but we never achieved closure because he'd fled too quickly for me to finish. I needed to soften that blow.

Eliot's knee tapped mine. "Poet?"

I dragged myself from those thoughts. "Eliot, I—"

"You saw the tension between the princess and me. I know as much. But that's not all you're troubled by."

"Nay, the main reason I asked you to join me is twofold. You might say everything's linked. And when is it bloody well not?"

"So there's something more." He licked his lips. "Poet, if you're ailing emotionally, I want you to know I'm your friend. I listen as much as I talk. It would be a pleasure to hear your troubles—I mean, not a pleasure per se. Not that it's a pleasure if you're troubled."

That wheedled a rueful grin out of me. "My plight doesn't matter. 'Tis you alone I want to talk about."

A fitful light kindled in his eyes—sudden, impulsive, and hopeful. "Me."

"You," I intoned. "The day I rejected you left something to be desired on my part. More than that, I hate to think it's plaguing you."

"You've been thinking about me?"

"Not in the way you expect."

He leaned forward and snatched my hands. "If that's true, I'm glad of it."

For fuck's sake. This was coming out wrong. And when the devil does anything ever come out wrong from me?

I slid my fingers from his. "Eliot, you shouldn't be. It's more complicated than that."

"I care not." On an exhale, Eliot lurched across the distance, clasped the back of my neck, and mashed his lips to mine.

Wicked. Fucking. Hell.

I froze as his mouth plastered itself against me, his lips puckered and trembling. Stunned, I waited him out, and waited, and waited.

And then I did something stupid.

My hands drifted to his jaw and cradled it. Holding him like this, sympathy trickled through my sternum, as well as a dose of sorrow. I yielded, my lips loosening and molding with his.

A small, wanting noise cut from Eliot's throat. Then his mouth moved with my own, fitting and folding in a slow pace.

I slanted and kissed him back. 'Twas sweet, how he moaned against the edge of my tongue when it glided between his lips. I flexed in, searching, pondering. His mouth gave with mine, our tongues sampling each other.

Yet my lips felt no spark, found no solace, lost not a shred of control. My mouth lagged, then stalled altogether.

Always, it was calmer with the minstrel, softer and easier than with the princess. We suited one another in many ways—all but one way.

He didn't drive me to fury and frustration. He didn't humble me. He didn't stir my blood with his moans. He didn't inspire me to thoughts I'd never had, to actions I never considered myself capable of.

He didn't smell of tart apples. He didn't have hair so red it glowed like a bonfire.

He didn't collect illuminated manuscripts. He didn't spend hours in the library until ink stained his fingers. He didn't have a chin that crinkled when he was upset.

He didn't make my son smile. He didn't alter the speed of my pulse—then shatter it to fucking pieces.

He wasn't her. No one else would ever be her.

Something heavy and helpless crushed my chest to a pulp. I unfastened my lips from Eliot's and pulled away.

His eyes remained closed, his mouth swollen. But when his lashes fanned open, the fog in his pupils cleared. It gave way to clarity as he searched my features, his own cinching with a mixture of grief, remorse, and denial. He knew what I was about to say, as I knew it wouldn't stop him from trying again, because he wanted to keep pretending for a few hours.

Alas. Broken hearts made faults and fools of us all.

I hardly fancied myself a shallow male specimen. If I let myself go with Eliot, I may never regret it the way I regretted the commotion of *her*.

But it wouldn't undo what I felt.

His crestfallen face was my doing. The kiss had been a selfish comfort and the very opposite of what I'd intended. I debated how to reply, how to apologize, how to discourage Eliot without breaking him again.

The fireplace bloomed with heat and light, none of which penetrated me. I opened my mouth just as someone's fist rapped on the door.

The noise chopped through the room, brisk to the count of three—willful, tenacious, and tempting. Whichever fool responded was doomed to great and terrible things.

Only one person made noise like that. Only one princess came to mind.

Everlasting fuck. Fate had spectacular timing.

Eliot gave a start. A livid noise sliced through my lips as I bent over in my chair and clasped the back of my neck, my elbows propping on my knees. Hunched over, I glowered at the floor, for I'd had plenty of great and terrible things to last me.

Every blow against the door brought unwanted memories of her to the surface. Each one manifested the princess's face as she had watched me leave the bell tower, as she'd watched me kneel in subordination to the Royals and make amends for something I hadn't felt the least bit sorry about.

The princess could go on knocking until her lovely fingers fell off. She didn't really want me to receive her. Not if she knew I had company.

In my periphery, Eliot thrust a hand through his hair, as though to tame it. He swiveled in his chair to inspect the door, then wheeled back. "Someone's calling for you. It sounds urgent."

"Ignore her," I muttered, my retinas burning into the rug.

If it surprised the minstrel that I knew who it was, I didn't sense it. Though, he was right. The pounding of her fist did sound urgent.

I lifted my head, listening as the knocks lost control and segued into desperation. Nay, *urgent* hadn't sent her here. *Tragic* had. As much as I wanted the relentless Royal to go away, something grieved her.

She needed me.

In seconds, I was yanking open the door and staring down at Briar. Blue crescents descended beneath her lower lashes, her braided bun had partially unraveled, and her breasts heaved as though she'd been running. The murderous glaze in her pupils, compiled with the flush racing up her throat and oxygen pushing from her lips, rendered me momentarily useless. Hellfire, she looked exquisite when inflamed, not to mention visibly primed to kill someone.

Briar pushed past me and flew into the room, unaware of Eliot. I opened my mouth to warn her. "Your Highness—"

"Where were you?!" She rounded on me. "I thought you were at the hill."

"I left. Your Highness—"

"Poet." Briar extended a hand, her palm on a dangerous course toward my chest, or toward that beating nuisance inside my chest. If her hand landed there, it would go through my skin and find what it was searching for. Then she would know it belonged to her.

I recovered from the alluring, infernal sight of this woman and recoiled with a hateful expression. To which she flinched, withdrawing with a pained one.

It wasn't that I'd forgotten the minstrel's presence. Her presence was simply bigger.

"Well, well," I mocked, slouching elegantly against the door jamb. "This is a trifle rash of you, coming here before the sun has set. People might see and think someone actually wants you here."

Briar winced but stampeded over that. "Poet—"

"I know my name, sweeting. You don't have to keep saying it."

"Poet, listen—"

"Frankly," I sneered, because fuck the charade, "the last time I listened to you lecture me, it didn't end well. Just tell me what's wrong and be done. The candles are melting, the hour is passing—"

She grabbed my face. "They have your son."

32

Poet

E very sound in the room dissolved. Only her turbulent voice
remained.

Oh, I heard her right. In fact, I'd heard those words countless times and in countless ways, in nightmares and spoken from
scores of mouths. From Jinny, from Nicu's mother, from the dead
Court Jester I'd replaced, from born souls in carnival troupes, and
from maddened prisoners caged in cells.

Fear was an emotion I'd learned most acutely. It had become a
perverse second language from the moment I first met my son.

I tilted my head. In my mind, this fear had been uttered by everyone but the princess. Hearing the words was one thing, yet it took
me several heartbeats to understand Briar. When I did, I choked the
knob behind me and slowly shut the door.

Then I bared my teeth. "I'm not amused, Princess."

Briar shook her head, and her eyes shimmered. "It's not a jest."

Nay. Quiet. Don't howl.

This woman wouldn't lie to me. She had wounded me too frequently and too surely to be capable of faking anything. I couldn't

fathom why I'd accused her of making a cruel joke.

Nay. Hush. Remember to hush.

It wasn't a jest. Damn her, it wasn't. I knew from the way her palms clasped my jaw, holding me steady lest I should splinter apart.

They have your son.

They were the Crown. They'd caught my son. They had him.

"Nicu," I hissed.

She nodded. "I'm sorry, Poet. I'm so sorry."

My trembling hands flattened over hers. Every vile thing that passed through me, she attempted to soak up, because I was about to be sick.

My son was here. He was in this court, away from his bed. The princess had found out before I'd had the chance, but I should have sensed it immediately. If Nicu was in danger, my instincts should have told me that.

He was here. I hadn't realized it.

A scream tightened in my stomach, then vaulted up my throat, about to blast out of me like shrapnel. The impending racket alerted the princess, prompting her to whisper, "Hush."

The scream thrashed across my tongue. I swallowed, forcing it down.

"You have a son?"

The stunned tenor jolted Briar. She reeled back, and her gaze landed on Eliot. The thunderstruck minstrel had risen from his seat, and his head jumped between the princess and me.

Briar gaped at him, then at the scene—the dim candlelight, the roasting fire, the chairs angled close to each other—then at me. Another streak of pain reflected in her eyes, for I'd once told her that I never brought anyone into this room. None but her.

Pardon this jester, who couldn't be bothered to explain himself. Not at this cursed moment.

She recovered quickly. "Eliot. Excuse me, I didn't know you were here."

"But you can't have a son," the minstrel insisted. "You're Poet."

Poet, the Court Jester of Spring. Sinful artist and silver-tongued advisor. Lover of lovers.

The Crown's darling. The court's whore.

He couldn't have a child.

Apologetically, the princess glanced at me too late. For the questions frothed in Eliot's head.

How could somebody like me have a son? Why had he been "taken"?

Stalking to the vanity, I braced my hands on the tabletop and bent forward. The princess translated my silence as permission to explain my secret. We could only hope that Eliot's affections ensured a measure of trust and that my rejection hadn't embittered him.

Behind me, their voices blurred. I glared at them in the mirror's reflection. "Where is he?"

Briar and Eliot wheeled toward me. She said, "They took him to a cell."

"Have you seen him? Did they hurt him?"

"He's unharmed, but—"

The back of my arm lashed out at the vials and pots of pigment. They launched off the vanity and crashed to the floor, where they shed glass and bled color across the stones. The piercing noise split the room in half.

The minstrel veered back. The princess hastened in my direction. "Don't," I said, halting her. "Get on with it."

Briar explained about Jinny and the ribbons. The scarlet one I had bestowed on her—which she'd tied to a bush whilst stalking me—had caught Nicu's attention. He saw the carnival, then the stronghold and its swarm of people.

I'd taught him to follow those bands. Because of that, my son slept in a dungeon whilst I stood multiple levels above him.

"We returned by the same path," I bit out. "You should have retrieved the ribbon."

"I was blindfolded," she reminded me. "I had been too distracted by that to bear the ribbon in mind, but you're right. I should have been prudent."

She wasn't the only one. If only she hadn't been blindfolded. If only one of us had remembered during our return.

The princess informed me of the guard positioned at the top of the stairway, plus the one stationed below amid the dungeon's cells. I felt an urge to charge toward the window, or back to my chair, or I didn't fucking know where. No corner of this room seemed favorable. My feet paced over the mess I'd made, my boots tracking golds, smearing reds, and coating everything in blacks.

If anyone touched my son, I would decimate them. If anyone so much as looked at Nicu the wrong way, they'd be dead once I found them.

My fingers itched for a weapon, for a hundred blades to throw, to hit my marks. I wouldn't miss, for I never did.

"Maybe you could speak to the Crown," Eliot suggested. "They treasure you. If you tell them, they might make an allowance."

"No," Briar protested. "Poet's been hiding this for a year. Even if that didn't offend Basil and Fatima, they won't make a public exception, and it doesn't change the law. Nicu would belong to them in some capacity." She turned to me. "Poet, don't take that chance."

"What, then?" Eliot demanded.

I spun toward him, peering into his face for a shred of deception. He gaped, baffled and wounded. I made no effort to disguise my skepticism, nor was I the person he thought, nor had I confided in him as I had Briar. Were he like a thousand other people in this palace, I would have expected resentment or disgust.

But he wasn't like them. Instead, Eliot took the brunt of my glower until I thawed. "I need your trust."

"Seasons, Poet," he murmured. "You don't have to ask."

Asking would have been the least of it. I would have gotten on my knees and begged. Without hesitation, I would kneel before an executioner, if it came to that.

Briar gripped my shoulder, "We're breaking Nicu out of there."

"Wait." Eliot swung toward her. "We're doing *what*?"

"It's our only choice."

"For shit's sake, you're a Royal. Use your authority and make something up. Say the boy's from Autumn."

"I did that to see him, but it won't get past my mother. She will know he's not Autumn's property. She'll *know* he's of Spring."

The means to determine an Autumn citizen from a Spring one stemmed from a person's lack of documentation and intimate knowledge of the culture. Though less official, certain overt facets of one's personality confirmed their roots as well.

My heart shouted and raged. Yet the new trade amendment offered another option.

"Then bargain for him," I whispered.

The princess blanched. "You cannot be serious."

"I'm Poet. You'll know when I'm not serious. That is, unless I'm being clever and a wiseass, which is most of the time, but not all the time."

"Autumn is the same cage."

"It's the lesser of the two evils. It's a wider cage and under your reign."

"Under my *mother's* reign."

"She's a tolerant woman from a mild-tempered land, and you're her daughter."

"You can't!" she cried. "You can't let him go like his mother did. You can't do that!"

"In an escape, he could be struck by an arrow meant for me," I spat. "Or if we don't make it, he could be punished more severely. Negotiation is safer."

"Temporarily, because if you do this, he'll grow up thinking he wasn't worth fighting for. That could break him. He needs you!"

"The knights are expert shots," Eliot pointed out. "If they aim for you, they'll strike you, no one else. And Spring won't blame your son for an attempted escape. He's a stripling. They won't suspect him of being savvy enough to have anything to do with it, which'll be the truth."

Muffled voices drifted through the crack under the door. One of them uttered the word, "simpleton."

We funneled to the entrance, eased it open, and listened to a group of servants mumbling.

"They say the Seasons can trade the likes of 'em now."

"You sure the wee thing caught today isn't being kept by Spring? The Crown likes the stupid ones."

"I just came from the hill what's set up for Lark's Night. Overheard the Royals myself, I did. Summer's traded with Spring—two of their elder simpletons for the one tyke. Wee hands make good net weavers, I s'pose. He's being carted off tonight."

My fingers curled. My fingernails impaled the wood.

Rhys. That miserable cocksucker hadn't wasted time claiming my son. Later, when the King of Summer discovered Nicu lacked the directional capacity to tie more than a simple ribbon—and only with someone's help—Rhys would take his irritation out on my child.

And I'd be tried for murder.

Briar's hand covered mine. "I have a plan."

With deadly precision, I whipped around and prowled to the wardrobe, where I kept my daggers. "As do I."

33

Poet

I whisked a hooded cloak the color of smoke around my shoulders. Briar changed into a dark mantle, a raven dress, and black velvet gloves that corresponded with the soft-heeled boots hugging her feet. Coupled with that inflammatory hair, which blazed as if someone had set a match to it, the ensemble made her look like a siren who recently broke from her coven.

Getting past every shithead in residence without being recognized left little to the imagination. Either we'd have to distract, immobilize, or draw blood.

Braced behind a wall, we glanced around the corner and gauged our first obstacle. In a rotunda where several thoroughfares converged, a guard paced the room's length, his footfalls echoing. A blade scar slashed through his mouth, his eyes were as brown as coffee, and his shoulder-length hair a rare shade of slate gray.

In my life, I had only seen a dozen residents with locks of notable colors, including Cadence and Vale. Though, it was said the Prince of Winter possessed an even rarer one—a deep, dominant blue—which hung in long a mane.

I scanned the guard's bulky outline for something worth prying from him. A medallion dangled from around his neck, the pendant tethered to an easily chewable thong. The strap's humble material suggested the medallion was of personal value.

Silently, I hand-signaled to Briar. Then I quietly snapped my fingers to the trained creature braced beside our boots. Tumble burst forward, dashed to the guard, and scaled his frame.

"What the feral fuck," the man sputtered.

The ferret snatched the chain between his fangs and chomped. The strap broke, and the medallion dropped to the ground, where it clattered across the stones. Our sidekick scooped the token into his mouth and darted down the hall.

The guard hustled after him. "You pissy little varmint!"

He moved fast, but Tumble was faster. The creature rounded pillars, slinked between railings, and vanished into a network of corridors that would lead the guard to the nearest turret.

Briar had explained how the ferret had come with Jinny but stayed behind in the princess's suite. Thereupon, I'd had an idea. Despite not knowing the layout, the agile little sidekick could make it through the niches of this castle without being seen, as he did in the forest. I'd left a crumb trail for him to follow, so he would deduce where to go and how to find Briar's chambers later.

Knowing the creature's stamina, the distraction would give us ten minutes. More if he succeeded in reaching the turret's ledge and flinging the medallion over the side, where the object would sink into the dung-infested moat.

I led the way to the stairwell. Briar's sure footfalls trailed after me, her shadow pursuing without hesitation. My lips slanted, despite everything that's happened. Earlier, she had braved the dungeon alone, hellbent on giving my son food and her cloak for warmth. She'd comforted and gave him a sleeping draught, sparing him from enduring another conscious minute of that shit-pit. Blatantly, she disregarded what the court would do if they found out.

At the shaft's entrance, I ceased too abruptly for the princess. She bumped into me, and I reached back, grasping Briar's hip to steady her. Her forehead fell in between my shoulder blades, her panting breath seeping through my clothes.

In the half-light, we took a moment to endure one another.

If something happens to me ...

If anything happens to you ...

Crimson would pool across the floor. Hearts would be ripped from chests. My daggers would maim and nail bodies to the wall for target practice.

That was assuming I showed mercy.

No one would be safe from me if they touched her.

As for my son, retribution would know no ends. I'd maul and shave the flesh from every soul who got in my way. Carnage would litter the halls like roadkill. What's more, this court would be reduced to rubble, torn from its foundation, and everyone who'd survived my wrath would be buried alive beneath it.

Briar's exhales cooled my temperature, calming the grisly visions. One squeeze of her hip, and I let go.

The princess kept watch as I descended into the veritable asshole of the castle. Torches bled orange across the cobbled floor, talons of light scratching across the final steps.

I sauntered into the alcove. There, I greeted the second obstacle—a man-bear with a brawny thicket of beard sagging from his jaw. Whereas I stood tall and athletic, this behemoth could dwarf an oak tree.

Seeing me, the guard rose from his bench. Even whilst he frowned my way, his impressive body flexed, as if to make a good impression. I caught his flicker of interest, how his pupils fattened whilst trailing down my form.

"Good evening, soldier," I purred.

The man licked his lips and genuflected. "What brings you here, Court Je—"

"I have a craving."

"State your business, then."

"My business is capitulation. My business is you."

Dumbfounded, the guard batted his lashes. "Beggin' your pardon?"

I smirked and prowled toward him, my gaze sliding over his sturdy frame with unbridled lust. "You know of my varied tastes. I've heard the guards talking about it. It must be a strain, wondering but not finding out, being stuck here by your lonesome, wanting for company. So much wanting."

The man-bear gripped his poleax, but his twitching member had other ideas. Given an invitation, he would gladly pound himself up my ass if I let him.

I gave his erect appendage a blatant once-over and quirked a brow. "Forgive me for daring to speak it, but your cock is magnificent."

"I would ask you to stay where you are," he warned. "Fraternizing while on duty is—"

"The Spring way," I provided, stalling inches from him. "Do you know how many times I've envisioned a strapping man taking me prisoner? I can't help myself any longer." My fingers spider-crawled up the cuirass plated over his chest. "Do I not appeal to you? Because you appeal to me, sweeting. You have no idea how a hairy man violates me in dreams."

His eyes tripped to my mouth. "I have a job."

I leaned in and whispered, "Who's to know?"

Capitulation, to be sure. The randy motherfucker changed his mind forthwith. With a healthy growl, the sod dropped his poleax. He grabbed and swung me around, pressing me into the wall.

I ejected a fake groan, to which he flashed his incisors. "You like playing captive, eh?"

Verily. Alas for him, it should be known by now: I liked playing the captor more.

His paws grappled for the straps of my leather pants.

"Ah, ah, ah." I produced a corked skin from the inside of my cloak and ran the tip over his mouth. "Let's make this more interesting."

In good faith, I tipped the skin and drank, letting some of the wine drizzle down my chin for effect. The man watched through glazed eyes.

From prior experience, this move had enticed many men who'd relished the opportunity to lick the alcohol wetting my lips.

The guard accepted the skin and guzzled with abandon. I gave him a wily, close-mouthed smile, leashing my temper as he landed on his knees and focused on my cock—before going cross-eyed and flopping sideways onto the stones. My grin dropped and then curdled into a sneer. I spit out the wine, tainted with the same sleeping draught the princess had used on Nicu. When I'd sought him out, the Court Physician had mused and mumbled something about potentially widespread insomnia.

From the reek of mead, the guard had exceeded his threshold a while ago. Hopefully, he would believe he'd been snoozing on the job—it wouldn't be the first time—and dreaming of me whilst an intruder had stolen into the dungeon. If not, I would spin my best words to convince him I hadn't been here.

My fingers prickled. Fortunately for this prick, I hadn't merely stalked behind him, braced his skull, and snapped his neck with a single twist. Even now, the prospect appealed to me. However, getting out of this unscathed and without leaving a trace behind would protect Briar from a death sentence.

Still, the daggers waited inside in the harnesses under my clothes. If I had to, I would be quick and quiet.

Around the corner, voices guffawed and hooted, chains scraping the floor as the sources paced. The prisoners couldn't see what had happened, but they'd heard the hints of a disturbance. For this original reason, I had lowered my voice and cut the guard off from identifying me within earshot.

I wrenched the guard's keys from his buckle and stepped over his limp body. I strode to the row of cells, the dark preventing the other inhabitants from seeing me. They sounded too far gone, either in madness or despair, to try anyway.

In one cell, a bundle rested on the floor. Cursing, I thrust each key into the lock. Naturally, it would be the last one that finally worked.

Ripping the door wide open, I vaulted inside, sank beside Nicu, and drank in his slumbering face and curled fists. My hand brushed through his matted hair. "I'm here, my love. Papa's here to take you home."

"Mmmfff," he mumbled.

Briar's cloak swaddled him. I secured his form in the garment, scooped him into my arms, and propped him upright so that his head nestled in the crook of my neck. My nostrils inhaled the scents of powder and sunlight.

I've got you now.

Grasping my son, I turned to find the princess's silhouette peeking at us from the alcove. Because I'd taken longer than expected, she must have come to see if I needed help. The angle hid her from everyone's notice but mine.

I admired her standing there with a small but solid stature, every bit the Royal and more than that. Far more.

In verse, I couldn't have conjured a braver person. Briar knew nothing of combat, nor did she have the physical training for it. This land would condemn her for helping me, for believing in something most people didn't.

Yet she was here.

She knelt and rifled through the watchman's clothes for weapons. Unfortunately, all he wielded was the poleax, which was too tall and heavy for Briar to bother with.

I strode to her. Balancing Nicu with one arm and snatching the dagger affixed to my spine, I pressed the weapon into her hand. I curled her fingers around the hilt, illustrating how to hold it. If we survived this, I would teach her later how to impale an enemy. For now, I had two darlings to protect, and this dagger would provide backup in case I failed to rip our opponents in half first.

Briar stared at me. She thrust out her chin, accepted the sheathe I also gave her, and fastened both objects to the belt of her skirt.

We cinched our hoods, preventing them from blowing off our heads and revealing us.

Whilst sprinting up the stairs and out of the murk, Briar predicted, "They'll sound the alarm once the guard wakes up, or once the other warden returns."

"For a born child?" I countered, scanning an adjacent passage crocheted in cobwebs. "To them, Nicu's not valuable enough to rouse the citadel and lower town."

After checking the hallway, we slipped along the passage, then down another shaft leading to the tunnel I'd often taken to visit Jinny and Nicu. One hundred paces later, a muffled gong shuddered through the air.

We stopped. Our gazes shot toward the ceiling, arrested by the tolling of the bell tower. The princess leveled me with an I-told-you-so look.

Shit. Well, I couldn't be right every time.

We ran. My legs pumped, my soles pounding over stone and gravel. Nicu's head jostled against my shoulder, so I cupped it, trying to keep him steady and praying he wouldn't wake up.

At the fork, we veered east but skidded in place at the overlapping bellows and pulsing lights dawning from an intersecting shaft. On a hiss, I spun and doubled-back, leading Briar toward the alternate route curving west, which would dump us near the glazier's forge outside the citadel. From there, we'd have to flee across the lower town and past the Dragonfly Pavilion, Spring's most frequented brothel, to get to the public stables.

We halted again. More lights and shouts clamored in the foreground. Twisting, I saw bodies advancing from behind as well.

"Fuck," I seethed, dread slicing through me.

The noise roused my son. "Papa?"

My palm clamped over his lips. My frantic eyes darted around the area. A niche embedded into the passage would have been our saving grace. But by the time I located it, they had encircled us, four armored soldiers drawing a circumference of spears and swords in our direction—mine and Nicu's.

Briar had disappeared.

I whirled and searched for her, panicked that she'd been caught.

The thought burned my knuckles, rage coalescing with fear. If they got to her, I'd be forced to smash my fist through their plated chests and yank out their vital organs.

I clutched Nicu, whose head shifted from left to right as he took in the scene. He would have been elated by this attention, except the guards' armor and whiskered features resembled that sod in the dungeon. 'Twas enough to trigger the opposite of excitement. He dug his trembling fingers into me, burrowing closer whilst making tiny, terrified noises.

The men sneered at me. Me, the cloaked specter who had rattled these castle walls.

The knots securing my hood would conceal my face, no matter how I moved. And move, I would.

But if I spoke, they would know who I was. Fame indeed had its drawbacks.

"You've led a merry chase, bloke," one of the guards acknowledged, dumping his torch into a wall bracket. "Now it's time to give up."

My nostrils flared. I clasped my son tighter and slowly shook my head.

"By order of the Crown, give us the half-wit!"

If you want what's mine, you'll have to kill me first. That is, if I haven't extracted your heart by then. And if you do take him anyway, my ghost will sever this world in half getting him back. Don't you know that, sweeting?

In training, a jester learned to be constantly aware of his props. My right boot concealed a surprise, the scabbard at my hip another. But against sets of armor, the vital areas I could target were limited. Hence, I would have to get creative.

Which weapon to use first? And how to defeat four assholes with only two means of defense? And how to do so whilst holding my son? And without him seeing his father likely commit murder?

"We're going to play a game," I whispered to Nicu. "Like when I spin you at home. Are you ready?"

"Uh-huh," he peeped.

"Good. Close your eyes."

He mashed his face into my chest and squeezed me with all his might.

Bowing my head, I gave my targets a one-armed performance.

Wheeling around so that my back shielded Nicu, I whipped the blade from my hip. Lashing my arm backward, I sent the weapon flying into the first guard. A fountain of blood spurted from the side of his face, where the blade hacked off one of his ears. Red spritzed the stones. With a howl, the man dropped his sword, tripped into a wall, and crashed to the ground, where he rolled and groaned.

The next one charged. A low, reverse-twirl dodged his spear, which I stole after the full revolution. My fingers pivoted the spear into a windmill, which cracked against the side of the guard's skull, dislodging his jaw and knocking him unconscious.

The third adversary caught me off guard. The man's sword rotated, caught my spear in a wide arc, and sent it careening. Tucking Nicu close, I rolled and ripped the second dagger from my boot, then slashed behind the man's knee, red spraying his limbs. He bellowed, but that didn't stop him.

The rock did. It clouted him in the face, crimson bursting from the well of his nose. Roaring, the dazed man pawed at the wound just as another heavy rock slammed into the back of his head. His eyes rolled before he collapsed.

The fourth guard barreled toward me with a lion's roar, swinging two swords at once. Baffled from where the rock came, I shot to my feet as he advanced. And then I dropped my second dagger on instinct and punched the man in the face. My knuckles rammed into him, bone crunching on impact. His swords fell beside him on the ground, and he went still.

Wheezing and stroking my frightened son's back, I discovered the princess abutting the tunnel's niche, with another rock poised in her hand.

Pebble-tosser, indeed. She'd neglected to tell me her aim was that good.

In a stupor, Briar glanced between her makeshift weapon and the man she had knocked unconscious. Or rather, *unconscious* providing he would survive the blow.

She must have rationalized that already. Her expression contorted, dread leaching the color from her face. "Did I …?" she whispered. "Did I …?"

"Briar," I panted. "Look at me."

"I couldn't grab Nicu from you fast enough," she rambled. "I thought, if I had a chance to distract them, or to do something. I don't know how to throw a knife, and …" She lifted the spare rock. "This was all I could find." But her hand shook so badly, the rock toppled from her fingers and struck the ground. "Seasons, did I …?"

I stalked to Briar, then held her gaze fast. "Deep breath, sweeting." I repeated this mantra until she heeded my words, inhalations and exhalations drafting from her lungs, then said, "You were protecting us."

Her throat contracted. "Yes."

"Keep your eyes on me and listen. You were protecting him."

She glanced at Nicu, who curled into my chest and watched her. With every steady breath, her features reinforced themselves. "I was."

"Papa, are we home?" Nicu whimpered. "I want home. Please."

Briar caressed Nicu's cheek. "We're going now."

We sprinted, taking the passage that we'd originally intended. Ripping my key from my belt, I thrust it into the lock and gave a violent twist, the gate groaning as I shoved it open. We bolted across the undergrowth, toward the public stables.

I'd borrowed horses from there so often, I knew the grooms' and stablehands' routines. At this hour, they would be placing bets at the tavern, if not shagging one of the resident courtesans.

Outside the stables, Eliot paced like a leenix. His ashen face testified to how much of a delay that ambush in the tunnel had caused. "What the seasoned fuck?" he groused as we reached him. "If you're ever going to be late for any reason, and I do mean *ever*, would you mind letting me know? Send a smoke signal or find a way to use telepathy. I truly don't give a shit what method works best for you."

"Now you know how I felt when you had a musical epiphany and went on a desperate hunt for ink instead of meeting me at the ruins," Briar lectured. "I had anxiety for two hours, worried that something bad had happened to you."

Eliot grimaced. "I told you, the muse is a wayward mistress. The siren's call must be answered, or it's lost forever. Poet, tell her."

"Two hours, Eliot," she repeated.

"That's called paranoia, Briar."

The pair of matching steeds he braced derailed my concentration. Why the hell did he have two with him?

"You could be pursued to Jinny's," the princess explained. "You'll need someone to divert the masses in case they gain ground. I'm a good rider."

I wanted to argue, and I would have, and I should have. But Nicu quivered against me, so I rubbed his back and murmured into his ear until he sagged, whilst Eliot watched in fascination.

Another gong of the bell tower and the cacophony of alarmed residents alerted us. Both horses were of the same chestnut coat. Riding our own mounts from the court stables would have identified us, whereas two unknown but identical animals served better.

"Be careful," Eliot begged us.

"And you," Briar replied, yanking him into a hug.

The minstrel reciprocated, clasping her to him. Over her shoulder, he glanced at me and my son.

I mouthed, *Thank you*.

Briar took one horse, Nicu and I on the other. We raced out of town, up the hill, and into the wildflower forest. My ride puffed off the main road. The animal's weight beat chunks of dirt and clusters of poppies, and its mane slapped my face. As we plowed through, the moon flashed at us between the shrubbery.

Another spark of terror flared at the shouts of pursuit. My ears perked, detecting the regal baritones, the number of riders and their speed, and the furious drumming of their mounts. These weren't watchmen, they were knights.

I calculated their distance. Three of them broke from the legion, gaining fast. Hooves bracing thousands of pounds rammed into the hard soil.

For devil's sake, all this for one child who now belonged to Summer.

Nay, also for the criminal who'd stolen the child.

Together, the princess and I dug our heels in and flew. With less weight to carry, Briar gained headway, the ties in her hood finally loosening, her red tresses flapping like ribbons as she swerved around the trees. By Seasons, the woman could ride.

I tailed until Briar remembered she couldn't navigate us to the cottage without my direction, and she slowed enough for me to reach her. We'd had enough of a head start. With any luck, our pursuers hadn't yet spotted a pair of horses and realized there were two of us. They searched for a single offender clad in a dark cloak, mounted on a chestnut steed.

The princess's skill on a horse surpassed mine. However, I knew the depth and breadth of these woods. I knew routes and corners that she and the knights didn't. Not that it made a difference to me, because I also knew what had to be done.

With a sigh, I yanked on the reins.

Briar stalled beside me and trotted back and forth, both she and her ride impatient. "What are you doing?" she demanded, her cheeks flushed and fog pumping from her mouth.

"You're lighter," I said. "Therefore, you'll get to Jinny quicker."

Briar's eyes bulged. "The plan was for me—"

"That's the problem," I tried to joke. "A jester never listens to anyone's plan but his own."

"Poet, don't. If they catch you—"

"Then bury me here and make sure the headstone is very big. And expensive."

"No! This is supposed to be my sacrifice, not yours!"

Hearing the frenzy in her voice, Nicu began to cry. He clawed at me as I pried him from my lap and handed him over to the princess. Despite her firm grip, Nicu flailed and reached for me, screaming,

"Papa! Papa!"

"I don't know the way," Briar cried. "You blindfolded me."

"Heed your lover," I told her. "Go southeast—that way." I pointed through the darkness. "Then trail the first brook you find. Listen for the sounds of the water and keep to it. When you reach a rather phallic looking boulder—trust me, you won't miss it—veer full east. No matter the obstructions, no matter how dense or narrow it gets, stay your course. You'll get there."

Her features collapsed like scaffolding. "Please, don't. Don't, Poet."

I grabbed the princess's nape and hauled her close. "Briar. Shut up and go."

My son wailed louder, scrambling for my cloak. I framed his cheeks and kissed his forehead.

Dear ones. Only ones.

I did my best, but I lost my way, for I'm not in your league. If this chase ends badly, and this tale ends worse, I might not see you again. So, remember, try to remember, my heart is yours.

Be good and happy. Be loved elsewhere.

Ignoring their pleas, I swerved my horse around. Slamming through the brush and back onto the main thoroughfare, I emptied my lungs and howled like a wolf into the canopy. The knights heard me and came thrashing, poppies exploding in their path. Needle-like objects whizzed over my shoulder from behind, likely darts pumped with a tranquilizer fabricated by Winter.

I leaned forward, urged my mount faster, and we soared down the road. I wasn't daft. I didn't expect to outride the handsome knights and steeds of Spring. This might be the lavish land of artistry and debauchery, but its soldiers rode with grit, passion, and strength.

However, after growing up in this woodland, I possessed a keener eye. A gust tore into my cloak, the chill racing over my sweat-coated skin. I swerved off the road again and slipped into the shadows, spurring my horse over a knoll and weaving around hedges.

Deeper and deeper we went. Those cursed knights kept coming, though their pace wavered as I led them astray by circling the area twice, then snaking down another condensed route. I sensed their hesitancy, which couldn't be from wariness over locating one of the copses or hollows that spurred reckless acts. Nay, most Spring citizens went searching for those places.

So possibly the knights were recalling the previous rumors I had spread about incubi and demons lurking in certain parts of the forest. I'd explained that to Briar when she fretted over a search party finding us at Jinny's.

I could have worn the soldiers out, tricked them into believing those rumors more keenly. Except my steed huffed. The beast would tire any moment, driven beyond its limits.

I balanced on the stirrups and scanned the trees, then stood, bent my limbs, and swung my arms. My hands hooked onto a branch overhead, and I pitched myself into an oak tree, a move I'd perfected when the princess had followed me. The boughs' jade leaves shivered as I flipped upright and crouched on the branch. My horse kept going and vanished into the forest, vegetation shuddering in the animal's wake.

Moments later, the knights arrived. Their black and dark green capes billowed. They cantered about, murmured to each other, then pointed and pursued my steed into the thicket.

I waited for them to double back. As a trickster and someone who had experience locking hips with a knight or two, I knew their tactics. They ranged from clever to commonplace, this one being the latter.

Several exhales later, the leaves quavered. The horses reemerged, plowing through the vegetation, the animals' coats glazed in a silvery nighttime sheen. Their muzzles puffed, tufts of undergrowth sank under their clopping hooves, and the knights astride them kept quiet. They circled the hollow, too exposed to signal one another, knowing an onlooker would see it.

Instead, their eyes skewered the offshoots.

I braced one hand on an overhead branch and held still, my joints fixing in place and my breath compressing. Always, jesters decided when they wanted to be seen and when they didn't. Be it a fortress or a wilderness, I could own the spotlight or melt into the environment.

Nevertheless, my face wrinkled into a frown. Something wasn't right. And about one second later, I realized the problem as I scanned their bulky forms.

Two males. There were two males present, but ...

My pulse seized at the same time the knights' shoulders hunched, and their grips loosened on the reins.

One of them shook his head in resignation. "Shit," he muttered. "Who the bloody hell vanishes into thin air?"

"Let's move on," the other replied, growing agitated. "Remember what the Court Jester had said."

"Bah. Fuck superstitions. This forest arouses visitors, it doesn't haunt them."

They steered the horses away. For good measure, the men scanned the hedges, never once raising their eyes to the canopy—until the scarlet ribbon untethered and slipped from my wrist.

It could have been any of the other cords affixed to my arm. But it wasn't.

I kept it close, tightly knotted. Only the battle with those guards in the tunnel could have eased the binding.

Nicu's ribbon fluttered like a plume, the color bleeding through the darkness. One of the knights must have caught sight of it in his periphery. The horses grumbled, wheeling around once more under the riders' command. Broadswords flashed at their hips, and the men's fists landed on the hilts. As they peered closer at the object, recognition caused their eyes to widen. Whilst they didn't know the ultimate significance of the bracelet, most at court had been privy to rumors about the ribbons, and everyone had seen me wear this one.

In slow motion, the knights swung their legs off the horses and lowered themselves to the ground, boots thudding as they landed. Small crossbows were harnessed to the equines, the instruments customized to eject those Winter darts that had flown my way. Yet for this present skirmish, the men required more sizable weapons.

They approached the keepsake whilst ripping out their swords, steel ringing through the wild. One of the men used the tip of his blade to scoop the frayed accessory off the grass and raise it to a beam of moonlight. My molars ground as the pair cast the object thunder-struck looks, then craned their heads upward.

Their eyes wandered, but the miserable sods would wait me out, assuming I didn't die of thirst before then. Either way, my son's ribbon slumped over the sword, in danger of being sheared in half or taken from me, like they'd tried to take him.

I clenched my eyes shut. "Motherfuck."

And then I jumped.

My feet smacked the ground between them. The men sprang apart, the ribbon slipping from the first one's weapon. I twisted and pitched to the grass, my legs propelling and clipping each of them in head.

The men groaned and staggered as I popped upright, but they recovered quickly. I swerved from an incoming sword, snatched the hilt mid-rotation, and maneuvered it to block the other knight's weapon. The blades crossed, the noise slicing through the air. Over the weapons, my opponent's eyes reflected shock because my hood had come undone, my face lurching from the fabric.

I slammed my head into his skull, then pivoted in the opposite direction, taking the second sword with me. Spiraling behind its owner, I rammed the hilt into his tailbone. He careened forward whilst his partner charged.

Swords weren't my craft, but I had wielded them to entertain the court before. I spun the weapon between my fingers, confusing the soldier and blocking his thrusts. Despite the haze, he maintained expert footing and quick reflexes. His knuckles cuffed my profile, blood spraying the grass and pain throbbing across my jaw.

We clashed and parried, his armor against my thin clothing, the sword in my grip nevertheless slicing open his cheek. Crimson spurt-ed as he groaned, momentarily veering from me.

A hulking weight launched my way from behind. I chucked the sword to a spot where it stabbed the ground beside the tree, then lunged into a series of single-handed backflips. My legs scissored the air, my boots punching the second knight's chest. The impact sent him flying whilst I kept flipping past him and snatched the ribbon from the grass.

Vaulting upright, I retrieved the sword, whisked behind the trunk, and knotted the ribbon around my wrist, then braced the weapon. Footfalls pounded toward the tree. This was going to take a bit more ingenuity and freedom to move.

I tugged the cords of my cloak. The garment dropped from my shoulders as I choked the weapon, then whirled in their path. As I did, the same harrowing fact resurfaced, the realization that had struck me earlier.

Two males. Presently, I clashed with two males.

But there'd also been a female.

34

Briar

We made it to Jinny's cottage. Poor Nicu had passed out during the ride, caught between chattering and crying himself into exhaustion.

The older woman nearly collapsed when she saw us. I didn't tell her what had happened with Poet, but from the way Jinny shrank into her chair by the fire, she knew. I promised everything would be all right but didn't blame her for not believing the lie.

On the way back to court, foreboding curdled in my gut. Poet might need help, but he could be anywhere. And if he'd taken cover, I might foil his plans or give him away.

But what if he was injured?

As my ride galloped back the way we came, my gaze landed on something flashing in a cradle of wildflowers. I jerked on the reins, stopping the horse and taking a closer look at the object.

A blade flashed through the lacing of flora. Poet had lost that weapon while fighting the leenix.

I jumped off the horse and stalked toward the object. Sinking to my knees, I picked it up and hesitated. Although I still harnessed the dagger Poet had given me, fate may have led me to this second weapon, to say I should go after him. Either that, or providence lured me here for another reason.

I glanced absently at a neighboring tree with exposed roots thatched in moss and braided into knots giant enough for a child to duck behind. A twelve-year-old girl who'd run away from her father on a stormy night. A memory so fresh that it might have happened yesterday.

My memory. My mistake.

I knew those roots. I hadn't recognized them the last time I was here, when the leenix wounded me, but I recognized them now.

I swayed on my knees and choked the blade. I gaped at my surroundings, at the place where my father died, the life bleeding from his face and changing me forever.

I stared at every detail. I stared and stared.

Just stared.

Just. Stared.

Something in my periphery whizzed through the air and pinched the side of my neck. The moss blurred, the forest tilted, and my eyelids dropped. And I stopped staring.

35

Briar

They dragged me before the court and shoved me to my knees. I blinked, woozy from the dart the knight had shot me with. Tall candelabras illuminated the stained glass windows in the throne room. The bonds at my wrists chafed.

Basil and Fatima stood on the dais, their faces tight with disbelief as they stared at me. They made a spectacle of this moment. Courtiers surrounded me, including the Seven, their faces bright with shock.

Even Eliot was here, his profile wrung out like a towel and his skin as green as celery. At least they hadn't apprehended him, too.

The guards Poet and I had battled stood in the foreground, bedraggled, bruised, bleeding, and bristling—but alive. That much was a relief. The one missing an ear managed to stay upright, and my rock hadn't vanquished the other male currently fuming from the sideline.

The Royals arranged themselves in a semicircle. My mother's eyes flashed with dismay, yet she ignored my pleading glance. She would not speak up for me. I had disgraced myself and dishonored her. I'd insulted Spring.

I was not sorry. I think they saw that from the lift of my shoulders and the dignified expression I mustered.

"Princess Briar," Basil lectured, his velvet mantle swishing around his feet. "Not for a century has a Royal passed judgment on another Royal. I can't believe I'm about to say this, but you've been accused of stealing the rightful property of Spring, of accosting the guards, and I can't begin to list the rest. What in Seasons got into you? Don't answer that yet," he said, turning to his wife. "Dearest, do help me. I've a headache."

"Your horse and mantle fit the thief's description," Fatima said, her crown glinting like a set of spikes and the fringed hem of her olive silk dress scraping the floor. "The dagger found in your hand, as well as the one in your belt, match the design of the ones used on the guards. What's more, your recent behavior has been noted by many."

People had seen. The day I'd fled the dungeon and raced through the halls like an apparition had been on my tail, the court had witnessed it.

Reluctantly, Posy, Vale, and Cadence confirmed that I had initially been wandering the corridors on the night we crossed paths. Because this was out of character for me, the Royals interpreted it as potentially malicious. Under duress, the ladies verified how I'd taken part in the escapade to the labyrinth, another example of my change in behavior.

Residents had observed me slink here and there, sometimes to the library, which accounted for the one time I'd felt someone trailing me. I hadn't been paranoid, after all. Members of the court had taken to watching me whenever I caught their attention.

But most times, I'd crept to the artist wing—to Poet. A few people had noticed my presence in that area as well, despite my having used the secret passage from my suite.

During the Peace Talks, I'd failed to compose myself and had suggested born souls be treated better. I got into a fight with the Court Jester.

I had quarreled with Mother in public. I'd slapped Cadence for mocking born souls. I stormed into the dungeon and bullied the guard into letting me see Nicu.

Eliot stepped forward and opened his mouth to interject. I shook my head, stopping him. I wouldn't allow my friend to place his head on the chopping block alongside me. Admitting to helping me and Poet commit treason would only cut short Eliot's life—and by agonizing means. Spring was prolific not only in the arts but in their executions.

That very fact pumped fear through my bloodstream. It doused me from the inside like ice water as my knees pressed into the foundation.

"Do you deny any of these accusations?" Queen Fatima asked.

By some miracle, I kept my reply steady. "A princess does not deny anything."

Murmurs and coughs spread through the room. The court shifted, their expressions varying from amazed to appalled.

King Basil puckered his lips. "Those were your daggers?"

"Yes," I answered.

"You acted alone?"

"I did, Your Majesties."

"Take care, Briar of Autumn. That's twice you've lied."

"It was all me. That's not a lie."

With a sigh, the king nodded at the sentinels standing post at the entrance. "Bring him."

Foreboding crawled like insects up my spine. No. No, no, no, no, no.

The double doors whipped apart. Unlike me, Poet didn't wait for his armed escorts to push him. Also cuffed in irons, he strode ahead of them and then swept to the floor, sliding gracefully across the polished surface on his knees. His arms spread as far as the chains allowed, blood dotting his knuckles.

Welts cluttered his visage. A purple bruise darkened his jaw, several lacerations diced his neck, and a red slash of blood crusted along his forehead.

The sight scalded my insides. Nevertheless, he coasted next to me with blithe indifference, straightened his sleeves, and fake-whispered, "Hello, sweeting. I think we've been caught."

"Stop that shit, both of you," Basil growled, his countenance bloating with umbrage. "Poet, we're severely disappointed. This is mutiny at best, treachery at worst. For your sake, tell us this a massive prank derived for Lark's Night."

"'Tis not," he answered, swinging his head toward the dais. "I give you my word as a man who jests."

"You cannot be serious."

"Hardly ever. But that's what you pay me for."

Nervous chuckles echoed through the assembly.

"Pity for you," His Majesty alleged. "If you had taken your escape more seriously, you would have outrun our knights."

"If you took humanity more seriously, I wouldn't have had to try."

The knights must have suspected two parties and split up when Poet created that diversion. They must have also decided this belatedly, since I'd succeeded in delivering Nicu to Jinny before being darted. Moreover, the knight who found me mightn't have spotted me at all, had I not been distracted by memories of my father.

"This is an affront to the Peace Talks, Princess Briar," Fatima censured. "What does Autumn have to say for itself?"

"Don't vilify her, Majesties," Poet drawled. "If she's gone rogue, the fault is with me. After I targeted the princess for ridicule on her first night here, she impressed me with her tenacity, and that impression stuck. Because her virtuous Autumn nature was no match for my conniving Spring ways, I manipulated her into helping my cause.

"As for why I committed mutiny—not that you asked, but I have a tender spot for children and a grudge against Summer. The Season and its monarch annoy me, so I decided to milk his temper for all the bullshit it's worth. I'll admit, he's such an easy target that I got carried away."

"You insufferable parasite!" King Rhys of Summer hollered, spittle flying from the black thatch of his mustache.

"The princess was under my spell." Poet raised an eyebrow, his voice cutting to the quick as he scrutinized the room. "And don't each

401

of you know what that fuckery is like."

I should have shut him up a while ago. I did not care to be portrayed as a damsel swooning under his influence. Nor was I going to let him take the blame alone.

"The jester's attempting to be heroic," I countered. "I was under no spell."

Basil ingested a thick breath, dismay wrinkling his visage. He and his wife had been pierced with a double-edged sword.

Poet's influence stretched beyond Spring's borders, and while half the court either desired Poet's body, feared his tongue, or resented his position, the citizenry was different. Unanimously, they idolized him. He was the talk of the tavern, an idol among the brothels, and the main event in each story that drifted from the castle into the surrounding villages and towns.

Also, the king and queen couldn't function without him. Poet was a member of their trusted council and the court's most valuable player. Pass judgment on their beloved and renowned fool, and the monarchy would lose him to a deadly end, not to mention guarantee widespread disorder.

Slap his wrist and do nothing, and the people of Spring would lose respect for their sovereigns, contrasting principles be damned. They felt scorned by Poet and sought compensation. Only not at the expense of forsaking him altogether.

Add the princess of an allied nation to the mix, and things got even more complicated.

The king shoved out the words. "You are both accused of conspiring to thievery of a simpleton. Theft of your sovereign's property and defiance against the Fools Decree are grounds for treason, the penalty of which is death."

"The simpleton belongs to Summer," Rhys reminded us. "Tell me, Court Idiot. In which manner would you like to die for stealing from a king?"

Poet cocked his head. "You'll let me choose?"

"I shall let you choose."

"Excellent. I'd prefer death by old age."

More sniggers arose from the congregation. Briefly, Basil and Fatima folded their lips inward, struggling to keep their amusement at bay. The joke alone might have tempted them to absolve him. But despite their adoration for Poet, these monarchs had their limits. They had to set the example, but how they would manage that without risking the public's wrath was anyone's guess. Though, I would not discredit them to find a way.

Rhys boomed, "You dare to mock me?"

Poet tsked. "Some might say I have a prowess for that, particularly the ones who've hired me to exploit my skills." His voice lowered, fatally calm. "And unlike you, I have respect for my profession."

"Keep going, then. For every insolent breach, I shall have your anatomy displayed on a fucking pike, starting with your tongue."

"Makes sense. It's the most valuable part."

"Poet." I elbowed him and muttered under my breath, "Stop."

But at this point, he was too livid to stop. Having his child sold like chattel will do that to any man. Because that was his right, I clammed up.

Basil checked himself, then made it clear. "If you wish to avoid retribution, you will inform us of the child's whereabouts."

"Do so promptly," Fatima instructed. "Comply, and we shall be merciful."

Poet and I held our tongues. They could do with us as they pleased, but we wouldn't tell them. Unless they considered Nicu worth combing the land to its borders, he would stay safe.

Somber looks passed over Spring's king and queen. Poet's deception had truly wounded them. And why not? For the past year, they've trusted him on matters political and social. For that, they must feel gullible at best, disgraced at worst.

"Well, then," Basil stammered, his grim features setting like stone. "Well."

"The princess and the jester," Rhys sneered. "It seems you two became quite the intimate allies during your jaunt in the wildflower forest. They say things happen there, isn't that so? People stumble upon certain copses, and it loosens inhibitions the way a slut might loosen the slit in their drawers."

"Do *not* go there," Poet growled, which had less to do with himself and more to do with me.

At the same time he spoke, Mother's teeth came out. "You will not speak that way about my daughter."

Rhys merely scoffed. I weathered the insult like a pebble bouncing off the surface of my skin.

Nonetheless, his pestilent accusation contaminated the room. Eliot winced, trenches burrowing into his countenance. Staring ahead prevented me from checking the Seven's reactions, but the court members who were visible glared at us. They regarded Poet like a lover who had been unfaithful, me like a princess who'd never respected them in the first place, and both of us like traitors.

Spring's meaning couldn't be missed. The details stacked against us, and the attention we'd paid one another over the past weeks pointed to the obvious.

They knew. We had been fools to think they wouldn't.

At Basil and Fatima's signal, several bodies headed our way. The instant one of the guards shackled my arms in a viselike grip, I yelped in pain.

Eliot stormed forward, but a soldier detained him. Posy, Vale, and even Cadence hollered protests. My mother was already halfway down the dais steps, her turbulent voice commanding them not to harm me.

Another second later, an elastic silhouette twisted in front of us. A set of airborne limbs rammed into the guard's breast. The knight's meaty hands vanished from my arms, and his body shot into the air like a lid blown from a pressurized cauldron.

He smacked the floor beside me. Blood spurted across the parquet. A cacophony of shocked noises erupted through the room.

Plastered on his back, the soldier cupped his broken nose while Poet knelt above him and dug his knee into the man's windpipe. Gargling, the man threw a fist toward the jester's face. Like a flicked switchblade, Poet's manacled arm blocked the attempt as though swatting a pesky fly.

With his chained leg nailing the man to the floor, Poet balanced a wrist casually over the opposite thigh. However, there was nothing casual about his expression as he leaned in. His instructive voice could have sliced through rock. "Sweeting, if the princess doesn't want to be touched—" he increased the pressure on the guard's trachea and enunciated, "—you do *not* touch her."

It had happened so fast, I'd barely had time to blink. One of the other knights sprang into action and charged at Poet from behind. I flung myself across the jester's back, threw my palms up, and shouted, "Stop!"

The jester floundered, astonished that I'd hurled myself on top of him like a shield.

Everyone gawked at us. Me and Poet, protecting one another as the guard flailed.

"We'll go," I swore, grabbing Poet and forcing him halfway around. "Poet, we'll go."

My plea tamed his expression, dulling its livid glint. He dislodged his knee from the knight's throat and sighed, offering his wrists to our wardens.

Reminded of what the Court Jester was kinetically capable of even while restrained, half a dozen fresh soldiers were assigned to us as an extra precaution. In a tower reserved for Royal and high-ranking prisoners, the fleet tossed us into neighboring cells separated by rails. Rushes covered the cubicles' floors and bars cut across a single window, though neither of these amenities obscured the dank air or the pungency of mold.

The iron doors screeched closed behind us. The moment the troop left, Poet and I flew at each other, pressing together through the barrier. My clamped wrists adhered to his chest, and he framed my head as we breathed one another in. Our mouths grazed and swapped heavy breaths.

"He's safe?" Poet asked.

"Yes," I whispered, then veered back to cup his wounded jaw. "You could have snapped that man's neck."

"If he'd bruised a single inch of your flesh, I would have. It's been a long night, and my tolerance threshold is at an all-time low. Not that it's ever been high concerning you and my offspring."

"And you're hurt."

"I'm inconvenienced."

"Who did this?" I hissed. "I shall have them flogged."

"Rest assured, the knights from the forest have it worse. I diverted the pissants, we had a little scrimmage, and then I realized one was missing. I knew the third had gone after my lady. I tried to find you in time, but the female's forsaken dart found me first."

"It found me, too."

"The desperate father in me neglected to retrieve my throwing knives before rushing from the tunnel. I've used them in front of the court, which makes them recognizable. It might have helped not to leave evidence behind, plus have some means of defense. I hear that's what smart people do. I failed incredibly well, if I say so."

"I found your missing blade, from the night of the leenix. I was kneeling on the grass and holding the knife, and I couldn't move. I just couldn't. That's how the soldier caught me."

Poet's mouth slanted. "Such a sentimental woman."

Tears broke from my eyes. "My father died there."

He tensed, then ushered me to the ground, where we huddled together. Because he couldn't wrap his arms around me, Poet slipped his hands through the bars, combed through my hair, and braided it over the front of my shoulder. While I cried, he tied the plait with one of his wrist ribbons, then hooked his palms over my hips, pulling me closer to him.

The corners of my eyes leaked. "On the path back from Jinny's, I found it. The spot where I watched him die. I never thought I'd see it again, and then there it was. I had forgotten what it looked like. It's strange how that happens, isn't it? You forget how something looks or smells or tastes or sounds."

"Until it's suddenly there again," he agreed.

"Like it was never gone."

"I've had that feeling a few times."

"Father and I liked to explore our home when I was little," I began, consoled. "He would wake me and take me anywhere I wanted to go. We pretended to be wanderers. I led the way."

My story continued in whispers.

Mother had often said I possessed an adventurous, impulsive streak like Father. She'd predicted I would grow up to be a daring female, ready to take chances and dismiss social rules. As a child, I enjoyed being around every class of people even when it wasn't my duty.

Ever prone to fits and laughter, my emotions left a trail behind me. Often, I said *no* and asked *why*. I wept in Mother's arms and ran circles around Father's legs. I talked over them, around them, right through them.

I was unpredictable, too vibrant for Autumn. I didn't hold back with them or anyone. My parents would quip that a stork had lost its way and delivered me from Spring.

When I was twelve, we traveled to that mischievous court, and there I met Eliot. I was so excited about making a new friend, I couldn't sleep for the thrill of it. That same night, I tiptoed into my parents' adjoining chamber and bounced between them in bed, demanding they hear all about Eliot.

At the time, I hadn't thought to keep my relationship with a minstrel secret. All the same, it hadn't mattered, because I never got to tell my parents.

Father's temper had been strained during the first Peace Talks meeting. He was in such a vile mood that he cut me off and barked at me to go to sleep, his voice booming like a great Summer horn. He'd never raised his voice like that before.

I yelled in kind. I ran out of their suite, my frame scrawny enough to get past the gate, down the castle hill, through town, and into the wildflower forest. I ran forever.

Although it was blooming season in Spring, clouds blanketed the sky, and fat sheets of rain doused the landscape. Father had searched the court's halls for me. He'd scouted the places we had explored together, then guessed that I fled outdoors. He caught up to me on his horse, knowing I liked those woods.

I'd ensconced myself behind a knot of exposed tree roots germinating with pillows of moss, a pretty place to hide. I thought to punish him, play with him—a grudge and a lark. I thought how sorry Father would feel when he couldn't find me, how wonderful it would be when he finally did, because fathers were supposed to find their children. He was a king, as invincible and timeless as our home. He was my very own stronghold.

Why *wouldn't* he locate me?

The storm lashed, creating a mudslide down a neighboring slope. Father bounded off his horse and gave a shout, horrified I might have gotten swept into the deluge.

"Briar!" he bellowed, twisting this way and that. "Briar!"

I thought, what a gift it would be when he saw me alive. What a happy gift I would give my father by popping up behind him.

Many giant tragedies killed people. Wars and assassinations, diseases and poisons, and curses from old legends.

People rarely considered the elements, despite how we worshiped the Seasons throughout this continent, despite its power and magic. While charging toward the mudslide, Father's foot snagged beneath one of the tree's exposed roots. His head cracked against a rock when he fell, the crunch of bone cleaving through my ears.

Yet I laughed. I thought it was a jest or a silly, harmless fall. I thought he would get up, but he didn't. And I laughed at him.

After crawling over the roots and tottering toward him, I plopped to my knees. "I'm here, Papa! I tricked you!"

Liquid pooled from his skull and seeped like ruby ink into my nightgown. His dazed eyes found me and glinted with relief, then with something soft and absolute—something I would later recognize as love.

Quickly, his expression became remote, those pupils turning to fog. And I stopped giggling.

When I did, his eyelids fluttered and then fell closed, no longer seeing me, no longer aware of how much I loved him back.

A brief loss of temper. A willful spirit. A trick.

The imprudent child I was had lost her father because she'd been playing. She hadn't killed him, but she could have saved him. She wasn't fit to be a daughter or anything else—certainly not a future leader.

That's when I changed. I folded myself up and stuck myself in a drawer. For eight years, I spurned revelry—dancing, laughter, and amusement. I had to, otherwise I'd revert and become someone unforgivable.

Mother and I shared the same dread of losing one another. So she kept me close, while I kept my distance.

Poet remained quiet, holding me. When I finished, he stroked his thumb across the rim of my ear. "Has it worked?" he intoned. "Erecting that wall? Keeping everyone at bay?"

I traced an invisible pattern on his thigh. "It's backfired."

"You were a child, sweeting. You didn't know better."

"I was foolish."

"You're foolish now if you think it's your fault."

"If I hadn't been that heedless girl—"

"If, if, if," he rattled gently. "If many things."

"I haven't felt him near in a long time, but I felt him today. It was like I needed to be that tempestuous child again to sense him close, to feel his presence. When I did, I was proud, not guilty or sad." I nestled into Poet as best I could, my head tucked against his solid chest. "I promised myself I wouldn't tell you this."

"We mere mortals all hide things."

No matter what he said, it often sounded like a clue to something else. As I contemplated the floor stained in torchlight and twilight, a hunch manifested. "Poet isn't your real name."

After a moment of silence, he murmured into my ear, "Nay."

"You won't tell me."

"'Tis embarrassing."

I chuckled weakly, then crumbled apart and glanced at him. "I'm sorry. I'm sorry about what I said in the bell tower. It was horrid and inexcusable, and I'm ashamed. Please believe that's not how I feel about Nicu."

His forehead fell against mine. "Thank you for that. What you said won't be forgotten any time soon, but thank you."

"I can't forgive myself."

"Work on that, my thorn. I've dealt my share of blows. I blamed you for what happened at the Peace Talks. I could have tried to persuade the Royals without you, but I fixated on losing your support. I refused to listen, to let you explain. It felt easier to hold something against you, punish the shit out of you. On the hill, I flaunted my friendship with Eliot." He paused in the manner he often did when measuring the weight of something pivotal. "Briar?"

I tensed. "Poet?"

"In my chambers, he kissed me. And I kissed him back."

The confession leached the oxygen from my lungs. He'd spoken tentatively, yet it failed to dull the words. Their sharpness lanced through my chest.

My best friend had attempted to enamor Poet. And Poet had let him try.

Not that I hadn't trespassed on Eliot's desires first or that Poet was mine to begin with. He never had been.

"Oh," was all that came out, my voice too fragmented to say more.

"Not *oh*," Poet said. "I deserve worse than *oh*."

The fact that I needed to ask, that there was a reason I should ask, was excruciating enough. "Do you have feelings for him?"

He thought about that. "Affectionate ones. If you didn't exist, then someday those feelings might grow. But not once have I been torn or doubted for whom my heart pumps, however futile."

His words lifted my spirits off the ground. Nevertheless ... "So much of me doesn't want you to care in that way."

"I would echo that sentiment if it weren't moot. Visiting my son in secret, deceiving the Crown for his protection. Those weren't acts of bravery—they were just necessary. What we have here and now? This isn't necessary. That's why it's brave. 'Tis the jester in me, but I have a theory. Are you ready for it?"

"No. Yes."

"The greatest courage a person can have is to love another, for there are only two outcomes. Either the love lasts, and our lives are compromised, or it doesn't, and our lives are emptied. Either way, we suffer more than we celebrate. I've enjoyed suffering with you. We are a tale for campfires." His mouth descended, pressing flush and hot against my own. "That is all. That is everything."

I shook my head, my lips grazing his. "It can't end here."

"Come now. It isn't that bad. We're finally allowed to have a fling without hiding it."

"We're in a jail cell and on trial for treason."

"Which means the hour is precious. If this is the only place we can happen, I'll take every drop of it."

"No. I won't let this go. I thought I could, but I can't."

A grin tilted his voice. "Who knew I would be the sensible one tonight."

"You're a hypocrite," I objected. "This isn't the extent of us unless we let it be. Unless you don't want me enough."

"Almighty Seasons, 'tis not about wanting. Oh aye, I'm afraid of never having more, never making you gasp with every stitch of clothing I peel from your flesh, never tasting every freckle shivering across your skin, never feeling your bare legs wrapped around my unclad hips, never knowing the ecstasy of being inside you, fucking you beautifully, giving you such deep euphoria until your mind is filled with every raw sensation in existence, and making love to you the way my body's been shrieking to for weeks. I'm afraid of that. From the beginning, I wanted you so intensely it drove me to the brink, and I'll keep wanting you until the Seasons fade. Alas, we don't get everything we want. This is it, sweeting."

What he said about fucking me, making love to me, eclipsed the rest of my argument. It returned me to all the enticing things we'd done to each other while in and out of the shadows.

All the staggering ways he had made me feel. All the heavy noises we'd elicited from one another. All the ways his body had fit to mine.

All but one.

Today, too many emotions had swarmed me, then been ripped from me. Endlessly, I took people for granted. I did not want to take this man for granted, too. I didn't want to lose this.

My response took on a husky note. I wanted him to hear it, then to do something about it. "Tell me about us. Take me there."

Poet emitted a throaty sound. He spoke, his breath pushing against the side of my neck. "I'm kissing a woman."

"That woman is kissing you back," I whispered.

"We're naked and entwined. That woman tastes of tart apples as her moans shudder across my tongue."

"Because she likes what your mouth is doing to her. She enjoys how you touch her in places she never imagined being touched, in places that come to life under your fingers."

"I'm dragging my lips down her throat," he rasped into my pulse point. "As I do, her whimpers vibrate against me, so that I discover the texture of her bliss, each sound telling me where to ply her, how hard or soft to consume her flesh."

"She wants both," I confided. "She wants it all."

"So that's what I shall offer. Her eyes reflect desire, her nipples tighten, and heat radiates between her legs. She's sitting on me, facing me astride my lap, her lovely wet cunt coating my aching cock as it pitches into her, and I'm going higher, deeper with each pass. And it's such a poignant, passionate, and privileged place to be."

"Yes," I muttered. "And her walls are surrounding his hard length, enclosing him within her damp heat."

"And I'm stroking into that heat, her open thighs hitched around my hips, her exquisite pussy spreading around me, soaking me to the base, her flesh throbbing from pleasure. And I'm losing my mind over her—*with* her."

"And she's riding his thrusts."

"And I'm desperate for her to come, for her to shout with rapture, and for the wild sound of both."

"And she's rolling her hips into him. And she's falling for him."

"And I'm loving her."

On a helpless sigh, I twisted at the same time he gripped my jaw and steered me toward him. Those clover eyes sizzled before his mouth slanted hotly against mine. At the contact, my insides liquified like a melting candle.

"I'm loving her everywhere," he murmured. "I feel the grip of her knees. I'm watching her vault upward, arching into me, her breasts pointed. She's digging into my shoulders as we let our hips go, her thighs catching each pump of my cock. I'm fucking her sweetly, making love to her roughly, putting every shred of myself into the motions, feeling her cunt contract as she comes long and loud, her face slack with ecstasy, her mouth unhinged for the whole foolish world to hear. I'm giving her everything she wants. And in turn, it's utter nirvana.

"Should she wish it, I shall do this to her forever, even as the walls crumble around us and the land burns to ash. I will stay with this woman, follow this princess into hell, and keep touching this future queen the whole time. I will keep wanting her, keep sparring with her, and keep coming back to her."

Poet whispers, "Right now, I'm loving her ... because I do, and have, and will."

My hands shook as they clasped his face. "Poet."

"I love her," he hissed, capturing my mouth.

Through the rails, my lips opened, and his tongue slipped past the seam. He probed inside, licking into me the way he once had between my legs, the way the rest of him could not. His tongue swooped against mine, the tempo sensuous, our mouth fusing—unbreakable.

I felt each long sweep, each heated flick, each way the jester kissed me.

And I loved it.

I loved him.

Seasons save me, I did. I loved this devilish man so much it hurt. He was everything that enflamed and emboldened me. He was my craving and my comfort, my abandon and my bedrock, utterly out of control yet safely rooted to the ground.

The emotion spun my body off its axis. It stripped me bare yet covered me in armor. It was all-consuming, feverish, and mine.

I loved Poet. I loved him desperately.

My panting lips untangled from his. I opened my mouth to say the words, to bare myself fully, but he pressed a finger to my lips and guided me onto the rushes.

We lay there, reaching between the bars. I traced his bruised jaw and lacerated throat with my fingertips, while he traced my mouth with words.

"Steadfast lady, sweet royal thorn,
how lovely-cruel you are.
My body's taut, my soul is worn,
from the lovely-cruel you are.
The highborn chose the lowest born,
'tis the lovely-cruel you are.
This trick unseen, this fated scorn,
of the lovely-cruel you are.
So, when you leave, I shall us mourn,
the lovely-cruel we are."

36

Briar

I awoke, bleary-eyed. Poet slept facing me, emitting the cutest snore. Over the bars, our manacled hands were clasped between us.

I stared, daring to wish for more than this, a morning folded beside him, quiet and still, as if it was an everyday occurrence. So simple a luxury.

This place should have stunk, but the traces of Spring and Autumn overpowered the tower's putridness. Notes of amber, vetiver, and green apples mingled. My lungs drew in his essence—and the fragrance of someone else. The perfume of cardamom drifted from beyond our huddle.

With his eyes still closed, Poet mumbled, "We have a guest."

I twisted. Mother stood outside my cell, her curvaceous figure wrapped in a pewter satin gown, with her hands folded over her navel—a pose I'd learned from her. The bars divided my mother's rigid face into sections as she stared at us.

I staggered to my feet. I heard Poet do the same.

Mother lifted one arm. In response, a reed-thin guard with an angry scar digging into his jawline materialized behind her. He wrestled with the keys and unlocked the door.

"Come, Daughter," my mother said.

I flinched to hear her address me formally. She gazed at me as she would a stranger, for which I couldn't blame her. Not after seeing my wrists bound.

I retreated a step. My shoulder knocked into the rails, prompting Poet to set his hands there. The picture we made did nothing to move Mother.

"Come," she ordered. "Now."

"No," I said. "Not without him."

"Do not test me, Briar. If necessary, I will have you dragged out."

Poet spoke in my ear. "I'd rather not come between you and yet another person. Family dramas are a sensitive trigger for me."

I whirled toward him. "I won't leave you."

"Ah, sweeting." He leveled my chin with his fingers. "Flattered as I am, I can't let that happen. I want you safe and out of here. Meaning, if your mother doesn't drag you out, I'll find a way to throw you out myself. Don't worry about me. Go and be a good daughter."

"I don't want to be good. I want to stay with you."

"I've never heard a more splendid compliment."

"What will they do to you?"

Poet's eyes flared. "Nothing I'll remotely let them do to you."

"If they hurt you—"

"They can't do anything I won't make them feel in return. They might have sharp objects at their disposal, but I wield something sharper than that, and they know it." He lowered his voice. "I'll be fine. Now get the fuck out of here, darling Briar."

Our fingers brushed. The guard barreled inside, pulled us apart, and hauled me toward Mother.

"I'll find a way to get you out of here," I swore over my shoulder to Poet. "I promise!"

He made no response as I vanished around the corner. The guard shoved me unceremoniously down the stairway. I wouldn't go unpunished by Spring or Autumn, but my punishment would be less severe than Poet's.

With that harrowing thought in mind, I jerked away from the brute. "I'm going, dammit," I snapped. "I won't fight. Only take your infernal fucking hands off me!"

Mother and the guard froze. I must have looked as enraged as I sounded, with my hair a nest, grime streaking my dress and hands, my teeth barred, and my tongue going rogue.

After a considerable moment, Mother nodded. The man unshackled me.

Two more escorts waited at the bottom. I followed them, marching ahead of Mother in a fury. The men stationed themselves outside my suite as she and I disappeared inside.

Morning light pelted through the stained glass windows and blasted in from the balcony.

The door shut. Because my rooms were in a recess with a private corridor, footfalls trailed to the hallway's entrance, far enough that the sentinels wouldn't overhear what was said, so long as I kept my voice civil.

The balcony doors gaped open. Beyond the facade, grass trembled across the hills, and clouds packed the overcast sky. The garden below was where I first saw Poet, and the distant forest was where I first discovered the agony of his touch.

Inside, the suite seemed to hold its breath. Steeling myself, I whirled to face my mother. Across the divide, we regarded each other in silence.

Then the brittle string snapped.

She surged toward me and choked, "Briar."

I rushed to her and croaked, "Mother."

The sorrowful noises chipped me to pieces as we crushed ourselves together. My head wedged against her shoulder, and tears sprang from my eyes, the onslaught soaking her gown.

She clutched me tighter. "Oh, Briar. Oh, my girl. Forgive me. I had to do it. I had to."

I nodded. I knew why she'd done what she had, treating me frigidly for the world to see. For this court, she'd had to play the Autumn Queen.

But I would be lying if I said I hadn't doubted her for a second. I missed the tenderness I'd been rejecting for years. I didn't want to miss it anymore. I cried for it. I cried because I got to be here with my mother, while Poet didn't get to be with Jinny and Nicu.

I cried so very hard. Mother did, too.

"I hadn't been informed of what happened until they caught you," Mother said. "The knights could have harmed you, or you could have fallen from your horse. Seasons, I want to strangle you!"

"I'm sorry," I wept. "I'm s-sorry, Mama."

"I'm infuriated and exhausted from pleading your case to Spring. Trust me, I've a score to settle with you about it, but right now, I'm only grateful that you're well." She retrieved a handkerchief from the dressing table, wiped my eyes, and spoke calmly. "What happened, Briar?"

I shook my head. "I don't know where to start."

She wadded the cloth into a ball and coaxed me to the bed. We climbed in, the linens and pillows caressing our cheeks. I told her everything. I told her about befriending Eliot, wanting and having Poet, protecting Nicu, and returning to the place where Father died.

Although I choked up a few more times, flushed at other times, I refused to censor myself. I explained why I'd pushed Mother away. I told her that I loved her, which pulled more tears from her eyes.

When we finished, we drifted into a watery type of calm, transparent and tranquil.

This life held room for many heroes. However, I had missed the signs about Mother. I did not remember her face after Father died, the things she said, how she'd coped without him or without me to mourn alongside her. Too gripped in my own grief, I hadn't paid attention. I had failed to recognize this heroine who recovered and ruled.

Bravely, she had survived it all.

"I thought bringing you here would be helpful," she admitted bleakly. "I thought facing the past each year would help us heal, but it only scarred you more. It was wrong of me."

"No. I shouldn't have avoided you," I argued. "I lamented not being home where I could make a difference. But in truth, I was afraid. If truly given a chance, I would have come with you anyway. I wanted to see Eliot, and I wanted to be near you, although it hadn't seemed that way."

Mother nodded, a warm light banking in her eyes before sharpening. "What about the jester? Did he coerce you?"

"He didn't do anything I didn't want," I stressed. "He's important to me."

"It looked as if there was a lot more than mere fondness between you. The things you've done and said, you wouldn't do for just anyone."

"I would do it again. And he only wanted to protect his son."

Bringing up Nicu softened Mother. "I encouraged you to embrace Spring, but I didn't mean like this. He may be a father, but he's also a seducer and a trickster, and—"

"I know everything that makes us different. It doesn't change how I feel." My next words rose from a place deeply entrenched like roots. "I'm in love with him."

Mother's eyes broadened, a thousand emotions flitting through her pupils—shock, empathy, tenderness, protectiveness, worry, and understanding—before they settled on a sorrowful one. "It's forbidden, Briar."

"He makes me laugh. That shouldn't be forbidden."

"And you're as stubborn as your father." For a moment, her gaze became remote, a wistful grin tilting her lips. "The way that man loved. He did it the same way he ruled, with resilience and tenacity, and yet it was effortless. It was unconditional."

My expression must be reverential, because her watery smile expanded. Then she sobered and cleared her throat. "Is there anything you wish to discuss with me about ...?"

Heat spread across my skin. Despite my being a grown woman, we had never talked about intimacy because every time she'd tried,

I erected a drawbridge. Even now, after every way Poet had touched me, I didn't know how to broach the subject with her.

My mother scooted nearer. "Briar, I won't insult you by speaking as if you're still a child. But giving yourself to a man—"

"I do not give myself," I told her gently but surely. "I share myself."

Pride alighted her features. "If I advise you to stay away from Poet, it will only accomplish the opposite. Without a doubt, your father would caution me as much. King or not, he'd be on your side." She focused on me, a crinkle forming between her brows. "As it is, you didn't tell me your secrets."

I swallowed. "I needed to keep secrets."

"We must conceal things, yes. We must do things that pain us, especially within our station, but please stop hiding from me when we're in private. You can talk to me. No matter what you do, you're everything to me, and I'm proud of you."

"Why?" I asked. "I disobeyed every written and unwritten law."

"Laws don't make us better. Our mistakes do, providing we rise above them," she sighed. "What you did—I can't say you handled it correctly. You've made poor choices but also valiant ones. If you're not passionate about anything, you can't be an honest queen. A ruler makes brave decisions, not merely cautious ones. You did what you believed was right. You sought to protect an innocent child from hate.

"Regardless of bloodlines or inheritance, we spend our lives learning how to be monarchs. But you've shown more determination during these past weeks than I've ever seen. That's why I'm not fretting about the queen you'll become." She swept a lock of hair from my cheek. "And I've suspected for a while about Poet."

"What will they do to him?" I implored.

"They haven't decided yet. They'll summon you both before the court again and offer to be lenient if you tell them where Nicu is. If you refuse, you'll be banned from Spring until your coronation."

That could take ages. Decades in which I would not see Eliot, in which Mother would have to come here alone. We'd never set foot in Spring together, because when I was crowned, she would be dead, if not incapacitated.

My chest constricted. Mother could fight me over this, but she must understand being torn between the heart and one's duty. It couldn't be helped. I would not give them Nicu.

"Briar." Mother cupped my face. "I hate to see this happen to you."

"What about Poet?" I persisted.

She hesitated. "Spring won't execute him. But the jester's recrimination will be physical, if anything."

They would string him in thorn vines and leave him in the square for hours. Or they'd gag him with fire pepper until his throat boiled and his tongue felt as if it were melting off. Whatever the torture or mutilation, Poet would heal, but he wouldn't forget. And he would never be the same.

To please the public, they wouldn't do permanent damage. Even though he had lied to the Crown, they would preserve his ability to talk and jest.

Or maybe they *would* deform him, turn him into someone unrecognizable.

Nausea roiled through me. Hysteria gripped my throat.

They could continue to search for Nicu without our help. They might eventually find him if Spring and Summer were militant about it.

Short of panicking, I buried my face in the pillow and struggled to breathe. Mother rubbed the back of my neck, murmuring things that escaped me. Not that it mattered. At the moment, I needed her touch more than her words.

Words. Written ones.

The Fools Decree. Unbidden, the document popped into my head. Intuition sent my mind racing.

I shook myself, recalling each line and searching for something. Just one thing.

"Fools, and all that they are, shall be bound to their new Season," I recited aloud. *"Fools, and all that they are ... bound to their new Season."*

Once more, I repeated, *"Fools, and all that they are ..."*

And all that they are.

All that they are.

I lurched upright. Blessed air returned to my lungs. Mother and Father were sympathetic to born souls, but it hadn't been their era to challenge that. I wouldn't convince our continent, much less the Royals, overnight. However, great feats began with tentative steps. This mightn't be Mother's legacy, but perhaps it was destined to be mine.

"Mother." I scooted closer. "I need to discuss something with you."

Two hours later, we strode into the great hall, where the Royals were breaking their fast. The guards flanked us, of course. Spring no longer wanted me out of its sight.

My satin gown had short sleeves, a skirt that swished around my legs, and a chain belt. I'd chosen silver, the color of sober Winter. Also, the color of armor.

But rather than a sword, I had words. I had a revelation.

The princess had a trick up her sleeve.

Basil and Rhys shot to their feet when we entered. The queens set aside their cutlery and gawked in surprise. Mother had been expected, but I had been banned from eating with them. That I'd disregarded this blazed across their faces.

Each of them appeared larger than usual, like monuments that would outlast time and eras of change. Poet's sly artifice worked for him, whereas my tactics had a disruptive effect. I prayed that unnerving the Royals would give me an edge. They weren't prepared for negotiation.

"Queen Avalea, this is anarchy," King Basil galled, slapping down his linen napkin. "Your daughter belongs in her suite. Can you not leash her for one damned day? For Season's sake—guards!"

I sank to my knees. Now was the time to show subservience.

My gaze lifted briefly to see Basil change his mind. Upon witnessing my genuflection, his hand shot up, halting the guards.

I forged ahead, speaking to the polished floor. "Your Majesties, I apologize. I regret showing you disrespect during this month of peace, especially after you honored me to participate. I'm most grateful for the invitation and remorseful to have caused the Seasons strain. Please, may I state my business?"

I'd been deliberately ambiguous, begging their pardon without referring to taking Nicu. I would never express regret for saving him. Not even as a lie.

The Royals consulted one another in silence. The Spring King nodded and bade me to continue.

I rose and clasped my hands behind my back, concealing how they shook. Only Mother, who stationed herself behind me, saw that. "Forgive my intrusion, but I won't reveal the child's whereabouts. Neither will your jester."

"Then I shall eat your humiliation for brunch," Rhys's mustache flapped.

"Autumn wants the boy," I announced. "We'll trade you for him."

The Summer tyrant barked with laughter. "This is preposterous. Negotiations take place in the throne room and between monarchs, not heiresses."

Mother moved to stand beside me. "She has my blessing."

Rhys peered at her, then his eyes clicked over to me. "You want that child awfully bad, as does your imbecile-loving jester. That alone is cause for me to refuse whatever Autumn has to offer. I'll hunt for the boy myself. I have no qualms about being spiteful. It's been a vexing four weeks."

"You want Summer's cells purged of the mad?" I contested. "Very well. Autumn will take a dozen souls off your hands. Send them to us."

Because we would treat them humanely, help them if we could, if it was possible. No matter what, we would try.

The king looked skeptical—and tempted. Other than including the mad in the trade amendment as a precaution, the Royals hadn't decided how to purge the kingdoms' dungeons and oubliettes of its least desirable inhabitants. Summer's cells especially, with the kingdom's mercurial population and fiery climate sparking more unlawful behavior than any other Season. For the price of Nicu, I'd handed Rhys a chance for more wiggle room in one of his prisons. Begrudging Poet and me wasn't more important to him.

I waited, my fingers trembling at the base of my spine.

Please, I thought. Please, I hoped.

Please, I silently begged.

Rhys mutely conferred with his wife and then puckered his lips, his mustache bunching like a shrub. "Two dozen," he countered.

My eyebrows snapped upward. "Eighteen."

"Twenty," the man threw back.

From the sound of it, we could have been haggling over the price of eggs.

Although Autumn currently housed the mad in dungeons, I'd convinced Mother to utilize an outlying settlement instead, an abandoned village a day's ride from court, where they could be treated fairly. Appointing guards and physicians, and employing willing commoners to oversee the place, would cause indignation. But the prospect of work and wages, with little depletion of resources, would appease our citizens.

I reasoned that our people would welcome a greater separation between the mad and themselves, particularly if we argued the points of safety and more cell space for actual fugitives. We were a calm land, but that didn't mean we lived free of criminals.

What Autumn would think when they found out I had traded for my lover's son—and with Mother's blessing—was another matter. I'd endure public scrutiny. But for those two males, I would do it a thousand times over.

Warning myself not to faint, I nodded. Another two hours later, the document was drawn up.

After signing it, Summer dropped the quill on the table, his fingers stained black. The bastard wouldn't be satisfied until he'd jabbed a few parting words at me. "You may be allowed to snatch that child out of hiding now, but don't look so smug. This doesn't change your own fate, nor the fate of your celebrated whore."

I tamped down a snarl. "That will prove difficult, seeing as Poet's now of Autumn."

The Royals blinked, shocked as I pricked them with a very sweet thorn. The trade amendment to the Fools Decree stated—I quoted for them, in case they'd forgotten—*"Fools, and all that they are, shall be bound to their new Season."*

"All that they are" meant their families. So being Nicu's father meant Poet was bound to Autumn.

At this news, Basil and Fatima whitened like a pair of onions.

Rhys's features suffused to an outraged shade of red. Scarlet came to mind.

"Prove it," he demanded.

"Disprove it," I volleyed.

No means existed to verify this. The Seasons relied on physical similarities and the divine acknowledgment of a monarch. To that, Mother chimed in and vouched for Nicu's parentage, now that she'd just become his sovereign.

That aside, Poet's actions proved he'd sired Nicu, as did their striking green irises. In fact, it boggled me that the Crown hadn't suspected as much.

"All that they are pertains to a fool's mind and body," Rhys fumed.

"Their body is their blood. Their blood is their family," I translated. "In and of itself, that's an irrefutable fact. Show me how it doesn't apply to families."

"That's not what the Decree says!"

"But that's how it reads."

"She's right," Fatima admitted after a moment's deliberation.

The monarchs looked dazed, chagrined to have missed this. It seemed even the most powerful could be foolish.

"We'll need to reword the amendment," Basil muttered. "We must accomplish that today. We can't have the relatives of fools swapped across the Seasons. This isn't about them."

Precisely why I'd had the Royals include that citation in my negotiation with Summer. They would make whatever changes they needed to the Decree, but the signed and dated trade document between us would still apply to Poet.

A princess should wait to be excused by her predecessors.

As the Royals turned to stare at me, I curtsied. "Your Majesties."

Before Rhys thought of burning it, I grabbed the scroll and strutted away in a circle of silver. As I did, my straight face lifted into a smirk.

Briar

Whispers invaded my sleep. I flopped over and yelped as three faces poked between the draperies of my canopy. Vale, Posy, and Cadence.

The latter female idled the furthest away, her evergreen green hair knitted in a lazy updo that nonetheless managed to look refined.

Vale sang, "Wakey, wakey."

"Your Highness," Posy finished.

Morning rays dragged through the room. Stunned, I hauled myself upright as the ladies swished aside the bed curtains, dropped onto the mattress, and banded around me. They wore airy dressing gowns in varying patterns of flora and fauna.

Cautious, I held the duvet to my chest. According to the brushfire of news spreading through the lands, I had lost my sense and virtue. I'd become a sympathizer. I stole Poet from the masses. The court mightn't worship him the same way anymore, but that didn't mean it celebrated his impending departure from sinful Spring.

Who knew what these ladies thought of me now?

"What's this about?" I asked.

"We have your clothes for today," Posy said.

"The perfect roughspun," Vale added, gesturing to a faded ensemble the color of kindling, along with a circlet of weeds.

Lark's Night. The sunset carnival.

But no. The king and queen certainly wouldn't let me attend that event.

And why would these ladies bring me such clothing? I didn't understand—until I did.

My visitors explained. Although the Crown would rather keep me away, that would also disrupt tradition, as every Royal in residence was expected to participate.

In addition, Basil and Fatima had plans for me—something they had every authority to request. I hadn't seen it coming, yet I wasn't surprised.

The roughspun outfit. Poet would see me in that.

Or would he see me at all? He'd been released from the tower, protected by Autumn from a Spring reckoning, but Mother had advised me to pace myself, that I shouldn't see him so soon after. And I assumed Poet had similar thoughts, since I hadn't heard from him, not even through a missive.

Mother told me that Basil and Fatima had summoned him for a private interview, but Mother had no idea what transpired. While the Royals couldn't fault her for what I did, and in public she maintained the aura of a contrite, disciplinary queen, her peers nevertheless treated her dubiously.

The trio of ladies had wanted to deliver my attire themselves, apparently to ease the blow of what was to come. Still, I marveled at Cadence's presence.

"Why are you being nice to me?" I pressed.

The female grunted. "Don't get your hopes up. None of us have ever endorsed the born, but the boy is Poet's son, so we're curious."

"Shamelessly curious," Posy emphasized, the blossoms inked over her collarbone peeking from her dressing gown. "We want the scandal."

"The drama," Vale corrected.

"The details," Cadence translated. "For one, I'd like to slap you as hard as you slapped me. You took him from us, but there are plenty of alphas to go around. If he prefers you, then you can't be the prude Royal we thought you were. For one, the last thing we expected was for you to rollick with us in the labyrinth or break the law. While Posy and Vale warmed to you sooner, clearly I misjudged."

"A rebellious heiress is thrilling," Vale championed, her burgundy eyes avid.

"Inspiring," Posy agreed, then teased, "And arousing."

"And impressive, especially when she's ruined," Cadence finished. "It sounds like quite the spicy enemies-to-lovers story. I can respect a princess who beds the most provocative trickster at court, then has the spine to smack me. It actually makes me tolerate you more."

Posy and Vale snorted. Cadence smirked at them and waited for my response.

My stomach jumped. "I haven't ... that is, we haven't ..."

Their brows stitched in confusion, then all three sets of eyes widened. "Wait," Cadence balked. "That's impossible. The way you two kept looking at each other on the night we were together—the tension was insufferably thick, which meant it could only have been spiteful or sexual."

"You noticed that?"

"It was obvious. And the way Poet watched you when you weren't aware; it wasn't the same way he chooses a mere conquest. I should know since I was once a candidate.

"Plus, how you acted in the throne room, like you would tear down the rafters for each other. Neither of you showed an ounce of regret. For Season's sake, you spent days in the forest, and they say you've been sneaking around these halls. Are you saying he hasn't fucked you? How the devil could nothing have happened?"

Morose, their foreheads wrinkled in disappointment. I watched my finger sketch the grooves in the duvet. "I didn't say nothing happened."

A gasp of satisfaction rushed from Vale. "Ohhh."

"So you marked each other, after all," Posy concluded, gratified. "You're roasting like someone who's experienced a wealth of cliteral satisfaction."

"A slow burn," Cadence interpreted with a wily grin of approval. "Every pleasure but the main one. I grant, that'll make for a greater climax later."

"Was Poet good at it?" Vale burst out. "That tongue of his must be good at it. I'm sure, I'd pass out before I had the chance to come."

"Look at her." Cadence flung an arm at me. "Of course, he was good at it. Superior, for certain."

Good didn't begin to describe all the things he'd done to me.

Heat scorched my flesh, yet my mouth quirked in amusement and a new sort of fondness. What I did with Poet was private, but I couldn't deny it felt nice to confide in them. "It's personal," I shared while tucking a lock of hair behind my ears. "Though, I'd very much like to know what the rest is like."

"In preparation?" Vale teased, a notion that caused my navel to pool with warmth.

"Listen to us," Posy realized. "We sound like the shallowest of creatures."

"How very Spring," Cadence remarked. "And well, Briar's flesh and blood, after all. She has secret passions, actually makes mistakes, and has smutty affairs with sexy jesters."

"It's more than that," Vale assured me.

Posy scooted to the bed's center and curled her legs beneath her. "We like you."

Cadence shrugged. "After what you and Poet risked for that sapling, maybe we shouldn't be quick to scorn. Maybe we should know more; that is, if you're willing to tell us what we've never considered. What do you think, Your Highness? Are you interested in liking us back?"

I wavered. As fans of Poet, that made them biased. Nevertheless, they were willing to listen. Cadence's ugly words at the carnival's hill still festered in my mind, but I had to believe people could change if given the chance.

I *needed* to believe that.

And I confess, I had been thirsting for such a moment, to have female companions lounge in my suite without an obligation to do so. It would be nice to have allies left in Spring, possibly kindreds.

"Friends," I mused, then cleared my throat. "Okay."

Despite everything, the ladies hadn't anticipated that. We glanced at one another, wondering what to do next, then sputtered into laughter.

The trio helped me into the roughspun dress. Tradition entailed that I forgo any grooming, so the ladies refrained from dusting my cheeks in rouge, rimming my eyes in pigment, painting my lips, or plaiting my hair. Instead, the layers hung in unkempt strands down my back, and the ladies placed the weed circlet atop my head.

After they wished me luck and swept from the room, I strayed to the balcony. My hands hooked over the ledge, the stone cool against my palms. I recalled my first day here, when I stood in this spot and wished desperately to be home, unaware of what was about to happen.

In every Season, contradictions existed. Savagery and beauty. Brutality and kindness. Pleasure and pain. Hate and love.

Every place had its scandalous courts and secret hideaways. They had their private alcoves and guarded halls. Their throne rooms and dungeons.

Spring had been heinous and bewitching. It had been intimidating, repulsive, hateful, inspiring, and alluring. Leaving would be a relief—and it would wreck me, because I couldn't take everyone I wanted along.

"You look like a notorious wood nymph," he joked from behind, his tenor easing my hold on the ledge.

"Many thanks," I said with a dry chuckle while gazing at the vista.

Eliot approached and idled beside me with his lute strapped over one shoulder. He'd never been in my suite before. I had called for him, which was another bold move on my part. Not that I had cared.

We stared ahead. The makings of the carnival, with its torches and streamers and pavilions, sprouted from the rolling hills. The tents' ornate shapes—some statuesque, others broad—looked as though they'd been spun from faeish glamour. Much later, flames would pulsate, illuminating the grounds. Drums would pound, firecrackers would burst, and inhibitions would flee the revelers. So many things were about to happen there, during periods of lightness and darkness.

Over the years, Eliot and I had enjoyed the Lark's Night festival together. Early sunset activities, at least.

As a minstrel, he played a regular part in it. A lengthy break in his performance and the massive throng of bodies allowed us to spend a few hours by one another's side, relishing the sights without anyone questioning us. At some point, we'd find a clandestine opportunity to hold hands, my smooth fingers laced with his callused ones.

Eliot had always had the opportunity to stay after nightfall, but although he was curious, he never did. He'd stuck by my side and walked me back to the ruins, where we parted ways.

My eyes watered. A host of unspoken words filtered through the silence.

Have I lost you? Have you slipped through my fingers?

"Eliot," I said, the sob cracking from my lips.

"Briar," he uttered.

We grabbed each other. His strong arms wove around me, and I clutched him in turn. He rubbed my back, and I brushed through his waves.

"Forgive me," I whispered. "There is so much to say."

"I feel the same," he answered. "I'm sorry too—for everything."

"I've missed you. I've missed you so much."

"And I missed you." He squeezed me closer. "I was hurt, and that hasn't gone away, but I wounded you as well. I was an asshole when you needed me most, and so I beg your pardon. Maybe it's different

432

between us now, but you mean everything to me. You do, Briar.

"I love him, and you love him, but that doesn't mean we've unloved each other. Friendships for the ages can survive this shitstorm. Did what I said make any sense? Because hugging you with this lute on my back is uncomfortable. I can't talk clearly."

"Perhaps after a minute, you'll grow accustomed to it," I croaked. "Eliot?"

"Hmm?"

"Do you remember when we were fourteen? That song we wrote?"

"The horse kingdom?" He groaned. "Shit, that was awful. Your lyrics."

"I know," I sniffled over his shoulder. "I didn't say it then, but thank you for using them."

He paused for a moment. "I still have the song."

I pulled back. "You do?"

"What do you take me for?" Eliot scolded while wiping his thumbs under my eyes. "You mean more to me than men and, well, even music. You mean more to me than my lute. I won't forget that, no matter how long we're separated."

It could be decades before my coronation, when I'd be welcomed back to Spring for the Peace Talks. In the meantime, the other heirs and heiresses would be permitted to join the Talks' closing meetings, to grow up with glimpses of their futures. I would be excluded from that right.

Mother would travel here by herself. I would not get to see Eliot.

I grasped his collar, thumbed his neck tattoo. "Then you'll have to come to me."

"How?" he asked, flattening his hands over mine. "It isn't possible. No one can travel between the Seasons without the Crown's permission."

"I've spoken with Mother. We'll invite Spring to Autumn when the time is right, however long that takes. I have no regrets about what I did, but to bring about a humane revolution, appeasing this court is necessary. I'll lavish your monarchs with flattery, appeal to their blithe nature, and urge them to bring their prized artists. For the sake of fealty and seeing Autumn grovel, they won't decline attending, nor at seeing Poet perform again, nor showing off their renowned lute player if the opportunity arises."

Eliot's eyes softened. "You believe that, don't you?"

"I will make it happen," I swore, my eyes stinging. "We will see each other again someday."

"You're dressed like a wood nymph, but you sound like a Royal."

"No." Balancing on my tiptoes, I brushed his lips with mine. "I sound like your friend."

"That, most of all," he whispered, grinning and kissing me back.

Our foreheads fell together. As my tears dried, I exhaled, blowing part of myself into the wind, so it would remain here with him.

38

Briar

The revels began. Thousands of people from the castle, the lower town, and outlying villages arrived pumping with energy.

I wondered if Poet had ever snuck from the woods to this carnival as a child. He might have. He might have even bumped elbows with me in passing.

The streamer garlands swung into the breeze. Lanterns and torches flapped with hot, orange light. Small fountains overflowed with wine and nectar.

Scantily clad aerial artists flew across the stages. Contortionists held themselves in impossible positions, acting as bars for their partners to tumble across.

Storytellers recited sultry tales from inside tents. Knights combatted bare-chested for onlookers. A puppeteer manipulated his marionettes, whirling them into a seductive waltz.

Artists sold beaded fans and sequined eye masks. Florists peddled edible blossoms that did more than merely taste good.

Musicians strummed, picked, pounded, and blew on their in-

435

struments. I craned my neck for a sight of Eliot, to no avail. Likely, he had been stationed on a different hill.

The lush ambience could have manifested from a darkly beautiful folktale, were it not for the gruesome parts that existed in another area.

Not far off, hogs chased a lad around a pen. He screamed as though they were monsters, perhaps because that was what he truly saw.

In another circle, two stocky women with features like Nicu's scratched at each other as the revelers cheered.

Sagging in the stocks, an elderly man looked puzzled by his surroundings while attendants cranked their arms, ready to fire eggs at him.

Those scenes rendered my own humiliation inconsequential. The crowd parted as I came through. Some gazed at me with sympathy because I was still a Royal. Others behaved more callously, pelting me with disapproving looks.

Me, the Fest Fool.

And him. Escorted by a guard, Poet materialized from the opposite end of the crowd. To my surprise, the welts had faded from his face—likely Jinny's doing. However, the bruise, the lacerations on his throat, and the cut on his forehead remained, the crimson lines dried.

All the same, those blemishes didn't offend Poet as much as other details. He raised his eyes skyward and pouted. And I saw why. They had dressed him in traditional jester's garb, including dark knee-length hose, stockings, and a motley-patterned jacket. Flaps hung from his neckline and wrists, and his bell cap chimed as he walked.

Only two details bespoke his true tastes. A single black tear dangled from his left eye, and his fingernails glinted black.

Spring had found a way to scorn us publicly. Basil and Fatima had shifted the rules to their convenience, appointing more than one Fest Fool.

How very Royal of them.

Poet caught my eye and winked. I mustered a smile.

The king and queen made their introductory speech and raised their arms. "Let the revels begin!"

Horns blared, and revelers erupted into shouts. With that, Poet and I belonged to the carnival, to any attendant in the mood to command or harass us. Since we'd dropped in favor, it was mostly the latter.

It went on and on. People halted and ordered us to fetch drinks or do tricks. They blindfolded him and me, then made us hunt for each other while a bunch of shouts misled us—or me, at least. In comparison, Poet found me swifter than the crowd preferred.

They tethered my right leg to his left, forcing us to walk as one for an hour. I wasn't as graceful about it as the jester was.

He growled at anyone who tried to get near me, his ferocious expression causing several hecklers to retreat. Though, not all of them registered this. One countess requested me to dance on a low-strung rope while dodging the staff she'd handed Poet, expecting him to prod me with it. When he ignored the stick, the noble poked me in the ribs herself.

I teetered, then stumbled off the rope.

Poet caught me and then ripped the staff from the countess's hand. His destructive grip suggested he might have swept it under her feet and sent the woman landing onto her backside. Instead, he spun the rod from hand to hand, rotated it across his shoulders, and windmilled it around his neck, all in a dizzying flourish that could turn deadly at any moment, should he use the staff as weapon.

With viperous reflexes, Poet thrust the object back at the countess. On gut reaction, the startled woman lurched backward, barely catching it in time.

"Be careful, sweeting," the jester cautioned, his voice low and lethal. "Keep your walking stick close, or someone might take it from you."

The female purpled with humiliation, and the scene earned a mixture of impressed and uneasy titters from onlookers. A trio of resident performers snorted with pride. Despite Poet's transgressions, the troupe hardly relished seeing their respected leader and mentor reduced to this.

I didn't need to read Poet's furious mind. His display was a silent warning.

No matter what they made us do, we would not break.

Be careful, because if he were so inclined, he could turn any jest on its head. It would backfire on the culprit and make that person the laughingstock. Deny it all they hoped, but this man could dazzle and mortify them if he wanted to.

His deadly glower said one other thing. *Touch the princess, and I shall impale you.*

My own deliberate scowl said something rather similar. *Touch the jester, and I will shatter you.*

Mother stayed away, as I had pleaded for her to do. She'd protested but gave in, agreeing to remain in her pavilion and mingle with visitors. The reason went beyond the pretense of being a repentant and punitive queen. I hadn't wanted her to see me ridiculed like this, even under the thin guise of celebration.

I'd done plenty to sour Autumn's relationship with Spring. Although I didn't regret doing it for Poet and Nicu, those relations had to be restored for my nation's sake. Moreover, it was essential for future widespread change. This degradation was a stepping stone.

As the hours passed, people let their guards down. Drugging petals melted on their tongues, inspiring visions and producing glazed eyes. Revelers twirled and gyrated to lutes and drums.

In his pavilion, the embittered Summer King requested us. He demanded a verse from Poet and ordered me to stand by and witness it. But as Poet began, King Rhys proceeded to ignore Poet and converse with Queen Giselle, talking loudly over the jester's words.

The rest of the attendants followed suit. It was a tactic meant to humble and humiliate. No one had ever ignored Poet before.

The Seven stood nearby. Freya, Questa, Rhiannon, and Lisette snickered. Like the majority, their admiration for Poet hadn't declined completely, but it had waned. As much as they didn't want to lose him to Autumn, nor were they ready to absolve him yet.

How easily one could rise to popularity, only to fall as quickly off the pedestal.

Vale, Posy, and Cadence did not find it funny. They tossed scowls at the company, including the rest of their clique, who swallowed their mirth instantly, their brows crimping with astonishment. The ladies' support drew an appreciative grin from me.

If Summer's disregard bothered Poet, he didn't let it show. He started another verse, weaving a tale that made me into a warrior—I rather liked that—and exaggerated the Summer King into a farcical sovereign. A monarch who couldn't see past his overgrown hedge of a mustache to locate his flaccid cock, much less read the fine print on the Fools Decree.

I ducked my head, trying not to laugh. So did the others who'd begun paying attention.

Poet finished to applause that caught King Rhys's attention. The monarch's forehead cinched, and his eyes narrowed in skeptical confusion.

Loudly, I clapped. My insolent jester glanced sideways at me and inclined his head.

No criminal law prevented what I was about to do. There were social codes of conduct, but we had already breached that. We'd had enough attention—and not enough.

Rules were meant to be upended today? We would oblige.

The people wanted two fools? We would give them two fools.

I strode over to Poet, grabbed his face, and seized his mouth with mine.

Poet

Her touch has always been irresistible, as have my deceptions. However, combine the two and drop them into the midst of a revel, and 'tis a whole new marvel.

Before the congregation, we threw one final trigger at the court, gave them one more felony to talk about …

Gasps broke through the tent. I stilled, then caught her face and kissed her the fuck back. My carnivorous teeth nipped her bottom lip, my shameless mouth parted hers wide, and my evil tongue committed heresy. It flexed in and licked against hers, tasting the sweet tartness of defiance.

Our mouths clutched and rocked, tongues swatting like flames. The tremulous curl of Briar's tongue slid down my spine, urging my fingers to vault through her hair. I sank my mouth into hers, undulating those lawless lips against mine.

The world didn't vanish. Oh nay, it came to life. It combusted like an inferno, bringing darkness and lightness into stark relief.

Our audience's rather volcanic reaction spurred us on. I crushed my mouth to Briar's, she shoved her lips against mine, and we strapped ourselves around each other.

Like this, she dominated me. And like this, I violated every restriction she'd ever followed.

Together, we smashed the rules to a fucking pulp.

A primeval sound tore out of King Rhys's gullet. It splintered the princess and me apart.

Although not the best way to appease Spring, our antics befitted the occasion. The festivities had intoxicated the revelers enough for them to watch us with stupefied intrigue. Ah, such was the glibness of court life.

From the sidelines, four members of Fatima's retinue gaped. Opposite them, Vale, Posy, and Cadence whistled and hooted naughty suggestions.

Rhys's jowls darkened to a pissed-off purple.

My lips curled, still tingling from the aftershocks of Briar's taste. "Any other requests, Your Majesty?" I intoned, husky. "I could offer another verse. Or my beautiful companion and I could keep binging on each other's mouths. Or perhaps you'd like us to render this merry company speechless in other ways. Unless you're sated and want us to—"

"Get the fuck out!" he barked.

"As you like," Briar and I complied.

I bowed, the princess curtsied, and we quit the pavilion. Outside, I ripped off that monstrosity of a bell cap and shoved it into the bloated womb of a bush. Though, there was nothing to be done about the tacky nightmare they'd dressed me in.

Soon, I predicted. It will come off soon.

As sunset thrived in its final hour, crowds swarmed the grounds. Bonfires blasted into the sky, sparks somersaulting through the air.

Mind-slothing drink and petal stimulants led to elation, flirtation, and copulation. Debauchery set the people into a distracted haze.

Drums pounded, torches writhed from poles, and lust saturated the atmosphere like the scent of lily wine.

The masks came out to play. Men exchanged their coats for horse, lion, and fox visors. Women unlaced their bodices, nipples peeking over the necklines and skirts lifting to reveal smocked garters. Couples ran barefooted, ground their hips into a dance, and lured each other into the recesses—or dry-humped outright for spectators.

Disheveled laughter. Indulgent moans. Wolfish singing.

I knew the gluttonous patterns of Spring. Too swept up in their inebriation and sexcapades, the throng had forgotten themselves.

They forgot us.

My jaw ticked. Briar and I exchanged looks, her features sketched in pulsing amber light. When she nodded, I clamped onto her hand and snuck past the masses with her.

Without stopping, I swiped a blade from someone's harness. A row of stocks held born souls, their heads bowing and arms dangling limply like puppets with severed strings.

At the first stock, I flipped the dagger and spun the hilt on one upright finger. Then I launched the weapon upward, caught the handle in my fist, and rammed it against the latch.

The closure snapped and fell open like a shocked mouth. One by one, we released the people trapped inside. They stumbled backward, expressions ranging from baffled to distrustful to frightened.

We stepped back and watched as they sprinted into the wilderness at last. Their outlines shrank to blots of movement before slipping away.

Some would be difficult for Spring to track down. Others not.

But at least we gave them the chance and the choice. 'Twas the most we could do on this eventide.

My head swung to the woman beside me, who stared back with lustrous eyes. One mutinous desire had been satisfied. Now a hotter need burned like embers across my fingers. Without another word, I snatched Briar's hand and dragged her out of there.

Mine.

She's mine now.

On the way through the quagmire, a passing figure balanced a tray of delicacies that included tonics and a bowl of berries. Briar recognized the morsels, swiped one of the enablers from the vessel, and tugged on me. I stopped, watching as she held my gaze and draped the bundleberry on her tongue. From within the burnished luster of a neighboring bonfire, her jaw rotated as she chewed.

The fantasy of juice swirling across her palate set my cock on edge. The morsels were effective for days, and I had planned to give her one later. But that she remembered the potent little berry from harvesting at the cottage, that she remembered its preventative clout, and that she consumed it without hesitation, smoldered my blood.

For what happened next, we'd be safe.

She swallowed. And we ran.

With my hand clasped to hers, we fled the whirlwind of that place, the divine and the corrupt, unable to help or save the rest who languished in the dungeon. Not tonight. Not yet. The knowledge charred us to the bone and accelerated our pace, inciting us to reach for something provocative, something capable of stifling the rage—something long overdue.

Something worth every ounce of pain that came before.

Desperation launched me forward. We barreled into the woodland, into the deep lung of Spring. Torch poles crackled between the foliage, scattered blazes painting the trees in blood red.

We would return to the carnival, but not before the celestials flashed like asterisks and the moon crawled up the midnight sky. Until then, we ran from it all.

Audible fragments of gaiety and atrocity subsided, fading into wisps of sound. Then all at once, the noise vanished. The quiet swallowed the forest whole, and mist coiled through the snarling brambles.

My heart became a violent thing. It thrashed like a caged beast, because I'd been wanting this for an eternity. Damn my fate to hell if I didn't shred through those bars, to grab what I thirsted for.

An urgent tremble rushed up Briar's fingers. Choppy breaths

pushed from her throat.

We raced through the mesh of undergrowth, our legs and arms pumping. I knew where to go. Briar had no idea yet surged through the wild with abandon, the skirt of her dress taking flight around her calves.

Ahead, a row of bent trees formed an arched bower. Black petal cords hung from the branches and shielded the entrance.

I slowed, clenched her hand, and prowled ahead. I whipped the cords apart, then grabbed Briar by the hips and whirled her inside. No sooner did we break through the vines, than we unleashed. As she flew into me, I grabbed for her.

Her arms linked around my shoulders, my fingers dug into her hips, and I walked her backward across the grass. My forehead dipped, trapping her in my gaze, which grew hooded. Little pants skittered from her throat, the sound blazing through my veins.

With a growl, I dove my head. My famished lips welded to hers and spread them wide. My tongue speared through her lips, enticing a moan from deep inside her. The noise quaked from her mouth to mine in a hot rush.

Briar dissolved against me, her digits climbing through my hair. Her lips folded under my own, her tongue flicking, lapping with me. At the taste of berries, I groaned. That mouth rode mine, heaving into the kiss, rocking into a breathless tempo.

Each of her curves pressed against me, heat emanating from the crux of her thighs. The force of it stiffened me to the point of agony, my cock wedging between us.

Jolting back, I framed her face in my hands. She did the same, and I couldn't tell whether this meant we were holding on or letting go. That mystery would be solved later.

Briar's gaze trickled momentarily, surveying the enclosure draped in cords. The ripe scents of jasmine and figs spritzed the bower like incense. Writhing orange light from distant torch flames squeezed through the mesh and dappled the area.

And she knew.

"This is ..." Briar trailed off, mesmerized, husky.

The answer ripped out of me. "Aye."

She gasped as I snagged her hip with one hand, hauled her forward, and sunk into her again. Sunset dripped through the canopy as we collided, a tumult of greedy lips and hectic fingers. I kissed her under a beam of sinking light, the force of my lips obsessive, destructive.

It wasn't nearly enough. It would never be enough.

I wanted her breath, wanted the taste of her branded on my tongue. I wanted her cries, wanted every sound this woman was capable of uttering. I wanted her loud and soft. I wanted her ruined, burned, and lost.

I wanted to step into that inferno with her.

The stories were true about the wildflower forest. The woods didn't manifest its secrets that easily, so I didn't know all the hidden pockets where recklessness permeated the air, its essence clinging to the foliage like sap.

But I did know this one.

My free hand made smooth work of the laces down her back. My fingers plucked, the bands falling limply from their grommets. With a flick of my wrist, I tossed them to the ground.

Her bodice sagged, breasts loosening. This roughspun wouldn't take long, but I moved slowly, needing to work for this, to reveal each piece of her skin like a forbidden secret. This had to take effort, to be earned.

Pulling back, I fastened my eyes to hers. I shed the bodice, chucking it aside before continuing with the skirt, which dropped to the grass. Briar's outtakes quickened with each divestment, as if I were touching her in new places.

Oh, but I hadn't begun to lay my hands on her. When I did, she would feel it to the marrow of her bones.

We kicked off our boots, then paused in a threadbare attempt to calm the hell down. She stood before me with a weed circlet lopsided atop her head and wearing nothing but a filmy chemise. Her nipples pitted through the sheer material. One shoulder drooped, exposing the knob of her shoulder, sprinkled with freckles.

Before I could properly relish the sight, an unspoken ambition lurked in her eyes.

My own gaze slitted. I swept my mouth against hers and muttered, "You want something from me, don't you?"

"I do," she confessed.

"Then take it, sweeting. Take what you want."

Briar nodded vehemently and grabbed the offensive jacket lined in flaps. She unclasped the front and peeled the vestment off my shoulders, fumbling with the atrocious thing until I wrenched my arms from the sleeves and slung the fabric aside.

I loomed over her in low-slung hose. My torso contracted, pecs bumping into her breasts. Briar's tongue peeked out to slip across her lower lip like she'd uncovered a delicacy. With her head pinned to mine, her palms dragged down the plate of muscles, etched the broad ridges of my pecs, and skidded over the stack of my abdomen. I clenched under her touch, tingles racing across my flesh.

Her exhalations puffed against my neck. She dipped her gaze and consumed the sight, riveted on each flex of skin and sinew. Desire pulled taut across her face, clashing with hesitancy.

Take what you want.

Remembering that, Briar bent her head and planted a kiss to my sternum. The hitch in my breath encouraged her, those gentle lips descending, plying me with innocent pecks. My chest rose and fell in a controlled frenzy as she traveled lower, her tongue following her mouth, licking a trail over my flesh.

Provoked by what must have been a buckling male groan—I'd grown too disorientated, my knees too weak, my cock too hard to register what my vocal cords were doing—Briar slayed me again. She flattened her tongue over my blasted nipple and licked as if it was sugar from a spoon.

The nipple toughened into a peg. I growled and snatched her waist like a vise. "Shit," I mumbled. "Briar."

She ignored the warning, branding me with her dangerous mouth, swabbing her lips and tongue over my nipple, between my collar-bones, and the rift under my jaw. Seasons, I wanted to shred her clothes and never look back.

But like the good devil I wasn't, I waited with a smirk. I let her explore and circle my body, her fingers tricking from the lattice of my ribs to the length of my back.

Dancing behind, fingers down my spine.

My hands itched, so I tamed them into fists. I wanted her to make this choice, not seduce her into it.

As she snuck behind me, Briar feathered her digits lower and draped them over my ass. She skimmed over the sides, gliding down the indentations, and then cupped the swells.

Almighty hell. My shoulder blades snapped inward, and my cock rose high against my abdomen.

Briar emerged in front of me, all blushing cheeks and flashing eyes. Meeting my gaze, she swallowed and gripped the straps of her chemise.

None of that. My hand swept up, the inside of my palm blocking her knuckles and ceasing her movements. Her eyebrows knitted in confusion. Without a word, I raised my opposite hand, pointed one finger toward the grass, and circled it.

Understanding simmered in her pupils. Nervous anticipation flushed her complexion. Her arms fell, and she turned for me, giving me an alluring view of her back.

Like a predator drawn to its mate, I stalked behind her, my pound-ing chest fitting to her spine. My frame spanned hers, one shadow casting over another on the grass like a shield. As long as I was near her, this beautiful body would never know pain, only pleasure.

Briar's lungs siphoned oxygen. My mouth quirked into a grin as I lowered my head and latched onto the juncture of her neck and shoul-der. A yelp broke from her. Incited by the fractured noise, I brushed my lips over her flesh until she shivered, then drew the delicate skin between my teeth and kissed as if the spot was her open mouth. I did it slowly, leisurely.

A whimper coiled from Briar's throat. Her scalp fell back and landed against me. Absently, her hand reached back to grasp my nape.

The pert shape of her ass pressed into my erection. I hissed and sucked on her, each tug of my lips extracting another disjointed moan. My mouth teased, incisors sketching the raw flesh and suckling anew.

Briar's profile squinted as though anguished. Her jaw hung open, those shaky moans a rhapsody to my ears.

A drugged sound ground from my throat as I feasted on her. My fingers climbed to her sagging neckline and towed on the material. A single breast popped from the garment, flushed and stiff at the peak.

My mouth skated up the side of her neck whilst my palm braced the weight of her, my thumb tracing the pink tip.

Briar unleashed a brittle sound and arched into me. "Oh," she grated.

"Shh," I implored, not truly meaning it.

I palmed both her lovely tits, one covered by the fabric, the other exposed to my searing gaze. That erotic nipple cinched, ruching under the pad of my thumb. I swiped at it, and we panted as the stud grew as dark as a cherry.

"Such a fine color," I mumbled. "Such tight skin."

"Poet," Briar keened.

Unable to stand that plea, I wheeled her around, our bodies rubbing together. Delirium blazed across Briar's features, but I gave her scarcely time to react before I batted the neckline aside once more. My mouth swooped down and caught that same nipple.

Briar cried out. Her hands thrust into my hair, and her chest pitched forward, shoving that breast into me. A deep rumble surged from my lungs. I snatched the nipple between my lips, fused it into the heat of my mouth, and sucked.

My thorn emitted pinched noises as my tongue repeatedly lashed at the crest. I tormented her, kissing the dainty point, licking it before switching to the opposite disk.

Briar's legs threatened to give out, but nay. She was made of sterner stuff than that. And it would be a while before I had her on the ground.

I hummed against the shell of her nipple. "Where else are you so dark and tight, hmm? Will you show me, love?"

Briar sighed, "I will."

Straightening to my full height, I gathered her close. With an arm anchored around her middle, I hooked one leg over my hip. The chemise's hem rucked up her thighs. My lips pressed to hers, kissing her lightly whilst my hand ducked into the vent of her drawers.

Thin material shrouded her cunt. Her arousal seeped through the scanty fabric.

My eyes lands on hers as a slow tear audibly pierced the air. I widened the fabric's slit, combed through the damp patch of hair, and dipped a finger into the ridge between her legs.

A fresh moan lurched from Briar's mouth. The slicks folds of her pussy spread over my digit, then suctioned around me.

I seethed, "Seasons help me."

More arousal coated her walls as I probed. My finger slipped into her slowly, then withdrew nice and patient, then flexed back into her slot. Watching her, I curled my digit, sketched the flanks inside Briar, and pulled out a second time. Retracting to the tip, I slipped in once more. And I did this again, and again, and again.

Briar clutched me and dropped her forehead atop my shoulder. Her body shook whilst I pumped gently, pitching my finger in and out, then adding another digit. Her walls throbbed, yielding around my rhythmic hand. My cock twitched, aching between my hips. I felt her moans like a touch, like a caress.

Instinctively, Briar's waist jutted. Harsh breaths chuffed against my shoulder as she worked herself on my fingers.

"That's it, Your Highness," I encouraged. "Ride them like you rule them."

Her waist gyrated. I speared a third finger into her, my arm slinging between her split thighs. Meanwhile, her clitoris swelled, so very delicate. The heel of my wrist pressed into the compact bud of skin and rubbed in tempo to my hand.

The flesh pulsated. Its percussion grew rampant, accelerating as I rolled it like a marble, massaging it just so. At the same time, my fingers plied her channel to my knuckles, the pliant flesh cushioning me.

With each lap of my digits, her pussy contracted like a single muscle. I felt the stimulation as if it were my own, every little jolt charging through her.

Spurred on, I picked up the pace with short, sweet jabs that hit a tapered spot inside her. She keened, her cries multiplying. My thorn swayed her hips onto me, and I cast my hand into her, and my wrist nudged her clitoris in tandem.

Her cunt bucked, leaked, and tightened around me. Oh, but she was about to come so beautifully.

My hand jolted faster, deeper. I surged my fingers between those shaky folds whilst thrusting against her peak. We labored in sync, pursuing what she desperately wanted, dashing after the orgasm.

"Ah," my thorn choked, her frame bobbing, quavering.

At last and too soon, Briar's moans cracked. Her body spasmed. The plush walls of her pussy unraveled around my hand, her walls rippling and seeping with her climax.

The glorious sound flooded my ears, my sac hung heavy with need, and blood overflowed to the roof of my cock. Euphoric, I kept pistoning, prolonging her orgasm until every drop of her spilled onto my fingers.

Briar collapsed into me, straining to catch her breath. As she curled against my chest, pride welled where her head rested. If I never made anyone feel anything ever again, so be it. I'd made her feel this. Nothing else would outdo that.

I combed through her hair and inquired, "Did that feel good? Has the jester pleased you?"

That priceless face craned back to gaze at me. "Who said you were done?"

My grin widened as Briar stepped backward, her vitality renewed. This time, I didn't stop her as she tugged on the straps of her chemise. The material trembled down her figure and splashed around her toes, wiping out the last vestiges of intelligent, civilized thought.

My canines slammed together, and my tongue plastered to the roof of my mouth. Straight hips. Steady hands. Small breasts with pert nipples. Freckles sprayed across her skin. That glistening swatch between her thighs.

She stood naked with only the weed circlet around her head.

So fucking ethereal. So fair, this woman of Autumn.

My sharp lady. My Briar.

I curled my fingers, beckoning her. "Closer."

She stepped nearer, allowing me to run the backs of my knuckles from her temple to her throat, to the dip between her tits, to her stomach. I snaked my arm around her midriff. And in one hard motion, I locked her to me.

A sexy gasp jumped from Briar's mouth, and her palms landed on my pecs.

My mouth veered to one ear. "May I indulge you, Highness?"

"You may," Briar permitted, her breathing acute.

"Then pay attention, for this is what's going to happen." I nipped her lobe and let my voice ooze like candle wax. "You're going tell me what you want, and I'm going to oblige. I'm going to ruin your body with my mouth, tongue, and hands until you're pent up, until the only thing your pussy craves is the part of me I haven't given it yet. Then I'll use this—" my free hand guided one of hers, bracing it against the solid width of my cock, "—to fill every wet edge inside you. I'll use it to push your body beyond its limits, then shatter those limits to pieces."

Her outtakes stalled as she palmed the hard column of flesh, feeling its heat brimming and its size stretching under her touch. "I don't think you'll fit."

My lips crooked against her lobe. "I'm flexible by trade. You're industrious by nature. We'll *make* ourselves fit."

"Poet."

"I've wanted you. I've been desperate for it. I've amassed so much want that it's scored on me," I rasped. "If you want it as much, nothing's going to stop us. I'll stroke into you so gradually, you'll feel every inch of my solid length—and every inch of your slick depth. I'll pump into you until it's all you know, until the only thing you concentrate on is my cock and your cunt moving together." My incisors scraped her flesh. "The softer you moan, the deeper I'll fuck you."

Briar drove her teeth into her lip, quelling a delectable sound.

I switched to the opposite ear. "Whatever it takes, you're not leaving this place without shouting. Because you see, my standards for your pleasure are rather high. It won't be enough to give you bliss. Nay, I want you to keep that bliss. I'll give you that hard kiss and sweet fuck I'd once promised. And I'll use both to make you come so wetly, so loudly—" my lips pressed a kiss to her lobe, "—you'll feel and hear yourself for days."

Her free digits bent, nails clawing into my sternum. As Briar pulled back, her attention dropped to my mouth, then to the waistband of my hose, then to the bulge shoving against the material.

Her tongue darted out, damping those lush lips. She glanced from my cock to my eyes in an unspoken request.

Longing swirled through my erection. Whatever she wished was my command.

I released her and picked apart the closures of my pants whilst my eyes fused with hers. The low waistband slumped. The flaps tented open. Without looking away, she joined her fingers with mine.

Keeping our attention fixed on each other, we drove the hose down. My cock released, rising from the vent and straining high against my pelvic bones.

Endearingly, Briar averted her gaze. But after a moment, her eyes fringed down, and her mouth parted to release a gust of air.

I wouldn't call myself as behemothly endowed as a giant, but I was a satisfying specimen, so I had been complimented. Nevertheless, suspense hindered my tongue. The princess's eyes roamed over the expanse of my cock, the stem long, its girth thick, the head broad and flushed.

The weight of Briar's gaze drew blood to my crown. I nearly lost my mind, stifling a groan as her fixation caused the enlarged cap to darken and coaxed a bead of arousal to surface through the slit.

Her throat contorted, and pink swam in her cheeks. At last, Briar's gaze lifted, irises heady with approval.

Relief and hunger swarmed my being. The princess liked what she saw.

Thusly, my cock twitched, hers for the taking.

Briar draped her fingers on my hips, urging us firmer together. Her pert tits grazed my tense frame, and her exhalations condensed, growing uneven. "Will you keep your promise now? Will you kiss me hard and fuck me sweetly?"

I pushed my torso against her breasts and strummed my lips over hers, my mouth lingering there. "Aye, I will," I hissed. Then I grabbed the back of her neck and hauled her mouth to mine.

A sigh cracked from Briar. Her fingers flew into my hair and wrenched on the roots, yanking me into her. The strength of my jaw kicked her head back as my tongue sliced through her lips.

Our tongues knitted, hers sweltering and ripe with that tart flavor. I swallowed her savory moan like an aphrodisiac, took it deep into me.

Humming, my mouth dislodged from hers and clamped onto the dip beneath her chin. I suckled her there before descending to her neck and along her shoulder. Open-mouth kisses quested across her body, sampling each freckle as though it were a morsel.

Briar's body quaked like a leaf, but she held herself aloft—a figure wrought of skin and steel. Like a future queen. And for a future queen, the jester would kneel.

She would know ecstasy by the time we were finished. She would know her pleasure like she knew her own voice. My words had touched her, and now the rest of me would worship her.

All for her.

I lowered myself, my mouth dancing everywhere, imprinting every curve, from her nipples to her navel. My teeth abraded her fingers, racing across them from knuckles to tips, teasing them one by one. Where my lips didn't reach, my hands did the rest. I traced her hips, cupped the shape of her ass, massaged the backs of her calves.

Setting my knees into the grass, I linked one thigh over my shoulder and kissed the inner flesh, drawing a path to her cunt. My mouth brushed through the red curls nestled at her juncture and spread those glistening lips with my tongue.

An intake of breath cut through Briar. "Oh!"

Her hands gripped back of my scalp whilst I licked the arousal from her body. Voracious, the plank of my tongue slid over the rift, running from her opening and along the groove. I ebbed back and forth, tucking myself into her flushed folds and sketching them. With purpose, my palate lapped the remnants of what my fingers had done to her earlier.

Briar's pussy trembled. She whimpered, the incoherent sounds hitting the treetops.

More. Louder, sweeting.

Louder came when I located that soft knot between her legs again. My tongue swept along the furrow in a single tender stroke that ended at her clit, the bud extending from her body. The instant I pressed the tip of my tongue against it, a shriek jumped out of Briar and punctured my cursed soul.

Her clit stretched, peeking from the thatch of curls. The pellet flushed under the point of my tongue, the skin throbbing. I felt the pressure of it, which increased with each indulgent lick. My mouth dabbed at her, the edge of my tongue swirling around the tiny oval.

Briar dissolved into sobs. Relentless, I preyed on that sound. I swabbed the fissure of her pussy until her body vibrated, roused anew and ready for me once more. She cleaved through my hair, pushed herself into my mouth.

With a ravenous grunt, I took what she generously offered. My mouth latched around the kernel and gave it a tender suck, not stopping as she tore through my roots. Her knees buckled, in danger of succumbing to gravity. Banding one arm around them, I secured her whilst towing on the crest, bobbing it into my mouth.

Briar's broken whine rang in my ears. By the time I released her from the clamp of my lips, her gritty exhalations scraped through the woods, and her clit was ruddy. I stopped before another surge could overtake her.

My thorn ejected a fretful noise. Though I would hardly call myself Poet if I made her satisfaction that easy, nor that expedited.

To beg the princess's pardon, I kissed the inflated peg and raised my gaze to hers. She stared, her expression bright with desire.

That look wiped any hint of a smirk from my face. Need surged up my cock and sizzled to the rims of my fingers. I flanked her hips and tugged.

Come here.

Obediently, Briar sank to the ground. I pulled her astride my lap, her thighs spreading around my waist. Her palms settled on my shoulders. Wet heat radiated from her slit as it aligned with my cock, which lifted high between us, the pommel aching.

Palming her ass, I nudged her forward, splaying her wider. Her pussy skidded over my crown. A tormented whine fell from Briar and a harsh grunt from me.

Our mouths rubbed, open and panting. Guttural, I positioned her above me, poising her drenched seam over the cusp of my cock. With a hiss, I framed her profile.

Face to face, skin on skin, level with one another, like equals.

No other words. Only this.

My gaze clamped onto hers. "Will you allow me to pleasure you now, Princess?"

"Yes," she entreated, her voice breaking. "Yes."

"Then tell me."

"Please my body. Give it to me." She licked her lips. "Fuck me sweetly, Poet."

The growl sliced from my lungs. I rolled my cock upward and probed. The head pushed through her folds and—fuck almighty—stretched them apart, the sleek lips spreading around me.

Briar grimaced in pain. "Ah."

"Sweeting, look at me," I gritted out.

Her eyelids fluttered. As she focused on me, I prodded higher, working the head slowly into her pussy. Dampness saturated my crown. Something serrated formed in my throat, ready to vault off my tongue, but I held back, held out for her.

Forcing myself to move carefully, I undulated with shallow jolts of my cock and murmured reassurances against her lips. "Keep looking at me. Keep your thighs parted like that. Keep watching whilst I open you."

Without breaking eye contact, Briar heeded my words.

That changed everything. My liquid voice and the rhythmic tilt of my hips loosened the princess. Her stitched brows smoothed out, her mouth parted, and her thighs relaxed around my waist.

My hips pitched deeper, sliding through her sodden walls inch by inch. She wound herself around me, squeezing when it hurt, sighing when it felt good.

At last, her cunt melted around me. Her body unwound, waist catching every sinuous snap of my body, hips rowing with mine. Quick puffs of air blew from her lungs and finally congealed into a single whimper.

"That's it," I hummed. "That's it, my princess. Open wide for me. Enjoy yourself."

Briar's fingers entwined in my hair. Taking that as encouragement, I slid my cock further ... higher ... deeper. Dampness spread around the head and suctioned it inside her.

My lips peeled back on a silent hiss, her warm grip so glorious it threatened to eviscerate my self-control. 'Twas all I could do not to butcher this moment by lurching the entirety of my cock into the soaked clutch of her body.

With measured swings of my hips, I spread her crease wider ... wider still.

Briar's sighs toughened into moans, each one in tempo to my waist. Her thighs shook, splaying further around my hips. The inner flanks of her pussy leaked, coating my erection.

My body knew about cadence and motion. Briar needed me longer, harder. She was ready, and I was long past the point of sanity.

Wicked hell, she was dripping all over me.

With a groan, I clasped her hips. In slow motion, I sank her fully onto me.

A cry sprang from her tongue. A grunt tore out of me as my cock pitched through her slit, the walls parting and then enwrapping me. Heat clamped my flesh from base to crown.

She felt mesmerizing, sexual, powerful. She felt like my destruction.

Briar's mouth unhinged against mine, small pants teetering from her lungs. Yet her focus never left mine as she spoke under bated breath. "Oh."

"Dear fuck," I uttered, haggard. "Briar."

"Oh, gods ... Poet."

I shook my head and grasped her face. My mouth seized hers. As promised, I kissed hard and began to fuck her sweetly.

My tongue swept into her mouth as my waist pitched into Briar. Both worked her, one deep, the other long. My lips reeled with hers as my cock lunged slowly, steadily, sensuously in and out of her. As I was about to leave her clutch completely, I rocked forward.

Again. And again. And again.

Brian's moans broke apart on my mouth. Her legs knitted around my waist and rode my thrusts. I paced myself, rolling my hips, withdrawing to the crest and slinging in to my base. With every languid pass of my cock, I tore gravely noises from both of us that cut through the forest.

My hips swiped upward, my cock plying through the pleats of her cunt. They parted, flexing around the column and clinging to every inch. I swiveled into her, my ass swinging back and forth, the rounded head tapping repeatedly against the tight hilt of her walls. Each time I nudged there, she wept in delirium.

My cock rowed in, glided out fully, and rowed in again. Her arousal glistened over the broad pommel of my erection, visible just before I sank back into her, to the top of my sac. I did this, and I did it more, and more, and more.

Endlessly, I cast inside Briar. My waist ground lazily with hers, my body impaling her gently, and her folds squeezing me mercilessly. I didn't let up, not even as she dilated around me, taking my cock effortlessly now.

Instead, I hardened my thrusts, pumping with a little more heft and maintaining a torturous rhythm. Briar's mouth hung ajar. She liked this pressure, the steady weight of it, how it pushed her upward.

She grabbed tufts of my hair. My fingers dug into her hips, which layered over mine and caught each measured jolt. Whilst I reeled my cock into her, our mouths cemented, our tongues swiping. We kissed in tandem, bodies adhering, pelvises bridled.

I lashed my waist patiently, my cock growing ever broader between her walls. Each collision of hips threw shockwaves up my vertebrae. I could perish, die a slow death like this.

Briar started to writhe, muffled sobs tumbling from her as she ground onto my lap and drenched my cock. My eyes slid back into my head. I wrested my mouth away to watch her unravel. She jostled above me, lips apart, breasts flushed, molten red hair spilling down her back.

Beads of sweat gathered between her clavicles and glazed my torso. Her cinched features screamed for more, more, more.

Obliging, I grasped her ass and unleashed, hauling her into me. The force spread her legs farther, my cock launching into her and doubling its pace.

Briar keened, crying to the beat of my hips. On each fluid stroke, her soaked body clenched me to the seat and released me to the slit.

So good. So wet. So mine.

My arms and limbs burned. Still, my cock struck into Briar at an unbridled pace.

Her head fell against mine, eyes squinting shut. Plaintive sounds pushed out of her.

"Wait for it, sweeting," I warned over her moans. "Stay with me."

"I can't," she gasped, labored breaths chopping between us.

"You can," I husked.

To prove it, I put my upper frame into the effort, levering deeper, so much deeper. I hurled her into me, my cock slanting at a new angle, hitting a spot that made her pussy compress and her head soar backward. She arched so far, the weed circlet toppled off her head. Her beautiful tits bounded toward the bower's canopy, and her thighs split, hips projecting into mine.

Her desire flooded my cock. She clung to the back of my neck, unwrapped her legs from around my waist, and braced her soles on the grass, using the leverage to ride me.

"Poet," she shrieked. "Yes!"

"Indeed, my thorn," I coaxed, jutting hot and high. "Spread yourself on me. Feel it."

But we couldn't anymore. It was impossible.

I pushed us to the brink but could stand it no longer. With another growl, I twisted her into the grass and balanced on my knees. Her limbs steepled, clasping onto me, burying me in the sleek depth of her body.

Lifting my torso upright, I held her hands on either side of her head and vaulted my cock into her. Briar sobbed and flexed off the grass as my body rode hers. Her heels hooked under my ass, and my hips snapped in a fierce tempo. I groaned with every fluid entry and retreat, her pleasure wrapping around me. The vision of her splayed, lost in rapture and taking the weight of my cock, drove me to sheer madness.

I might die. Or I might just kill us both.

I wanted her on every forsaken surface available. I wanted her beneath me like *now*, above me like *before*, bent in front of me like *someday*. I wanted her hair unruly and pouring like lava down her freckled skin.

I wanted to see her lovingly fucked by me.

I wanted her padding through my chambers in nothing but my shirt, the sleeves dangling past her wrists, the hem billowing around her thighs.

I wanted her fast and slow. I wanted her hard and soft.

I wanted her crazed and peaceful. I wanted her in darkness and daylight.

I wanted Briar against a wall. I wanted her sprawled across a desk. I wanted her astride my cock, riding me on her throne. I wanted Briar in her bed and in my bed.

But this patch of grass had to suffice. Thrusting into her, I lived the fantasy. I prolonged it with a harsh sigh and a hard snatch of my hips, making sure her lovely pussy would feel me well into the night.

Briar curled forward, pressing her forehead to mine. The position hoisted her knees higher and changed the slope of our hips. I snarled and hunched over her, flinging my waist, fucking so deeply into her, the tight walls dousing my erection.

I released her wrists, grabbed her face, and pumped my cocked swiftly. Our waists slammed together, charging helplessly. Her thighs fell apart, and she clung to my ass, urging me faster, harder.

Seasons, she was drenching me. My heart and crown threatened to explode.

Hectic moans coiled from Briar, each one rising an octave. That sound raced from my sac to my crest. I swept my body into hers, covetous of the noises she emitted, desperate for them.

Her expression pleaded with me. *Finish this.*

Her ragged features begged. *Never finish this.*

"Almost," I panted. "Almost there."

My muscles shook as I chased after her lovely cunt, the pome of my cock hitting the right spot, hitting it sweetly. I flung my waist, throwing sharp, shallow thrusts inside Briar, grinding her into the grass. Her walls tensed, and spasms rushed up my erection, the force mounting—and scattering.

"Now, sweeting," I hollered. "Now."

Briar shattered. Her folds convulsed, her pussy coming around my cock. Her head flung backward, body contorting off the ground as she shouted.

I whipped my hips quicker, pistoning into her, lengthening her climax.

As her cunt pulsated, my cock shuddered. I stilled, my mouth falling open against hers. Then I shot into oblivion, a chain reaction firing through my blood. With a final pitch of my ass, a bellow ripped from my lungs as I came. My release spilled into Briar whilst she cried out, her moans like sobs, like screams.

My growls and her moans collided, the catastrophic noises smashing through forest. I drowned myself in them, wanting to hear every wild thing we did to each other, hoping the whole forsaken world heard us, too. For at last, we didn't have to be silent.

With a final cry, Briar sagged onto the grass, and I fell into her. We lay there in a boneless, mindless heap. Sweat coated my spine, and my hips rested in the hot valley of her sprawled legs as we panted into each other, straining to catch our breaths.

Briar's fingers draped over my ass, and her free hand combed through the damp layers at my nape, the sensation among my new favorites.

Wicked. Hell.

This was how it felt like to fuck someone I loved.

We heaved, shockwaves coursing through us. Minutes or hours passed. I couldn't say, nor give an infernal shit.

Still inside her, I hauled myself up on one bent arm. Briar's eyes sparkled at me, her face radiating awe and pleasure. I had done that. I'd given her every bit of myself, stripped myself raw in nearly every way.

All except one. I caught her wrist and raised it, my mouth skimming the place where the iron shackles had cut into her. Quietly, I spoke against her pulse and told her my name.

Not Poet. Not the Court Jester of Spring.

My real name.

40

Briar

His breath swept through my ears like a breeze. His voice warmed my skin like rising steam. His name poured into me like melted honey.

Pleasure unlike anything I'd ever known coursed through my veins, the shock of it oozing from my scalp, to my heart, to my toes. A million silken wings fanned in my navel. My eyes closed, listening to the sound of him, letting this final secret envelope me.

His name. I felt it like a touch, like a confession, like a promise.

At last, my lashes fringed open. The jester materialized above, his features unveiled, slack with reverence. No mask. No artifice. Sex had loosened the whetted edges of his jawline, desire swam in his pupils, and something more bobbed in his throat. The emotion surfaced like an exposed root.

His name. He'd given that to me.

I smiled and traced the ledge of his chin. "Hello, sir."

An indentation burrowed into the crook of his mouth. "Evening, sweeting." The backs of his knuckles pushed a strand of hair from my temple, fingernails enameled in the half-light. "How do you feel?"

It came out effortlessly, honestly, and without reservation. "I feel in love."

His eyes flashed. "What a coincidence."

Only that tear painted black and dangling under one orb betrayed the raw expression reflected at me. But even that couldn't hide the magnitude of his stare, as open as a chasm. The jester lay naked, with his cock primed inside me and his secret lingering on his tongue.

I stored the knowledge inside, as though it were a keepsake clasped within a locket. Yet always, he would remain as I'd known him.

My jester. My Poet.

Mine. All mine.

A fresh wave coursed up my limbs, rushing to the juncture where our hips joined, our pelvises locked in heat. Seasons, he was still hard. The realization pooled liquid through my walls, renewing the throb in my core.

My palms draped atop the ovals of his buttocks and swayed to the dip in his spine, which beaded with sweat. A sudden urge crept through my fingers, and the notion scorched across my cheeks. Whatever hints showed across my countenance, Poet's eyes squinted with intrigue.

I gave him no merciful warning. Impulsively, I angled my hips to release his length and drifted my hand down to catch his erection.

And I held on.

The wet evidence of my climax laminated his flesh. His cock rose between my fingers, the column slick and the crown fevered in a ruddy tint. It stretched along my palm, firm as a finial with a slender cut across the top.

I had given the jester my virginity, and now I wanted to take something from him. A thrilling sort of curiosity directed my hand. I glided it over the stem, slowly, gently.

Poet sucked in a breath. Those eyes narrowed into harsh lines that distorted the tear painted on his countenance. And when I drew a path to his sac, then to the pome at the top, his hips vaulted.

"Briar," he warned, dropping his hand over mine. "If you keep doing that—"

"I know," I confided with feigned innocence. "Let me have you. Please?"

His orbs hooded. Awe and longing swirled in the green scythes.

How I loved rendering his silver tongue speechless.

Without waiting for a response, I unhooked my legs from around his waist and nudged his frame backward into the grass. We switched positions, me hovering over his side and Poet sprawling underneath.

I admired his body, sculpted to dance and trained to wield knives. The smooth cliff of skin spanned before me, his long cock lifting between those solid hips and that steep V.

Gluttony overcame me. Love and lust coiled in the rift of my legs.

I sketched the inclines of his hips, threaded my fingers through the slender trickle of dark hair leading to the ridge projecting from his body, so much heat originating from there.

A defeated sound pushed from Poet's lips, the noise satin and gritty in a way only he could achieve. Transfixed, he bracketed his elbows and braced himself, his pulse ramming into his throat. The vision teased a grin across my mouth.

Yes. Watch me.

My digits traced his width, starting at the base where his sac hung and scaling its height to the apex. His cock jolted, thickening for me. My heart sprinted, and fluid raced between my thighs.

I feathered around the crest, the pads of my fingers brushing its mass. The swollen head flushed, a droplet of rekindled arousal budding from the slit. I thumbed the incision, sweeping lightly.

A captivated groan engulfed Poet's lungs. Something severe cast across his face, as if the ministrations pained him.

Torment. That was it.

Touching him felt like touching myself. Strong. Invincible. The memory of telling Poet how it felt to gratify my body and then showing him in the library replayed.

The same craving led my digits over his crown, spurring them to flick his crease. And as he leaked onto my finger, my core respond-

464

ed. I sought his weak spots and powerful spots, wanting them both.

Emboldened, I rolled my palm down his column and strapped my digits around him. The flesh yielded, stiff but pliable. It enlarged, nearly too wide for me to encase him fully, his girth wetting the slot of my thighs.

I licked my lips, braced him in my hand, and stalled. The enigmas of pressure and pacing funneled through my mind.

Poet sensed my indecision and molded his fingers with mine. He urged them tighter and strummed our hands up and down his cock. Once the tempo became clear, he withdrew and offered me leave to take control. He rested his weight on those bent arms, keeping himself partway aloft, panting and willfully at my behest.

I ensconced him in my grip and siphoned his erection. Another groan rumbled from Poet's mouth, then another, and another. One free hand curled around my hip, as if needing the additional leverage to hold himself up, lest he should evaporate.

I pumped him, maintaining a steady tempo. With each assent to his crown, my thumb glided over the inflated knob of skin. Then I plunged again, over and over.

He lost himself in my touch, and his face clenched, eyeing the hand that encased his length. Unable to stand it, Poet snapped his hips into my fingers, jutting through them as though it was my pussy.

I sighed with relish and quickened the tempo. My hand tugged on the hardness, yanking hoarse moans from his lungs, each new one amplifying. His backside clenched, and his abdomen contracted as his cock bucked into my hand.

The jester's moans roughened into growls. "Damnation. Aye, love. Like that."

My forehead landed against his, and one of his legs steepled for balance as he leaned into me. I trapped him in my gaze and squeezed, my wrist flexing as he rode my fingers to the hilt.

Tremors raked up his limbs and tracked across his chest. I savored the rupture of noise, the tightening of his erection, the way he launched into my hand.

Convulsions sprinted over his frame, his cock so hard and on the brink of unleashing. I wanted him seeping onto me. I wanted his shouts. And so, he surrendered them as well.

Yes. Show me.

His mouth fell open, nearly there, so close.

I dashed my hand up and down his length until Poet tensed—and unleashed a string of jagged hollers. They unraveled, inundating the forest bower. His body rocked, and his cock spasmed. Warmth spurted from his slit to my knuckles.

Triumph and yearning converged low in my stomach. As he yelled, I choose that moment to kiss his mouth, taste his orgasm, and whisper, "You're beautiful."

Poet's being transformed, snapping him out of the haze. His shouts tapered to a single, sinful grunt. Before he could finish on my hand, the jester yanked me top of him.

My legs bridged his waist. My thighs split around his hips.

Trapping me above him, Poet emitted another husky noise and vaulted his erection upward. His length plied into me, the force stunning the air from my lungs. My spine snapped backward as I sat on his cock.

The friction shot pleasure from my core to my scalp. A cry shook from my being.

While watching my hand drain Poet, I'd wanted this again. And he must have known.

Poet dissolved into the grass, splaying himself completely. Under me, he twisted his hips and began a deft sequence of pumps. On instinct, my palms flattened atop his pectorals, nails clawing into the flesh above his nipples.

Unable to contain it, I opened myself to the flexing strokes of Poet's hips. His buttocks careened sinuously as he whipped into me, rousing my moans into an uproar. He steered the backs of my thighs, vaulting them against him until I caught on to the cadence.

Earlier, Poet had done what he'd vowed, kissing me hard and fucking me sweetly. At length, he eased his grip and beseeched me to take over—to make love to him sharply.

I answered the plea. With my hands planted against him, I used the momentum to glide my hips back and forth. My pussy clutched his width, drenching it to the seat.

We sealed our walls together and lurched. Poet casted in and out, his hardness slipping through my folds, abrading the inner flesh. My sobs collided with his growls, just like his cock and my pussy collided—just like we've always collided yet managed to fit.

We'll make ourselves fit.

Poet fastened onto my backside as I moved faster. I moaned in tandem to the swift lurch of his lower half, his waist snapping into me. The groans intensified, so that I could no longer tell which were his or mine.

I leaned forward, caught his shoulders, and rode my folds on his cock. As we bounded into one, chants escaped my mouth, and entreaties poured from his lips. I didn't know how he managed so soon after his second climax, but Poet's vigor filled me to the brim. I straddled his lap and flew into him, the pleasure amplifying, tangling into a knot.

Yet it went on, and on, and on. Delirium unfurled around me, the world reducing to a blur.

Suddenly, Poet shot upright. In a seamless chain of movements, he got to his feet, pitching us off the ground. I yelped, my ankles linking around his lower back.

His arms banded around me like iron, securing me to him. With our bodies still connected, he strode to the nearest tree, its branches dripping with ropes of black petals. Flattening me against a column of smooth bark, Poet cupped the back of my head. Like this, he used the foundation for balance and hauled his cock into me.

I shrieked into the canopy, the force of his thrusts jostling me into the dark, blossoming curtain. The tilt of his erection in this position seemed to reach another new area, which penetrated nerve endings I hadn't known existed. It couldn't be real, couldn't be endured.

Still, I bobbed my hips. The impact of my core and his cock ramming together shot me higher, higher, higher into the tree. Several foliage cords sagged over our shoulders, the vines shaking around us.

Unable to stand it, I bunched my fist into my mouth. My teeth sank into my knuckles, because otherwise I would lose my voice.

Poet muttered something and plucked my hand from my lips. No barriers. No restraint. He wanted me to hear myself, wanted me to feel it all.

But heavens. We pounded into each other, his growls beating against my moans.

My joints burned, and my head levitated. I tried rolling my waist more, but it proved difficult with Poet's body pinning me.

To that end, my chin crinkled. He saw this and smirked through his groan.

Whirling us around, he switched our positions. He skirted us beneath a lower branch and pressed his spine into the tree trunk. "Grab it," he panted.

I flung up my arms and latched onto the overhead branch. Hooking my fingers onto the bough enabled my waist to move freely. With an eager sigh, I pelted my waist against his, driving my folds onto his upright cock.

And we erupted into motion.

Poet surged into me. I catapulted above him. Our mouths unleashed, my cries and his shouts coalescing.

We watched each other succumb to the hysteria. Nothing left to hide. Nothing to hold back. His pupils mushroomed, the irises vanishing behind a pair of black wells.

Momentarily, my gaze strayed to his erection glazed in my arousal. The flesh glistened as it soared up my walls. He filled me from the roof of his cock to the hilt, so wonderous, so good.

My attention leaped back to Poet's face, which tensed with the impending climax. I felt every wet inch of his cock jutting between my pussy, his entire length spasming for release. The sight of him threw flames across my skin, infusing me to my bones.

I gripped the branch and hurled myself at him. My hips slammed onto his, wanting this pleasure, wanting it all.

Poet's eyebrows crimped in pain. His fingers spanned my back-side, lifting me up and down on his cock. And I thought, *Come for me.*

He arched into the trunk, digits burrowing into me as if hang-ing on for dear life. My lips split in ecstasy, his erection so hard, so broad as it speared into me. I moaned, bowed my head toward Poet, and flung my core at him. I met every one of his thrusts, pitching us together at a breakneck pace.

Hot tingles whirled through my folds and crackled at the tip of my clitoris. I hastened after it and took the jester with me.

"Poet," I wept.

"Briar," he grated.

And everything exploded. Our hips crashed, locked, and held. We seized up, then burst into a great convulsion of heat.

My pussy fluttered around Poet's lunging cock, the combustion washing through me. The climax rushed in like an avalanche, drown-ing out all thought, all other sensations. I cried out so loud, so hard, so long. He roared to the treetops, his backside lurching with each jolt.

While grinding onto Poet, I soaked him and heard his own final rasp of completion. He stroked his cock into me slower, shallower until the eddies subsided. I let go of the branch and collapsed into him, oxygen depleted and heart wedged in my throat.

Something else filled the crevices inside me. Something elated.

My hair spilled across his chest. Air blasted through us as we slumped against the tree.

I tilted my head and met his heady gaze. Drowsy, I glimpsed the bruise swimming across his jaw from battling the knights and that black tear sliding from his lower eyelid. I curled into Poet and brushed my mouth over the wound. Then I used my thumb to smudge the dark paint, wiping away the tear as if it were nothing more than a stain.

Poet

My sweeting, this is where I've led us. In this secluded bower, I've been drifting and remembering this tale with you as my company.

I don't know how this story continues, but 'tis time we find out. Also, there is one thing I haven't yet confessed ...

The princess and I dozed in the grass. I rested beneath Briar, with her legs nestling my hips. As the eventide light threw shadows over us, I drowsed in and out of her scent, in and out of our story.

Seasons help me. It had never been like that with anyone.

Briar had wiped my past clean. Only she existed now.

After the tree, we spent an indulgent amount of time staring and touching. Then I fucked her for a third time.

If we didn't come up for air soon, neither of us would be able to function for days. Nevertheless, I welcomed the mutiny. I thirsted for more nights like this, easy and eternal.

For anyone else, belonging to Autumn should guarantee it. Living in the same court should close the divide.

If only it were that simple.

A throaty groan spread from my chest. Briar's fingers wound through my hair as she blinked at me. "Hi," she whispered, her voice worn from exertion and saturated with pleasure.

This woman couldn't know how delirious and devastated that word made me. I wanted to tether that intimate *Hi* into a knot and unravel it every day, unspooling it from her like a ribbon—a rare and secret gift.

She spread herself over me, my body still partially fitted to hers. Her head rested on my shoulder, her hair a red mess across my chest, the locks matted as though she'd walked through a tornado. A fragrant mist of apples and sweat wafted from her naked skin.

Like a trickster, she fingered the inclines of my hips. Damnation, how I liked that.

Matter of fact, I liked it so much that it was beginning to show yet again. My insatiable cock twitched inside her, and my plaintive growl made her chuckle. Seasons, I could do this forever, listen to that laugh and make love to her until the sun rose. Sensuous and slow. Rough and fast. There remained at least half a dozen evil things I'd like to do to this female.

But soon the bell would toll midnight, and eventually dawn would sneak over the horizon. One by one, carnival revelers would notice our absence.

But there was much to discuss, namely that Briar had bargained me and my son to Autumn. She had my gratitude for that—to an extent.

Once released from prison and questioned by the Crown, I had rushed to Jinny and Nicu. Plagued by nightmares, my son hadn't yet recovered from what happened. I'd held him and coaxed him to sleep, the wrathful father in me plotting ways to make my former sovereigns bleed from their fucking ears.

As desperate as I had been to see Briar, the only reason I returned to the castle before our journey to Autumn was that I'd been hand-picked to be the Fest Fool. That had robbed me of hours comforting

Nicu and bidding Jinny farewell.

Although lying about our blood relations could enable Jinny to come with us, her bones were too old to make the trip. The woman who had raised me, whom I'd sworn never to abandon—as my parents did to me, as Nicu's mother did to him—would end her days alone.

The grief had been immeasurable. When I gave her the news, I cried more than she had.

Jinny had smiled bravely. She'd rubbed a poultice into my wounds, then held my face and told me to be well, to stay together and make a home for Nicu.

Intolerance existed on a quieter note in Autumn—up to this point, at least. Ultimately, it was still intolerance in a climate that hadn't been tested yet. Not only would I be prying Nicu from the only place he'd known, but the threats wouldn't end in another court. The risks would only take on a different shape, a new sharpness no one could predict.

Through us, Briar would be put in danger, too.

The backs of my retinas burned. Mercenary impulses clawed through my fingers. If anything happened to them, I'd slit throats and draw rivers of blood.

But for the time being, the sight of Briar's flushed face rinsed away those instincts. I tapped her nose. "I suppose I'm under your command now. But then, I've always been."

She propped herself above me, her breasts skimming my ribs. "It was the only way."

"Indeed."

"And us?"

I wavered. Seasons no longer came between us. But that left three-hundred and fifty-three other conflicts to deal with.

She was royalty. I was the professional butt of a joke, the court's precious whore, and a pricey trinket to be shown off at feasts. At all times, I was the most worshipped, the most desired, the most envied, the most hated, and the most controversial person in the room. This was nothing new in Spring.

But not in Autumn. What upheaval I'd cause there remained to be seen. But whatever happened, whatever I did intentionally or unintentionally, it would affect Briar.

Pain rippled through me. I balanced myself beside her, wanting to take the words back even as I spoke them. "I'll be your Court Jester. I'll entertain and advise. I'll gain countless fans and foes, as befits my station. And on some fateful day, I'll watch you marry an archetypal suitor with immaculate teeth and table manners. And whilst the wedding guests fill themselves with bucketloads of alcohol, I'll mock everyone within a twenty-foot radius, and they'll despise me for it, as much as they'll lust after me for it, as much as they'll resent me for it."

Denial clambered across Briar's face. "In the bell tower, you asked what you meant to me."

"I merely wanted to know. I wasn't counting on it for more, however much I fancied the idea. You were the one who reminded me of our differences."

"And then I changed my mind."

"Sneaking into alcoves under the cover of night and hiking up your skirt for a quickie? Speaking in riddles to communicate, or manipulating the system to send missives? Slipping into your suite, covering your mouth so no one but me shall hear you moan, and leaving before dawn? Romance is labor intensive, don't you agree?"

"Be serious for one minute," Briar snapped.

If I did that, I'd have to tell her it would be worth it. Every secret moment, every effort to steal a moment with her. I would do it a thousand times and more. It wouldn't be difficult. Nay, it would be instinctual.

But if I went there, I would only delay the inevitable.

"I don't want to conceal what we have," Briar persisted. "Not again, and not in my court. It may take years, but someday the people will accept it."

"We'll have enough of a battle ahead with our grand plans for humanity," I countered. "Pushing those limits will leave scant room for much else."

"Like you said, a princess has harsher things to deal with. Riots, assassins, dissention—"

"Indeed, those will be on the agenda. If so, I'll need my energy to dismember anyone who gets near you or Nicu. Where you're both concerned, I tend to do things thoroughly, which means however much I'd love the task, I can't have my stamina depleted by making you come every night."

Briar flushed. Reproach nevertheless dug into her face. "I know what you're doing."

"I'd expect nothing less."

"You're trying to distract me."

"Get used to it, sweeting."

"And I can look out for myself."

"I know you can," I assured her. "That doesn't mean I won't take up where you left off and do damage to anyone who so much as sneezes in your direction. That's what allies do, if not lovers."

"I don't want you only as an ally or a guardian." Briar cleared her throat. "But thank you for wanting to protect me."

"My pleasure." I quirked a naughty brow. "Always, my *pleasure*."

Her flush deepened. "The court doesn't have to celebrate us. But if I prove myself as a Royal, they'll respect my choices."

"Once upon a spicy time, a princess and a jester fell in love," I narrated. *"They waited a lifetime to have their court's blessing, the jester watching and waiting as the princess grew into her role. Soon enough, her days became busier, filled with new faces and obligations. She met warriors and noblemen, debated with them at roundtables, and invited them to the revels. She received her peers and her subjects, with less and less freedom to idle in the arms of her jester. By the time they realized they'd grown apart, the feast had grown cold."*

"That won't happen," she insisted.

"'Tis how these stories end, as they aren't truly stories."

"I know you don't want to be a king."

"Good Seasons, nay," I balked. "I am, and will always be, a jester."

"Fine. But you know you're so much more than a centerpiece to

474

rulers—so much more to *me*. And Mother reigns without a husband. Queens can be leaders on their own."

That wasn't unheard of in our history. Ever since the Seasons were united a century ago, power and peace hadn't required alliances.

Elitist standards, on the other hand, were quite welcome.

"You're willing to forsake a king in favor of a fallen jester," I summarized. "A lowborn orphan with a so-called bastard 'fool' of a son. There couldn't be a worse combination to toss at the people."

"I don't see either of you that way."

"I know, but 'tis how your world shall see us."

"That's bullshit!" she spewed rather impressively. "You cultivated power and influence in Spring. The people are upset with you now, but eventually that will fade. Don't deny that if given the choice, most denizens would ultimately follow you over the Crown. If you can do that here, you can do that in Autumn. The only difference is we'll be on level with each other."

"I hate to admit this, but Sinful Spring isn't as morally strict as Proper Autumn."

"The court won't disapprove forever. You're Poet. You can bewitch anybody. And I'm a smart leader. I can sway the rest. And when the day comes, I'll appoint an heir, because I don't have to give birth to one. I'll be married to Autumn and loving you."

My throat contorted. "That's not enough."

"What?" she gasped, recoiling from me as though I'd slapped her.

I snatched her wrists. "Listen to me, Briar."

"Don't!" she jerked back, withdrawing herself from around my cock and scrambling off my chest to sit upright beside me. "After everything that's happened, I offer you my heart. I offer to rule without a king so I can be with you, and that's your reply? That I'm—that we're not enough?"

My own grief reflected in her eyes. Trying to explain this away felt wrong.

And yet. "It won't be enough for either of us."

"I make my own decisions," she rioted. "I chose this. Why doesn't that suffice? I kissed you in that pavilion. I shared my body with you. The Dark Seasons know about us."

"We are performers, you and me. With artistry and resilience, we'll undo the impression we've made until the world reduces us to a brief, passionate tryst that ended as quickly as it began. Nobles will court you, and you'll let them—for appearances' sake to begin with.

"But soon, you'll have admirers in earnest, handsome fops with golden hair and golden pockets. Even their snot will be priceless. You'll gain the approval of your people, who hope for a pristine match. For the sake of a nation, you won't be able to reject that. I'm not telling you anything you don't already know."

"You're telling me everything I don't believe," she spat. "That's what you're telling me."

"We'll bicker about how little time you have for us, how each smile you share with another man was merely a facade. You'll resent me for questioning it, and I'll resent you for scowling at every man and woman who bats their lashes at me. You'll hate that I haven't ceased flirting and teasing, although you know it's my craft.

"I'll want the luxury of holding your hand in the halls and the privilege of climbing into your bed without having to wear a disguise and scale a wall. However willingly and eternally I'd do anything for you, the yearning for more shall grow. We'll argue, misinterpret actions and words, go days and then weeks without having a moment alone. We'll say the wrong things and react stubbornly, and as much as I fancy make-up sex as much as the next person, interludes will become riddled with tension. It will get messy, and it will happen before we've realized it."

I drove the blade in. "And Nicu will see it happen."

Briar's face crumbled. She covered her mouth and twisted away, those snarled locks draping over her naked breasts.

The sight was hell on earth. I wanted her to stop me from ruining this, but she couldn't, and I couldn't let her.

"He'll be heartbroken," I said. "He'll want you for a mother and wonder why he doesn't get to see you. I'll be in agony, knowing I can't explain it in a way he'll understand.

"And whilst I'm kneeling at your feet, juggling and dancing for you, or throwing blades at targets—when I'd rather be hurling them at the insolent pricks whispering platitudes in your ear—I'll also want to shake you, yell at you, touch you, kiss you, fuck you. I'll want to do deep, illicit, naked things to you. But with each sunrise, I'll feel us slipping away from each other, word by word, look by look." I spoke around the needles in my throat. "It will break Nicu, torture me, and push your limits. In turn, that will hurt you, which is a dealbreaker. I'll never allow myself to be the reason for your torment, and I'll never allow Nicu to feel the brunt of it. Don't make that our future."

Briar surged to her feet. Shaking up a storm, she threw on her chemise and rounded on me. "Get dressed."

Well, well. Her first order.

"If it pleases you, Your Highness."

"It does not please me. I would like to keep you bare for at least several consecutive hours, but then I won't be able to say what I have to say. Get dressed, Poet."

I stood and slipped into the horrible pants, omitting the jacket because I just couldn't with that rubbish. Finished, I spread my arms and waited.

Briar puffed and squared her shoulders. "You're a coward," she clipped. "You said if I wanted things to change, I should change them. You said I shouldn't cling to past ways. You told me that you loved me."

"Aye," I murmured softly. "I did say that."

"And you said loving took courage. We have the chance to become something different, yet you insist upon tucking tail. Well, I won't let you. You might beautify your words, but I *stand by* mine. If I make a vow, I do not break it. My will is as strong as my promise, and if you don't know that by now, then you don't know me!"

My throat stung. "Briar—"

But I shut up when she knelt before me. "Give me your hand."

Mesmerized, I placed it in hers, gobsmacked as she spoke. "I swear I won't abandon either of you. Nicu will have my adoration every morning. He will have me at his bedside every night. I will sit with him. I will listen to his stories. I will tie ribbons through every corridor. I will hold his hand and bring him to the dais, so that he may see his father dominate the great hall. I won't let anyone harm him. I'm his. I'm yours. You come first because you're my family, as are my mother and my father and Eliot. You are my *family*."

Her eyes glistened. "I'm not ashamed to love you, and I will fight for that with everything I am, and I won't hide it. I have pretended long enough. I'm not afraid of Autumn's judgment or retaliation.

"And this isn't purely for us, it's for the people. Someday we'll make a difference together, be a finer nation for it, and show them that no other match could have existed for me than with you. We'll rule and love like warriors." Briar sucked in air. "All right?"

When her day came, she would make an inspiring queen. Lucky for me, I would be there to witness it.

Transfixed, I stared at her. The worst reply in history wavered on my tongue, but I thought back to something Jinny had said before I left her.

"You tell me," she had said. "Now that nobody can hear you but Old Jinny. Without your fancy clothes and thoughts, you tell me now that it's just us."

"I can't love her," I'd whispered, although it was too late for that.

Jinny had studied me with weathered eyes. The scents of herbs and woodsmoke had clung to her shawl, the first gift I'd purchased for her from my income as a jester. "Remember when I told you that you'd know what to do without me? It's time you found that out. If not, what will that teach Nicu?"

What would denial teach him about passion and freedom? About himself?

Most days in our world, between courts and peasants, there existed wisdom in restraint, for it granted power. Other days, it stripped us of our souls. For what we thought of as safe could often be a greater danger than to live, to try, to dare.

For such an adept person, I'd proven remarkably fucking stupid.

If Briar chose me, she chose my son.

None wanted us as she did. None wanted her the way we could.

To deny this was to deny our worth. *That* would be lying.

Sinking to one knee, I leveled myself with Briar. Then I twisted her hand to brush my mouth over her knuckles, to drop a kiss there, and give her my answer.

42

Briar

I took a deep, wheat-filled breath. My eyes closed as I inhaled the scent, letting it weave through my lungs as if I were already there—already home. Orchards dripping with apples. Foxes traipsing through the grounds at court. Legendary treehouse colonies, flora and fauna imbued with their own magic, and misty grey skies.

Autumn. Soon.

A current of air dashed through my skirt, flouncing the twill material. The gold and black pattern danced, then settled around my boots.

I exhaled. My eyes opened to a twilit sky capped in thickets of clouds and a deep sapphire blue. The sun had yet to rise, but I sensed it coming. I felt the impending dawn as I felt many things ahead, some of them unknown.

Murmured voices and the clank of steel reached my ears, the noises returning me to the present. My gaze dropped from the firmament to survey the activity. Spring servants and Autumn knights moved in and out of the sconce lights illuminating from a procession of carriages. Horses affixed to the vehicles stood tall and robust. The equines were ready to embark on a long journey.

The second I registered the scene, my attention swept from one end of the caravan to the other. My heart skittered as I searched amid the strings of faces. Hope trickled across my chest. I swallowed hard and began to fidget, the black leather gloves encasing my fingers straining with the motions.

He would not break his promise. He would never do that.

Where are you?

Then I saw it. As my gaze bypassed the carriage stationed in front of me, a flash of red caught my eye. The door to my private transport was poised open, the sumptuous interior upholstered in velvet.

Resting atop the left seat cushion was a band of scarlet.

My pulse spiked. Happiness unlike anything I'd ever known rushed through my veins, the visual stinging my eyes.

"You're late," a smooth timbre said.

I slanted my head toward that voice. He leaned against the front profile of the carriage, his back reclining casually against the vehicle as if he'd been there the whole time. As usual, the jester perfected his customary sprawl—lazy, cunning, refined. So impeccably disheveled.

Poet twisted his head my way, tossing me a sidelong glance. His tousled hair fell across his face, but there was no hiding the impish glitter in his pupils.

My fingers ceased their restless movements. I folded my hands in front of me and raised a single eyebrow. "And you jest."

A fiendish half-smile cut across his lips. "'Tis my job, Princess."

He wore an ankle-length coat of crimson, the cuffs rolled up his forearms, and dark leather pants tucked into his boots. The vision robbed me of air, so much that every nearby figure and neighboring commotion vanished.

I knew you'd come.

In the forest, Poet had told me yes. Despite that, anxiousness and eagerness to see him had overtaken me this morning.

Those green irises teased, *Did you miss me?*

My own gaze declared, *I'll never have to.*

Poet's countenance slid over my traveling dress, admiring the opulent style and the way it accentuated my body. Most especially, he strayed to my hair, which fell unbound. A pair of gold spade earrings ornamented the ensemble, the jewels dangling behind my locks.

The jester's hot gaze burned right through my clothing. Seasons, my thighs tightened, and the nexus of my legs warmed. This man never failed to rouse me, even while fully dressed and in public. We would have quite a challenge ahead of us, as prudent Autumn would hardly fail to notice such exchanges, nor be accustomed to them.

Nonetheless, his stare emboldened me. It spurred me to respond, to play in kind.

Clearing my throat, I reached into the carriage, extracted the ribbon, and presented the evidence. "You cannot do anything simply, can you?"

"Perish the thought." Poet broke from his leisurely stance and sauntered my way. "Would you say you're fond of me?"

"Yes," I laughed. "A thousand times, yes."

"Splendid. In that case ..."

With reverence, the jester stopped inches from me, his scent lacing through my senses. I watched, my heart knotting as he tied the length of red material around my leather-bound wrist. His fingers blazed through the textile, so that I pooled with need beneath my dress. No one melted me as he did.

To be sure, no other gift would ever be as precious as the bracelet. My expression swore as much. And his answering gaze simmered, assuring me that my clothes would be off by now, were we alone. To which my temperature rose, agreeing with him.

Our fate would not be easy, nor would the struggles that awaited us. We might face a lapse in Autumn's benevolent nature. Civil disorder could erupt. Either that, or the danger might surface from within the court through veiled threats masked in politeness, the lingering looks of courtiers, or who knew what else.

Change would take longer than we wished. Our actions had earned us a fair share of enemies across The Dark Seasons.

I thought of similar mornings in Autumn, the air laced in fog and the sky dim. However tranquil it felt, I'd forgotten how a subdued canopy shielded one's world right before the turbulence barreled in, whisking everything that was once settled into a new frenzy. This intermission felt like a quite before the storm.

However, Poet and I would endure. We knew how to do that now.

"Briar," he murmured, snapping me out of the haze.

I marshalled my thoughts, fell into his green gaze, and sunk into the strong arms that encased me. "Poet."

"Where did you go just now?"

"It doesn't matter. I'll always come back."

At that, he clasped me tighter. "Speaking of which, you haven't asked what sort of mischief I intend for this trip."

I feigned astonishment. "Jesters do not wait to be asked. And princesses never inquire, they command."

"Clever woman," he complimented. "I thought of a story. Verily, I've had it in my mind for a while. Bits and pieces have entered my thoughts but never the larger scope. I've realized there's more to it now. I'd like your approval to recite it for tonight's meal whilst we make camp." He leaned in and whispered, "A warning. I'm a father, and some parts aren't fit for a child's ears."

"I would not fret."

To demonstrate, I glanced over his shoulder and jutted my chin toward the display behind him. Poet twisted and followed my trajectory to where Nicu ran across the cobbled pavement and slammed into my mother's side. She gasped in surprise while servants and knights stalled, their features lifting in bewilderment.

Yet Mother smiled and strapped her arms around Nicu, who had charmed her the second Poet introduced them. Then she knelt before the child and whispered, her words muffled but discernable. "Would you like to ride with me?"

Nicu's eyes flared wide. His head jumped between the queen and the grand, lacquered carriage. At last, he pivoted toward us, his visage alight with excitement.

Poet nodded, silently giving his permission.

Elated, the boy snapped his fingers. At the sound, Tumble galloped from the castle's threshold and sprang into the vehicle, followed by Nicu.

Mother cast the pair a dazed but fond look. Noticing her audience, she glanced at the hovering figures with a protective frown until the entourage jumped back into motion.

Before she ascended into the carriage, Mother transferred her regard to Poet and me. Pride kindled there, despite how she worried for us. With a private wink, she slipped into the transport, the jacquard folds of her cloak sweeping behind her.

One of the knights appeared beside us and grunted. "There is a carriage assigned and waiting, Your Highness."

A thin layer of dutiful respect concealed the scandalized tone lurking under the surface. He meant, there was a separate transport for Poet. That arrangement would be the thing to do. However, Mother knew as well as we did. This was the time to set a precedent, one that we wouldn't apologize for. One small step forward.

Then again, neither of us presently cared what the cavalry thought.

While keeping his focus pinned on me, Poet intoned, "No need."

To which the man's speechlessness incited a grin from my lips. "We're together," I clarified.

Disgruntled and with a sliver of hesitancy, the knight refrained from insisting and merely genuflected before departing. Poet's mouth twisted as he bowed with a flourish and swung his arm toward the cabin. I buried my incisors into my lower lip, stifling a chuckle.

Glancing over my shoulder, I committed Spring's castle to memory. The ivy-laced palace where we'd met. The place where old and new friends resided. My aching chest kept them close.

I would see Posy, Vale, and Cadence again. I would know Eliot's embrace once more when the time came.

Swerving back, I climbed into the carriage with Poet. He lounged across from me, our gazes locking as the coachman closed the door, insulating us in candlelight and blessed privacy.

Knights swung themselves atop the horses. The line of transports kicked into motion across the isolated lane reserved for Royal travelers. It stretched from the court, along the outskirts of the lower town, and up the hill into the wildflower forest.

Poet and I continued to stare. We paced ourselves, knowing what would happen.

In his face, I saw a hundred expressions. I'd been collecting them over the past three days since we left the woodland bower.

Impatience with me. Impatience to be inside me.

Determination in the throne room. Private humor from across the great hall. Heat in our chambers as he thrust into me.

He infuriated and pushed me. He made me laugh.

He kissed me hard, made love to me roughly, fucked me sweetly. In my bed. In his bed.

On my desk. Against the wall.

Angry and hectic, we would rush into each other, our turbulent limbs pounding away. Other times, it had been patient—slow, long, and torturous. Our mouths would graze, open and panting while our hips whipped together.

Endless torture. Exquisite depth.

Already, he had taken me in numerous ways. I'd made him climax with a shout, attuning myself to each part of him. Every sound, every taste.

Currently, the trees shrouded us on either side. The instant this happened, we lurched into action. With a growl, Poet grabbed my wrists and hauled me across the divide. I chortled while landing astride his lap, my legs flying around his hips.

Poet snatched my lips in a spine-tingling kiss. I dove into him, clasping my thighs around his waist and parting myself for him. Our mouths fused, tongues stroking in and flexing together. I hunched over his frame and speared my hands in his hair, pulling his face closer and opening wider, desperate to taste him, to drown out the world outside.

The carriage trundled through the wild. The sconce flames writhed. The wildflower forest flanked us in a vignette of muted sages and golds.

Our bodies rocked with the vehicle. My breasts crushed against the jester's drumming chest. Arousal seeped from my walls, my core rubbing onto his cock, which grew firm and high.

Poet released my mouth on a groan. "I could make you come right here."

I caressed his flushed lips with mine. "The procession could halt at any moment."

"I do love risking my life with you."

"Insatiable," I laughed breathlessly while combing my fingers through his messy layers.

"And yet I love prolonging the agony just as much. In which case, I shall up the ante." His tongue flicked over my earlobe, and I shivered as he whispered a promise into the shell. "When next we're alone, I'm going to fuck you on your throne."

I gasped, a thrill eddying between my folds. "That would be even riskier."

"Ah, but I believe we can find a way around it. We're quite the rebellious pair."

Because I couldn't disagree with that, I took his mouth again. Poet hummed and licked into me. The kiss dissolved every shred of fear and trepidation that had been creeping in and out of my consciousness for days, leaving only desire, elation, and strength in their wake.

Whatever dangers lay ahead, and whatever gambles we took when the sun rose fully, those worries vanished for the ride. Right now, only this existed—the jester's firm mouth folding over me and his naughty tongue stroking mine.

Once more, Poet pried his lips from me. "Briar," he husked. "The tale."

"Hmm?" I exhaled against his own stunted outtakes. "Oh, yes. You were telling me about a story." I looped a stray lock over his ear. "How does it begin?"

Those trickster irises glinted. "Allow me, Your Highness."

Both of us had been touching mindlessly. But now he took my hand and kissed the ribbon encircling my wrist. And although this man preferred being the centerpiece, he drew the window draperies of the carriage door shut, blotting out the passing woods as though he were about to impart a forbidden tale.

He really was incapable of doing things simply, I thought in amusement.

Spreading his arms, Poet inclined his head and flashed me a wicked grin. "It begins with a ribbon."

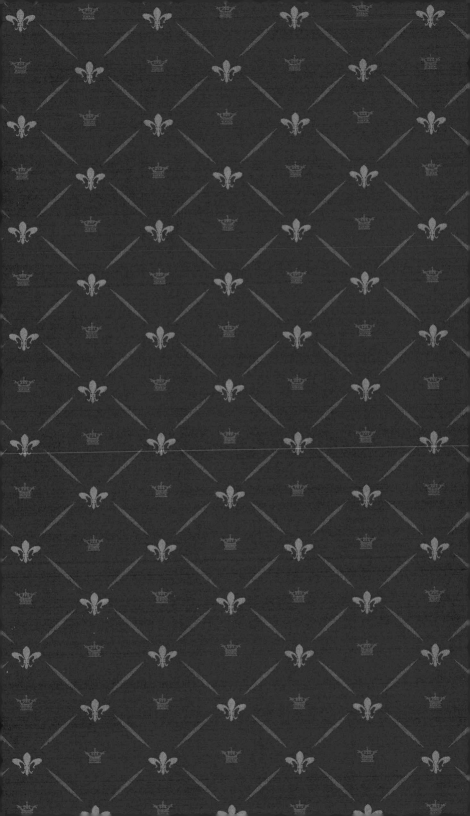

EPILOGUE

Poet

As you see, the tale didn't end in that Spring forest. It went on, and it shall go on if I have anything to say about it. You know, I always have something to say.

There's more ahead for us—some of it entrancing, some of it ruthless. There will be violent dangers, ruinous secrets, and dark passions.

Let it happen. I'm ready.

For I'm not the same fool who started this story. I'm still devastatingly pretty, ever a glittering and devious thing, but also whole. I'm of a new Season, new Crown, new purpose.

I'm a superior father for the world to see. I'm a lover to only one.

To many, my name is Poet. To others, it's something else.

I like to think I'm improving with age. 'Tis mostly your doing. You've slayed me, bested me in a stunning way. My silver tongue has lost this sinful battle—for now, at least. You're a pleasure to spar with. And I'm not done with you yet, my sweeting.

My thorn. My Briar.

In fact, I shall never be done with you. For our story has only begun.

The first time I spun this tale, you'd been naked and sleeping beside me in that secluded forest bower. Thus, I'd replayed the heated story quietly in my mind, a prelude of sorts.

Tonight, it will be revealed to an audience beside a blazing camp-fire, from unknown enemies to unspoken allies. It shall be a stepping stone, the first spark of what's to come. But you'll always be the one who knew first how it began, long before they did.

I could promise to withhold privileged details, to keep them purely between us. I could promise to be humble and discreet, to restrain myself from bragging.

But you're not afraid of the truth. And I'm not that good of a liar.

Poet and Briar's spicy story continues in book 2

Want steamy NSFW character art of Poet and Briar?
Sign up for my newsletter to unlock an exclusive
digital download for subscribers' eyes only:
nataliajaster.com/newsletter

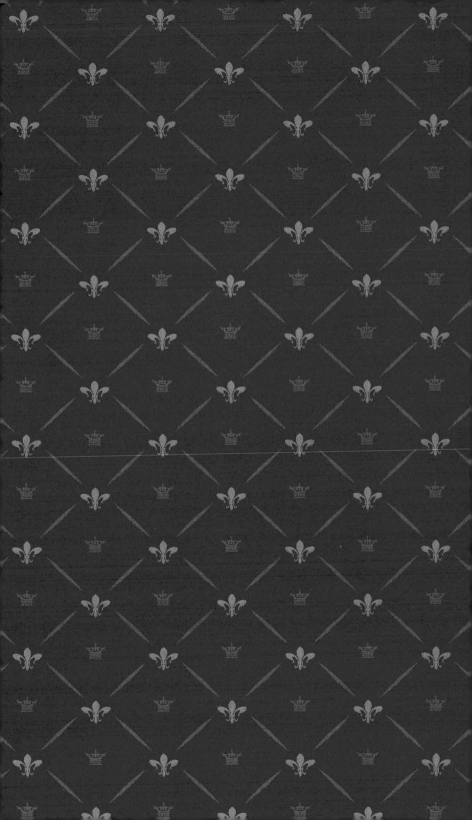

AUTHOR'S NOTE

even years ago, I wrote a book about a jester and a princess. Creating a story with the most unlikely hero archetype—and then defying expectations of that archetype—was a risk. Then again, I've always been a writer who gravitates toward the unconventional.

I made a court jester sexy. But I didn't know if readers would agree with me.

Wicked hell, did they ever!

To this day, Poet remains one of my top beloved MCs among readers. He and Briar are one of the most popular couples I've ever written. After all this time, people still tell me how much this pair means to them. Nothing could fuel a writer's heart more.

And while I LOVED writing the story, one thing still nagged at me years after its release: the spice!

The more books I wrote, the more steam I wanted between the pages. So when I became a fully-fledged adult fantasy romance author, I returned to *Trick* to give this couple the heat they deserved! That created a domino effect. I got ideas for more books about Poet and Briar, plus the urge to revamp every installment in the Foolish Kingdoms series. To make them deeper, edgier, sexier.

Returning to *Trick* became a monumental task that I hadn't foreseen. I revised, rewrote, and reimagined. From refining the world-building and its characters to meticulously editing, fleshing out, and extending the original content; creating whole new scenes; and comforting myself with copious amounts of pastries, this became a magnum opus of a project. It was as intense as writing a brand new book—and it became my heftiest at

145,000 words.

Can you tell I'm addicted to romance? Slow-burn passion. Angst with heart. Enemies to lovers. Darkly sumptuous settings. Not least of all, a whole lot of spice leading up to that well-earned HEA.

I also can't seem to stop taking chances. Reworking a completed series is a pretty wild example of that. I went through cycles of excitement, fear, doubt, giddy joy, and panicky tears while working on this book. But ohhhh, it was worth it.

I'm in love with this story more than even. It's richer, denser, lusher, and yes, SO MUCH hotter. My greatest hope is that you feel the same.

So get ready. I'm not done with you yet, sweeting. This is only the beginning.

If you've been here from the start, thank you for sticking with me and returning to this universe. And if you're discovering this world for the first time, welcome to The Dark Seasons.

All the bows and curtsies to the court of a dozen beta and sensitivity readers, including hardcore fans of the first edition, who generously read and offered feedback. I'm eternally grateful to you.

Hugs to Michelle, for your jester love, your beta prowess, and your friendship. I heart you, my queen.

To my family, for being everything in this world.

To Roman, my silver-tongued troublemaker and soul mate.

To my ARC team, the Myths & Tricksters and Vicious Faeries FB groups, and every reader who opens my books and turns the page. You are Royals.

See you on the other side of Poet & Briar's journey…

Their spicy story continues in *Ruin* (Dark Seasons: Foolish Kingdoms #2).

To the generous supporters who contributed to Trick's first edition crowdfunding campaign. I am most humbled by you:

Alanna L. Boyle

Alia Kreisel

Alison (readaroundtherosie)

Ana Hernandez

Angela Bell

Anonymous 1

Anonymous 2

Bridget Crawford

Diane Clark-Sutton

Hartmut & Renate Jaster

Jackie Gilliam

Jayme Bussing

Kathryn McElveen

Kaylyn Peterson

Kika

Kimberly E. A.

Maria O'Brien

Mika K.

Miriam K.

Norbertsmom

Pooks

Selma Wolff

Shirley Wu

Steffen Wätzold & Arlette Moser

Suzanne Kyro & Niklas Hallberg

The Rendon & Usera Families

TomiStaccato

About Natalia

Natalia Jaster is a fantasy romance author who routinely swoons for the villain.

She lives in a dark forest, where she writes steamy New Adult tales about rakish jesters, immortal deities, and vicious fae. Wicked heroes are her weakness, and rebellious heroines are her best friends.

When she's not writing, you'll probably find her perched atop a castle tower, guzzling caramel apple tea, and counting the stars.

COME SAY HI!

Bookbub: www.bookbub.com/authors/natalia-jaster

Facebook: www.facebook.com/NataliaJasterAuthor

Instagram: www.instagram.com/nataliajaster

TikTok: www.tiktok.com/@nataliajasterauthor

Website: www.nataliajaster.com

See the boards for Natalia's novels on
Pinterest: www.pinterest.com/andshewaits

Made in the USA
Las Vegas, NV
10 March 2023

68855333R00289